BUY ME, MASTER

Erotic Tales from a Slave Girl

For all the lovely voices
who have performed these tales as erotic audio
dramas at /r/gonewildaudio on reddit.

PART I -
THE TALE OF A SLAVEGIRL

BUY ME, MASTER

1

Buy Me, Master

We hear gentle, exotic music ... or else, soft and muted in the background, the sounds of a slave fair. Optionally, we might occasionally hear the gentle clinking of the slavegirl's delicate chains.

the audio opens with the soft, rapid breathing of the slavegirl

gasps Wait ... no, wait, Sir ... don't pass by. Please! Don't leave the pavilion, you haven't bought a slavegirl yet. Wait!

Here. I'll lift my body for you. See? They've chained me, naked for you. With just a blossom in my hair. With this collar locked about my throat and my wrists fastened behind me. The chains holding me captive for your pleasure are pure silver, to keep any werewolf from entering the tent and trying to buy me. *a soft whimper* These chains are delicate ... like me ... but strong. I can hardly move. But I can tilt my head back and lift my breasts ... like a gift ... Here. See them naked ... and soft. I can feel every touch of the cool evening breeze through this open tent like a caress across my tits. Do you like my breasts? Do you like how they move as I breathe? *breathing softly*

My breasts are young ... and full ... and so naked and available to you. You can ... *swallows* ... you can touch them if you want, Sir. The slavers won't mind. As long as you don't ... *she takes a quivery little breath* ... fuck ... me before you buy me, they will let you touch me however you desire. Do ... do you desire me, Sir?

When they burned my village, the raiders dragged me screaming to their ship. I lay bound and weeping while the waves rocked beneath the keel. They brought me here, across the sea, to sell me. Because they said I had a body that would give men pleasure. Does my body please you, Sir? *whispers* Do you want me, Sir? Do you want to touch me? Do you want to ... fuck me?

See me kneeling prettily on this platform for you, Sir? Raised just a little above the ground, so you don't have to stoop or bend if you wish to fondle me. ...

gasps Open ... open my legs for you, Sir? *hesitates* I ...

smack!!!

her sharp cry

frightened Forgive me, Sir! Yes, Sir. It will be my pleasure, Sir. Here, I'm parting my thighs for you, Sir ...

smack!!!

cries out Yes, wider, Sir. Of course, Sir, as it pleases you, Sir. Here. *fearful* My legs are spread so wide. I'm naked for you. My soft young cunt is on display for you, Sir. My soft petals. My swollen, sensitive little clit. They had me oiled and aroused, and my whole body glistens in the light from that lantern, Sir. My nipples are swollen and hard … and my soft thighs … I … I feel so exposed. And vulnerable. I'm bound, Sir, and helpless … and available to your EVERY touch. *quivers* Do I interest you, Sir? Do you want to buy me, Sir?

whispers I will please you, Sir. I will. I will give you SUCH pleasure. I will be the wettest, the most giving, the most … sensual … pleasure-slut in this entire slave fair. I promise. I am here for your pleasure. To be a DREAM of pleasure to you, Sir.

Do you see me dripping onto my thighs?

You've stepped closer. *quivers* I'm so glad. Can you smell me, Sir? Can you smell my wet heat? Please touch me, Sir?

…That? On my thigh? Yes, Sir, that's blood, dried on my thigh. *shy, blushing* It's my virgin's blood. The slavers left it drying on my skin because … *quivers* … they wanted my buyer to know how freshly deflowered I am, how innocent and young and still frightened at the touch of a cock. *breathing in little gasps*

Yes, Sir. Yes. It does … frighten me. That you might buy me and chain me to your bed and fuck me like an animal. That you might rut in me like a feral beast. That you might force my thighs open and cover me with your muscled body and rape me. *whimpers* But if … *frightened* … if you don't buy me, Sir … if … if no one buys me, if I'm one of the girls who doesn't get sold … they'll sell me at discount to the hunting guild, to use as bait for wild animals and werewolves in the dark forest.

whispers Please don't let them.

Please buy me.

No, Sir, I ... I don't know how much they're selling me for. They haven't told me. But I ... *frightened, a little desperate* ... I promise, I will be worth every last coin. I will be so good for you, Sir. Every pleasure you have ever wanted from a woman, it is yours. I will be YOURS.

The other maidens from my village have already been sold. In a single lot to an innkeeper, to dance on his tables or be rented sluts for a night, included in the price of a room.

sniffles I miss them. So much.

a slow, shivery breath to regain her control

The slavers ... *takes a breath* ... they kept me for this pavilion, this evening, where private pleasure-kittens are sold. Here I am, on display, naked, oiled and glistening, ... *quivery* ... wet ... the sweetest exotic young girl to own and fuck. But no one's bought me yet.

I want it to be you who buys me. Please. You are gazing at me ravenously ... HUNGRILY ... as a wild animal, but you look less ... less cruel than the other men here. You're strong. *reverently* Powerful. The way you stalked into this tent like a panther. I might not be able to bend you or persuade you or beg you to be gentle. You will just do what you want with me. With my body. With my soft little mouth and my tight ... young ... cunt.

a soft, soft moan How you look at me ...

I wouldn't be able to escape you or fight you. You're too strong. But you don't look cruel.

You … you wouldn't be cruel to me, would you?

I would do anything to please you, Sir. *whispers* …Master.

whispers May I call you Master?

May I be your slavegirl? Will you take me, Master?

Will you buy me?

cries out Ahhh! How you squeeze my tits! *whimpers* Oh gods. Do they please you … Master? My tits, warm and full in your hands? I am so naked for you. I am dripping for you. *whimpers* Oh! *cries out* My nipples are sensitive. Please be gentle, Master. *cries out again* Oh how you twist them.

Yes, Master. Yes. I'll … I'll take it for you.

whimpering as he pinches and twists her nipples

panting

moans How you cup my breasts…

They're yours, Master. My tits are yours to enjoy.

SMACK!

cries out

Yes, Master. Yours to smack.

SMACK!

cries out

Yes, Master, smack my tits.

improv some hard smacks and yelps and whimpers

vulnerable Do I please you, Master? Does this slavegirl please you?

whispers May I give you pleasure, Master? With my soft … small … wet little mouth?

Please, Master?

slowly, seductively Do you want to be in my mouth?

Ohhh … your cock … you've taken out your cock. It's so hard. So … thick … and warm as you press it to my cheek. If I turn my head … just feel my breath warm on your cock. *exhaling soft and slow*

aroused You smell like such a … man.

so softly, so sweetly, so yearningly May I kiss your cock?

Thank you, Master.

soft, gentle kissing sounds … kissing his shaft

My Master. *kissing*

See my eyes gaze up at you. This blossom in my hair. My eyes soft. My mouth small … and open. *kissing*

whispers And wet.

As I lick … *licking slowly*

after a moment And kiss … *kissing*

… your beautiful, hard cock. *kissing*

breathless, quivery I'm your slavegirl, Master. My mouth is for your pleasure. If I please you so well, will you buy me, Master?

whispers Buy me.

licking him gently

aroused May I please you?

breathless, pleading I want to worship this cock with my mouth.

…Yes, Master. It will be my pleasure, Master. *taking his cock in her mouth*

soft, sensual blowjob sounds

Do I please you, Master?

blowjob sounds

My mouth is so small. *whimpers* And your cock is so big.

blowjob sounds … slow and sensual

Buy me, Master. Please buy me.

blowjob sounds

a sudden, muffled moan around his cock

Master! Master! You're touching my … my cunt. You're touching my cunt! *squeals* Your finger! Inside me! *moans* T-Two … Master! Master! I'm so tight. I've only been fucked once in all my life, Master, please be gentl-MMMMPHH MMMPHHH

blowjob sounds … and she moans around his cock, muffled and burning with heat and need

MMMPHHH Master … Master, I'm so wet. I'm so wet!

blowjob sounds

MMMPHHHH Oh Master, your fingers in me! I can't! I can't take it! MMMMPHHH MMMPHHHH

her whimpering moans around his cock

frantic little gasps of arousal and fright and need all at once I've never … I've never … never felt this … you're going to make me cum, you're going to make me cum! Does … does Master wish me to gush on his fingers? MMMPHHH MMMPHHHH Do you want me to flood your hand, Master, the way I would flood your cock? Are you going to make me cum, Master? While I suck your cock? MMMPHHH MMMPHHHH MMMPHHH Do you want me to squeeze your fingers and show you how I would clench and milk your cock with my tight little cunt? Is that what you want, Master? MMMPHHHH MMMPHHH MMMMM Do you want me to cum for you, Master? While you fuck my mouth? MMMPHH MMPHHHH MMMPHHH

she gags a little

whimpers Yes, Master. Master may be rough with me if he pleases. I will do my best to take it like a good girl. MMMPHHH! MMMPHHH!

improv a rougher fucking of her mouth

in the following lines, she keeps trying to talk or plead, and he keeps interrupting her with a hard thrust of his cock ... her muffled moans around his cock get more intense

MMMPHHH Yes, Master. I'm a good girl. I'm a good gir-MMMPHHH MMMPHHHH

Do you like this, Master? Do you like being in my mou-MMMPHHH! MMMPHHH!!! MMMPHH!

MMMPHH! Buy me, Mast-MMMPHH MMMPHHH MMMPHHHHHH

MMMPHHH Your fingers! Your fingers! MMPHH MMMPHHHHH

MMMPHH Your cock is SO big ... too big MMMPHH MMMPHHH

MMMPHHH Yes, Master, I'll take it deeper, yes, Master, plea-MMMPHHH MMMPHHHH MMMPHHHHHH

choking

spluttering I can't breathe. I can't brea-MMMPHHH MMMPHHH

improv a hard throatfuck

at one point he shoves deep and she stops breathing for a count of five, then splutters and chokes

she comes up heaving for air

gasping Master! Master! MMMPHHH MMMPHHHHHHHH

vigorous, fast facefucking… he ENJOYS her, fucking her mouth hard

she is nearing her orgasm, and so is he … her wild whimpers around his cock

MMMPHHHH Are you going to cum, Master? MMMPHH MMPHHH Are you going to fill my mou-MMPHHH MMPHHHHH MMPHHH

muffled around his cock, talking with her mouth full Cum in my mouth … Master … Cum in my mouth … Cum in my mouth … Cum in my mouth … Cum in my mouth … Cum in my mouth … Cum in my mouth … Cum in my mouth … Cum in my mouth … Cum in my mouth …

she orgasms, wild and intense, her squeals of pleasure muffled around his cock

as she whimpers around his cock in post-orgasmic bliss, he cums in her mouth and we hear several loud swallows

panting afterward

You … you filled my mouth. Tasting like the sea. So salty and … sticky. *a last little swallow*

tearful Did I please you, Master?

Did my soft little mouth please you?

Did my tight little cunt please you when I spasmed around your fingers?

Master ... Master ... you gave me an orgasm. I've ... I've never cum before. *tearful* Thank you, Master. Thank you. *almost sobbing from the shock of it*

Master ... *vulnerably* ... I'm yours.

I came for you.

My body was made for you, Master.

a little frightened It's getting dark. I know my eyes must be so large and frightened in the lantern light. Soon they'll be closing the pavilion for the night, and any girl who hasn't been sold will be handed over to the hunters. *whispers* As wolf-bait.

breathing fast It that going to happen to me, Master?

To this luscious, wet, captive slavegirl who swallowed your cum? *breathless* Who swallowed everything you gave her? Who came at your touch?

Is that what's going to happen to me?

softly Do you want me? Do you want to buy me?

Please buy me. Own me, Master.

I'm yours.

slow, sultry, with every ounce of seduction she has Take me home,

Master. Burn the mark of your brand in my soft thigh. *a scared whimper* Teach me my duties. I will be such … a good … slavegirl. I will be so open and wet for you. To grip … and squeeze … and clench around your cock … whenever you want. Please, Master. May I be your pleasure-kitten? May I be your love-slave? Please, Master? You can fuck me until dawn and I … helpless, chained, in your collar … I would have to take it all. Every thrust of your cock. Every bruising kiss on my breasts. Every smack of your hand. Chain me to your bed and break me, Master. Ravish me until my thighs are shaking. Make me soak your bed with my wet little cunt until your bed smells like me. Until your bed smells like you fucking me. I am yours, Master. I am so yours. Buy me. Don't let any other have me. I don't want to quiver under any other man. I don't want to squirm as werewolf bait on a forest hunt. I want to squirm and moan and arch my back for you, Master. Only for you. I belong in your bed, as YOUR slut. I belong under your hard body, clasped tightly around your thrusting cock. Squealing for you as you FUCK me. Your hot, melted little pleasure-slave.

I belong to you.

Please buy me.

a soft, soft sigh May I kiss your cock, Master?

gentle kisses I love your cock.

kissing

Please, Master.

kissing

Please thrust this cock in me tonight. Make me yours with this cock. This magnificent … thick … cock. *kissing* Please buy me. Buy me, Master. Buy me.

Please, please. I'll be so good. I will be such a good slavegirl. Please, Master. Please will you buy me, Master?

whispers Buy me. Buy me, Master.

the episode ends

2

Whip Me, Master

We hear gentle, exotic music. Possibly (optionally) the quiet, gentle trickle of fountain water.

the audio opens with the soft, rapid breathing of the slavegirl, both aroused and frightened

Here, I stand naked for you, Master, in your pleasure garden. My breasts and thighs kissed by the night air. My wrists still chained behind me. Your collar clasping my neck, as firmly as the grip of your hand. *whimpers* It's locked on me, Master. Locked. You've bought me. You own me. I belong to you. I am ... *swallows* ... so glad. If you ... if you hadn't bought me ... *frightened* ... I ... I tremble thinking of what might have happened to me. Girls who aren't sold get used as bait in the forest at night. *a scared little sound*

But you've bought me. And taken me home. I'm yours. What do you wish of me, Master? How may your slavegirl give you pleasure?

You want me to ... look around at your garden? At ... at my new home? *quivers*

Yes, Master. Your pleasure garden is lovely in the moonlight, Master. I hear the music of instruments … and the music of water, but I don't see any fountains, Master. You … want me to look more closely at the pools? *gasps* Oh. *blushing hotly, flustered* I see. The water trickles from between the thighs of those marble nymphs. Goddesses sculpted and curved with their breasts full and their thighs open. They stand naked in the pools, cupping their stone breasts in their hands. One of them has a hand reaching out to beckon your guests near.

And beyond, I see my Master's guests reclining beneath blossoming trees, and my Master's other pleasure-slaves dancing on the grass. Dancing naked and graceful by moonlight to entertain your guests, each of them a sensual delight. Is that what you wish of me, Master? Am I to be one of your dancing slaves tonight? *softly* Am I to dance naked for you, Master? Will I tease your guests with the sway of my breasts? With a glimpse of my naked cunt as I spin and pivot? Will you arouse me first, so that my warm honey drips down my thighs as I dance?

quivers Will my Master's guests be permitted to touch me? Caress me? Taste me? Or … am I reserved for your touch only, Master?

Is that what you want, Master?

breathing faster I'm not dancing tonight? That … that isn't why you bought me? That isn't what you decided when you sampled the pleasures of my body at the slave pavilion? When you fingered me? When you thrust your magnificent hard cock in my mouth and gave me my first hot, sticky meal as your slavegirl?

frightened but desperate to please What did you decide, Master? What will you do with me? What pleasures may I provide you, Master?

Your private ... bed-slave? *quivery* To wake my Master in the morning with my soft warm little mouth? To massage your shoulders and back and hips ... and cock ... with warm, scented oils? To dress my Master, placing a loving kiss on each part of your body before arranging your garments? And then, while Master is at the market, I am to be bathed in milk, my skin made so soft, my nipples ... *gasps* ... pierced, so that Master may string silver jewelry from my nipples. Protecting me from werewolves ... and displaying my breasts beautifully for my Master's pleasure. I am to be prepared all day for Master's return. The hair between my thighs trimmed and perfume dripped on my soft petals. And then I am to kneel by Master's bed, waiting for his pleasure, my arms chained delicately behind me, as they are now, my head lifted, my lips parted, my mouth open and soft and ready for my Master's cock. *trembling* Yes, Master. I will give you such pleasure, Master. I will be your oasis and your voluptuous slavegirl, Master, each evening, when your business is finished and you desire pleasure.

The night is late. Do you want me in your bed now, Master? To please and delight you?

No? ... There is ... something you wish to do with me first? Here, in your garden?

Yes, Master. Whatever you wish, Master.

clinking of chains

hopeful Are you unchaining my wrists, Master? I … I promise I won't … I won't try to escape you. Here, in your walled villa, I am … safe. Protected. Yours. Outside, anything might happen to me. I might be seized and sold as a pleasure-toy for the men in the mines, to be fondled and groped and fucked by dozens of rough men in the dark beneath the earth. *whimpers* I might be grabbed while hiding in an alley, a hood pulled over my head, thrown over a slaver's shoulder and carried to be sold as a tavern girl, to give men pleasure with my mouth while they drink their ale and beer, a new man in my mouth every hour. *whimpers* Or I might be sold to the hunters, to be wolf-bait, to help them capture feral, brutal werewolves who scream and howl at the moon. Who run miles under the trees tracking the scent of a woman, lusting to grab her by her neck, throw her to her belly on the mossy ground, and violate her … and fuck her and tear at her small, vulnerable body with their claws and teeth. All while the hunters form a trap, a circle around the beast and the slavegirl he is ripping apart. *a frightened almost-sob* That might have happened to me, if you hadn't bought me.

I don't want to escape, Master. I want to be here, my body naked and oiled and adorned with slave jewelry for your pleasure. I will do anything to please you. To excite you.

Do I excite you, Master? Do I please you, standing naked in your garden, my breasts lifting … and falling … as I breathe? *she breathes slowly for a moment, inviting the listener to imagine her breasts*

With my hands unchained, I can … cup my breasts. I can lift them … *moans* … I can entice my Master. See my soft, feminine hands holding my breasts, so much smaller than your hands, Master. I can caress and tease my nipples … *moans* … for you, Master. *moans* I can pinch … *a sweet little gasping cry* … for you, Master …

Do I … delight you, Master?

Do you want to take me?

Oh! You've taken hold of me! Ah! You're pressing me back against one of the marble nymphs. Her stone skin is cool against my shoulders and ass. *a slow inhale* I can feel the swell of her breasts against my back. Lift my hands, Master? Yes, Master.

clinking of chains

Yes, Master, you may chain me the way you wish. I won't resist you, Master. *a soft little quivery moan* Her marble arms are extended above her head, her wrists crossed, and you've lifted my arms above my head, crossing my wrists and chaining my wrists to hers. So that she holds me, my warm soft flesh against cool, hard, naked stone. My arms high, my breasts lifted. Only the sweet kiss of my thighs pressed together conceals my naked, wet cunt from my Master's guests and his dancing slaves, if they should glance at us …

nervous little sounds

Yes, Master, I'm closing my eyes. I can hear the music for the dancing girls. The water dripping from the cunt of this marble nymph you've chained me to. I can hear you stepping close.

inhales

quivery and so aroused I can smell you … hot and sweaty and male. My Master.

May I open my eyes, Master? *whispers* Thank you, Master.

Oh! You've taken a fistful of my hair and forced my head back … your gaze burns with such HEAT, like I've lit a forest fire in your loins, Master - mmmphhhh

he kisses her, roughly and loudly and long, and she whimpers sweetly into his kiss

panting softly

softly The way you kiss me makes me drip down my thighs for you, Master.

softly You … own me.

frightened What is that in your hand, Master? Its touch on my nipple … *moans* … like worn leather, smoothed and warmed from your hand. *whimpers* How you tease and circle my nipple … *moans* … how you trail it down my belly … *a gasping little cry* … teasing open my thighs … yes, Master, I will open my legs for you, if you wish. I know if I hesitate, you will smack my little clit with your hand …

SMACK!!!

she screams

Like that, yes, Master.

SMACK!!! screams

SMACK!! screams

little gasps My thighs are spread wide for you, Master, my cunt naked and hot to your touch… Whatever you h-h-have in your h-hand, how you nudge my tight entrance with it. Will … will you be gentle with me, Master? Please, Master. Please. Do you feel my warm honey dripping onto your fingers, Master? I am here for your pleasure, Mast-MMMPHHHHH

he interrupts her with another rough, passionate kiss. We hear her whimpers muffled by his mouth as he teases her wet folds and entrance.

gasping for breath after the long kiss

You've … released my hair and stepped back. *a sudden, terrified whimper* And I - I can see what you have in your hand. What you were teasing me with. What you … what you are going to use on me. Master. Master. You … *quivers* … you don't need to whip me, Master. I will obey you completely, perfect and pleasing, without hesitation or delay. I … I will be SUCH a good slavegirl. I will do anything, surrender anything. You don't need to kiss my body with your whip, Master. Please.

whimpering I'm squirming a little against the marble nymph who holds me. I … I can't help it. I'm … I'm frightened. That whip is long and when you crack it in the air … it will hurt me, Master! Please don't whip me.

trembling You … you're going to teach me who I belong to? You want every cell in my body to know who I belong to?

Master … Master, out here … in your garden … all your guests, your dancing-slaves, they will all see me dance at the whip's touch, they'll all hear my screams! I have been displayed in a slave tent, fondled, my mouth filled with a cock … but I have never been whipped, Master. The screams you'll force from my lips … I will be so naked. So NAKED.

They'll HEAR. Please. Master, I beg you.

CRACK!!!!

a shrill scream

soft little sob M-Master, your whip's fire across my tits!

CRACK!!!!

squeals

My thighs! *panting* My thighs!

whimpers

Yes, yes, I understand, Master. I will submit to you. I will cry out my surrender, loudly, so that everyone in your garden can hear, … at each crack of your whip.

whimpers Yes, Master.

CRACK!!!

I'm yours, Master!

CRACK!!!

I'm yours, Master!

CRACK!!!

frantic Master, I'm yours, I'm yours, I'm y-

CRACK!!!

I'm yours, Master!

CRACK!!!

I'm your slavegirl!

CRACK!!!

Your pleasure-slut!

CRACK!!!

Your kitten!

CRACK!!!

Yes, Master! Your slut! Your SLUT!

CRACK!!!

sobs You own me, Master!

CRACK!!!

squeals

tearful and aroused and trembling You own my tight, young cunt.

My warm, wet little mouth. My breasts that are heaving for you right now. *breathing hard* My thighs that burrrn when you lash them. My every breath. My every scream.

sobs I'm yours, Master.

frightened gasps You're … you're going to whip my cunt?

I'm sorry! I'm sorry! I don't mean to press my thighs together again. I'm … I'm scared. Master …

CRACK!!!!!!

shrieks

breathless, talking fast Yes, Master, I'll open my legs, I'll open my legs, I'll open my legs …

My skin burns where you've struck me, Master! My thighs are open for you, Master. And wet. And my cunt is exposed … bared … to each caress of the night air. My soaked, swollen folds naked and hot and available to each kiss of your whip.

a whimper

CRACK!!!!

an anguished, moaning cry

Masterrrr!

quivery, sobbing, moaning breaths

CRACK!!!

she shrieks

CRACK!!!!

a wild, high-pitched moan

sobbing softly

tearful, aroused How you press my body between yours and the marble nymph ... you're so strong. I am captured, helplessly yours. Your hand cupping my chin, lifting my eyes to you. Your eyes deep as the sea at midnight. Dark as the ocean the slavers took me across, to sell me to you. To sell me to my Master.

Master, you whipped me. *whimpers* You whipped me.

quivers I will always be SO pleasing, Master. I will be so good for you.

whispers You own me.

These welts forming in my skin ... My body will be marked by my owner for a week.

a rough passionate kiss, muffling her tearful little whimpers

softly The dancers in the garden have stopped? They're ... *swallows* ... they're all watching us? I ... I submit to you, Master. Even if the whole world watches. Only your eyes matter to me. Your eyes that smolder in the dark.

My body burns for you, Master.

The stone girl you've chained me to is cool against my skin, her breasts and thighs are cold, but mine burn like molten flame. I drip down my legs. I am your melted, soaked little slavegirl. Please, Master. Please take me.

Please ... fuck me.

whispers Take what's already yours.

breathing softly

whispers Master ...

a wild cry

Ahhh! Master, y-y-you've thrust the handle of your whip INSIDE me!

he starts fucking her with the whip handle ... we hear her wild, abandoned cries

Masterr! *quivering* Masterrr! I ... I am so ... so aroused by ... by the whipping ... I ... I ... every touch is fire! I can't ... I can't take it! Master, please, be gentle! Master! Please!

wild, desperate moans

Ohhh! That whip handle ... it's so LONG ... it's so DEEP in me ... So WARM from my Master's hand ... as you fuck me with it.

improv her frantic moans as he fucks her with the whip

after a few moments Yes, Master, yes, fuck me with the whip, Master! Fuck me with your whip!

Master! Master! I ... I can't ... *panting* I ... I ... I ... I'm going to yield, I'm going to cum! Master, Master, Master,

I'm clenching down on that whip in my cunt, please, please, let me cum, let me cum, PLEASE Master let me cum, please may I cum, please! Master!

screams YES! Yes! Master! Feel my hips buck against your hand! Master, make me cum! Make me CUM!

her passionate cries as she orgasms

panting afterward

almost sobbing from the intensity of it

quivery The whip ... and your hand ... are covered in my warm honey.

reverently Master gave me pleasure. You gave me pleasure, Master. Here, in your garden, under the bright moon, chained to a marble pleasure-nymph, while your guests watched me writhe naked on your whip.

whispers I'm yours, Master.

a low moan Ohhhh ... you've pulled the handle out of me ... I ... I feel so empty with it gone.

breathless You're holding it near my eyes. Master, it's ... dripping with me.

Yes, Master. Yes, I'll kiss the whip. *blushing* Whatever Master fucks me with deserves my worship and my gratitude. Press the whip to my lips, Master.

kissing ... small, gentle kisses

a little whimper Yes, Master. I'll lick … *licking* … the whip … *licking* … with my warm, wet little tongue. *licking* Just like I would lick … *licking* … your thick … *licking* … hard … *licking* … cock … *licking*

draws a quivery breath You're teasing my lower lip with it. Do … do you want it in my mouth, Master? Do you want the handle of your whip in my mouth?

she whimpers and takes it in her mouth

improv a slow, sensual blowjob for that whip handle

after a few moments I'm yours, Master. *sucking gently* You beat me with this whip. *sucking* You … fucked … me with this whip. *sucking* You own me, Master.

sucking for another few moments

he takes it from her mouth, to a little whimper of protest from her

moans Your hands are warm on my tits, Master. My nipples are so hard…

Caress me, Master. Fondle me, Master…

moaning as he does

I'm flushed … and slick with sweat … and chained naked to this nymph in the moonlight. Your guests are going in to sleep, though the dancing girls are still watching me quiver for you … Ohhhhh … Yes, I'm lifting my hips, Master, craving your touch. I need your touch. I need your mouth on my breasts …

cries out

Like that …

shrieks Y-you bit my nipple! You bit me!

Master!

another shriek as he bites her again

panting You may do whatever you want with me, and I will take it, Master. I will take it like a good slavegirl.

In my village, the other girls and I daydreamed about being kissed by a man. But … we never imagined … I never imagined being so naked … so helpless and chained … so wet. *quivery* Do I please you, Master?

soft little sounds as he touches her

The night is getting chill. Will you keep me hot, Master? Will you take me inside to your bedchamber? Do you … do you want to fuck me, Master? *whispers* Do you want to put your cock in me?

moans Do you want me to squeeze and ripple around your hard cock?

May I give you pleasure, Master?

grateful Yes, Master, YES, kiss me … mmmphh

a slow, sensual kiss

her voice soft and needing Take me inside, Master. Please Master, take me to your bed.

Take me to your bed and fuck me.

the episode ends

3

Brand Me, Master

We hear soft, exotic music and the sounds of a fire, a hearth. The slavegirl is nervous but very aroused.

You wish to bind me, Master? In silk rope, soft but unyielding against my naked flesh? Here in your bedchamber, by this fire in your hearth that burns as hot as my Master's desire for his slavegirl? The moon has set outside your window, Master. The whole world sleeps. Only the werewolves in the forest beyond your walls are awake now. Only the wolves … and my Master. The night is so quiet. Just your slaves' music in the garden below. And here, by your bed, there's only you and me, and your fire.

quivery I am your pleasure-slave, Master. You bought me. Your collar is locked about my throat. Your whip kissed my skin in the garden. I will not defy you, Master. You may do whatever you want with me. I submit to you.

she takes a steadying breath

Here, I will kneel prettily for you, Master. *rustling* Your silk carpets under my knees. *a soft sigh* So soft … I will lift my arms ... *breathes in* ... lifting my full young breasts as I breathe. *breathes slow and deep* ... I'll push my hair back from my shoulders, let my hair tumble down my back, so that my body isn't hidden from you. I'm naked, Master. You may see all of me. See my nipples harden and swell as you gaze on me with such heat? See the sheen of your collar at my throat, holding me captive. Do I please you, Master? See the firelight on my skin, Master. See how my breasts and thighs, oiled for your pleasure, glow in the light of your hearth? The marks of your whip ... *quivery breath* ... are on my body, Master, from how you whipped me earlier tonight, when you desired to break in your new slave. *a frightened little sound at the memory* I will be a good and pleasing slavegirl. I will part my thighs for you. Spreading my knees wide, my cunt glistening and warm and available to you. You own me, Master. You own this soft ... tight ... cunt.

softly My cunt will caress and grip and squeeze your cock tonight, if you wish it, Master. I quiver at the thought of you in me. Warm honey drips from my cunt as I await your touch. I will be a sensual delight for you, Master.

I can see this bedchamber you've brought me to is a temple to your pleasure, Master, a place my Master comes to be worshipped. The silks on the bed. *her breathing gets more aroused as she says these next lines* And the headboard, carved in the shape of a slavegirl, naked, cupping her breasts in her small delicate hands. Her legs spread wide, the blossom between her thighs carved so realistically, her cunt open and soft by my Master's head when he sleeps. In the firelight, she looks so real. As if she might moan if you touch her.

And the footboard. Carved like a woman kneeling, on her knees like me, her hands lifted to present a shallow silver basin. Water for Master to drink if he wakes? Or is it oil in her basin, for me to dip my hands in, to soothe and caress your feet, Master?

And two marble nymphs standing to either side of your hearth, one with her wrists captive behind her, the other with her wrists crossed and bound above her head. Both with their legs open, their bodies displayed for your pleasure. Their marble skin shimmers like milk in the firelight.

And in the floor, on the walls, in the headboard of the bed attached to the nymph's wrists, are metal rings where you might bind me as you please.

softly This room, your bed … this is where I must give you such pleasure.

That silk rope in your hand, Master. Do you wish to bind me, like the pleasure-nymphs carved against the wall? I will offer you my wrists. Lifting them above my head, crossing them, my body completely open to the man who bought me.

I tremble as you step near me, Master. I know you might do anything you want with me. *gasps* Your grip on my wrists! You're so strong, Master, as you wind the silk rope around my hands. Binding me. *gasps* So tightly. *aroused and slightly frightened* Your rope feels … different … from the chains I wore for you earlier, Master. More … intimate.

soft little sounds as she squirms Do I excite you, Master, as I wriggle and squirm, testing the bonds on my wrists? My breasts moving soft and gentle in the firelight as my breath quickens? Master, you've tied me. I feel so … helpless.

You wish me to lie down, Master? On your silk carpets? Your trembling, helpless pleasure-slave? *breathing faster* Yes, Master. *rustling* Is this how Master wants me? Lying open and wet by your fire, my arms above my head, my breasts and soft cunt ready for your touch?

quivery I belong to you, Master. *frightened and aroused* What will you do with me tonight?

Your gaze flicked to the hearth. I don't understand, Master. There's just your fire there, the wood cracking at the flames' caress. And a metal poker lying half on the hearth, half buried in the coals' heat. What are you looking at, Master, with such hunger in your eyes?

Oh! You're bringing more rope. And binding me as I lie here.

soft feminine sounds for a moment as he binds her

The rope is so soft … but it doesn't give at all … it holds me, helpless to your touch.

trembles Master, these loops of rope under my breasts, lifting them for your pleasure. The rope around my thighs, my legs, my shins…binding my legs together so tightly. Why do you wish to bind me so? Are you … *vulnerable* … are you not going to fuck your new slavegirl, Master? *frightened* Have … have my delicate curves and my soft gasps and moans failed to delight you, Master? *more frightened* H-have I displeased you?

SMACK!!!

a squeal at the pain

SMACK!!

she cries out

I'm sorry, Master! I will be silent, Master, as you bind me.

her soft little whimpers as he continues binding her

after a few moments, her breathing comes in little gasps

quivery May … may I speak, Master?

Thank you, Master. I … I'm frightened, Master.

very softly You've tied my wrists to … to a metal ring in your floor, high above my head. And my ankles … to another ring near the wall. Stretching me by your fire. On my back, the silk carpet soft beneath my shoulders and ass. You've stretched me so tightly, I … I can't move. I can barely wriggle at all. *she whimpers as she tries* I can barely breathe.

How you crouch beside me like a panther, your hand warm and so firm … *gasp* … gripping my thigh. *moans* Caressing me. *moans* Fondling me.

I'm so hot and wet between my thighs, Master. *a whine of need* But you've tied me so tightly I can't even rub my thighs together, one against the other.

whispers Master, I'm so wet. I'm so wet for you, Master.

You've made me so ... helpless. *reverently* You've bound me. *quiver* What... what is going to happen to me tonight, Master?

frightened Master? *gasps and squirms* Master! You're reaching for that poker, taking it in your hand! Master, why?! No, Master, please don't lift it from the fire, please! You can't!

SMACK!!!

squeals Master!

SMACK!!!

screams Master, wait!

a third, sharp SMACK!!!!

she cries out Please!!!!!

breathing fast I'm scared, Master!

whimpers Yes, Master, I can feel ... I can feel the h-h-heat, radiating from that .. that iron, as you hold it close to show me. I see the design worked in metal on its tip ... feminine, and small, and sweetly curved, like me. A symbol to tell the world that the woman you've marked is your pleasure-slave. *terrified, whimpering* The metal glows r-red with h-h-heat. Master, please! Please!

You're moving it down along my body, held an inch above my skin so I can feel the heat... Master, are you going to burn me? Are you going to brand me? Are you going to put that mark in my soft, trembling flesh?

I'm squirming but I'm tied so tightly I can't move. *a sobbing breath* You … you've paused … with the iron just above my thigh. My sensitive, soft, naked, feminine thigh.

rapid, frightened breathing, almost hyperventilating Master! I'm scared! I'm scared! I'm scared! Master, please don't kiss my thigh with the iron, please, please! Master please, you own me, I'm yours, I will do anything for you, give you any pleasure you desire, any delight you crave. You don't need to mark your slavegirl, Master, I'm already yours, I'm yours!

whimpers You're going to cover my mouth with your hand? Wait, Master, plea-MMMMPHHHHHHHHHHH

he covers her mouth with his hand and for a moment we hear her frantic little gasps of fear through her nose

Then a soft hiss of the brand against flesh, and her wild, short scream of shocked pain as he brands her. Her shriek is muffled by his hand.

followed by sobbing whimpers into his hand for a few moments.

he lifts his hand from her mouth

pained little gasps as she gulps in great breaths of air, sobbing the word "Master" between them Master. Master. Master.

tearful I feel the fire of it in my flesh, Master. In my thigh. *a shaky breath* Your mark, your ownership, burned into my body.

sobbing softly, sweetly

tearful I am your slavegirl, Master.

You're ... you're untying my ankles. ... *soft sounds, overwhelmed at what's happened to her* ... my legs ...

But my wrists remain captive above my head. My breasts are lifted for your pleasure, heaving with my every breath.

outside, distant, a wolf howl

she gasps loudly at the sound

speaking softly, a little quickly, frightened and overwhelmed You bought me, Master. You saved me from being wolf-bait in the forest. You whipped me ... *half a sob* ... and branded me. *quivery, awed* Your brand is on my body. I am yours, Master. I want to please you. *a sobbing breath* How may I give you pleasure, Master?

breathing, whimpers

a sudden cry You've thrust my legs apart! Master! Are you going to fuck me, Master? *she cries out* Your weight on me! You're on top of me! Your eyes above mine, your hands gripping my tits, I can hardly breathe, you're so big, you're so BIG. Pressed against my folds. *breathing in little gasps* Master, I feel your mark warm in my thigh ... *whimpers* ... painful and deep ... and your cock hot and thick against my soft cunt. *frightened and aroused* Master, I'm so tight. Will you be gentle with me? Master, will you be gent-AHHHHH! *he interrupts her with a deep, savage thrust, and she cries out as he takes her*

Master!

a squeal as he thrusts again

Master!

a squeal

Oh gods, Master!

for a few moments, hard, pounding thrusts, and her wordless cries at each thrust inside her, then she starts to cry out "Master!" at each thrust

Master! Master! The surge of your hips! Your cock! Your cock is so deep! *a wild cry* Master!!!

Oh, Master!

Master!

Yes, grip my tits! Grip my tits, Master! *cries out* Bruise my breasts with your fingerprints, Master. Master!

overwhelmed The pain in my thigh! The pleasure in my cunt! Master, break me! Break me! I'm yours! I'm yours! My Master is fucking me! You're fucking me!

Fuck me, Master! Use me!

he kisses her ... we hear her grunts of pleasure muffled by the kiss as he fucks her

Yes, Master, enjoy my mouth! *crying out loudly* I'm your slavegirl! Enjoy my mouth!

he kisses her again, hard, and she whimpers into the kiss at each thrust

Master, you own me! Do I please you? Does my tight young cunt give you pleasure? Feel me clench down on your cock, Master! I'm so close! Master, Master, will you make me surrender? Will you make me cum? May I cum, Master, may I cum, may I cum?

gasping cry Your hand on my throat! *panting* Your firm, strong fingers! Are you going to choke me, Master? You w-won't hurt me? Yes, Master, yes, you own my air, you own the very breath in my body!!! I understand, I get to breathe when I cum, I get to breathe when I cum!

choking

a count of ten hard thrusts as she fights for air, as the pleasure builds like a tidal wave inside her body

she cums in a squeal, a shriek of pleasure so intense it could just destroy her

after, she is panting desperately for air, lightheaded and overwhelmed

between gulps of air Master … Master … Master …

little gasping, moaning sounds as her Master keeps fucking her

Is Master close, too? Are you close, Master? Does my tight hot cunt feel good on your cock? Do I give you pleasure?

a wild moan as he pulls out of her

Oh, Master, you've pulled out of me, you're crouched over me with your cock in your fist, stroking so powerfully. Oh your cock is so big, so massive. Master, Master, you look so masculine and so powerful above me, with the fire glowing on your muscled shoulders and arms and chest and hips, and Master, cum, please cum, Master! Cum on me, cum on me, cum on my tits, Master, cum on my tits! Cum on your slavegirl's soft, heaving tits! Please, Master! Please cum on my tits! My tits are yours, Master! I'm arching my back, lifting my body to you for your pleasure, Master! Cum on me! Cum on me! Cum on me!

her soft cry of delight as he does

Master! Your seed! Your seed splashing warm and sticky over my tits! On my throat! *gasps* My lips! Salty on my tongue! *a small, sweet sound as she tastes it* Master! Master!

panting

quivering You came…

proud, awed, grateful I gave my Master pleasure. *whispers* I gave you pleasure.

gaspy breathing as she recovers from the intensity of this experience

My thighs are shaking, Master. How you fucked me. How you FUCKED me!

Your hands, how they caress me .. strong and warm on my thighs … *whimpers* … Master! My left thigh is so sore where you burned me. Master, it hurts when you touch. *emotional* If … if I lift my head I can see it, the mark. Delicate and feminine. Telling the world I am your girl and you own me and desire me.

he kisses her, and she whimpers faintly into the kiss

in the distance, a little louder than before, the howl of a wolf

in response, hearing it, she whimpers louder into his mouth as he kisses her

after the kiss, breathless The werewolves hunt in the forest outside, wanting a woman to fuck and devour and tear apart. But I do not fear them, Master. *quivers* Not with your hands on my body. Not with your brand in my thigh, your collar on my throat. When you sunk that iron into my flesh *tearful* I screamed into your hand, Master. But … but I … the brand … your mark on me, it means … if I displease you, you won't sell me or give me away to the hunters? You'll simply whip me, whip my thighs and my tits and my helpless wet cunt, until I please you again … because you own me. *whispers* You take pleasure in me.

I'm bound beneath you. Naked and flushed, my body slick with sweat, my breasts sticky with your seed, my thighs soaked with my juices, my cunt sore from your vigorous enjoyment of me. *a shaky breath*

a soft, shaky breath You'll … you'll keep me, won't you, Master? *pleading* I will give you night after night of pleasure. I'll cry out as you take me. I will worship you with my soft, warm mouth … whenever you desire. I will sleep when you permit me, with your cum drying on my body. I will be the most loving, surrendered pleasure-slut you could ever desire. I am yours.

Your seed glistens on my body in the firelight. Am I beautiful, Master? Do I please you?

a sensual kiss, as her Master enjoys her mouth again

vulnerably, yearningly I am yours. Will you … keep me, Master? *quivery* Will you keep me?

the episode ends

4

Display Me, Master

We hear gentle, exotic music and possibly the soft, low guttering of flames in lamps. The slavegirl is aroused and quivery at all the eyes on her, but is proud of her beauty and her new status as her Master's bed-slave.

The audio opens with the sound of massive heavy doors opening, then closing.

You called for me, Master? Here I am. Your slavegirl, your pleasure-kitten, stepping naked into your banquet hall where your guests are feasting. I'll wait just inside the door until you summon me nearer. I will stand beautifully for you, Master, so you will be proud of your slavegirl, and all your dinner guests can see what a lovely pleasure-slut wears your collar. Do you see this blush in my cheeks, Master? All your guests are gazing at me with hunger and heat in their eyes. Admiring … wanting … what belongs to my Master.

Do I please you, Master, standing here obediently while you talk with the other men? I am YOUR beautiful slavegirl. *softly* Gaze on me, Master. I'll roll my shoulders back, my young breasts moving gently as I breathe, to entice and delight you, Master. My feet are small and bare, and the silk carpets that cover the floor of this hall feel like a caress against my skin. One hip turned toward you to display the sweet curves of your slavegirl's body. And the brand you burned into my flesh last night. *quivers* Red and small and lovely in the curve of my thigh. You burned this mark into me, Master. When you claimed me. *softly, aroused* When you made me yours.

I am my Master's pleasure-slave. I made my Master moan with the warm caress of my body, again and again, all night. You chained me by my ankle to the bed, and woke me this morning with your powerful thrusts, the surge and roll of your hips. You woke me with your cock, Master. I woke to the singing of the dawn birds in your garden outside, to the warm sun kissing my skin, to the grunts and growls of my Master as he fucked me. As you took such pleasure in your slavegirl. You fucked me, and I spasmed around your cock and screamed under you on your bed as you made me yield and surrender.

I am your pleasure-slut, Master.

Your dancing girls prepared me for you tonight, while you were away at market. They oiled my body and perfumed me and aroused me for you with their soft, delicate hands. They strung these decorative chains of silver about my belly and hips. But your slave jewelry and your collar, clasped securely around my throat, are all I wear, Master. The welts from your whip are still faint across my thighs and tits. My cunt is naked and ... soft ... and glistening with my warm honey in the light of the lamps above your banquet table, Master.

a soft sigh of arousal Those lamps. Held high above your guests' heads by the shackled hands of stone slavegirls, marble women taller than living girls, ten along each side of your long banquet hall. They are all naked. Like me. Some of their mouths are open in eternal orgasm. Others have their mouths gagged with marble imitations of leather straps. Any woman who enters this hall does so for my Master's pleasure and delight.

When I chopped onions and heated stew in my father's small house ... as a free girl, before the slavers took me ... I never imagined such a banquet hall. Such a table, with a dozen men dining in their elegant garments and jewels. And there you are, my Master, at the head of the table, seated in your oak chair carved in the shape of intertwined slavegirls, caressing and fondling each other, their backs arched in orgasm. With that huge window behind your chair, and the red sun setting behind you like a world on fire. *breathless* You look like a god, Master. With your eyes deep as the sea and your powerful body and that sable cloak you wear.

You beckon to me with a look. Yes, Master. I will approach you, Master. It will be my pleasure, Master. *softly, yearningly* My Master. See me walk toward your table with slow grace. My wrists crossed behind my back as if you've bound them, Master. My hips swaying at each soft step. I do not conceal my soft wet cunt from you or your guests as I walk. My cunt is yours. It belongs to you, Master, and you do not want it hidden. I have been bathed in warm milk, but for hours this morning your semen still covered my breasts. My neck. My cheek. Dried on my skin, wherever you splashed it over me last night, after each time you took me.

Each time you thrust in me and ravished me, again and again and AGAIN. Each time my young, tight body gave you pleasure, Master.

Your guests gaze at me, like fire on my body, as I walk down the table, Master. They can smell my heat. They can smell me dripping for you as I walk past the naked thighs of the stone slavegirls. They want to touch me. *quivery, aroused breathing*If you weren't here to protect me, they would caress me with their fingers as I pass or grip my ass and my tits. *gasps softly*Maybe even pull me onto the table and fuck me.

They all want me, Master.

shyly Do YOU want me, Master?

I'll kneel beside you, Master, on your silk carpet. *a soft little sound* I'm parting my thighs for you, Master, kneeling with my legs open. All your guests are gazing at my soft, naked thighs and my soaked little cunt, and I am yours to display as you wish. My wrists crossed gracefully behind me, my breasts high and inviting, my lips soft and full. The cool evening breeze through the window licks at my cunt.

a soft, soft moan Your hand in my hair, Master. Mmmmm, and caressing my cheek … Master, my Master. Your hand is so warm … and strong. May I rest my cheek on your thigh, Master, while you dine? *so softly, so sweetly* I yearn for you, Master.

You … you want me in your lap, Master?

But won't your guests … ?

SMACK!!!

a cry or yelp from her Yes, Master, forgive me, Master. I'll rise gracefully to my feet, turning my body so you can see my breasts and cunt fully in the red light of the sunset. Look, Master, I'm dripping onto my thighs. It's because my Master is near. My Master who bought me, who branded me, who fucked me all night.

I am yours, Master. Your guests may watch the curves of my ass as I settle into your lap, my thighs open, one knee to either side of you, Master, in this enormous oak chair. Yes, Master, I'll cross my wrists behind my back. You make me feel so … helpless. Your body is so … massive. And I am so small in your arms. My body naked and available and open to your every touch. *gasps* You've taken my hair! Forcing my head back, lifting my breasts toward your face. Master, Master! Are you going to kiss my tits in front of all your guests?

moans Master, your mouth … *panting* … hot and wet on my nipples! *a cry of need* Masterrr!

a few moments of soft little moans and cries as he touches her

Your kisses on my throat and breasts … Master!

moaning softly

Master, I melt at your touch. My cunt is hot as the setting sun. Please, Master, touch me. Touch me. *a whimper* Touch my cunt, Master. *quivery* Let them all see how I surrender to you, Master. All those men gazing at me, wishing I was captive in THEIR laps. Fondle me, Master! I belong to you!

I want to please you!

a cry of arousal Master, your fingers! *panting* My folds are so soft and slick at your touch. Do I delight you, Master?

Am I lovely in the sunset, Master?

moans passionately Yes, Master, yes, fill me with your fingers, Master. Thrust them in me. Two. Th-th-three, three of your fingers inside me. *shaking with need, on fire with sensation* I'm so tight! I'm so wet and so tight! You fill me so full! So full, Master! You own me. I will submit to each caress. I will surrender to your every desire. Feel me grip and squeeze your fingers. Your fingers thrusting and THRUSTING inside me! You are my everything, Master. My only desire is to give you pleasure. I am your pleasure-slut, helpless and naked at your banquet table. My warm honey is dripping down your hand! Master, enjoy me! Enjoy me!

her moans intensify

whimpering Yes, Master, yes, I'll be silent. So you and the men can talk. Forgive me, Master. Yes, Master, I understand. Your slavegirl is here to give you pleasure, not to disturb your guests' dinner with her cries of joy at your touch.

whimpering helplessly, passionately, her lips closed to hold back her cries, as he touches her

Master, Master, I can't, I can't hold it in. Master, please! Let me moan, Master …

SMACK!!

she squeals

SMACK!!!!!

she squeals and nearly cums but just barely holds back

panting, gaspy, just above a whisper, desperately I'm sorry, Master! I'm sorry, Master! I'll be good! I'll be your good girl, Master. I'll be such a good girl.

SMACK!!!

yelps

whispers I'll be quiet, Master.

holding back a whine of NEED

whimpering at the thrusts of his fingers

a desperate, anguished moan erupts from her lips

Master, please, please, you're … you're going to force me to yield! I'm going to cum on your fingers, Master! I can't … I can't hold back. I can't keep quiet. You want me silent and I can't, I can't, I can't! Please cover my mouth, Master. Cover my mouth with your hand! Make me obey you. Make me subm-MMMPHHHHHH

he covers her mouth with his hand

she squeals into his hand as she cums

soft little whimpers into his palm afterward, for a few long moments

breathing hard when he releases her mouth

breathy, reverent Master.

small, soft licking sounds

whispers Feel my wet little tongue, Master? Licking your hand that kept me silent for you? *licking* While I came on your fingers? *licking* Your fingers that are resting inside me, thick and full. *licking* I'm licking your strong, masculine palm. *licking* Licking the fingers you held over my mouth, Master, but I want to lick the fingers you have inside me. *licking* I want to taste the pleasure you forced from my body. *licking* I want to taste my juices, Master, I want to taste what a good girl I am for you. Please, Master? Please? Will you put those fingers in my mouth?

a soft whimpering moan Yes, Master, pull your hand from my cunt … ohhhh … you're lifting your hand to my face, rubbing my wetness across my cheek. *so, so aroused* Feel me nuzzle my cheek into your hand, Master, like the softest, most pleasing kitten. *a low, feminine sound of adoration* My Master.

You're tracing my lips with your fingers. *a soft exhale, then sweet, gentle licking* I can taste myself on them, Master. *moans* May I have them in my mouth, Master? Your fingers? While you talk business with your guests?

sweetly Thank you, Master. I will suck my juices from them like a good … obedient … slavegirl.

gentle sucking sounds … she spends a few moments cleaning his fingers, moaning sweetly around his fingers

at last he withdraws them

she breathes softly Do I please you, Master? Do I make you proud of your slavegirl, here in front of all your guests?

Mmm, the way you're pressing my head to your shoulder. Yes, Master. I'll be quiet. I'll snuggle into my Master and be a good, silent slavegirl while you talk with your guests.

soft little noises from her as she snuggles

soft kissing sounds

slight teasing in her voice Master doesn't wish me to kiss his neck? Am I distracting you, Master?

SMACK!!!

yelps

whispers My ass!

SMACK!!!

squeals

Yes, Master, I'm sorry. I'll be good.

her soft breathing for a moment

the softest whisper I'm dripping onto your lap, Master. And I can feel your cock … how hard you are beneath me. *whispers*Hard as a god.

Do you wish you were fucking your pleasure-slut in your bed, this very moment, Master?

the softest sigh That makes me happy.

her soft breathing and soft, aroused and arousing little sounds for a few moments

then, a sudden gasp as she hears something in the talk at the table

sound of her squirming a little in his grasp

an anguished whimper, followed by hushed, frightened pleading Master! I know I'm supposed to be quiet, but Master! Master! I'm frightened! I overheard! I heard! Your guests! They're wolf hunters, Master! These men! They use women as bait for werewolves in the dark forest! Master, they take slavegirls ... like me! ... under the trees at night and they arouse us and make us run and RUN to attract werewolves. To attract feral animals out of the dark who would fuck us and tear us open with their cocks and rip us open with their claws and teeth! So the hunters can capture them while they rape us and eat us. And Master, these men, these hunters, they're looking at me! *squeaks* At ME! They heard me cum for you! They can smell my wet heat! They want to take me from here, bound and hooded and terrified, to use me as prey! And that one with the dark beard, he just implied ... he ... he ... *an anguished cry of fear* Master! Master! He's making you an offer to buy me!!!

Master, no! Master, don't sell me! Don't sell me, Master, please!!!!!

frantic, pleading I'm yours! Your brand is in my skin! I gave you pleasure all night, squeezed and milked your cock with my tight young cunt! Please don't let them have me, Master! I'm scared!

You ... you meet with them before each full moon to help

plan the hunts near your estate? And you sell them dancing girls who have been displeasing? *anguished* But not me, Master! Not me!

sniffling I will be the most pleasing, obedient, wet little slut for you, Master. *sob* Don't sell me, Master.

That hunter! The way he looks at me! My tears just excite him!

nearly hyperventilating with fear Don't take his offer, Master, don't-don't-don't, please don't, please don't …

SMACK!!!

screams

SMACK!!!

screams

panting Master, you smacked my clit!

SMACK!! … squeal … SMACK!! … shriek … SMACK!! … whimpering cry

sobs I'm sorry, Master! I'm sorry, I'll be silent!

SMACK!!

screams

I'll be a good slavegirl!

SMACK!!!

squeals

breathing hard Yes, Master, yes, I'll climb onto the table, Master. As Master wishes. *sniffling* Here I am, Master, standing naked and trembling among all your delicacies and desserts. *fearful little breaths*

Dance? You … you want me to dance? To dance on your banquet table for your pleasure and your guests' delight?

pleading I don't want to display my curves and my soft cunt for these men! These men want to buy me, Master! As wolf-bait! Master, please!

gasps No, Master, no! no! you don't need to whip me. Forgive me, Master! I will dance for you, Master.

sniffles Yes, Master. It will be my pleasure, Master.

taking a slower, steadying breath I will entice you, Master. I will make you crave me. I will make your loins burn for me. Keep me, Master. Own me. Take pleasure in me. See me dancing for your delight, Master. See me pivot and spin. See my jewelry flash in the warmth of the lamps, see your brand burned deep in my thigh.

soft, soft clinking of chain jewelry. Optionally, the music may change or increase in tempo here.

quivery, seductive, trying to entice her Master My hips sway for you, Master. My breasts rise and fall sweetly for you as I dance. See the flash of my cunt as I lift a long, smooth leg. The gentle music of the delicate chains hung about my hips. The sun has set, Master, and my oiled skin glows for you beneath your lamps. Am I beautiful, Master? Do you desire me?

I raise my arms high above my head, lifting my breasts like a gift … crossing my wrists like a captive … as I sway … and turn … and dance for your pleasure, Master. See my warm honey drip down my legs. My cunt soft … and swollen … from your attentions, Master.

Your guests watch me, gazing heatedly at my naked, wet cunt. Are you watching me too, Master?

I'll dance faster, swifter, every movement of my body a promise of pleasure and heat. See me lower my arms, holding them behind my back. I'm yours, Master. Helpless. Captive. Your slavegirl. See me sway as I walk toward the edge of the table, toward you, careful not to disturb your bowls and plates as I bring Master his most delicious dessert. Here I am, Master. Leaning back, my breasts high, my hips rolling for you, Master, my legs open. *aroused and heated* My folds glistening. Do you want me, Master? I'll kneel on the table, Master, and just sway and undulate for you like a willow in a night wind. Enjoy the fullness of my breasts, Master. Enjoy the wet heat of my cunt. I can hear your guests panting, Master. Every one of them must have a hard, engorged cock under his garments. Every one of them wants to touch me. Taste me. Fuck me.

They want to fuck YOUR pleasure-slave, Master.

I'll lean back until my head touches the table, my knees spread wide, my cunt right in front of you, Master. *moans* Yes, Master, take hold of my hips with your warm, strong hands. My breasts are heaving as I breathe! Watch me bring my hand between my thighs and … ahhhh … open my cunt for you. Spreading my folds with my fingers. Look, Master. I'm open. I'm tight and small and ready to be taken.

Claim me, Master! Claim me!

she cries out

Master! *a cry of surprise and delight and fearful anticipation* You've thrust me down on my back and climbed onto me! Onto the banquet table! Master!

a cry of need Yes! Cover me with your body, Master! Crush me beneath you! My Master!

moans My hip has landed in a dessert, Master, in something creamy and cool to the touch. Ohhh! You've grabbed my breasts! *she cries out* Squeezing them! Oh! You'll bruise me! Your hips muscling in between my thighs and … Master, your cock! It's so big, your cock! Master, I'm yours! *almost sobbing with need* Ravish me, Master! I'm yours! I'm your slavegirl!

her wild moaning cry of "I'm yours!!" as he penetrates her

the sound of her being fucked hard against the wooden table

her breathless cries I'm yours, Master, I'm yours! Whatever you desire of me is yours! *moaning* Make them watch, Master! Make them watch! I'll lift my hips into your thrusts! *cries of wild pleasure as she does* I'll clench down on your cock! Master, take me, take me!

moaning

a gasping whimper Master? You've … you've pulled it out of me ... what are you ...? What do you mean, Master, you only needed to get your cock wet and slippery inside me before you ... *gasps!*

You've flipped me onto my belly! My tits shoved into a sticky cream pastry on your table! Ah!!! And wrenched my head back by my hair! *panting* Master, Master, what will you do with me, Master? *whimpers* Master, your cock, slick with my honey ... you're pressing it to my ... to my ... !!! ... Master, I've never been opened there! Master, I've never had a man in my ass! Master!

a squealing, pained cry as he thrusts into her

fast little gasps of air Master, the head of your cock is in my ass! The tight heat of my ass!

squeals

Master, are you going to fuck my ass, in front of all your guests?

pleads Master!!!

grunts

No, Master, please, don't thrust the rest of your cock inside me, you're too big, you're too big, Master plea-MMMPHHH!!!

he covers her mouth with his hand, and we hear her muffled grunts and whimpers as he works his cock in her...

...and then THRUSTS

DEEP!!!

we hear her SQUEAL into his hand. Imagine her eyes wide and her scream as her Master's cock is shoved SO DEEP into her ass. Her cry muffled erotically by his palm pressed firmly over her lips

once he is all the way in, she lets out a low whine into his hand

he begins to fuck her in rhythmic, pounding thrusts, not fast but deep and hard, taking her ass as he pleases. At each thrust, we hear an animal grunt from her, muffled into his hand. Her grunts and whimpers and moans become more and more animal, feral, a slavegirl in heat being FUCKED in the ass by her Master. He fucks her on the banquet table until she is reduced to a shaking, quivering female animal. The listener should hear the rhythm of his thrusts by her short, muffled, breathless grunts and cries.

at last he lifts his hand, moving it under her instead to fondle her. The lines that follow are delivered in quick little gasps as he rides her hard and urgently

Master! Master! You own me! You own me! You own me! You're in my ASS! Yes, grip my breast, Master! Squeeze the cream into my skin! *panting and grunting* And my clit! My clit! Your fingers under me, on my clit! Master! Master! Master! You're so DEEP! You're so DEEP! I can barely breathe!

SMACK!!!!

squeals

Yes, Master, smack my ass! My body belongs to you, Master! My cunt, my mouth, my breath, my ass, everything I am is yours, Master, yours, yours, yours!

several hard SMACKs and squealing cries from her

squeals You fill my ASS!

Stretching me! STRETCHING me! Master! MASTER!

screams You pinched my clit! Oh gods fuck me Master fuck me FUCK ME FUCK ME FUCK ME FUCK ME

Master, may I yield? May I cum? Master, may I cum?! I NEED TO CUM! Master! Master! Cum with me, Master, cum with me!Cum in my ass! Master cum in my ass, cum in my ass! May I cum, Master? May I cum may I cum may I cum yes yes YES YES YES!!!!!

her screams of pleasure as she cums, as he cums IN her

panting, barely conscious

M-Master …

quivers Yes, Master, caress my thigh … feel your brand in my thigh, under your fingertips, Master. Feel your mark in my skin. You own me.

a moaning cry You've pulled out of me. Out of my ass. *panting* You've climbed off of me. Youre standing by the table, Master, leaving me a shaken, quivering mess. Lying with cream desserts squished under my cunt and tits. With your hot, sticky semen leaking from my ass.

a long, quivery inhale I'm so s-sore. *breathes in again, shaky* So well-fucked. I … I don't think I can move.

whimpers

You've broken me on your banquet table, Master. If I turn my face, I can see the wolf hunters. Their faces flushed. I

… I think some of them came in their garments, watching you fuck me. Watching you pound me like a wolf's she-bitch under the lamps, under the blind eyes of the stone slavegirls. *a soft whimper of fear* These men … they all want me so. Gazing at me as I lie here shaking while the werewolves howl under the trees outside and the lamps gutter and the first stars appear in the dark through the window.

gasps Master! What … what are you telling them?!

a little sob of happiness, relief, desperate gratitude Master!

I heard! I heard what you said! The pleasure-slut on the table, you've fucked her. You've claimed her. You've BURNED your ownership into her tight young body. No one, wolf or man, may touch this woman but you.

sobs Master. Master. My Master.

You stand by your banquet table like a god, your muscles rippling, your body glowing with sweat, your face flushed from fucking me. Your cock naked and hard and twitching in the air. And your eyes … your eyes are fire. Daring any of them to challenge you, daring any to anger you by trying to buy me.

shaky breaths I'll get up on my elbows … crawling weakly over the spilled desserts, to the edge of the table. Master, I need to be near you. My Master, you own me. *happy tears*

Master, I cling to the edge of your table and press my lips to your thighs where you stand. *kissing* Master. My Master. *kissing* Feel my mouth small and wet and sweet on your thighs.

a few moments of gentle, small kisses on his thighs

I am your adoring slavegirl.

reverently, gratefully, overwhelmed Master. My Master. My Master.

a few more soft gentle little kisses

the episode ends

5

Save Me, Master: Part I

The audio opens with the soft music of her Master's home, the warm crackle of a fire, and the soft breathing of the slavegirl.

Do I delight you, Master? Lying naked in your bed, my body perfumed and adorned with silver jewelry, slender chains around my hips, an anklet above my small foot. My cheek soft against your thigh, while the first stars burn like sparks of fire, and the night breeze through your window caresses my body. I lift my fingertips to my neck and caress the collar you've locked on me, Master. I am your voluptuous slavegirl, helpless in your bed in the dark delicious night.

reverently, softly Master.

Feel my young, supple breasts pressed sweetly to your leg, my cunt warm and wet against your shin. This wet cunt that you own. I'm aroused, Master, with you near me. *she lets out a breath, quivering with arousal* Do you smell me, Master? Do you smell my cunt, my heat? You've lit fire inside my body, Master. I can't help it. I need your touch.

Oh, Master. You lie naked and magnificent as a god on these silk sheets. Your skin looks so … *reverently* warm … in the firelight from your hearth. *quivers* The fire you branded me by. My Master. Even lying in your bed, you look so … big. So impossibly BIG. Muscled. *purrs the word* Male.

breathing in deeply

The way you smell makes my cunt melt and drip with warm honey, Master.

exhales slowly Do you feel my breath warm across your thigh, Master?

Do you feel my fingertips caress the inside of your thigh?

I'm yours, Master. You own me.

Tonight … *trembles* … tonight will be the full moon. If you hadn't bought me, Master, if you hadn't brought me to your bed, to moan and squirm beneath your thrusting hips as your helpless pleasure-slut … if you hadn't claimed me … tonight I would have been one of the slavegirls taken by the hunters into the forest, aroused and set loose under the dark trees to be chased … *frightened* … and fucked … and savaged by werewolves. I would have been bait for wolves, Master.

But instead I am here in your bed, your sensual slavegirl. Safe and … wet. My thighs open like a gift. Your mark burned into my thigh. *whispers* Making me yours.

Have I pleased you, Master? … *a soft, adoring sound* … Your hand stroking my hair … *a soft sigh* … and your cock … *a soft moan* oh, your cock … thick and resting like a sleeping beast across your thigh.

aroused How brutal it was inside me last night … and how wonderful. Your cock.

It's hard. *a soft sigh of need* You're so hard. Are you thinking about fucking me, Master? Are you thinking of how you fucked your naked, trembling pleasure-slave on your table in the banquet hall last night?

a soft plea Fuck me again, Master. Put your cock in me.

moans I need your cock, Master.

If I turn my cheek, I can kiss the inside of your thigh, Master.

kissing sweetly

Like this.

kissing

Gentle little kisses…

kissing

My mouth soft and open. My warm, wet tongue …

licking

Licking your thigh, Master …

she takes a few moments kissing and licking his thigh and making soft, feminine sounds of need as she does breathing in deeply The way you smell.

May I please you, Master? May I take your balls in my soft, warm mouth?

sucking gently, the sweetest little moan of pleasure around his balls in her mouth

whispers Master.

sucking

whispers Do you like being in my mouth?

sucking

Will you enjoy your slavegirl, Master? Your trembling, devoted slavegirl?

sucking

Night has fallen, Master. The whole world is soft and quiet. The marble nymphs to either side of your hearth are watching us. *giggles* Waiting for me to give their Master pleasure.

whispers Do you want pleasure … Master?

sultry Your slavegirrrl is dripping her honey onto your leg. *whispers* Please touch me.

Yes, Master. Yes. I will lick and please your cock.

licking

Do you like my small wet tongue, Master?

licking

Do I please you? Licking up and down your shaft …

licking

trembling Your cock is so thick, Master.

I'll swirl my warm tongue around your sensitive tip.

licking

breathless You own me, Master. You own my mouth.

My small, warm mouth.

for a few long, mmmm, delicious moments, we hear the sounds of the sensual, adoring blowjob she is giving her Master.

Mmm. Am I a good girl, Master? Am I a good girl?

blowjob sounds

gasps You're … you're taking my hands! Binding my wrists! In soft, silk rope … *aroused* … like the night you branded me …

quivers as she is bound

You've tied me, Master! *soft sounds as she squirms*

My soft tits bounce for you as I squirm, Master. My wrists tied in front of me where you can enjoy the sight of me captive and ready to be taken. Do you like me tied, Master? Bound tightly for your delight?

a soft moan of need I submit to you, Master. Bound on your bed in the night, far from the wolves and the forest, your brand on my body, my mouth soft … and open … for your cock. You are my Master and my god. I am surrendered and open and will take whatever you put in me.

gasps Your hand … you're tugging at my hair. Master? Do … do you want more of my mouth, Master? Are you going to use my mouth while I'm tied up? *a quivery moan* How may your love-slave please you, Master? mmmphhh mmmphhh

mmmphhh mmmphh

gasping for air Yes, Master! I'll take it deeper! Whatever you wish, Master! mmmphh mmmphhhh

a few moments of deeper blowjob sounds as he slowly but powerfully fucks her mouth

gagging

Master, you're thrusting your hips! I don't know if I can take it, I don't know if mmmphhh mmmphhh mmm MMMPHH!!!! MMMMPHHH!!!

he fucks her mouth hard, choking her

spluttering, sobbing from the intensity of it Yes, Master! I understand, I don't need to breathe right now, I just need to please you! I need to please you with my mou - MMMMMPHHH!!!

for long moments, a rough, demanding throatfuck, the sounds of her taking it, choking, whimpering around his cock, fighting to breathe, struggling to give her Master pleasure.

MMPHH MMMMPHHH *spluttering* You're so big, you're so BI - MMMPHHH MMMPHHHH

choking sounds

MMMPHH *heaving for air* I can feel your cock pulsing! Master! Master, cum in my mouth! Cum in my mou - MMMPHHHH

another few moments of deep, relentless throatfucking, then her muffled squeal around his cock as he fills her mouth with his hot, sticky pleasure

loud gulps as she swallows what he gives her

the sound of his cock leaving her mouth

her desperate gasps of air

a soft little sob

gasping, panting Master, you … your hand warm on my face, caressing my cheek. Did … did I please you, Master? Did I give you pleasure?

when she hears his answer, she breathes the word adoringly, breathlessly: Master!

You tasted so good in my mouth.

catching her breath

quivery, adoring Master, I could swallow your seed all night.

worshipfully You filled my mouth.

Master. Oh, my Master. Each time your cock is in my mouth … *moans* in my body … it's as if I've waited a hundred nights for you to fill me again. I yearn for you in me. Taking pleasure in me. *proudly* Enjoying me!

How else may I serve you tonight, Master, before the full moon rises?

her soft breathing as she listens

You … you wish to bathe now, Master?

her voice goes slooow and seductive You want me to prepare your bath, caress and grip and massage your hard shoulders and your strong back … rub oils into your body … trail my fingertips down your arms and chest … tease and delight your cock with my small, soft, oiled hands …

Mmmmmmm.

Yes, Master.

It will be my pleasure, Master. To bathe you. To worship your powerful body and soothe away every care.

I will give you SUCH pleasure, Master.

Oh! Master is taking my chin in his hand … Mmmmm *he kisses her*

a long … wet … sensual kiss

a soft, happy little sigh after it

You're untying me, Master?

quivery soft sounds as he does

My hands are free. My soft, small hands … feel me press them gently to your chest. *a soft, happy little noise*

another kiss, this one a little rougher, hungrier. She whimpers sweetly into his mouth.

Yes, Master, I will go at once for bath salts and oils to please you with, Master. I will bring them from the supply room. Your slavegirl will be so quick, Master, running soft and naked over the silk carpets in your halls. I'll hurry and come back to you, Master! And give you EVerything you need.

the sounds of her rising from the bed, her soft feet against the carpets, the opening and closing of a door. Then the sound of the fire is gone, and she is running lightly down the halls

another door opens

She hums softly to herself. She hums so happily! And we hear jars on a shelf as she sorts through them.

Hmm. Lavender. Vanilla. Rosemary. What should I pour into Master's bath? *giggles* Don't worry, Master. I'll find the perfect one.

a soft sigh of yearning Master, your bath and your slavegirl will be an oasis tonight. I will soothe you and relax you and satisfy you. I will make you so proud of your slavegirl.

more sounds of jars on the shelf

a sudden, frightened, startled gasp as she turns and catches sight of unexpected visitors behind her

Who … Who are you? You men in those black garments! What are you doing in the door to my Master's supply room? Gazing at me as if I'm a cornered deer! *terrified* Why are you carrying that chain … and that hood?

No! … no, don't come in here! Don't! … stay back! … *panicked breathing* I'll throw this jar at you! Stay back!

she throws the jar. We hear it shatter.

we hear her grabbing more jars from the shelf

she grunts, hurling another, it shatters

then her whimper and struggle as the men grab her

No! Let go of me! Master! Master, HEL-MMMPHHHHH

A hand covers her mouth as she screams for help! Her shrieks are muffled under her abductor's firm hand

scuffling sounds and muffled grunts as she fights them. The click of chains or shackles locking about her wrists, and her anguished whimpering cry as they click shut. Her mouth is free for the briefest instant.

she gulps in a breath, then tries to scream Master HELP! Hel-MMMPHHH!

they force a wadded cloth into her mouth. Fabric rustling as a hood is pulled over her head. She whimpers in the dark

sounds of quick footsteps and her muffled cries for help as the men drag her quickly down a hall a door opens, then closes

ambient night-time noises, to show they are outside. Footsteps.

after a moment, the whicker of a horse. A distant wolf howl. A muffled grunt as she is thrown into a wagon. A desperate, muffled shriek of "Master!" half-smothered by the gag.

another shriek of "Master!!!" muffled under the gag, interrupted by several harsh SLAPS against her naked flesh, making her yelp and whimper into the gag.

She sobs.

Now, the sounds of horses' hooves and wagon wheels creaking as her abductors take her away from her Master's villa. Ambient night noises. Distant wolf howls. Possibly new music in the background, quiet, a little ominous, maybe stringed instruments. The clinking of chains. The slavegirl's muffled sobs for a few moments. Then another muffled, anguished scream for help. A whimper. Then the soft sounds of her working the gag out of her mouth.

she gets her mouth free, her breathing is quivery and fast I've … I've worked the gag out of my mouth, but I can't see. I can hardly breathe under this hood. Please … please … who are you? Where are you taking me? Why are you doing this?! Why have you chained my wrists?

she listens a moment

I … I don't understand! What do you mean, my Master has been distracted from his duties to your guild? And you mean to remove the distraction. *talking quickly* Whatever is wrong, I can tell my Master about it! I can help him focus. He'll listen. He treasures me!

gasps I … I'm the distraction?

a soft sob

terrified How … how do you intend to "remove" me?

gasps Wait, why … why are you taking off my jewelry? Unclasping the delicate silver chains from around my belly and hips … and my anklet! Why? Please, don't take them away! My Master put those on my body to adorn me for his pleasure, to excite him when he calls me to his bed, jewelry small and delicate as I am, and purest silver … to protect me from werewolves.

a wolf howl, louder than before

She is breathing fast and quivery. She is frightened. That howl … that wolf is close. Where … where are you taking me? *holding back panic* What kind of place are you taking me to, where you'd want me stripped of my silver chains and anklet? Naked except for my steel collar and this leather hood and the shackles holding my wrists?

whimpers and clinking of chains as she squirms

It's so quiet out here. Except … except for the wolves. Where are we?!

breathes in deeply I smell … *frightened* … moss and cedar and pine. A f-forest.

whispers in horror You're hunters.

a terrified cry You're wolf hunters!

No! No! Please! Please, please, please! *begging, sobbing* Please, don't take me there! Not to the trees! PLEASE! I'll do anything. Please don't do this to me, PLEASE!! I just want to go home to my Master! *tearful* I'm supposed to bathing my Master and oiling his shoulders and his hips and his cock, and pleasing him with my soft mouth! Pleasing him with my body! Not squirming in this wagon in the dark! Please!

fighting her chains

whimpers No, no, I don't want to run from the wolves.

gasps, and a soft moan of startled arousal No … Why are you touching me? You can't!

a soft moan

Don't … don't do that. Tracing your fingertips teasingly over my breast … *a quivering sigh* … and caressing my soft thighs. Please don't touch me. *whimpers* Please don't arouse me!

desperate, anguished Why are you doing this to me?!

trembling You … you have to excite me for the hunt?! You need my nectar dripping down my legs? To … to lure ravenous wolves with the scent of my wet cunt!

No! No, stop! *a low moan* I don't want to be wet! I don't want to be wet for you! No! *moans* Please! Please! They say werewolves can track the scent of a woman for miles. THey'll find me! They'll tear me apart! You can't! You can't!!!

moaning No, don't touch me, don't, don't, no please, please stop … *squirming* … don't fondle my breasts, don't squeeze them … *moans* … please … your hands are so firm … so many hands … too many hands … on my tits … on my ass … on my soft, naked thighs! Oh my gods, how many of you ARE there? *moaning* Don't … don't caress me with your fingertips, please! Not my cunt, not my cunt! *moaning*

Let GO of me!

SMACK!!!

her shriek

angry, scared, aroused No! Only my Master gets to smack my clit! *tearful* I BELONG to him! His brand is in my flesh! This is HIS collar on my throat! Get your hands OFF me! Please!

SMACK!!

her sharp cry

NO!!!

SMACK!! SMACK!!!

her sharp squeals at the slaps across her clit

No! I'm not yours! *a grunt as she lands a kick*

struggling I can kick! If I wasn't hooded, I could bite you! Let me go!!

wolf howls

anguished, hearing the howls NO!!!!

panting Don't grab my legs, please, please don't pin my legs, don't spread them, no, no, I'll keep my thighs pressed together, you can't have me, you can't! Please, please don't do this to me ... *sobbing* You have my legs forced apart ... I'm so ... open ... please, please don't, don't touch me, I don't want this ...

Master, help! Help me, Master! Find me!

moaning No ... *a wild cry as one of the men fingers her* ahhh!!! Don't force your fingers in me! No! Get them OUT of me! Oh gods! My cunt is tight around your fingers, don't fuck me with them, please!!

improv a few moments of desperate, reluctant moans that she can't hold back

tearful, defiant My Master will KILL you! He will find me and save me and kill all of you!

they force another moan from her

Let me GO!

moans Ahhh! How you work your fingers in me! In my tight wet cunt! Please!

she moans as they play with her

Ohhh ... two mouths on my nipples ... ohhh ... your wet, warm mouths ... *helpless moaning* ... please ... please ... ah-ah-ah! *panting* What? what? What? That mouth! A mouth! On my clit! Your lips, they're too soft, too soft, oohhhhhhh ... your warm, wet tongue! *her wild cry* Oh you can't!!!

her moans are so erotic and intense as they all fondle and arouse her

Ohh, how you lick me … ahhh! Tongues laving my nipples, a tongue at my neck, tongues on my belly and h-h-hips, a tongue caressing my swollen little clit … so many … tongues …

breathless, lost in pleasure you can't … you can't … my warm, dripping honey is for my Master! Please! *moans*

squirming, pleading, as her moans overtake her and overwhelm her

Please! PLEASE! My pleasure is overtaking me, I can't, it's like a spring flood and I am the smallest leaf! I can't! I'm going to yield! I'm going to CUM! Please, please, stop!

Master! Master, I'm sorry! I'm sorry, Master! I'm sorry, Master!

a desperate wail as she cums, as the pleasure shatters her Masterrrr!

quivery, pleading gasps Master … Master … Master …

You're … you're all still … t-touching me … licking me … fondling me … my body flushed and quivering under your lips and your hands … why? why? I came! I came! Why are you still touching me?

panting You're … you're going to make me cum again? Again?! *sobs* And again? Until my legs are soaked with my pleasure?!

wails No!! Don't enjoy me, don't!

moans as they enjoy her

Oh you can't, you can't! I can smell my own wet heat, even through the hood! And my moans! My cries will wake the whole forest!

wolf howls

The werewolves will WANT me! *sobs* They'll WANT me! They'll want to chase me! Dark silent beasts smelling their way through the forest! They'll hunt me, they'll HUNT me! I'll be their prey! Their helpless quivering prey, weak from orgasms, still dripping from your touch, my wrists captive behind me, my soft full breasts bouncing as I run! Sobbing as I trip over a root or a rock! Weeping as they pursue me in the dark!

One will catch me! He'll catch me! He'll grip my slender throat in his teeth and pull me to the mossy ground and fuck me! He'll want to force his massive, beast-like cock in my slick cunt while I squirm and kick and scream! He'll rape me! He'll ravage my cunt, and he'll tear at me with his teeth and eat me!

moans Please don't EAT me!

moaning helplessly as they ravish her with their mouths and hands

shrieks You bit my clit! You bit my clit! *shrieks* My nipples!

Stop!

wildly aroused at the biting

Oh gods, no, no, no-no-no-no

for a couple of minutes, she cums ... and CUMS ... their touch slamming her from one orgasm into another, her cries filling the night

panting, unable even to catch her breath, losing her mind from orgasm after orgasm Oh your hands! Your hands! So much pleasure! I never imagined so much pleasure! I'm on fire! I burn! I BURN! Oh gods. Oh GODS! Please, untie me! Let me touch you, as you make me yield and yield and yield! Let me caress your faces! Let me grip and clutch at your shoulders and ass! Let me touch and worship your hard cocks! Please untie me!

moaning and soft pleas until yet another orgasm is forced on her, as they get her so aroused for the hunt

Everything in me is melted h-heat!! *cries out* Do I taste good to you, men? Does the soft flesh of my breasts excite you! My trembling thighs? My soaked, helpless cunt? Do you like my taste in your mouths? Taste me, men, taste me!

quivery Caress and lick my body with your warm tongues!

I-I-I'm a pleasure s-slut ... a good slavegirrl ... I'm a good girl ... I'm a good girl ... I'm a good girl ... I'm a good girl ...

She cums, squealing sweetly, heartbreakingly. The sounds of the wagon wheels and horses' hooves stop and fall silent while she does.

After, she is shaking, panting, in a nearly "ahegao" state, completely overcome

quivery, almost a whisper, awed You've broken me. You've broken me, broken me.

panting

breathless A cup? Pressed to my lips?

the sound of her gulping water, desperately, because they've dried her out with orgasms

shaky You've … you've taken your hands from me. Your mouths.

We … we've stopped?

trembles We're deep in the forest? I … I can't see through the hood. *whimpers, aroused and frightened* You … you say I lie sweaty and gorgeous in the moonlight? In the light of the full moon.

wolf howls, close and loud

an exhausted little sob

the sounds of them lifting her

You've taken my arms!

a creak from the wagon, and her startled cry as she thrown to the ground. The thud of her impact and her grunt

quivery You … you've thrown me from the wagon! This moss is so cold against my tits and my thighs, and the pine needles are sharp against my soft, sensitive skin! Please! Please, let me back in the wagon! Please!

sounds of a few men jumping down, then their footsteps receding

And some of you are running away under the trees with your

nets! *terrified* To form your perimeter, to get ready for the hunt! And … *squeaks with fear* and I'm the bait! Bound and hooded and … naked!!! With my cum on my thighs!

rustling as she gets to her knees

I will kneel and beg. With my wrists chained behind me. Please. Please. I'll do anything. You've touched me. Tasted me. Am I not a dream of pleasure? See me on my knees, naked, a hood over my head! You can't see my face or the pleading in my eyes, just my body. My breasts lifting as I gasp and whimper! See, I'll … I'll spread my legs! Look! Look how my warm cunt glistens for you! Open and soft and TIGHT … and yours if you take me! Don't … don't you want me? You don't want the wolves to have me. You all want to fuck me! I heard it in your voices, in your breathing as you fondled me and made me cum! Please! I'll be your slavegirl! I'll be your little pleasure-slut! For all of you! Kiss my thighs and breasts with your whips! Break me with your cocks! I will take them ALL! I'll take each of your warm, thick cocks in my mouth! In my throat! Choke me and fuck me and spill your semen down my soft, tight throat! I will swallow it! All of it! All of your hot, sticky seed! Shove your cocks between my soft breasts, each of you, one after another! Thrust yourselves in my tight young cunt! In … *whimpers* … in my ass! Please! Just save me! Save me! Fuck me in the wagon, all of you, fuck me until I shatter, force as much cock in me as I can take! Anything you want! As rough and violent as you want! I know you crave me! Take what you desire! Just bring me home to my Master! *sobs* Please! Save me, please! I'm begging you! I'm begging you like such a sweet, good slavegirl! Please!

the sound of the hooves and the wagon wheels, receding a little

her anguished cry Don't leave me!

sobs Don't leave me here alone in the forest! Blind in the dark! With no silver to protect me! Clothed in nothing but moonlight and a collar! *crying* Surrounded by prowling beasts! Please!

the hooves and wheels are gone.

whimpers Don't leave me.

sniffles I've … I've dripped so much warm honey down my thighs. The wh - whole f-forest can smell me.

wolf howls

frightened at the sound I have to get away from here! With … with this hood over my face, I can't see! I can't see! But if I stay here, they'll get me, they'll GET me! *whimpers*

scrambling, wrists bound, to her feet, trembling The … the howls came from … from over there. Maybe if I … if I run this way, I can … I can get away … *crying* … maybe if I run fast enough! I'm young … and lithe … if I just run swiftly under the trees on my soft, naked feet … if I run until my sides burn! If I don't trip or break my hip against a tree!

starting to pant as she runs. We hear the sound of her feet and the pursuing howls

a soft, soft moan of fear Find me, Master, please! Find me! Don't let them get me! I'm scared, Master! I'm scared! Save me, Master!

a wolf howl, and her frightened, breathless whimpers

Save me. Save me.

the episode ends

6

Save Me, Master: Part 2

We hear the night sounds of a forest and the panting, shivery gasping of a frightened, fleeing slavegirl. Her running footsteps, bare feet. The clinking of chains or shackles at her wrists. She is hooded. Possibly, we hear quiet background music, maybe ominous strings, a fast tempo for the chase.

A wolf howls, close, and the slavegirl cries out in fright

Master, save me! Find me, save me, Master! Don't let the wolves get me! Don't let them get me, Master, don't let them get me!

My heart's pounding so fast! So fast! *terrified* The forest air is cold, and I'm wet from slipping on the moss, and I'm wet between my thighs where the hunters fondled me! The werewolves can smell me! *sobs* Master, help me! *whispers* Help me.

My wrists are locked behind me! I'm hooded in the dark, and I can't see! I can't see where to go, how to get away. I'm scared, Master, I'm scared!

the sound of her crashing her hip into a tree, yelping and falling

My leg! *a moan of pain*

whimpers That hurt.

sudden, scared, tearful anger There are too many trees in this forest!!

crying softly, shivering I'm so cold, I'm so cold. If I could only see…

wolf howls

whimpers No, no, no, so close! So close! *sounds of her scrambling* I have to get up, I have to get up! I have to RUN! *whimpers* I can be in pain later, I have to run NOW!

sounds of her bare feet running, her panting and whimpers, the pursuing wolves

They're hunting me! They're HUNTING me while I run naked in the moonlight! I'm blind under this little red hood and I'm so shaky and weak from the orgasms the wolf hunters forced on my body! I can't catch my breath, I can't! I can't!

her panting, then a wolf howl, LOUD

No! It's in front of me! *panting to herself* Turn around, turn around, run, run, RUN! Oh gods! *sobbing with fear*

sound of paws following her

No, please! Please! *sobbing* Run faster, if I run faster …

a wolf growl behind her

Oh no! No, no!

the sound of impact, the wolf bearing her to the ground, her cry as the wolf slams into her, her grunt as she hits the forest floor. The wolf's low deep grrowl and her cries of fright as she squirms under the beast!

the wolf's growling

panting No! No! This can't be happening! No! Help! Someone help! *her gasp* Your claws, your claws on my thighs! Holding me down, my belly and tits to the wet forest moss. Pleeeease! Please don't eat me! Don't eat me, don't eat me…!

almost hyperventilating with fear

Oh gods! *squeals* Oh gods! Your breath hot on my neck! *moans* Don't do that, don't do that, don't lick my neck … *a moaning whimper, then little gasps* No … no … no, your tongue is so hot on my skin … don't … I don't want to be licked … *whimpers* I don't taste good …

shrieks No! No! I can feel your jaws around my neck … your t-t-t-teeth pressing into my skin … please … please … please!

her whimpers of fear and the low growl of the wolf

then a shivery sob Thank you … thank you … for not biting me, for not tearing out my throat. Thank you, wolf, thank you, wolf … *crying*

the wolf's growl stops, replaced with sniffing, the wolf smelling her whimpers No ... no ... don't smell me. Ahhh! Don't press your snout to the inside of my thigh. Your warm breath washing across my clit. *a whimpering moan* Please! Please, I don't smell good. I don't smell like a tasty meal. Please let me go, let me go! Don't SMELL me!

a low growl from the wolf

little gasps of fear I know you've chased me all through this forest. After hunting me, you probably have a wolfish appetite, but you don't want me. You don't want me! I'm not a deer or a rabbit, I'm a woman. I'm a slavegirl. Please! You were human once, weren't you? Just like me?

a louder GROWL from the wolf

whimpers No-no-no, you don't want to do this to me! You don't want to eat me or fuck me or tear me apart ... please ... *sobbing* I'm not for you! I'm for my Master!

I know the wolf hunters touched me and TOUCHED me until my warm honey ran down my legs, I know that snout of yours can smell my wet heat.

I-I-I can smell you too. Your overpowering musk, your hair damp with sweat from running me down. *whimpers* I can't see you, you're just this massive beast above me, on top of me. You're so ... big! Please! I can hardly breathe under you!

sobbing Wolf, wolf, please, please listen. I'm bait. Do you understand my words? Please, please understand. The wolf hunters ... they use slavegirls as bait. Please, nooo! Don't press your snout to my cunt, *gasping* you have to listen to me! You have to!! They're coming, the hunters! They're closing in on you with nets and spears! If you take me, wolf, if you ravage me, they'll BE here soon! They'll take you! *pleading* Don't you want to stay free? Don't you want to run through the forest with your pack in the cold, cold night? Under the full moon? You can stay free if you let me go! Please! You have to understand! You have to LISTEN to me!!!!

a sharp cry from her Ahhh! Your claws are so sharp! Don't dig them into my thighs, please! Don't cut me with them, don't!*frantic* I don't want to bleed! I don't want to bleed! I don't want to bleed! *screams* No! Don't force my legs apart! No! No! Master, save me!

we hear low, quiet wolf growls throughout the lines that follow

sobs There isn't ANYthing human left in you, is there? Not under the full moon. The moon I can't see, the cold moon I feel on my skin, the wild moon I hear in your growls. You're so ... feral! Like darkness and hunger and every nightmare that ever chased me in my dreams as a girl! I can't get away, I can't get away! You're like the wild midnight and the wilderness itself and you've caught me, you've GOT me. And you don't even know I'm a woman, a beautiful slavegirl! I'm just soft wet flesh for you to enjoy and ravage! *sobs* You're just a BEAST! Just a big, hungry beast!

whimpers I'm a woman, I'm not food! Please!

shrieks

Your teeth! Your teeth grazed my thigh! Please! Don't BITE me! No! Not there, not there, not there ... *sobs*

I know, I'm soft and tender and trembling. *sobs* My Master has me bathed in warm milk each day to keep me soft and delicate and lovely to his touch. Am I lovely to your touch too? *whispers* Don't eat me, don't eat me …

a shocked, aroused moan

You … you licked me! *a wild moan* You licked my cunt! My clit! *moans* Oh, your tongue! Your long, warm … tongue! Wolf, wolf, don't … don't … *moans*

her wild moans as the wolf licks her

Wolf! Wolf! *panting* You wild wolf! Please! You h-h-have to st-stop! I've already cum so many times tonight! If you do this to me, if you taste me, if you make me cum, I'll shatter! I'll break like glass! Please! If you do that to me, I might not even be human anymore, just a wet whimpering little bitch in heat, cumming and cumming and cumming, like one of your own she-wolves in your pack!

breathlessly Please don't do this to me, please …

moans of pleasure too fierce to hold back or resist

Oh … oh … you're holding me down … with your claws in my thighs and your tongue ravishing my cunt! Licking me from behind while my nipples harden against the cold moss beneath me. Please … this can't be happening … this can't …

moaning

panting Do I taste good to you then? You animal, do I taste good to you? Oh GODS! *moaning* It's too much, it's too much …

whimpers I'm SOAKED! My honey dripping over your warm snout. Wolf, please …

Master, please … help …

quivery Wolf, the way you lick me … my cries are going to shake the forest!

moaning, her arousal overpowering her as he LICKS her

wails No, no, you can't! You can't!

You beast! You beast! You BEAST! *she cums, her cries of orgasm loud in the dark*

her gasping breaths

then her low, almost animal whine No … don't mount me. Don't mount me, wolf! Ahhh!

terrified Your jaws are closed around my neck again, no, no, no, holding me pinned by my neck! Your teeth clicking against my collar! *panicked* No! No! I feel that swollen, hard beast-cock! No! Nudging at my thighs, at my thighs where I bleed, at my soft, vulnerable cunt! Please don't, don't, don't, you won't fit, you won't fit, you won't, you won't …

her scream as he penetrates her, an agonized animal cry

You're in me! *a wild cry as he thrusts*

You're INSIDE me! *a wild cry*

her wordless, desperate cries as the wild wolf fucks her

then No! You can't! You can't!! My throat is in your MOUTH! My life held between your teeth! Please! Don't fuck me! Don't break me with that cock! Don't tear me open for a meal! Please!

desperate cries as she is FUCKED

moaning in terror and approaching orgasm I can't see! I can't see! I can't breathe! So heavy on me! So thick inside me! Like a dark forest god is FUCKING me! Fucking me in the dark! Fucking me in the dark! Help!

panting "help, help" for a few moments between gasping cries as the wolf takes her

panting, just animal gasps from her, fucked nearly mindless You're so … BIG! Wolf, wolf, you're tearing me apart! You're too big! Too big in me, too big in me, stretching me, stretching my cun - *she wails, a long desperate WAIL as she cums*

panting Clenching! Clenching! Squeezing your cock!

SOAKING your cock!

gasping, panting as the wolf keeps taking her

then, her little gasps Master, save me, save me, save me …

the sound of a horse's hooves approaching

panting

whimpers Wolf, no, no, no, how you're grunting, nooo! Don't cum in me, wolf … don't cum in me … *wails* … please!

the hooves get close, then the swing of a blade and the thunk of it in the wolf's flesh

her little gasps as the wolf's thrusts go still

What … what's happened? What's happening? All this blood pouring hot over my hips … I'm shaking, crushed beneath this wolf …

The sound of a man sliding from the saddle. The whicker of the horse.

frightened little gaspy breaths from her

footsteps approach her

Who … who's there?

whimpers Help me.

the sound of the wolf's body heaved off her, aside onto the ground

… No, don't grab me! Don't grab me! Whoever you are! Don't flip me over on my back! No more, no more, no more! *crying*Don't hurt me!!!

a little whimper of terror that would nearly break a protective Master's heart

the rustle as the hood is removed

You're … taking off my hood … ?

a gasp!

M - Master?!!!

Master!

a sob of relief Master, it's you! It's you! I can see your eyes deep as the sea and the full moon above your hair! You're holding me! You're HOLDING me! Master! Master! *crying* You found me! You saved me!

Take me in your arms, yes, hold me. I'm your slavegirl! Master! Master!

crying softly for a moment as he holds her

gasps The wolf! You cut its throat with your long knives. How terrible he looks, bleeding there on the moss. I couldn't … couldn't see him before, under my hood. He ravaged me while I was blind in the dark. He's so big, so cruel. *sniffles* His fur damp with blood. And his … I can see his cock. *whimpers* So big. So horribly big! He was IN me. *whispers* That wolf fucked me, Master. That wolf fucked me … H-he was going to EAT me … *sobs* The wolf hunters, they kidnapped me, Master! I was going to make you a bath. And they grabbed me! They fondled me and tore off my silver anklet, the silver chains you strung about my hips to protect me! They brought me here to the forest to be fucked and eaten. My wrists are still locked behind me, Master.

panting The way you caress my hair … telling me I'm safe, you'll keep me safe … Hold me, Master, hold me … keep me safe … *sniffles* … please hold me so tight …

Master, you found me. You saved me!

Master, I was so scared. I thought I was going to die tonight.

sniffling I've soaked your sable cloak in my tears and I'm … I'm sticky with the wolf's hot blood, I'm getting it all over you, all over your arms and your beautiful clothes, Master. Please don't be mad. *a heartbreaking little whimper* I was supposed to give you a bath tonight.

You're taking my chin.

vulnerably Master?

he kisses her. A long, sensual kiss, long and long, leaving her breathless after

softly You're being so gentle with me, Master. I'm sore and … *sniffles* … and shaken, and bleeding a little from claw marks in my thighs, and you're being so gentle. Your soft tongue and your lips caress mine, and your mouth on me is so … tender. *a brief, gentle kiss* Mmmm.

Your eyes are so deep and so warm, even in the cold light of the moon. *breathlessly* My Master.

You didn't let them have me. You came for me.

he kisses her again

the softest little whisper from her, as if she barely dares even breathe the words, yet she can't hold them inside I love you, Master.

her voice gentle and adoring I love you, Master, like I love water and air and sunlight. This is your collar on my throat, your brand on my thigh. I am YOUR love-slave. Master, I love you!

kissing, her soft little moans of love muffled into his mouth breathless Kiss me, Master, kiss me until I can't breathe. *kissing* My mouth belongs to you, Master, and my kisses, as many kisses as you could ever want. My kisses are yours, Master! *kissing* You own my mouth. *kissing* Yes, caress me. *tearful* Cup my breasts in your hands. My breasts are safe in your warm hands. You own my breasts. *kissing, a little moan into the kiss* Yes, my nipples. Ahh, under your fingers! You own my nipples, Master. *low and breathy* They're yours.

moans

You own my body. My hips and my soft tight cunt. *kissing* You own my breath and my heart. *kissing* You own my everything. You own me, Master. *kissing* I am yours, Master, I am yours.

sweet little whimpers into his kiss, and we hear wolf howls while they kiss. She gasps at the sound and breaks free of the kiss.

Wolves! *her little gasp as she remembers danger* Master! Master, the wolf hunters! They're still out there under the trees! They might be watching us! They wanted to hurt you, Master! They took me because they wanted to hurt you!

sounds of footsteps around them

Oh no! Master, they're here! Oh Master! Master, there's four of them! With nets and knives! Master, we have to get away! We have to get out of here!

No, Master, no, don't set me down! Don't fight them, there are too many! Master, no! You have to take me to your horse, we have to ride away! That fury in your eyes, Master, like your soul on fire! It frightens me! Don't fight them! Master, please! I'm scared for you! Master!

the ring of metal as her Master unsheathes two long knives

breathless Two long knives, one in each of your hands. The way you hold them … like they're part of your body, like you might dance with them and slice open the gods themselves. Master!

sounds of clashing blades

Wolf hunters, you ANIMALS, leave my Master alone! *tearful, angry* Leave him ALONE!

rustling as she gets up I'll scramble to my feet. *quietly, tearful and determined* I may be bound, but my legs are free. I can run at them, kick them, entangle them!

her quick, running footsteps, then the whistle of a net closing about her

No! *her furious cry* NOO! Get this net off me!

her grunt as she falls to the ground No! I don't want to squirm and wriggle in a net on the ground! I want to help my Master! You animals! You animals! *her cries and grunts as she struggles* I will get OUT of this net and I will KICK you! I will bite your faces! That is MY Master you're fighting! I am his slavegirl! I have to get to him! *shouts* Master! Master, I love you!

the thud of a body falling

Master, you slew one! *a happy cry* Master!

grunting as she struggles You wolf hunters, my Master will CUT you! You TOUCHED his slavegirl!!!! You took me from his HOUSE! My Master will kill you all!

squirming in the net I am going to get OUT of this!

Master, behind you!

a thud

her cry of relief and worship Kill them, Master! Yes!

reverently My Master. The way you battle these men who took me! You dance over the mossy ground as gracefully as I danced on your banquet table at home. How you fight! Fighting for ME. Such masculine power in every movement, every spin of your hips, each crouch and pivot and slash! None of them dance the blades as you do, Master. Destroy them!

Master! You are a god. My Master. My owner. My love!

squirming more, grunting

Oh! I've got my legs free! Kicking in the dark! *triumphant* I may still be tangled but I can STAND!

scrambling up

Master, I'll help, I'll help! I'll run at this wolf hunter from behind, slam my shoulder into his back, shove him right into my Master's knife! *her cry of anger as she does*

a thud.

a moment later, a last clash of blades, and a final thud

panting You slew them, Master. All of them. The wolf hunters. They're gone.

a soft, frightened gasp You … you're wounded! Master!

A … a scratch?

ablaze with fright and anger and adrenaline That is NOT a scratch! That gash in your side! You're hurt! Master, you're hurt!!! I would bind it for you, Master, but my hands are chained!

the sound of her Master's long knife cutting through the ropes of her net

Yes, my Master, my Master, saw through the net! *breathless* Set me free!

metal sounds You're picking the lock on my wrists with your knife!

Master, free me … free me … I'm yours. I don't want other men's bonds on my wrists. Only yours. Only ever yours.

a sweet cry of happiness My wrists are free! Master! Oh, Master! Let me grab your hair and mmmphhhh *kissing him ferociously*

I love you Master! *kissing, breathless* I love you! *kissing* I love you!

May your slavegirl tend your wounds, Master?

Not … not yet? Other wolves may come? You have to get

me out of here first? But Master, you're hurt! You're bleeding! Master, let me help! Please!

a soft cry No, Master, put me down! I have to bind your wounds! Where are you carrying me, Master? Master, don't carry me, you're hurt!

a quick smack!

Yes, Master, I'll be quiet. I'll be quiet. *whispers* But Master wait! Wait! That little red hood on the ground, the one the hunters tied over my face! Take it with us, Master! Please!

whispers Thank you, Master.

the whicker of the horse, and sounds of them mounting the horse

softly You're settling me in front of you in the saddle, naked as the night, wearing only your collar and your brand in my skin. Your arms around me, warm and strong, protecting me. Yes, Master. Take me from here. I don't ever want to be in this forest again! *tearful* I want to go home with my Master.

worried for him But Master, you're bleeding! Don't bleed through my fingers! Don't die, Master, don't die! Hand me the hood, Master, please, hurry! Here. I'll press this leather to the gash above your hip while we ride. *angry, tearful* Those men intended this hood to make me their helpless wolfbait, but I'll use it to save my Master!

rapid hoofbeats, the horse galloping from here through to the end of the audio

Faster! Ride faster, please! I won't fall, I know I won't, not with your arms around me! We have to ride FAST!

You're so pale. Master! *frightened but trying to reassure her Master* You HAVE me, Master. I'm safe. No wolf is going to get me. I'm here, Master, I'm here. I'm safe. *whispers* I'm yours.

I'm pressing my lips to your neck … *kissing gently* … kissing my Master … *kissing* … keeping your blood, your life, inside your body with the gentle pressure of my hand, holding the leather hood to your wound. I'll keep you safe too, Master.

I love you. I love you with every beat of my heart, every breath in my body. I am your melted, obedient, loving slavegirl. I am yours, Master. I am yours. Always and forever yours. You saved me.

kissing

Ride with me in your arms, Master, under the full moon, until you've taken me far away and this forest is only a nightmare behind us. Take us home, Master. Take me where I can dress your wound and kiss you and be a dream of pleasure to you, safe in the arms of the man I love, the man who owns me.

Take us home. I love you. I love you!

I love you, Master.

the episode ends

7

Lock Me, Master

We hear soft, exotic music. A heavy door opens and closes as the slavegirl steps into her Master's library. For a moment, we hear the quiet flipping of book pages until her Master sets the book aside. We hear the very aroused breathing of the slavegirl. She is quivering with arousal.

You called for me, Master? I'm here. How may your slavegirl delight you, Master? ... Oh! *a gasp of surprise*

in wonder Master, your library! It's ... it's beautiful! I ... *breathless* ... I've never seen so many books and scrolls and ... stories. *quivery* Bookshelves on your walls and ... and Master, those trees. You have trees in your library! Growing out of vast silver pots, slender trees with white bark, pale like moonlight, shimmering in lamps hung from their branches. And ... *breathing in* ... the scent of their fruit. It's like the perfumes you have ME scented with, Master. You have juicy delicacies growing right here in your library ... so that my Master may enjoy succulent, delicious fruit while he reads.

whispers Is that why you've summoned ME to your library, Master? *quivers* So that you might enjoy your succulent, obedient slavegirl … with my soft breasts … my open, inviting thighs … while you read your books?

softly Master.

You … you want me to look closer at the trees? Oh! *surprised and delighted* Oh, Master! Each tree is carved in the shape of a naked slavegirl. The branches are her hair. *giggles* She has fruit in her hair. Her breasts are pale and full, carved delicately from her living wood. Her arms make two shelves for books, and she holds more books for my Master in her small, feminine hands. And … her legs are half carved from the tree, open, a tiny shelf set between her soft, naked thighs, holding tales of adventure or erotic pleasure for my Master to read and enjoy. Master, your wooden slavegirls … their soft blossoms are carved so realistically, their little clits swollen and sensitive. Their pussies look wet as they shimmer in the lamplight. *giggles* Master, those slavegirls are going to drip their warm honey onto your books!

giggles

Your library is wonderful.

And *breathless* you look so powerful, my Master, in your sable cloak, with a long knife in its sheath at your hip. As you watch me, your deep eyes smolder like coals at midnight. *quivers* Your wound from battle has healed so well, these past few weeks, Master. You look strong and … pleased. *whispers* That makes me happy.

My wounds have healed too. They were just bruises and scratches. Except ... *quivery* ... I still have the nightmares. Night after night. But ... *draws in a steadying breath* ... I am a brave slavegirl for my Master.

At first I was frightened. ... Afraid you might not want me, after I was touched by others ... *whimpers* ... But the way you're looking at me, the way you've looked at me every night since and every morning when we wake, like I am the most beautiful thing in the whole world, more beautiful than starlight or rain falling on leaves, more beautiful than the sunset or a tempest at sea. I am your beautiful slavegirl, Master, and I melt and drip down my thighs when you look at me.

You sit there like a lion at rest, relaxed beneath the branches with their scented fruit, a book open on your lap, in your ivory chair. A chair shaped like a woman, her arms open for my Master, her lap making a gentle seat for you, Master, her eyes lidded, her face sleepy.

Everything in this library is here for my Master's pleasure. *softly* Including his devoted, collared slavegirl.

a thought takes hold of her Master ... all these books. *trembling* May ... may I ask you for something, Master?

nervous, wanting this SO much Master, would ... would you teach me to read, Master? Would you teach your pleasure-kitten to read? There was no one to teach me in my village before I was taken. *wistful* My father said I was more needed in the kitchen than dreaming over a book. And the slavers certainly never taught me. But ... I ... I've seen some of your dancing-slaves reading in the afternoons in your pleasure garden, Master!

excited Master, may I? May I read? Please, Master? I will curl at your feet, sweet and soft, and read you the most delicious stories while you rest by your fire in the evening. Or I can sit in your lap, your naked, delectable pleasure-slave, and whisper stories in your ear. And you can breathe in the scent of your library ... mmm ... and the scent of me ... the scent of wet heat between my thighs as I read to you, Master. And when you are so happy and full of stories, Master, I will kneel like a good girl between your powerful legs. I'll kiss and lick at your thighs with my soft, wet little tongue ... and then my Master can fill ME, whenever you choose. Please, Master. Please will you teach me to read?

a soft gasp, and a small, feminine sound of pleasure

almost tearful Thank you, Master. I love you, Master. I will learn so quickly, and I will read naked to you whenever you desire, Master.

May I approach your chair, Master? May your slavegirl give you pleasure?

Not ... not yet? You ... you want to gaze on me a while? Yes, Master. I will stand beautifully for you, Master, as you've taught me. One hip turned gently toward you, displaying the small, red brand in my thigh. My shoulders back, wrists crossed behind me, my full young breasts lifting and falling as I breathe.

breathing softly, letting him watch her breasts

whispers Do my tits please you, Master? Do you want your strong hands ... *an aroused inhale* ... your ravenous mouth ... your teeth .. on my tits, Master?

Master, please, I have been aroused for you all day. Yearning for you to come home from the market. When your other pleasure-slaves bathed me and oiled me for my Master, their soft hands cupping and squeezing and caressing my breasts, my warm thighs ... *moans* ... I wanted to slide my hand between my legs and touch this wet, hot little cunt that belongs to my Master. *needy whimper* But you didn't let me, Master.

See me open my thighs for you, Master, let you see clearly what you've locked on me, its smooth metal shimmering in the light of those lamps. How your eyes burn as you gaze on me. Master, this metal slave belt you have locked on my cunt ... it fits me so snugly. *whimpers* It is small and delicate ... like me ... but unyielding in its clasp, cupping my cunt firmly like my Master's hand. Holding me captive. And yours.

It is made of purest silver and it is locked on me. *a reverent, aroused, quivering breath* You locked it on me, Master, reserving my body for your touch only. The lock is heavy and shaped like a heart, and only my Master has the key. So that no wolf hunter might ever remove this belt. No wolf or man may ever touch me where I am so soft, so wet, so intimate. Only my Master. Only your fingers, Master. Only YOUR mouth. Only YOUR cock.

whispers You own me.

The inside of the belt is lined with the softest velvet, rubbing gently against my wet little blossom each time I take a step. Each time I BREATHE, Master. The gentle velvet is rubbing against my clit and my folds now, Master. Exciting me. Making me crave your touch.

whispers Please let me walk to your chair, Master. Please let me have your touch.

Please. I want to be such a wet, quivering, submissive pleasure-slut for you tonight, Master. I want to kneel like a good girl and open my soft, wet mouth for your cock. I want to beg you to unlock me so I can open my soft, tight cunt for your hard, thrusting cock, Master. I need you in me so much. If you don't touch me, I might die of need, Master. All day I've felt this slave belt rub against me, felt it LOCKED on me, heating me, keeping me melted and wet, reminding me at every moment that I am my Master's slavegirl.

The velvet inside the belt is soaked with my warm honey. Please, Master. Please will you unlock me? Please will you put your cock in me? And ravish me? Here in your library, surrounded by all your books. Make me scream for you, Master. I want to cry out as I spasm around your cock. I want you to remind me who owns me, with each hard, pounding thrust. Please, Master, please.

breathless I may approach? Thank you, Master! As you wish, Master.

See me walk toward you, Master, slow and graceful, gentle as moonlight. See how lovely I am, how feminine and soft and naked for my Master. See your brand in my thigh, Master. Delicate and deep, where you burned me. How I cried into your hand when you marked your ownership in my body! Do you remember, Master?

See my nipples, pierced because you desired it, Master. A silver chain running from one to the other, tugging gently as I walk. *moans*

See your collar holding my throat securely. Each time I breathe, each time I swallow your seed, I feel its gentle pressure on my neck and I know who owns me.

I'm here, Master. You wish me in your lap?

Yes, Master. *whispers* It will be my pleasure.

gently Will you set your book aside by your chair, Master? *teasing* I don't want to get your book wet, Master.

Mmmm, thank you, Master.

her quivery, aroused breathing Feel me slide into your lap .. ahhh .. one leg to either side, my thighs open. If this belt wasn't locked on me, my cunt would be dripping onto your lap, Master.

I love being in your lap. Naked while my Master is still clothed. Here for your pleasure and delight.

gasps Oh Master, how you squeeze my breasts. Your hands are so firm! Are my breasts soft to your touch? My nipples swollen and sensitive against your palms? *gasping little noises and moans* Oh Master, your touch sets fires to burn in me. My insides melt and drip for you, Master. *moans* Touch me, yes, touch me, Master! *quick little gasps* When you pinch my nipples, I can hardly bear it … *desperate little sounds*

moans How you caress my sides, moving your hands down my body, like you desire to enjoy ALL of your slavegirl.

a soft, bewildered sound What … what are you doing, Master? Tracing your fingertip along my thigh in that strange pattern?

It's … it's a rune?!

gasps You're teaching me a rune! A letter!

tearful and happy You're teaching me to read, Master?!

Yes, Master, yes! *sniffles* I'm so happy. I understand! The first rune in my name. It's the shape you just traced with your fingertip, writing on my body. And it makes that sound. *the voice actress pronounces the sound of the first letter of her GWA name.* Yes, I'll remember, Master. I'll remember because my Master traced it on my body. I will never, never forget.

… And that's the second letter. *she makes the sound of the second letter in her name* Yes, Master!

… And the third…

she finishes her name, repeating each sound after her Master traces the letter in her thigh. She says the name at the end.

reverently Master.

in wonder I know how to read my name. You've taught me to read my name.

loving You gave me my name.

I'll learn so quickly for you, Master! I'll read you every book in your library! I promise! I will read naked in your lap! I will be such a good girl, Master!

And you'll teach me more later tonight, after I've given you pleasure?

a soft, sweet, happy sound

I love you, Master. I love you so much.

Do you want to kiss me, Master? *softly* Please kiss me. Please kiss your pleasure-kitten.

He kisses her. Soft little moans muffled into his mouth. She gets more and more aroused as he kisses her, as he touches her, so that we hear her muffled whimpers and moans get more excited during this long kiss.

after the kiss Master! Master! Having your fingers caress the soft insides of my thighs, so close … so close to my blossom … but not touching me! It's torture, Master! It's torture! *whimpering with need*

Oh Master! Oh Master!

a sob of need

I will be such a loving, obedient slavegirl for you tonight, Master!

I missed you when you were at the market, Master! I missed your touch!

moans

I'll kiss your neck, Master. As you caress me!

soft, gentle, wet little kisses

low and breathy Do you like my mouth, soft and wet, on your throat, Master?

kisses

Do you like how your slavegirl teases your neck? Mmmm …

kisses

moans softly

whispers And my lips at your ear, Master …

kissing and licking gently

My soft little tongue …

licking

a quivery breath My teeth …

biting, with little whimpers of need

Do you like when your slavegirl nibbles your ear, Master?

kissing and nibbling

I like the sounds you make, Master, when I nibble and lick. Do I please you, Master?

kissing his ear

quivery moans Please, Master. Please unlock me. I need you. I need you like I need air in my body. Please, Master.

This belt has held me safe for you, all day. I am so wet … and I feel so safe when you are away, locked by my Master. At night after you enjoy me, when you lock this belt on me again, when I am chained by my ankle to your bed, I am so thankful. Because often I toss and turn in my sleep, whimpering while my nightmares grab me. In my sleep, I am in the wagon again, touched and fondled by men who don't own me. *frightened, aroused* Or I'm in the forest, crushed under the body of that werewolf, his hips thrusting at me! … But if I wake shivering in the moonlight, I feel the belt you've locked on me, the belt you've locked on my cunt, its cool silver protecting me. And I see you sleeping beside me like a very satisfied god, Master. I tremble and press myself to your body as you sleep, my breasts naked against your side, my thigh pressed to your hip. My Master. My owner. And I know I'm safe, so safe. Locked and yours. That no one will ever touch me again, against my Master's will.

a soft sigh You keep me so safe.

Sometimes, I wake you as I thrash in the grip of my nightmares. The first time, I trembled, thinking you might tie me to the metal rings in your floor and whip me for disturbing your rest, Master. But … you only held me, and caressed me, and stroked my hair and kissed my young breasts until the shaking from my nightmares subsided. You whispered in my ear that I was beautiful, and safe, and yours. That you treasure me. That I will never be lost in the dark forest again. That I belong in your arms, in your collar, and there I will stay.

whispers I love you.

Will you unlock me, Master? May I give you pleasure with my tight ... wet ... cunt?

a soft quivery gasp Yes, Master. Yes, the key. In your hand. Please. Please. That hard, thick key. Thrust it in my tiny, heart-shaped lock, Master. Open me. *quivering* Open my cunt. Open my heart. Open me. Open me.

the sound of the key in the lock

she moans

Master.

the sound of the belt coming off of her, and set aside on the table with a metallic sound

her quivery, excited breathing

I'm yours, Master. I'm yours.

whispers Please touch me. I belong to you.

a moaning cry of pleasure Your fingers! Oh, Master, Master! Ahhhhh! Inside me! Your fingers thrusting inside me! Master, Master, I love you!

her soft cries for a few moments as he fucks her with his fingers ... she is almost sobbing from need and pleasure

Ahhhhh! Master, when you pinch my clit ... *she squeals* ...

Master!

sobbing with need Master, may I yield? May I yield? May I surrender and cum at your touch? Please, Master, please! May I flood your hand in my warm honey? I've waited all day! I was WET all day! Master, I can't ... I can't hold back ... I need ... I need ... please, Master, PLEASE let your pleasure-kitten cum! Please, Master, please!

Yes! Yes! I love you, Master! Yes! Yes! YES!

she cries out these words helplessly as she orgasms You own me!!!

panting after her orgasm

whispers You own me, Master. You own me, you own me, you own me.

rustling sounds, and aroused little sounds from the slavegirl

You're binding me, Master? Tying my wrists behind me with your sash?

Yes, Master. As it pleases you, Master. I want to be bound by you.

wriggling, making soft sounds You always tie me so tightly, Master. You make me so helpless. You make me so yours. You make me cum and cum.

whimpers

I'm your slavegirl, Master. I can feel your cock beneath me, beneath your garments, hard and hungry as I wriggle naked and tied in your lap.

a little gasp at something he says

softly, submissively What do you mean, Master? That your … your heart breaks at my nightmares, my night terrors, my memories of the werewolf in the forest? *quivery, touched, shaken* I … I didn't know … that my screams in the night upset you so, Master. The way you're looking at me right now, Master. So tender and so … heated. And … you're not just going to teach to read tonight, you're going to teach me how safe I am? You'll teach your slavegirl that she's protected? So that I will know it deep in my cunt and deep in my heart, so that every night, even as I sleep, I'll know my Master is keeping me safe?

trembly Master?

the softest little gasp You're unsheathing your knife from your hip, Master? *quivery breathing* That knife is so long, so sharp. Steel, delicate and deadly, with a tracery of silver on the blade, to slay werewolves. And the hilt is ivory, ribbed for an easy grip.

her voice overflowing with love It's one of the two knives you brought with you to the forest, Master, when you saved me. It's the knife that cut the net from me, the knife that slew my captors. *breathless* This is my Master's knife, the knife that protects my Master's woman. *whispers* The knife that protects me.

The knife my Master uses to keep me safe.

gasps You're taking my hair and … ah! … forcing me down on the floor, on my back beneath you on your silk carpets, with your bookshelves and your trees carved like slavegirls all around us. My hands tied under me … You're so powerful above me, so muscled and male … my Master … *whispers* Yes, Master, I see the knife. I see the knife. Just above my face, glinting in the lamplight.

What will you do with me, Master, here in the quiet peace of your library at night, surrounded by your books? What will you do with your trembling, naked pleasure-kitten?

whimpers You have a fistful of my hair … so I can't squirm away… *little gasps of fearful excitement and arousal* … while you caress my cheek with your blade. The metal is so cold against my warm flesh, Master.

trembles The edge against my cheek … I don't have a beard for you to shave away, Master.

gaspy Your hand is so firm around that hilt, each movement deliberate. Careful. Strong. *whispers* I trust you, Master.

so softly, sinking into a deeply submissive space Yes, Master. I will kiss the blade of your knife, Master. Your long, hard knife. Your slavegirl will kiss the knife her Master uses to keep her safe.

slow, gentle kissing sounds as she kisses the knife

softly The metal is so cool against my lips. Mmmmm. Not like my Master's cock that pulses hot in my mouth.

But strong. *whispers* The blade is strong. Like you, Master.

quivery breaths What are you going to do with me, Master?

quivery gasps Yes, Master, I feel the tip of the knife caress the line of my jaw. *gasps* And cold … lethal … sharp … against my soft, vulnerable throat. The gentle pressure of your blade into my skin. If you pressed harder, I would bleed for my Master. … I'm tied and held and completely helpless. *frightened but submissive* Will you keep me safe, Master? Will you keep me safe?

Yes, Master. I trust you. I submit to you. You own me.

All of me. My breath, my heart, the life in my body.

shaky breathing

I feel my Master's knife tease along my collarbone … ahhh … and down … ahhh! … across the swell of my breasts.

whispers, vulnerably Master, it's so sharp.

whimpers

Men have died on this knife. This knife that protects me. As my Master protects me.

a soft little cry Master, those slow circles of the knifetip around my nipple … Master, Master!

quivery little breaths, aroused and completely stimulated

Every cell in my body quivers, Master. How you tease my breasts with your knife. I'm … I'm frightened. I'm scared, Master.

breathing fast

Yes, Master.

Yes.

You will keep me safe.

repeating so softly You will keep me safe. You will keep me safe.

I'm yours, Master.

whispers My nipples are so hard. ahh-ahh-ahh, when the knife teases across them ... *whispers* ... so sharp ... so sharp ...

Yes, Master, I'll repeat what you tell me, like a good slavegirl, as you trail the blade across the underside of my breasts. *quivering*

My Master owns me.

My Master treasures me.

My Master takes such delight in me.

And you will keep me safe.

she breathes the word like it's a magic word, like it's the most beautiful and important word in the whole universe: Safe ...

whispers I'm so wet, Master.

My honey is dripping down my thighs. *moans* I'm so wet, so wet.

quivery I belong to you, Master. You own me. You own me.

gasps Master! The knife ... I ... I feel it ... tracing down over my smooth belly ... Master ... *quick little gasps* ... Master, where are you taking it? Where are you taking your knife, Master?

whimpering Oh my gods.

Oh my gods.

Ohhhhhh ...

Yes, Master, yes, I ... I .... I feel the flat ... of the blade ... teasing my soft mound. *whimpers* Master, keep me safe. Keep me safe. Keep me safe!

moans

Yes, Master.

I am my M-Master's pleasure-kitten.

My Master's love-slave.

You will never let anything hurt me. My Master takes good care of what he owns. My Master will keep me safe.

whimpers

then MOANS

Oh, Master! The edge of the knife caresses my soft, trembling thighs, where I'm still soaked from your fingers in me, Master. *breathing fast* You press the knife into my skin so firmly, waking everything in my body, yet you're so ... careful. Not to cut me. Master. Master, I love you!

a cry of pleasure and fearful arousal

My clit! My clit! The flat of your knife is rubbing across my c-c-clit! My clit is under your knife, Master!

repeating in fast little whimpers I'm yours, Master. I'm yours, Master. I'm yours, Master.

whisper You will keep me safe. Master will keep me safe.

whimpers

a quivery plea, in wonder at her own body and at her Master's touch Master, I'm ... soaked. I'm SOAKED. I ... I didn't know I could get this wet. Master. *awed* I'm wet. I'm wet, Master.

I'm trembling. I might cum at a touch, Master.

Yes, Master. Yes, I understand. *whimpers* I won't cum without your permission, Master. You own my pleasure. My cunt is yours to unlock, my clit is yours to caress. My pleasure is a gift from you, and I am a good, loving, submissive slavegirl who does NOT steal from her Master.

whimpers Please, Master. Please give me pleasure. Please.

Please give your slavegirl pleasure.

whimpers

I'm so wet for you. Only for you. Only ever for you. No one else, no man or wolf or nightmare. I belong to YOU. You're my Master. I love you.

squeaks Master? Master? I feel ... I feel the hilt of the knife, the ivory handle pressed thick against my soft, tight heat. Master! The hilt is warm from your hand. Master, are you ... *desperate little gasps ...* are you going to put it in me, Master?

Are you going to fuck me with the hilt of your knife?

whispers Are you going to fuck me with your knife, Master? With the knife that keeps me safe?

Master, oh my gods, Master, I trust you, I trust you! *she squeals as he thrusts it inside her*

panting Master! It's so big in me! So big in me!

gasping the words between quick moans at each thrust of the hilt Master! Master! Master! You're fucking me with the hilt! You're fucking me with your knife, Master!

little screams of pleasure

Yes, Master! Yes, I'll rock my hips. *moans* I'll SOAK the hilt of your knife in my warm honey. *moans* I'll grip *moans* and squeeze *moans* and ripple around the ivory hilt *moans* like I'm squeezing your cock! *moans*

Yes, Master! I'll make love to your knife!

I'll FUCK your knife!

This knife that keeps me safe!

moaning

My hips lift for you, Master. Oh Master, take me! Take me! Take your tied pleasure-slave! Master! Master!

her moaning cries, intense and hot and desperate

Oh Master, the way you flick your wrist, making the hilt swivel and turn inside me! I can feel each rib along the hilt caress me from inside! *a wild cry* I feel it! I feel it! So deep in me! So thick and warm!

Master, please, may I surrender for you?

May I cum on your knife, Master? May I cum while all those trees you've carved into slavegirls watch? May I cum screaming in your library, Master?

May I yield and shatter for you? Shatter on this knife that keeps me safe? You keep me safe, Master. You keep me so safe! I have been h-hunted by wolves, by nightmares as I sleep, but no nightmare can stand against my Master! You keep me safe! You keep me safe! Master, PLEASE let me cum! PLEASE! I am soaked! I am c-c-clenching down on the knife! Master! I can't! I can't hold back! Please please please I want to obey, I want to obey you! I want to be such a good obedient slavegirl! Please! You're going to BREAK me! Please let me cum, let me cum, let me CUM! Please, my Master!!!!

Yes!

screams Yes, Master! YES! I'll cum! I'll cum! I - I - *she screams as he orgasms for her Master, cumming on the hilt of his knife*

panting the words after her orgasm, under her breath, like the words are just pouring out of her heart I'm your slavegirl, I'm your slavegirl, I'm your slavegirl …

a soft, sweet cry Master, you're taking the hilt out of me … taking it out of my cunt … *moans* … leaving me empty … so empty … *cries out* But you're getting on top of me! Covering my body with yours! Yes, Master, yes, I'll spread my thighs SO wide! So wide! *panting* Your cock! Your cock against my soft folds! Master! Are you going to fuck me? Are you going to - *she moans desperately as he penetrates her*

a few moments of her cries at each hard, pounding thrust, and fucked nearly out of her mind, she gasps after each thrust words like "I love you!" … "Master!" … "I'm yours!" … "Yours!" … "Yours!"

a wild moan Yes, Master, I'm safe in your arms, Master! Fuck me in your library! Fuck me, Master! Fuck me, fuck me, FUCK me! Master, fuck me!

Master, Master, Master, may I cum? May I cum? May I cum again? Thank you, Master, thank you, aahhhhhhh! *she wails in pleasure as she cums*

he keeps thrusting vigorously

Oh Master, feel me tighten and grip your cock … spasming around your cock … your cock! your cock! … your cock feels so good in me, caressing me from the inside! … I love your cock … I love your cock, Master! Fuck me with that hard cock, Master! Fuck your slavegirl! Own me, own me, OWN ME! I love you! I love you!

a brief choking sound

Master, yes! Grip my throat! Choke me! My breath belongs to you! All of me! All of me! All of me is yours!

choking sounds

whimpering when she gets to breathe at last

Master, Master, please cum! Please! I want to give you pleasure! I want you to cum! Cum on my breasts, Master! Cum on my thighs! Splash your semen over my body! I want to be sticky with my Master for the rest of the night! Master, please! Please! Please! Cum for me! Cum for me! Cum for me! Master, I'm going to cum, I'm going to cum …

another wild orgasm

panting

he pulls out of her and she whimpers You're pulling out of me … oh Master … you're so hard … so throbbing and hard and so hot …

Yes, Master, lift your hips to my face. Yes, Master, my mouth is for your pleasure! mmmphh mmmphhhh mmphhhhhhh

improv a swift blowjob, gagging a couple of times. Her muffled pleas "cum in my mouth … cum in my mouth … cum in my mouth

when he does, we hear her moan as he fills her mouth, then her loud swallows

gasping for air after

breathless My Master. My Master.

My legs are so wet. From how you made me cum.

You make me cum so hard, Master. *whimpers* Each time you touch me, you make me yours. Each time you caress me, each time you take me, each time you make me swallow your seed, each time I am more helpless, more surrendered. Your love-slave. You own me.

the rattle of metal

The slave belt? You're going to lock it on me, Master? You're going to lock it over my soft, soaked little cunt?

And then ... you're going to hold me and teach me to read ... until the night has grown old and your slavegirl falls asleep in your arms?

sniffles Yes, Master. Put it on me. Protect me.

the sound of him putting the belt on her, not locking it yet, just putting it on her

soft, happy crying Master. My Master, my Master. You make me feel so ... safe.

You take such good care of what you own. You protect me. You keep me safe. *breathless* I love you, Master. I love you.

I'm yours. Every breath in my body, every beat of my heart is yours.

This metal belt with velvet inside that holds my cunt so tightly, so softly ... please lock it, Master. *whispers* Please lock me. Lock me, Master.

My soft … wet … cunt belongs to you, Master. Only you.

the loud sound of the chastity belt LOCKING

her quivery little gasp in response

softly, saying this with all of her heart You own me, Master. I love you.

the episode ends

8

Inflame Me, Master

We hear soft, exotic music. The opening of a heavy door. Then it closes. In the distance, roaring fire. In the foreground, the soft, aroused, needy breathing of the slavegirl.

I'm here, Master. Your pleasure-kitten. Do you wish me to kneel beneath your banquet table, Master, and please you with my soft, wet little mouth while you dine with your guests? All day, Master, I have burned for you. All day while you were at the market, while I waited and whimpered and moaned for you. Beneath this slave belt you locked on me, my cunt burns for you, Master. I am dripping for you, Master! Locked, unable even to touch myself, I am wet and helpless for you, Master. I am in heat for you, Master.

My Master, my owner. I will gladly kneel and give you pleasure with my mouth.

May I approach the table, Master?

a happy sound Thank you, Master.

Master, you look so powerful, so intense. With the flame of

sunset in the window behind you and the dark heat in your eyes.

But your guests ... they're so silent. They're ... *nervous* ... they're not even turning to look at me as I step near, my breasts soft and full, a chain of purest silver strung between my nipples. I am naked, my body glistening with oil. Surely your guests desire me, Master? Surely they lust for your slavegirl? Why aren't they turning their heads to gaze at my soft, smooth thighs as I walk?

gasps Master? What ... what is wrong with the guests, Master?

frightened They all sit so still. With their backs to me.

gasps I recognize them! Their garments, their jewelry! Master, Master! These are the wolf hunters! *quivers, frightened* The men of the hunting guild who conspired to steal me from you! These men took me from your home! These men want to hurt you ... by hurting me! I don't want to be here with these men! Master, I'm scared!

breathless How you rise from your seat, towering over me like a god. Master ... such fury in your eyes! Like a forest fire burns inside your heart. Master, are you angry with me?

gasps You're taking me by my arms! So strong, gripping me just below my shoulders. Master! What's wrong, Master? Mmmphhhhhh!!!!!

he silences her with a rough, demanding kiss, a powerful kiss, an ownership kiss, and she whimpers sweetly, muffled, into his mouth breathless after

whispers My Master.

I love the taste of your mouth.

Master, you're turning me to face your guests. And … *gasps* … they're … Master! Are your guests … ? Your guests, they're dead, Master! They're all dead?

Poison?

By your hand?

quivers The way you pull me against your chest. Like you burn to possess and protect me. Your eyes like a world on fire. *in wonder* Master, the fury in your eyes. Such fury at those who would hurt your slavegirl. Such rage at these men. These men who hurt me, Master. *in wonder* You invited them here, and … and poisoned them.

quivering They didn't know what a dangerous man owns me.

kissing

Oh Master, your mouth on my throat …

moans

You own me, Master. I am yours.

I know. No man will EVER steal me from my Master again.

whispers, emphasizing the word "I" … I know how dangerous my Master is.

I saw a werewolf dead at your feet. I saw men who had fondled me against your will cut down like autumn wheat by your long knives, Master. I have felt your whip kiss my breasts and my thighs and my naked cunt. *quivers* I felt you burn your mark of ownership into my body, the first night you took me, when you branded me, then fucked me by your fire all night. I feel your touch, ahhhh, your lips on my neck, burning me now. Your hands on my breasts. *moans* Squeezing my breasts. *a helpless, hot little moan* Making me captive, making me yours. *moans* Masterrrrr, how you touch me!!

How you protect me.

How you keep me safe.

quivers You killed all these men for me.

a frightened breath But Master, if you kill all the wolf hunters, who will keep your villa safe from werewolves? What if they overrun your walls? *whimpers* What if the wild wolves run through your gardens by moonlight, hunting your dancing-slaves, hunting me?

You … you've taken care of the werewolves?

What do you mean, Master?

Why are you drawing me to the window, your hand firm on the back of my neck?

sounds of fire get louder

Oh, Master. You stand behind me, holding my breasts so firmly, your mouth kissing my hair … mmmm, and I am naked and bare at the window of your banquet hall, where any guest or dancing girl in the pleasure gardens below us might see me. *whimpers* You display me naked and yours before the whole world, Master!

Master, when I lift my eyes and look past the gardens, past the wall of your villa … out to the horizon … *gasps* … Master, the forest! The dark forest where the werewolves howl at night! It's on fire! Master, the trees burn! Not with the sunset but with flames red against the dusk! I can smell the woodsmoke and hear the roar of it.

whispers Master, what have you done?

Your whisper in my ear. That no werewolf will ever hunt me again.

You've set the world to burn. To protect me.

softly, worshipfully Master.

If there are no wolves, no dark trees for werewolves to hunt beneath, then we don't need wolf hunters. We don't need a hunting guild to send naked slavegirls sobbing as they run, aroused and helpless and luring monsters out of the dark with the scent of the wet slave-heat between their thighs.

Master … the forest burns.

whispers For me.

trembles You did this for ME.

My strong, violent, terrifying Master.

Yet your hands are so gentle on me, so gentle on my body.

breathless Master, I am shaken.

gasps Your hands on my hips. Pulling me into you. I can feel your cock against my ass. And you hold something cool and metal in your fingers. Master? *excited* Is that the key to my belt? Are you going to unlock me? *a sigh of need* Are you going to take it off me, Master? Are you going to open my soft, wet cunt for your touch and your pleasure?

whispers Please, Master. Please.

Only not here. With the ghosts of dead men watching us.

SMACK!!!

she cries out

SMACK!!!

she yelps

I'm sorry, Master! Yes, Master, I know you may take me where you wish, however you wish. You own me, Master.

softly I'm just frightened, Master. Their dead faces scare me.

soft, frightened breathing

You … you want me to keep my eyes on the forest? On the fire blazing in the cedars and pine? Watching the fire you lit, while you light fires inside me?

You inflame me! I'm on fire, Master! I'm ON FIRE!

whimpers

Yes, Master. As you wish, Master.

the sound of a key in a lock

whimpers, so needy she can barely speak Yes, Master, yes. Unlock me.

Open me, Master, please!

the sound of the belt being taken off her, then clattering to the ground

Ah-ah! I am so naked! So NAKED!

a wild moan Master, your hand! … *gasps* … your hand sliding between my thighs … *moans* … Master, are you going to touch me right here, at your window?! Master, the heat of that distant fire against my skin, the heat of your fingers … *she cries out* … sliding inside me! So thick! *moans* So hot! Master, you burn me, you burn me! I am your slavegirl! Enjoy me, Master!

moaning with all the pleasure of a woman who hasn't been allowed to touch herself for too long Oh, Master, Master, Master, your fingers! Your fingers feel so good in me! So thick and so warm! Oh! Oh!

SMACK!!!!

whimpers Yes, Master, yes, I'll be quiet, I'll be quiet and take what you give me like a good girl. I am your soaked little pleasure-slut, Master! How you touch me!

SMACK!!!

she squeals

SMACK!!!!

squeals

improv her soft little whimpers, fighting to stay quiet as her Master wishes and failing some as he fingers her wet heat

desperately Master, Master, I can't stay quiet, I can't. Screams of need claw their way up my throat at your touch! Your touch makes me wild as a cat in heat! Your hand, your breath on my neck, your cock hard against my ass! Master, your touch burns me hotter than the forest in flames! Please, Master, please, let me moan. Let me moan!

SMACK!!!

whimpering wildly into her closed lips

improv her frantic whimpers of need, her arousal taking her right to the brink of orgasm before he pulls his fingers out of her

panting M-Master? You … you stopped. You took your hand from my cunt. Master? *breathing hard, needing to cum*

gasps Yes, Master, yes I'll taste my fingers for you - mmmm mmm mmmm mmmmmmmmmmmm

the sound of gentle sucking and her arousal moaned around her fingers

breathing in little pants of need

just above a whisper I taste like my Master's pleasure-slut. I taste so hot, so hot. You make me so hot, Master!

Do you want to taste me, Master?

Soon? You … you're taking me to another room first? Yes, Master.

a soft, aroused moans Pulling my arms behind me. Master, you're binding me! In the sash you wear, its fabric soft against my wrists but …

soft little whimpers as she squirms

… but strong as my Master's will, holding me secure. … Yours … Safe. Tied so tightly, I can't move my wrists!

the sound of a chain clinking, and the click as he leashes her

breathless, so aroused You've leashed me, Master. Clipped that chain to my collar. *footsteps, and a soft little cry!* Yes, Master! Tug me. Pull on the collar at my neck! I will follow you, my Master, my love. Wherever you take me, I'll follow. I am yours. Your slavegirl! Leashed and owned and yours.

the door opens, closes. Their footsteps down the hall outside. Her soft, quivery breathing

I am on your leash, Master. Bound. Naked, my warm honey dripping down my thighs.

breathes So helpless.

Where are you taking me, Master?

Down … down these stairs? I've … I've never been to your cellar, Master. Do you wish to open a flask of blood-red wine to drink deep while you enjoy your slavegirl? *aroused* Do you wish to pour the wine over my full, naked tits, let the wine run down my body cool and dark as desire, until my hard nipples and my soft thighs are scented like grapes? Do you want to pour wine over my cunt tonight before you taste me, Master?

breathes Oh, Masterrr … I drip down my legs for you, Master. *whispers* I am so wet.

Your cellar door, Master.

the sound of a heavy door swinging open

in the background, the sounds of gagged women whimpering softly, from here through the end of the scene

the slavegirl gasps Master! These women! Your cellar is filled of women, chained to the walls and gagged! Some of them naked, some in dresses torn open to bare their soft breasts. How they wriggle and fight against the chains, their eyes wild with fear. Their breasts bouncing as they struggle.

I've never seen these women in your pleasure gardens. Are they new, Master? Who are these slavegirls?

They're … *a deep inhale* … the loving wives and virgin daughters of the wolf hunters? My Master! You raided the hunters' houses, seized their possessions … and their women! You brought them here to squirm helpless in your cellar while their men choked on poisoned food in the banquet hall above.

What … what will happen to all these women, Master?

Master, Master, the fury in your eyes! *a little frightened* I know you want the world to know how you will protect me, Master. I know their men hurt me, but Master, these are just captive girls, they're just like me, Master. You wouldn't … kill them, Master?

a sigh of relief at his answer I am glad. Oh I am glad, my Master.

You … you're going to have them sold? At the slave market?

… Yes, Master. Yes, I'll … I'll speak to them. For you, Master.

Girls, I know you're scared. Squirming, sobbing here in my Master's cellar. You can't get your wrists free, you can't even scream for help. The cellar air is chill against your exposed, naked breasts. And my Master's eyes blaze with heat and rage as he looks at you. You're scared. You don't know what's going to happen to you.

I … I'm my Master's pleasure-slut. His love-kitten, his love-slave. He … has done this, he has taken you from your homes because your men hurt me, gave me to werewolves to fuck and devour. *sniffles* But my Master, he … he won't hurt you, I know he won't. He'll make sure you are sold to good men.

hearing her say that, the whimpers from the women get louder for a moment

she raises her voice, too My Master, he … he treasures me. And he won't want me to be worried about you, so he'll set a high price on each of you and make sure good Masters buy you. Men of wealth, like him. You won't be tavern sluts, forced to take a different man in your mouth each hour of the night. You won't be slavegirls in the mines, pinned down and fucked brutally beneath sweating men in the dark under the earth. And … *a flash of anger* … you won't be wolfbait! You won't be fondled and sent running in the dark, screaming and sobbing and terrified, like I was!

My Master says … he wants each of you to know much his love-slave means to him. How deeply your husbands and fathers wronged him when they took me. And he wants you to see what will happen to each of you after you are sold, if you're sold to a Master who will care for you and protect you and WANT you.

Girls, look at my soft thighs. See how I glisten and drip like a honeycomb? See how my desire trickles down my legs for him? My Master has done that to me. *whispers* He owns me. He keeps me safe and his.

she cries out suddenly as her Master bends her over

Master! You've bent me over a wine barrel! On my belly! Tied and helpless and naked! With my cunt SOAKED! Master! *trembling* Master, are … are you going to fuck me? Right here? While these captive women watch you take me? While they watch me buck and moan and yield for you, Master?

SMACK!!

yelps

SMACK!!!

a sweet little scream

Yes, Master! Whatever you wish, Master! I won't defy you, Master!

three more hard, rapid smacks and squeals

I understand, Master! I can moan as loudly as I want now! You want them all to hear me! But Master, but Master they're all staring at me! All the women you've chained to the cellar walls!

SMACK!!!

she cries out

Yes, Master, yes, I'm yours, I'm yours! Master! Master, you're gripping my thighs, your fingers warm on my skin where you branded me … spreading my legs … crouching behind me! AHHH! Your warm breath on my clit! Master! Master, Master, are you going to … *she squeals with sudden pleasure as he licks her*

moaning Master, your mouth on me! Master, taste me! Drink me! Get drunk on my honey like warm wine, Master! Drink me! I'll gush into your mouth, Master! I'm so wet for you, Master! Master, Master, ohhhhhhhhhh … your tongue is so strong and so warm … Master!

her wild cries, and the whimpers of the captives in the background

Lick me, Master! Lick me, please! Lick me, lick me! Your mouth burns me! Burn me, burn me, burn me!

panting, desperate I'm yours, I'm yours!

Master, I'm going to yield! I'm going to cum! I'm going to cum! They'll see me cum! I'm so naked! I'm so naked! Master! Master! Yes! Yes! As you wish, Master, AS YOU WISH! YOU WISH! YES! YES!

screaming the words as she orgasms You own me!!!

panting after You own me, you own me ...

I feel you getting up, *cries out* ... grasping my hips, Master, your cock! Your cock is so hard, right there, Master! Feel my blossom wet and soft as a kiss against the tip of your cock! Master, please, please put it in me, Master, please ravish your slavegirl, please, Mast-ahhhhhH! ... *she squeals as he penetrates her*

we hear her quick cries of pleasure he pumps into her hard and fast and the creaking of the wine barrel beneath her

Master! Master! Yes! Show them your heat, your desire, your lust, your hunger for me, Master! Show them how you fuck your slavegirl! The slavegirl their men tried to hurt! Show them how you own me, Master! Show the whole world who I belong to! Who owns me! Who protects me! Master, I'm YOURS! Master, fuck me! Fuck me harder, please! Break me!

moaning

My tits slap against the side of the barrel as you pound me! The slave chain strung between them tugging at my nipples!

her wild cries of heat

You're so hot in me! You're so hot in me! Master, I burn! I burn! Burn me, Master! Fuck me! You're SO BIG IN ME! *squeals as he gives her an especially hard thrust* GODS! Masterrrrr!

Master, may I cum on your cock? May I cum on your cock while they watch? May I yield, may I yield for you, please???! PLEASE!

Masterrrrr! *she cums, wildly*

panting little gasps and moans as he keeps fucking her Master, yes, yes, take me, take me, take me, take me, I'll cum for you again, I'll please you! I'll please you! I'm your good girl! I'm your good girl! I'm your good girl, Master! I'm-a-good-girl I'm-a-good-girl I'm-a-good-girl I'm-a-good-girl I'm-a-good-girl I'm-a-good-girl I'm-a-good-girl *CUMS*

exhausted, aroused little whimpers as he keeps fucking her

Master, Master, I've f-flooded your cock. You own me. Ravaging me over this barrel in your cellar. Master! You are so hard in me, feel me tighten around you, tight and hot and wet and YOURS. I'm gripping you, clenching, squeezing my Master's hard cock! I love your cock, I love your COCK! Master! Enjoy me, enjoy me... *moans until she cums* I'm cumming, I'm cumming, I'M CUMMING!!!! *an orgasm that leaves her shaken*

in an "ahegao" state, just panting

her whining whimper as he pulls out of her

Master. Ah! You've grasped my hair, pulling me to the cellar floor beside the barrel! *panting reverently* Master, your cock is so hard … so big in your fist. Are you going to cum on me, Master? *moans* Are you going to cum on my face and tits while they watch?

breathless with pride Girls, chained helpless girls, look at my Master! Look at his hard cock! Look at him about to cum! See how I please him! I give my Master SUCH pleasure!!

I'm your pleasure-slave, Master. Mark me with your semen. Splash it over my body! Master, cover what's yours! Cum on me! *her moaning need for him, pleading so sweetly* Cum on me, Master! Cum on me! Please cum on your slavegirl! Cum on your devoted, loving, soaked little slavegirl! Cum on me while my tits bounce for you as I gasp for breath! Master, cum on me! Cum on me! Cum on me CUM ON ME!!!!

her moan of enjoyment, of submissive pride, as he does

Yes! Masterrrrr!

Ahh! Another spurt of your seed!

panting Another!

cries out, then giggles Another!

giggling softly, exhaustedly Oh Master, oh Master. I feel the gift of your pleasure hot and sticky across my cheek, on my lips … *a licking sound* … mmmmmmmm, Master, you taste like the sea … like the SEA … Master, I feel your semen dripping down my soft, full breasts … *a low sighing moan* … on my belly … oh Master.

I will lie with your semen drying on my body, Master, reminding me all night of how you desire you, how you protect me, how you FUCKED me. My cunt is sore from how you FUCKED me. I'm a wet, shaky, sticky mess at your feet, Master.

Master, I love you. I love you!

suddenly emotional, sweet and needful and emotional and slightly tearful You keep me safe. You keep me burning in heat at your touch … and you burn anyone who tries to hurt me. My Master, my Master.

breathless Yes! You're tugging on my leash. I obey, Master. I will crawl to you, Master, on my knees, my wrists bound behind me, my body sticky with your pleasure.

whimpers I'll lower my face and press my soft, warm lips to your foot, Master.

the sound of the sweetest, gentlest kiss, soft and wet

Master. You own me. I love you, Master. I yearn only to kiss your feet and give you every pleasure you desire. Every night, Master.

kissing his feet

I adore you.

kissing and licking

Feel my soft, wet little tongue. Master, you stand over me like a GOD.

kissing and licking

My Master, my powerful Master.

kissing, with little gaspy breaths, overcome

softly Girls wriggling in your chains on the walls ... don't, don't be scared. One day you might love a Master as I love and adore mine. A Master who will protect you better than your husbands or fathers did. A Master who will conquer you and inflame you and break you and own you as mine owns me, down to each beat of my heart and every drop of heat in my cunt. Don't be scared, girls. I love him so.

Master, see my eyes gaze up at you. Worshipping you. Your slavegirl, your pleasure-kitten is at your feet. How may I give you more pleasure, my Master? How may I delight you and serve you? How may I love you tonight?

yearning I love you.

the sounds of her reverent, soft breathing and the whimpers of the captives for a few moments.

whispers I love you, Master.

The episode ends.

9

Breed Me, Master

We hear the gentle noises of water against the sides of a boat on the lake. The slavegirl's breathing, a little frightened. We may hear soft strains of music from the shore, carried over the water. Occasionally we hear the calls of lake birds or marsh birds. The slavegirl is frightened of being out on the water and also, as the script reveals, she needs reassurance from her Master today.

quivery No, I'm all right, Master. I just … I'm just a little scared today. I haven't been in a boat since the slavers took me over the sea. They tied me, helpless, with water everywhere, all around me, nowhere to run. I used to cry myself to sleep, knowing they meant to sell me when we reached the shore, fearing a storm might come and sink us first. You … you won't let me drown, Master? *whispers* Don't let me drown.

Yes, Master. I'm touching my collar with my fingertips, like you told me. The cool metal locked on my throat. Keeping me safe. You keep me safe.

It's so quiet out here. Just the soft music from your pleasure gardens on the shore, and the cries of those marsh birds.

And this boat is so small, and the lake is so big … *frightened breathing* The shore is so far away … the boat could tip! And I'd drown. Or … or there could be … monsters. Blind, scaly fish large enough to swallow me whole. One big gulp, and your beautiful pleasure-kitten might be gone, Master! *shivers*

But I know … this … this isn't like being in the slavers' ship. I don't … I don't need to run anywhere or get away. I belong to you. I am yours. Your beautiful slavegirl. *almost pleading* I need to stay with my Master. I need to please you, Master. And if that means kneeling naked in your boat, with nothing but … *whimpers* but water … beneath me … then … I will be brave. I will be brave for you, Master. *quick breaths* I will be so, so brave.

frightened breathing, and then she tries to calm her breathing

It … it IS very beautiful, your lake. This lake on your estate. The water is such a deep purple. I've never seen water that color. It … it's tiny creatures? Sprites in the water? Will … will they hurt me, if I touch the water, Master?

Yes, Master. I'll be brave and … dip my hand into the water.

We hear her hand dip into the water

a soft gasp It's … it's warm! The water's warm!

Do the sprites keep it warm?

Yes, Master.

No, Master. No monsters bit my hand. *blushing* It isn't … kind … to laugh at your slavegirl, Master. When she's scared.

she listens

Yes, Master. Thank you for … helping me be brave.

softly Why have you brought me out in your boat, Master? I thought Master wished me in the library today, to practice my reading, what you've taught me. And to sit naked and soft in your lap and read a story in soft whispers in your ear. I've been practicing so much, Master. I want to please you. I want you to be so proud of your slavegirl.

a quivery breath You ARE proud of me?

her shaky breathing as she tries to accept it

whispers, with all of her heart naked in her voice Thank you, Master.

she listens … We're here because … because you've been tense, from the strain of your assassins' war with the last of the hunters' guild. And you come out here when you need to relax and think.

softly Master, you brought me out here with you this time. It's the first time I have ever been here on your lake, in your boat, Master. I'm naked and soft and scented; your dancing-slaves oiled me for your pleasure with their small delicate hands on my body, arousing me before sending me to you, Master. And you have unlocked my slave belt. It lies there in the bottom of the boat, Master. There is nothing to keep your mouth … or your fingers … or your hard cock … from touching me, from sinking into me, Master. If I part my soft thighs … *a quivery breath* … like this … you can see my blossom glisten for you, Master.

You can see my breasts lift and fall as I breathe.

breathing softly, letting the listener imagine the movement of her breasts, of her naked body in that boat

How may your pleasure-kitten help you relax and think, Master? Here, naked, helplessly yours, surrounded by all this water? Is there any pleasure your slavegirl can give you that would soothe you, Master? Is there any way I can ease your stress, Master, with my soft, feminine warmth?

Yes, Master. It will be my pleasure, Master.

the sounds of his garments rustling … then soft licking and kissing sounds from her

gently Do you like my kisses on your thighs, Master?

kissing and licking

she draws in a deep breath

softly, seductively Master, the scent of you … of your cock … your musk … it makes me quiver, Master. It makes me so wet for you.

May I delight your cock, Master? May I make you feel good? Please, Master? *whispers* Please put it in my mouth.

he does, and we hear soft, sensual blowjob sounds

Master …

blowjob sounds

Master, I love your cock.

I love the gentle pressure of your cock on my tongue.

I love how you smell and taste. *quivery* I love it so much.

licking and sucking

I love you in my mouth.

shy, needy Do you love being in my mouth, Master? Master, does my small, wet mouth give you pleasure?

blowjob sounds and lake sounds for a little while

her voice is so soft and loving Master, feel me cup your balls in my hands, caressing you with my warm, gentle fingers. Oh Master, my hands aren't like yours. They are soft … and small. And so gentle. Feel me just soothe your balls with my touch. As I caress the length of your cock with my tongue …

a needy little moan as she licks him, then takes his tip in her mouth, sucking warmly

breathing softly with him resting on her tongue My Master.

sucking gently

Don't think about the assassins, Master, or the hunters, or any of your cares and worries. You have done so much to protect me, to take care of me. I want to take care of you, Master.

With my full breasts moving gently as I breathe, to delight you … My nipples hard for my Master.

With my soft, feminine hands.

kissing With my warm … wet … mouth.

a few moments of sensual blowjob

gasps Yes … grip my head, Master, in your powerful hands. Do … do you want to use my mouth, Master?

whispers Please, please, use my mouth.

rougher blowjob sounds … and some gagging

spluttering for air Yes, Master. Yes! I won't be frightened of the water beneath us, or the wolf hunters, or ANYthing if my throat is full of your cock, if I'm focusing on every breath through my nose, if I am focused on giving you so much pleasure. I'm not scared, I'm not scared! My Master has me in his hands!

talking fast, aroused and breathless Yes, Master, yes! I'll spit on your cock, Master! *she does, loudly* I'll get your cock so sloppy and wet, I'll be such a good slavegirl, here on your lake, Master! *more spitting, then sucking sounds* Master, can you smell me? Can you smell my wet heat, my warm honey? Master, I'm so wet, so wet at what you are about to do to me, Master!

spitting on his cock again

almost panting Master, fuck my mouth! fuck my m- mmmphh mmmphhh mmmphhh

a deep, urgent blowjob, throatfucking

gasping for air Yes, Master, you own my throat! You own my thr-MMPHH MMPHHHH!!!!

throatfucking for long moments, her sounds exciting him as he uses her throat for his pleasure, as she breathes in little gasps through her nose and struggles to give her Master everything

mmmphhh mmmmphhh Master yes, take me, take my thr-

mmphh mmmphh urggkk urrgggk

mmphh mmm *struggling to breathe* Yes, Master! Take what you desire! Everything you need, everything you crave, I'm yours, I'm yours! Make me please you! Mnmmphh mmmphhhhh

a hot, hard, long throatfuck … and then her squeal as he cums in her mouth

several slow, loud swallows

gasping for air

heartfelt, almost tearful from the hard throatfucking and the emotions wild inside her Master, I love you! I love you! I swallowed your cum, Master, I swallowed all of it! *breathing hard*

Yes, Master, yes. I'll kiss your thighs.

gentle kisses for a few moments

How your cock throbs against my cheek! I'll kiss and clean your cock, Master.

kissing and licking sounds

shy Did … did I please you, Master?

a soft sigh at his reply

I want to please you. I want to give you such pleasure, Master.

Master, always.

tears, soft crying for a moment, quiet little sobs

I'm sorry. I'm sorry.

No, you didn't hurt me, Master. You didn't hurt me with your cock.

almost a little feminine growl I LOVE how you hurt me with your cock.

I ... I ... *sobs* ... I've just been so scared. So scared.

a soft little cry Oh, you've gripped my collar ... ahhh! ... pulling me to you.

whimpers Your arms around me ... feel so good, so strong. Yes, Master, yes, hold me.

sniffles I've felt like I'm ... drowning.

Like I'm drowning in that purple water.

I'm sorry, I'm sorry. I'm getting tears all over your sable cloak and your vest, Master. *sniffles* No, no it isn't the wolf hunters. I know I'm safe. I KNOW I'm safe. You make me safe.

T-tell you what's ... what's wrong? Master! Master, I can't! *panic* I can't be that naked! I can't! I can't!

SMACK!!!

she squeals

SMACK!!!

yelps I'm sorry, Master!

SMACK!!! SMACK!! SMACK!!

sobs

Yes, I'm sorry! I'm sorry! Yes, Master owns me. You own my … my soft wet little cunt. And my ass. And my mouth. And my breath. And my heart. Every secret in my heart. I have to be … COMPLETELY … naked for my Master. I don't hide anything from my Master. You own all of me.

whimpers Yes, Master. *sniffles* Yes, Master, I'll tell you.

It's … it's that GIRL.

a little angry and frightened You KNOW what girl.

All the wolf hunters' wives and daughters that you took and enslaved, you sent them to the market and sold them. All but one. That little virgin with the … with the raven hair and the big, frightened eyes. *she sniffles, then swallows back a sob* You visited her in the slave rooms. And later, when I ran into her in the hall on my way to get oils for you, Master, she walked like she was sore, and there was a red stain on her thigh, her virgin's blood, from where you tore her with your cock. I saw the bruises your fingers left on her tits. She looked … dazed.

And that night at dinner, as I knelt, while you fed me bites from your plate, Master, pressing succulent little bits into my soft mouth with your fingers, Master, you looked flushed and ... happy.

sniffles

I don't want that little raven-haired slut to please you, Master. With her high breasts and her soft, creamy thighs, and her voice like an angel in heat. I don't want her to. I want to give you pleasure.

angry, frightened I BURN with jealousy, Master!

quivers And I'm scared. What if I displease you? *softly* What if you no longer want me?

I ... I don't want to be left tied, naked, trembling on the furs tossed across the cold stone floor in the slave rooms, alone in my bonds while you enjoy that quivery little slave in brutal thrusts on your bed, night after night.

What if some night soon, you call HER, and ... and you don't summon me to your bed? *cries softly* I belong in your bed, Master! Chained by my ankle to your bed, just where Master put me, my soft mouth around your cock, Master. I want you to enjoy me, my soft feminine body, fully relentlessly every night! I want to wake each morning to your cock in me! To your possessive, demanding thrusts inside my tight, slick cunt!

Master, my Master, I want you! My heart burns thinking you might want that new slavegirl! Master, I will please you like she could never dream possible. I will be so pleasing, Master!

soft gaspy little breaths I feel like I'm drowning.

fervently Master, you own me.

You bought me.

You collared me.

You whipped me. You branded your mark in my body, in my soft thigh, right here, under my fingertips.

softly I want to delight you, Master.

Feel my breath warm and … soft … at your neck. *breathing softly on his neck*

My fingertips trailing along your arms like the gentlest promise of pleasure.

she makes a soft, longing, yearning moan

Master, I need you … Won't you take my body and let me please you? Right here, in this boat, while that scary, deep water rocks us? *softly* I won't be scared of … anything … with my Master inside me.

the sounds of a deep, hungry kiss. Her little whimpers against his mouth

Yes, kiss me … *kissing*

so gently Kiss me, Master.

kissing

Ahhh, how you bite my lip … taste me, Master.

kissing

Kiss me until I can't breathe.

a long, long kiss

whispers You are my everything.

Do you want me, Master?

she cries out softly as we hear him thrust her onto her back in the bottom of the boat

Master!

Yes, Master, push me down on my back! I am your pleasure-slut, yours! See my breasts heave for you, so soft and full! See my soft eyes gazing up at you through my eyelashes. Looking up at the strong, powerful man who OWNS me.

Yes! Cover my body with yours, Master! Your body is so sweaty and muscled on top of me. Oh, Master, Master! Yes! Bite my breasts! Ah! Ah! Nip at my soft skin with your teeth! Mark me! Claim me! I'm yours! Always yours! Feel me squirm and writhe under you, blushing hot as you … ahhhh! … as you thrust open my legs! Oh Master!

I need you, Master! I NEED you!

fiercely I will grip and squeeze your cock like no other slavegirl EVER will! I am your PLEASURE-KITTEN! TAKE ME, MASTER, PLEASE!

Your cock rubbing against the inside of my thigh … so close … it is torture, Master, it is torture.

very aroused sounds

Here. See me reach down between my thighs, Master … for you … my breasts pressed together between my arms, lifted for your pleasure, my fingers touching my soft blossom … *moans* Look, Master, look. I'm opening myself for you. Opening my body like a flower opens to the sun. Master. Burn me with your heat, Master. *softly* I am so open … and slick … and tight … and wet. And it's so hot inside me, so hot inside my cunt, I can't bear it, Master. I need you in me, Master.

I'm holding my cunt open for you with my fingers, Master. My fingers hot and soaked in my warm honey. Inviting you to use your slavegirl.

moans … Master, please, you know I'll do anything to pleasure you. Use me, ravish me, devour me, Master! And the next time another slavegirl glances over her shoulder at you, at my Master, remember the soft warmth of my breasts in your hands, the gentle pressure of my tongue on your cock when you rape my mouth and throat … the tight, slick grip of my cunt when you fuck me … Take me, and remember only me, Master … Only me. Only me!

a long, squealing cry as he penetrates her

crying out wildly at each thrust Master! Master! Take me! Take me!

Only me! Only me! Only me!

squealing and moaning under him as he fucks her

Master! How you lift my legs to my shoulders, each thrust taking you so DEEP in me! So deep! Master, you're so big! SO BIG! Hurt me, Master! Hurt me! Just … don't break the boat! *a breathless, moaning laugh* Don't let me drown!

Oh gods! Oh gods! Oh gods! My breasts bounce for you! My cunt GRIPS you! Make me squeal, Master! Make me squeal! Feel me reach and dig my fingers into your hips, pulling you into me, Master! Deeper, Master! Please, deeper! I want to be SO open for you! Master, please fill me! I'm yours, I'm yours, I love you, I love you, you're so deep and powerful inside me! Master! Ah! Your hand! On my throat! Ah!

choking

little gasps of air

Master, more.

Please.

Please more.

Choke me. Please own me. Own even the breath in my body. Please, Master, please.

choking … long

heaving for air

You own me, you own me. Take me, take my body, fuck me and fill me and make me scream! I'm yours, I'm yours, I want to give you pleasure, I want to give you pleasure!

You … you cherish me?!

You cherish me!

Master, what are you saying? You cherish me? Master! Master!

improv wild moans and cries as he takes her roughly in the boat. Louder sounds of water sloshing against the boat

gasping between cries I … I can't! … I can't even … speak! You're … you're fucking me … owning me … so hard … I can't even speak! I can't even speak!

Yes, Master!!!

Yes! Cover my mouth! With your hand! Cover my nose! You own the air in my body, you own my every whimper, my every squeal, all of it, all of me is yours, all of me, all of me, all of me, mmmphhh mmmphhhhhh

muffled squeals into his hand over her mouth, then breathless desperate whimpers at each thrust as he keeps her breath captive … he doesn't let her breathe until fifteen thrusts … fifteen whimpers without air

the sound of her breathing, explosively, a breathless moan

My Master! My Master! I don't need to breathe, I don't need to breathe, I just need to give you pleasure! I know you'll keep me safe, you would never let me drown, never, never! Oh Master, Master, how you throb in me! How you throb in me! mmmphhh mmmphhhhhh

again. He holds her breath. Twelve whimpers without air, muffled under his hand her wild HEAVING for air

she squeaks Master! Master!

improv desperate, desperate moans from her as he thrusts and thrusts

Yes, thrust in me, thrust in me! Master, oh Master Master Master please please please please cum in me. Cum in me. You've never cum in me. You've never spilled your seed into my body! Master, I'm young! I'm fertile! You own me! You've taken me! Take my womb!

Take my womb, Master!

Fill me with your seed! Fill my cunt with your seed! Put your potent seed in me! Make me swell with new life for you, Master!

her voice is passionate and wild with arousal Master, love me! Love me as I love you! Please, please I love you! I love you! Get me with child, Master! Please, I want to make a baby for you, I want to make such a strong GOOD baby for you! A baby that will grow to be a powerful strong man like you, Master, a man who takes care of what he owns, a man who protects his woman! And keeps her! And cherishes her! And FUCKS her!

Breed me, Master! Please! Please! Let me give you a baby! Please! Let my womb grow round and my breasts full with warm milk! Master, own me! Own me! Impregnate me! Please cum in me! Please cum in me! How you're thrusting, how the muscles in your hips are tensing, how you GRIP my breasts so roughly, bruising me! Master, I know you're close! I know you're close! Master, it's all right, I surrender!

I surrender even my womb. Even my WOMB! It is yours! My womb is yours! Fill it, Master! Fill me with your cock, fill me, FILL ME! I BELONG TO YOU! MAKE ME PREGNANT! CUM INSIDE ME! CUM IN YOUR LOVE-SLAVE! CUM IN ME! CUM IN ME!

her wild cries as he cums in her You're spurting in me! I feel it, I feel it! I'm going to cum, I'm going to cum, I'm going to milk all your wild heat from your cock! Give it to me, please give it ALL to me, please! Master!!! *screaming the words as she orgasms* I LOVE YOU!

afterward, she draws in shuddering breaths of air

Master … how you CAME in me.

Filling me in spurt after spurt, gripping me close, nearly crushing me in your arms as you spasmed inside me. And now you lie on top of me panting. Your hot, flushed face resting on the soft swell of my breasts.

whispers, overcome My Master. My Master.

a few moments of soft breathing

Ahh. Lifting your head to look at my face?

hushed My Master is so beautiful.

The sky is so … open … *reverently* and blue and big … above your head, Master. Your eyes … gazing down at me, at your slavegirl … your eyes as deep and open as the sky. Master, I can see your heart. I can see your heart in your eyes. *trembles* My Master is naked.

she starts to cry very, very softly

after a moment or two, she sniffles and says: It's ... it's all right. I'm crying because I'm happy.

sniffles ... trembly I'm so happy.

her voice is so soft With your cock in me. With the man I love inside me. Your weight on top of me.

With your warm semen in my cunt, in my womb.

quivery I will give you such a strong, good baby, Master. I promise. I will make the most beautiful baby for you.

sniffles happily

Yes, hold me close. Kiss my neck.

I am yours. I belong to you. You own me. You OWN me, Master. I gave you pleasure.

she emphasizes the word "I," a little fiercely I am the slavegirl who gives my Master pleasure.

sound of a long, sensual kiss

Master, how you kiss me. *quivery* Kiss me.

kissing

sniffles, then a nervous giggle I'm glad ... I'm glad we didn't tip the boat ... the way you were fucking me so vigorously, Master. And I ... I'm glad the only monster out on this lake is my Master's cock ... *giggles* ... stretching me until I'm sore.

All that deep, dark water beneath us is still … frightening. But I … I have my Master's cock in me. My Master's lips on my throat. My Master's hands holding my breasts, holding me safe. Mmmm. Since you haven't tied me, I'll reach my arms around your neck, Master. *tenderly* And hold YOU.

whispers Stay inside me, Master.

Please, please stay inside your slavegirl.

Master, I feel so safe with you in me.

Nothing in the whole wide world can hurt me, when you're in me.

Please stay in me.

giggles And don't let any of your seed leak out of me.

I don't care how long I lie here, flushed, with my thighs shaking and my cunt so tight around your cock, here in your boat, Master. Stay in me til dusk, til they light lamps in the pleasure gardens over on the shore and your dancing girls undulate and writhe beneath the hot stars and the cold marble nymphs. Stay in me until midnight. Until the water mirrors every star in the sky…

loving Let me see the starlight reflected in your eyes, Master.

whispers Stay in me until dawn.

I am yours forever. Your slavegirl. Your pleasure-kitten and your devoted, wet little breeding-slut.

with all her heart Master. I am your love-slave. You own my heart.

a soft quivery sigh And my cunt.

Do I make you happy, Master?

Do I please you?

My heart and my body melt for you, under you, each time you ravish me. My cunt is so full of you and my heart is so f-full of you, I can barely speak.

soft, whispery I'm melted for you. Please stay inside me. I belong to you.

I love you.

whispers I love you, Master.

Happy little noises from her that get muffled by a warm, loving kiss. The soft sounds of the water against the boat.

The episode ends.

10

Love Me, Master

A rooftop at night. Ambient night noises. Possibly soft, exotic music. The soft breathing of the slavegirl.

Master, you called for me, Master? I'm here. On your rooftop. Naked as the night, holding a bowl of fresh, succulent fruit, berries to delight my Master. I've come up the stair, Master, collared and yours.

Your rooftop, it's so beautiful. So many silk cushions to lie on in the warm night under the stars, and sculptures of naked slavegirls, marble nymphs in ecstasy or resting sweetly. There's one with her thighs spread for my Master, her soft carved pussy gleaming in the starlight. And another with her head back, her small feminine hands cupping her breasts, her lips parted, as though she wants to scream with pleasure.

quivers This is the roof of my Master's house. Below, your dancing girls practice barefoot in your pleasure gardens. I can hear their music, soft and sweet as desire.

And far away, beyond the walls of your villa, Master, I can see two curls of smoke against the night sky. Other houses that you have burned. You are still the hunting the wolf hunters. Hunting the men who hurt me. Who hurt your slavegirl.

softly My Master protects me.

You keep me safe.

takes in a breath My beautiful Master. How you rest naked and masculine and mighty as a god across your cushions, propped on one powerful arm, watching your pleasure-kitten approach.

My thighs quiver with love for you, Master.

Do I please you, Master?

I am different now, Master, than when you bought me. Your brand is burned into my thigh. Your slave belt is locked around my cunt, its cool metal keeping me safe … and reserved for my Master's touch. And my belly has grown a soft swell from the new life you've planted inside me, Master. From your child in my womb, Master. I feel your child sometimes at night as we sleep, turning inside me. A beautiful, loving little girl like me with a heart full of fire. Or a strong son like you, Master, a boy who will grow into a powerful man who protects the woman he owns. *a soft little sigh of happiness* I might be bearing your son, Master. You put such a strong baby inside me.

My breasts are swelling, and they're always so sensitive now. Each caress of the night air on my nipples is sensual as a kiss.

whispers I need to be touched, Master.

Will you touch me, Master? Will you touch your slavegirl?

... Yes, Master. It will be my pleasure, Master. I will kneel beside you, Master, mmm. Yes, Master, lay your head on my naked thigh. I will caress your hair, Master, and I will soothe and relax you. *a soft intake of breath* Yes, Master, kiss my belly. I feel so cherished when you do that.

All the stars are out ... but no moon for wolves to howl at. It feels so peaceful and ... safe ... kneeling for you in the starlight. It has been hours since dinner, Master. Are you hungry, Master? I've brought fruit.

tenderly Here. I'll lift a berry and bring it to your lips, Master, and press it into your mouth with my soft fingertips. Mmm, yes, Master ... *a quivery breath* ... close your lips around my fingers, mmmm, sucking the berry's juices from my skin. *quivers* So juicy ... like me. *a soft, soft moan of need* My wet, tight cunt is hot with my juices tonight. I want to delight you, Master.

whispers I'll get another berry for you, Master.

a soft gasp Not with my fingers, Master? I'm to offer this to you with my mouth?

Yes, Master.

It will be my pleasure, Master.

I'll ... just place it between my lips and then you may take the berry, Master, and my mouth ... as gently ... or roughly ... as you please, Master. *whispers* I am yours.

Here it is, Master. *whispers* The berry. … mmmm …

the sound of a long, sensual kiss … gentle at first, then rougher and rougher, until the slavegirl is whimpering into his mouth

panting breaths Master! Are … are you trying to heat your slavegirl? Because I am … hot … Master, so hot between my soft thighs. How you kiss me.

Would … would you like another berry, Master?

Yes, Master. Here it is. In my mouth … mmm …

another kiss, shorter but passionate

almost panting I love you, Master.

kissing

sniffles

My … my eyes, Master? They … look swollen?

I … I am all right, Master.

SMACK!!

squeals You smacked my tit! My sensitive, swollen tit!

I'm sorry, Master!

several sharp smacks and squeals

trembly Forgive me, Master! I know you own me. You own my body. You own my heart. I'm not permitted to hide my heart from you, Master, any more than my tits or my cunt.

I'm sorry.

SMACK!

squeals

Yes, Master. I was crying earlier. Yes, I'll say why.

sniffles

Forgive me, Master. I know I am to be perfectly beautiful and perfectly pleasing. But my eyes are still red and swollen. I was crying, Master, while you were at the market. I missed you. And I … I was remembering the girls from my village, who were taken by the slavers, as I was. My friends. My … sisters. The girls I grew up with, girls I laughed and dreamed with. They would have been so happy to see my womb full like this, my belly round, my eyes shining with joy. It would have made my sisters so happy. They were my family. And now they're gone. Until you took me and claimed me, I was so … so alone.

crying softly

I'm sorry, Master. I … I'm here to give you pleasure, not drip tears on your shoulders. *sniffles* I don't know why I'm so tearful. Maybe it's because of the baby growing inside me. *sniffles* It's only … I … I miss them, the other girls. And here I am … happy. *breathes the words* So happy. And I don't know where they are, whether they are hurting or afraid or even alive.

she is spiraling into worries and fears

How can I deserve to be happy, when they aren't, Master? And what ... what if I don't make you as happy as you make me? What if ... what if you ever tire of me, Master?!

I would be so alone!

frightened, talking faster My body is changing, Master. I'm more round and full ... you ... you might not want me. Master, what if ... what if I keep swelling rounder and rounder and I become hideous to you, Master? What if you don't want m-MMMPHHHHHH MMMPHHHH

he covers her mouth with his hand and she whimpers quietly into his hand for a few moments

he lifts his hand

quivery and quiet You're fondling my thigh, where you've branded me. Where your mark is burned into my flesh. Reminding me you OWN me.

Yes, Master. Yes, I'll be quiet.

soft, shaky breaths

There are ... things you want me to hear, Master? Tonight, under the stars?

quivery You don't want me to speak.

Yes, Master.

softly, repeating what he tells her You're going to cover my mouth with your firm hand ... and talk softly in my ear. And I will listen like a good girl to everything my Master tells me.

Yes, Master. I understand.

MMMPHHH

he covers her mouth

for a few moments, we hear her sniffling softly as she listens to him, then she gasps a little, then whimpers something grateful and wordless into his palm.

for a moment or two, she cries ever so softly, muffled.

he takes his hand from her mouth

whispers, tearful, barely able to speak Thank you, Master. Thank you.

whispers, shaky Your words. Your beautiful words. What you said. That I'm … not alone.

I'm safe.

tearful I'm WANTED.

Treasured.

Owned.

breathing softly, in wonder That I'm as hot to you as the sunrise and the sunset and the moon by night. As beautiful as rain falling on the sea.

awed Master.

sniffles

And my Master thinks his slavegirl has a … a beautiful heart.

A heart my ... *sniffles happily* ... my Master loves.

And you ... you know I will make good children for you.

fervently Oh Master, my Master. It's true. I will make the most beautiful, strong children for you, Master. I promise!

whispers, shaken Yes, Master. Thank you, Master.

You wish your slavegirl to kiss your mouth, Master? To press my small, wet mouth to yours? Yes, Master.

kissing

a long, long sensual kiss

her soft whimpers of happiness into his kiss

whispers after I'm so happy. I'm so happy. *sniffles*

My ... my lips taste like tears, Master? Forgive me, Master.

You ... you don't mind?

whispers Thank you for loving me, Master. For keeping me safe. For owning me.

You hold my warm cunt locked in this belt by day, and you hold my body at night while I quiver and shudder and surrender to the hard thrusts of your cock in me. And you hold my heart. You hold my heart, Master! Cupped in your hands, so firmly.

whispers Like you'll never drop my heart or wound it. My Master.

Yes, Master. I am sorry. Your slavegirl is full of tears and soft sobbing little whimpers and feelings tonight. *blushes* I know you desire pleasure, Master. You're so good to me.

You're so good to me.

Yes, Master. I will give you such pleasure.

Settle back in your cushions, Master. I will get you another berry. Here, I will press my body to you, warm and soft… I will submit to you, opening my soft mouth, and giving you a small, juicy berry on my wet little tongue. Master.

a passionate kiss … we hear her soft noises as she gets more aroused

Oh Master.

Do you like my berries, Master?

Mmmm.

sultry I have something to give my Master that is more succulent, more delicious than any berry in the whole world …

Mmmm.

Feel me … trailing my nipple across your lips … Master …

pleading Master …

gasps Yes, Master! Your mouth!

soft, quivering little gasps of pleasure

My Master! My Master!

moans I will put my nipple in your mouth like a small, ripe berry!

moans, then cries out sharply ... You BITE me! ...

Master!

panting I'm not REALLY made of berries, Master! You can't BITE me.

she cries out

Master!

squeals

Master!

breathing fast Yes, Master, yes, you can do whatever you want me. You own me. You own my breasts. You own my soft, full tits. Master ... *moans* Master ... I love your mouth on my tits.

a soft, sighing moan Oh yes, Master, take my breasts in your hands. Your strong hands! My breasts are yours, Master. Do you feel my warm tits, Master, their soft weight in your palms? *moaning*

softly My tits have grown, Master. They're swelling for you. Do you really like them ... like this, Master? Full and aching at your touch?

soft moans as he touches her

How you grip me, Master! How you fondle me!

Yes, Master. Squeeze my tits!

gasps Use me!

moaning Oh Master! Soon my tits will be full of warm milk.

Master!

moaning

a gasping cry Master, my nipples!

she cries out

Yes, Master! Yes!

she cries out

Yes, you can do as you please with my body, Master. My nipples are for your pleasure! Master, take what you desire!

a wild little scream

You're twisting them!

squeals

Master! Master, I'm so sensitive! Please be gentle, Mast- *squeals*

breathing faster I'm yours, Master. I'm yours! I'm yours, I'm yours, I'm yours!

panting Oh, Master. Oh, Master. I'm so wet.

whispers I'm so wet.

I'm soaking the soft velvet inside the slave belt that you've locked on me.

shaky, aroused breathing

a gasp Master!

excited Master! The baby! The baby kicked inside me, Master! I felt your baby in me!

Yes, Master, please, touch my belly. Press your hand warm to my belly. Master! Can you feel your child, Master? Can you feel the baby your love-slave is making for you? Master! Master! This is your child!

soft, quivery breaths

It's all right, Master. You'll feel him soon, when he's just a little larger inside me. I feel him, Master, he's so … strong. As he kicks. Strong like you, Master.

tearful Master, I love you so much.

My body is full of your child.

Oh my Master.

Master … *whispers* … will you hold me tonight? Will you hold me so tightly, with your child inside me? Please, Master? I … I need to be held.

Yes, Master, I'll give you my wrists. *moans* You're binding them in that silk rope you've pulled from beneath the cushions. Bind me, Master. Bind me. I'm yours.

Hold me captive all night in your ropes.

soft moans and squirm as he binds her

And loops of rope around my breasts ... Master. My full breasts. Master, your rope on my body is so firm ... so soft but unyielding. You hold me so gently but so strong ...

gasps You're ... binding my wrists to my ankles, Master?

Yes, Master.

You may bind me as you wish, Master.

moans

I submit to you.

I am yours.

soft moans

You're binding me! My elbows to my knees. Master, I feel so held! And so helpless. You could open me so easily, like this. You could thrust my knees apart and fill me with your cock!

gasps You ... you're holding the key! The key to my slave belt!

Master! Are you going to unlock me? Are you going to fuck me? Are you going to fuck your pleasure-slave, Master? Are you going to surge and thrust inside me while your child moves in my belly?

a metal unlocking

soft little gasps of need Master! Master! Master!

metal sounds as he removes the slave belt

so, so quivery You've removed my belt! My soft, soaked little cunt is naked to the night air, Master. And to your … *moans* … to your touch! Yes, touch me! Oh gods, Master, PLEASE! *moaning* Just caressing my folds lightly with your fingertips is TORTURE! Please, Master, take me! Take your pleasure-kitten and fuck her, Master, please!!!

I … I have to beg more prettily?

a low whimper

Yes, Master. As Master wishes.

Master, please! I need you in me! I need your cock! I need your powerful hard cock! I need you, I NEED you! Right here on your roof under the stars, while your marble nymphs watch, while the dancing slaves in the gardens below listen to my screams! I need to feel your thick heat penetrating me, fucking me! Thrust your cock in me, Master, please! Thrust inside my slick cunt, into my wet tight cunt, I need to FEEL you, I need to GRIP you, I need to clench around your cock and scream to the night sky as I surrender to you, Master! I need you, Master! I need you inside me! PLEASE! I love your cock!

a sharp smack

a wild little cry

Master! You smacked my clit!

SMACK!

squeals

Yes, Master! You can smack me as you please!

SMACK

squeals

I'm your pleasure-slut, Master!

SMACK!

squeals

I'm your kitten! Your treasured, tight, wet little kitten!

SMACK!

screams I'm your kitten, I'm your kitten!!!!

SMACK!

yelps

I love you, Master!

SMACK

screams Your pleasure-slave adores you!

SMACK

screams I love you!

SMACK

squeals Yes, Master! I love you, I love you!

SMACK

shrieks

I love you!

SMACK

screams

tearfully, joyously I love you!

SMACK

squeals I love you! *a whining moan* Master, Master, I'm so wet, I'm so wet, I'm so WET! Master, please! I love you!

SMACK

screams I love you!

SMACK

screams I love you!

SMACK

screams I love you!

Yes! Yes! Your weight on me! Take me! Take me! Your cock hard against my folds, oh Master, I burn for you! My warm honey runs down my legs! Yes! Spread my bound legs, with my wrists still tied to my ankles! Master, take me! Take me, Master!

Master, I … I …

her wild scream as he penetrates her, screaming the words as he fills her I love you!!!!

little grunts and moans from her as he takes her hard and fast

she starts to gasp the words between moans I love you! I love you! I love you!

I love you!

I'm so sensitive! I'm so sensitive! I can't … I can't …

Master! Master! Fuck me, fuck me, FUCK me! BREAK ME, Master!

Gods, Master, you're so BIG in me! You're so deep! My Master!

squeals

My Master!

squeals

My Master! My Master! *moans* My Master!

Oh Master, oh Master, you're in me, you're in me, so thick, so full, you're caressing my body from the inside, Master, Master, you own me, you own me!

I'm tied so tightly, so tightly! I can't move! I can't even wriggle as you hold my legs spread far apart and FUCK me under the stars!

Master! Fuck your slave!

Fuck your slavegirl!

improv mindless, passionate moans

moaning Master, you melt me, you melt me, I am molten HEAT, Master, Master! Ohhhh ohhhh ... Master, your hand ... your hand slipping between us, fondling my clit ... Master!!!!!

wild squeals of pleasure

Master, I'm clenched so tight around your cock! Master, your thrusts! Master, I need to yield, I need to yield I need to yield I need to yield please please please please please yes yes yes Master!! Master!!! MMMPHHH MMMMPHHHHHHHHHH!!!!!

he covers her mouth with his hand and TAKES her, HARD, and we hear her muffled squeals at each rapid, hard thrust, and then she cums and cums and CUMS, screaming muffled into his hand

soft little panting grunts afterward as he keeps taking her

he lifts his hand

desperate little moans Master, your mouth on my throat ... on my full breasts ... Master! Your body sweats on top of me, rolling and thrusting into me! *tearful and wild with heat* Master, you are my god! You are my god! I worship you, Master! Please don't ever stop! Please, please, I'm yours! I'm yours!

her next orgasm rolls into her like THUNDER fuck, fuck, fuck fuck fuck fuck fuck fuckkk Master I'm yours! I'm yours-

AHHHHHHHHHH!!!!!!!!!!!!

panting afterward

little gasps I'm your slavegirl. I'm your slavegirl. I'm your wet tight loving slavegirl. Master, how you fuck me! How you own me! How you HOLD me! I feel so safe, with you on top of me … and in me … with you wanting me!

Want me, Master!

Want me!

Please cum in me!

Please, let me give you pleasure! Let me give you all the pleasure in my body! Let me SOAK your cock! I want to milk your cock dry! Please, Master, please cum in me! Fill me with your hot semen, the way you did when you put your baby in me! Master, cum in me! Please! I want you! I want your seed! I want your seed! Master, let me please you!

moaning Master, do I please you?!

Master, ahhh! Biting my nipples! Ahhh! Master! Master! I'm … I'm … I'm …

she screams as she cums I love you!

Yes!

Yes!

Pulse in me!

I love your cock! I love your cock! I love your cock!

Fill me!

Oh gods!

panting Master … Master … Master …

Oh, I'm soaked in sweat. Oh, I'm a wet shaky little mess for my Master.

I felt your cock empty in me. Oh, Master. How flushed and beautiful your face is. I wish I were untied and I could hold your face in my hands. Oh, Master. My beautiful Master. My love. My god. I love you, I love you.

Oh, Master. Your eyes. Smoldering in the dark above mine. Oh, Master. Oh, Master. The way you're holding MY face in YOUR hands. I could cry, I could cry.

kissing

whispers My Master. Kiss me forever and forever.

kissing

gaspy, emotional What are you saying, my Master? … You love your slavegirl? You're proud of her? Because she is smart and brave and beautiful … *whispers* … and she gives you pleasure.

kissing

sniffles I love you.

kissing

suddenly giggling breathlessly The baby is dancing in my belly, Master. Do you … do you feel him now?

giggling Ouch, little baby.

He … he says we're keeping him awake.

breathless, loving, happy giggles

moans Ohhh … you're pulling out of me.

soft, exhausted quivery breaths

gasps Your breath across my clit!

moans

Master, are you going to lick me?

moaning

Oh Master, your mouth is so hot. So hot…

moaning and mewling with pleasure

Master … I'm tied … I'm tied … and so open … and so hot … and so wet … Master, love me with your mouth. Love me with your mouth, Master. *moaning cry* I want to fill your mouth with my warm honey, Master!

Master!

Master!

approaching a relentless, wild orgasm

Master! May I yield? May I yield for you, Master?

I … I have to wait!

Master, I can't wait! I can't! I can't! My whole lower body is on FIRE, Master! Master, please! I can't hold back, I can't!

SMACK

a wild, desperate, pre-orgasmic scream!

SMACK!!!

SQUEALS!

Forgive me, Master! I'll obey! I'll obey!

squeals Your FINGERS in me! Master!

Master, you'll break me! Master, Master!

Yes, Master! Yes! Yes! I won't cum! I won't cum, I won't cum! I won't cum until you tell me. I'll be a good girl. I'll be your good girl.

her wild whimpers of heat as he licks and sucks at her clit I'm your good girl! I'm your good girl! I'm your good girl! I'm your good girl! I'm your good girl! I'm your good girl! I'm your good girl! I'm your good girl! I'm your good girl! I'm your good girl! I'm your good girl! I'm your good girl! I'm your good girl! I'm your good girl! I'm your good GIRL!

Now? I can cum now? I can cum now? I can cum NOW???

she screams as she cums

her orgasm leaves her shaking

quivery I love you …

You make me the wettest, most desperate little pleasure-slut who has ever had a man inside her or worn his collar.

almost sobbing from exhaustion and pleasure

Yes, Master. Ahhh. Ahhh. I know you'll keep me. I know you'll keep me.

I love you so much.

metal rattling

her low moan of dismay and obedience

You're locking me again …

Oh, Master.

Oh Master I want to so naked for you.

I want to be so naked for you.

I want my tight cunt to be naked for you every moment of every night.

whispers Don't lock me yet. Don't lock me yet.

the sound of the lock

quivery Yes, Master. I am yours. *sniffles* Locked. And safe. And yours.

moans Yes, hold me.

Hold me tied in your arms. My Master.

You own me.

I love you.

panting softly Oh Master. Your marble nymphs are watching us, and they look so happy. With their legs spread wide and their hands full of their tits and their soft little mouths open and ready for your cock. They're proud of me. I gave our Master pleasure.

a soft giggle

Hold me, Master. Hold me.

Your cock is still hard against my thigh.

Mmmm. If you hadn't locked me, Master ... *teases* ... I could give you more pleasure. I know I could. I could please you ALL night.

Oh ... I ... I will?

With my wet little mouth?

Yes, Master. I'll be a good slavegirl.

But you mean to hold me first? Bound. *a pained gasp* While the baby kicks.

You want to press your belly to mine and feel him kick inside me.

You put him inside me.

You put a baby in me.

I am so full, Master. So full of everything you give me.

My womb is full.

My heart. My heart is so full I can barely speak.

he covers her mouth with his hand

mmmphh mmmphh mmmphhh mmmmmmmm

mmmm mmmm mmmphh

he lifts his hand

her voice is gentle and reverent Did you like my small, wet tongue licking your palm? My Master …

How you hold me.

Captive.

Mmmmm.

Yes, Master. I understand.

I don't need to speak. Not when my heart is so full. I don't need to speak. I just need to open my soft, wet mouth and give you pleasure.

Yes, Master.

Fill my mouth.

improv a slow, sensual blowjob, her soft whimpers around his cock … an occasional breathless "I love you" … "I love you" … "I love you" … and then he cums in her mouth. We hear her whimper of pleasure as he fills her soft mouth with his hot, sticky seed. Then her gulps as she swallows for him.

catching her breath

low and sultry I swallowed everything you gave me, Master. I'm a good girl.

whispers lovingly Oh, Master. How you cup my cheek in your hand.

I'll turn my face and kiss ... *kissing* ... your palm ... *kissing* ... your fingertips ... *kissing*

Your strong hand.

kissing

Master.

kissing

I am my Master's good girl.

Mmmm.

soft rustling

Yes ...

Hold me, Master. Mmmmmmm. Your arms around me, protecting me ... keeping me warm with your body on your rooftop while the stars burn like lovers in the sky. Your hard body behind me, your cock settled against my naked, warm ass. Your hands cup my tits, holding my swollen breasts safe in your grip ... letting me know you desire me. You desire my full, pregnant body.

Oh Master, I can cum for you a thousand times and I won't have even begun to give you the pleasure you deserve. My love, the man who owns me, who branded me, who saved me from werewolves and put a baby in me. I could give you pleasure every night and every morning until the hair tumbling down my back and the soft, sweet down between my thighs turns silver, Master, and it still wouldn't be nearly enough to show you how much I love you. I want to give you everything, Master. My every breath, every beat of my heart, every drop of warm honey that drips from my cunt. I love you.

I love you, Master.

kissing

It's so dark out tonight … with no moon … and I am so safe in your ropes, Master, binding me, holding me open for your pleasure all night. I am safe in my Master's collar. Safe in your powerful arms.

soft little gaspy moans Yes, kiss my neck, kiss my neck…

whimpers of pleasure

I'm bound. Helplessly yours. Your love-slave. Please, kiss my mouth, Master. Kiss my m-Mmmmphhhhhh

a warm, loving kiss

softly, lovingly, pouring her heart into the words:

You own me.

11

Milk Me, Master

The sounds of a thunderstorm through an open window. Possibly soft music from inside the villa. The slavegirl is asleep, but she is moaning softly in her sleep. Her Master has just thrust himself inside her, gentle and slow in the night.

After a few dreaming moans at his thrusts, she wakes with a soft gasp. The light clinking of chains.

surprised, sleepy, loving Master! *moans* Master! You're inside me! Your cock is inside me! And your collar around my throat! *moaning* I love you, Master! How you hold me safe under your body as you thrust! The swell of my belly and my breasts full of milk. *moaning* My wrists still chained from your enjoyment of me before we slept! Master, Master! Oh Master, take me!

soft moans

Oh Master, I love you in me.

Take me, Master. Take me.

Yes, Master, I'll be quiet for you. Here in the middle of the night, while thunder cracks open the sky.

thunder

moans loudly Master!!!

Yes, Master, yes, press your powerful hand over my mouth. Keep me quiet while you enjoy me. *moans* Cover my mouth, Master. Cover my m-mmmphhhhhhhhhhh

improv a few minutes of loving, intense sex on her Master's bed, her moans into his palm as he thrusts, as he takes her. The sounds of rain. The clink of her delicate chains.

She moans into his hand, enjoying his thrusts very much. Mostly wordless, but a few muffled whimpers of "Master" and a sweet, smothered cry of "I love you, Master!" as she approaches orgasm

She cums, squealing loudly into his palm.

she whimpers sweetly into his hand afterward

Rain falling in the garden outside. He lifts his hand from her lips.

Quivery little gasps I love you, Master. My thighs are shaking. I love you. I love you.

moans You're still thrusting in me. Inside my warm, pregnant body. It's so dark, and your body is so warm on top of me … and inside me! Every one of your thrusts so loving and so deep! My Master! *breathy* I'm yours! Chained in your bed, my wrists chained to the wrists of the mahogany slavegirl carved into the headboard of your bed, Master. My thighs … *moans*… open around your surging hips! As you plunge inside me again and again, Master! I'm sweaty and naked for your pleasure, soaked and swollen with new life! The life you put in me, Master.

moaning

I am surrendered to you, Master. I want to wake up like this every night, to your thrusts inside me. I want to surface from my dreams with you inside me. Master. Master.

moaning

I feel the marks in my soft thighs where you whipped me before bed, Master. You whipped me, just to remind me that you OWN me. *moans* But you whipped so lightly. Were you afraid of hurting the baby, Master? I can take more, Master. *breathless* More. More. The baby and I both are strong. *sultry* I don't mind hurting for you, Master.

a sudden cry Oh! How you THRUST in me! Master!

I'm as wet as the storm inside! I'm so wet for you, Master!

Here, I'll spread my legs wider for you, Master. *gasping and whimpering with raw NEED* I'd spread them wider yet if my hands weren't chained! I want to open for you as a blossom opens to the sun! I want to give you all my sweet nectar, all my warm honey! I'm so open for you! So open! I want you in me deeper. Deeper! Please, Master! My breasts are bouncing beneath you in the dark. Master, take me! You won't hurt the baby. Fuck me, Master! Fuck me! Enjoy me!

crying out as he takes her harder

her wild cries and the thunder and the rain

Do you want to finish inside me, Master? I love you. Oh, Master. Let me whisper in your ear.

whispers hotly You are such a good, strong, loving man. I am so glad you own me. You own me, Master. Please cum in me. Please, please cum in me. I want your seed in me. I want to leak your seed down my thighs all night.

My Master, my Master.

panting Please, Master. Please. Fill your pleasure-kitten with your seed! Please FILL me! I need you pulsing in me, Master! Please let me give you pleasure! Please! Please? May I give you pleasure, Master?!

squeals You're biting my calves! Masterrrr! Yes, yes, bite me! Bite the soft insides of my legs! Devour me, Master! I love you! I love you!

Yes! Yes! Cum in me! Cum in me! Please, Master, please cum in me! Cum in me! Cum in me!

she squeals as she cums

panting

gaspy and loving I'm yours. I'm yours. I'm yours.

Yes, Master, I'm shaking. My thighs. I … the way you fuck me is so intense. I love you so much. I love being captive in your arms.

kissing Do you like my soft, wet mouth on your neck, Master? *kissing the sweetest little mew of need* May I kiss my Master? Do you want my mouth, Master?

a long sensual kiss with her soft little noises of pleasure and love and need muffled by his mouth

Ohhhhh, Master. *her voice trembling with passion* I love you.

she makes a soft, feminine noise and then her voice goes very sultry Yes, Master, I'm lifting my hips into you … ahhhhhh! … and clenching around your cock with my soft, tight little cunt. *a happy noise* Do you like my cunt, Master? *teases* Do you like your slavegirl's wet little cunt? *whisper* You own my cunt, Master. *moans* Do you like this warm, gentle cunt you just fucked? This cunt you fucked so full of your hot semen, Master?

purrs Masterrrr…

Are you glad you bought me, Master?

reverently I'm your slavegirl.

thunder, and the rainstorm gets more violent, a downpour

That rain! *giggles* All your marble nymphs are getting rained on, Master. *teases* All that water dripping down their smooth stone breasts and their naked thighs. *softly* MY thighs are wet, too, Master … and my cunt is wet … so wet …

giggles I hope your dancing slaves are all inside, Master. Warm and naked in their silk bedding and not soaked in Master's pleasure gardens. *giggles* My Master has so many dancing slaves, each as luscious as a dream, but I am the only slavegirl chained to my Master's bed and shoved full of his cock. *a soft sighing moan of love* I am the only slavegirl with her belly warm and round with my Master's child. The only slavegirl with her breasts full of milk for my Master. *breathes* Oh, Master. I am your love-slave.

a soft moan Your hands … so warm on my breasts. Mmmm, Master. *quivering* Do you feel how swollen my tits are? *moans*Your seed in me did this, Master. Made my body so full and so hot. *quivery* My breasts are full of warm milk, Master.

moans Yes, Master, squeeze my breasts.

soft little noises

giggles Yes, Master. I'm going to keep … mmmm … squeezing your cock … ohhh … until you have me again, Master.

sultry I want to milk you dry, Master. I want to please my Master. I want to fuck my Master until he's exhausted.

smack

she yelps

Yes, Master. *giggles* I'll be a good girl and let Master rest a moment. *teasing* Since my Master isn't ready to satisfy his slavegirl.

SMACK!!!

squeals

SMACK!!!

squeals

giggling I'm sorry, Master!

SMACK!!!

squeals

SMACK!!!

squeals

Masterrr! My breasts are so full of milk, Master! *giggling* They're too sensitive to smack, Master!

SMACK!!!

squeals

I'll be a good girl, Master!

SMACK!!! SMACK!!! SMACK!!! SMACK!!! SMACK!!! SMACK!!!

squealing

softly Yes, Master. Yes, I am your sweet, surrendered slavegirl. I'm only giggling because I'm so happy. You make me so happy. And so full of baby. *giggling*

she takes a breath after the giggles, makes a happy noise

softly, worshipfully How may I please you, my Master?

a soft little noise My breasts are swollen and sore, and they're leaking milk.

softly, slowly I'm leaking warm milk, Master.

a quivery little whimper Your m-mouth … warm on my nipple … Master … *a long, long quivery moan* M-Masterrrrrr … are you … *gasps* … drinking from me? Master … Master … the way you suckle … my warm milk is flowing out of me, filling your hot, hungry mouth, Master. Drink from me, Master. Drink from me. *quivering* How your h-hand grips and squeezes my tit. *moans* Milk me, Master. Milk me.

You own me. You own my breasts.

she starts to moan and moan

Yes, Master, I'm rocking my hips. I can't help it. This … this feeling … of your mouth on my tits, drinking from my body … it's so … so intimate. Please, Master, I love you. Please ravish me again. Please thrust in me. Please fuck me. I'm yours. *a little sob* I'm yours.

barely able to speak I'm so happy. I'm so happy.

moaning as he thrusts inside her, again and again

Master … drink my milk … oh Master … Master … How you squeeze my tits … Milk flowing into your hot mouth, milk from my other nipple flowing over my naked breast … oh, Master! oh, Master! I'm so full of milk for you! I'm so full of milk! I'm so full of life! Master, Master, I'm making life for you! And milk! I'm making milk!

a soft little cry Feel me grip you, Master!

her voice goes fierce with love I'm milking your cock while you milk me, Master! My Master who keeps me safe, who protects me, who bred me, who LOVES me! I'm milking your cock! Feel me squeeze … and ripple around your cock … *panting moans* Master, I want to give you so much pleasure! Here, chained and naked and fucked in your bed! I want to give you more pleasure than any man has ever had from a woman! Master! Will you unchain me? Please? I want to rake my nails down your back and your thighs! I want to bite your shoulders while you ravish me, while you suck my milk from my tits! Master, please! Unchain me and just pin you to your bed with your cock! I love you! I love you!

rattling and unlocking of chains

gasping with need Thank you, Master! Thank you, Master!

I'll ravish you, too, Master! Bucking my hips! Digging my fingers into your ass! Ahhhh! Pulling you into me! Fuck me, Master! Fuck me! Milk me! Milk my breasts! Milk me dry, Master! My body will make more! More! More! More for you and the baby inside me! Milk me, Master! I'm going to milk your cock! *each cry of this phrase louder than the last* I'm going to milk your cock! I'm going to milk your cock!

Fuck me in your bed, Master! I'm yours! I love you! I'm your pleasure-slut! Your pleasure-kitten! Your milk-slut! Fuck me! Fuck me! FUCK ME!

screams Yes, bite me, Master! Bite me! *squeals* My tits are yours, Master! My tits belong to you! USE ME!

squealing and biting as he fucks her

Feel my teeth in your arm, Master! *biting with a sweet, desperate little feminine growl* I can't help it! I can't help it! I'm so wet! I'm so in heat! The way you fuck me! So possessive and strong! So hot inside me! Master, Master, my cunt burns for you! I need you in my mouth, in my cunt, in my ass! I need you, I need you, I need you! *biting and panting*

thunder loud outside, and more downpour

Master, fuck me like thunder, Master! Fuck me like the thunder fucks the world! Just fuck me, fuck me, fuck me! *screaming* I love your cock! I love your cock! I love your cock! FUCK ME, MASTER!!!! I'm milking your cock, squeezing and milking your cock! Please, Master, give me your milk! Give me YOUR cream, Master, please! Please! Cream in me, Master! Master! MASTERRR!

she cums screaming, gripping and squeezing his cock as he drinks from her. Milking his cock while he milks her, his hands caressing and gripping her breasts, his mouth hot around her nipple.

the rain is gentler outside now

she is shaking and making soft, feminine, well-fucked little noises

Did I please you, Master? *emotional and vulnerable and loving* Did you like the taste of my milk, Master?

her voice tearful and emotional I love you.

I love you.

I'm so happy.

sniffles and cries a little in his arms

You're kissing my tears from my cheeks. *sniffles* My eyelids.

kissing

My lips.

kissing

softly, so softly My mouth is soft and open for you, Master. Like my cunt. Always.

kissing

I belong to you. Only you.

kissing

happy sniffles, then a giggle My breasts are warm and sticky with my milk. *giggles* I'm Master's wet, sticky milk-slut.

softly, more erotically I am your milk-slut, Master.

breathy I am so, so full of milk.

You've filled me with your cock and filled me with life. I love you, Master. I love you so much. I wish you could drink me and drink me until you're so full of me. *quivery* Like I'm so full of you. So full of you.

giggles I don't even know what words are spilling from my mouth, Master. I'm probably the silliest slavegirl with this baby in me. *breathy* I'm just so in love with you.

I love you, Master.

a low moan Ohhh, you're pulling out of me …

a soft little whimper Don't. *whispers* Don't.

Stay inside me.

Come back.

clinking of chains

Oh, you're chaining me again, Master?

Are we going to sleep, Master? While it rains in the garden? *sultry* Until Master wakes hungry again and fucks me before dawn?

Yes, Master. *softly* Whatever you wish, Master.

I am your pleasure-slut. *softly* Your love-slave.

My body is for your pleasure.

Mmmmmmm, ohhh, you're rolling me on my side … ohhh … settling behind me … your arms around me, ahhhh … one cradling my belly … the other caressing my warm, full breast. Oh Master. Oh Master. Your warm, strong hands keep me safe. Your hand on my breast, your hand on my womb. Keeping me and the baby so safe. My Master who protects me.

a low, startled, loving moan

Oh yes, Master! Ease into me from behind … *moans*

Oh Master, your cock is so warm and so good.

slow, sensual moaning

So slow and so deep. Like you're caressing me with your cock. *moans* Oh, Masterrr. I can feel you slide in … and out … *moans* … and into me … so warm and so thick. Mmmmmmm. Yes, Master. I'll be a good girl and take your cock. As slow or as hard as you please. I am yours, Master. OHHHH your hips are so muscled and strong, fucking me from behind. *moans*

giggles suddenly Your baby is kicking inside me, Master. Do you feel him under your hand?

a loving moan

He knows you love his mother so much.

Love me, Master. Love me.

moaning for a moment

Yes, Master. Cover my mouth. I love your hand strong and warm over my mouth. My Mast-mmmmphhhhhhh

mmmmphhh mmmmphhhhhhh

for a minute, we hear her soft, slow, loving moans into his palm, muffled and sweet, as he makes love to her. We hear rainfall outside. He takes her slow, slow and lovingly.

she cums again, sensitive and hot, surprising herself

she moans into his palm

whimpers

soft, quivery little noises after her orgasm

a muffled "I love you, Master" into his palm

the episode ends

12

Fuck Me in the Bath, Master

The audio opens with gentle music. The slavegirl is humming softly. We hear the gentle splashing of water with her hand, and water pouring slow and sweet into the bath

Mmm, I think that's hot enough. Now to pour in sea salt and fragrances … mmmm … oh, this bath smells so good … And Master's bath room is hot with steam. There's a slavegirl carved in marble at the foot of the bath, luscious and naked like me, with her thighs spread open and the water pouring into the bath from her slick, wet cunt.

giggles Just the place to relax my Master. I've put petals in the bath, and I've lit candles along the wall so the light shimmers on the water … and on my Master's slavegirl. I glow with love for my Master.

Mmmmmm.

Master has left my belt unlocked and waiting by the bed since the baby came. I … I'm naked. Unlocked. I could … *whispers* I could touch myself.

If Master hadn't told me not to.

whimpers

But I could. I could. Master wouldn't know. He isn't here
…

whimpers

Oh, I'm so wet. So wet. My soft petals are swollen with
need.

whimpers I could just … for a moment … just with my
fingertips …

moans and quivers

I… I… *struggles with herself*

frustrated-determined … I need to finish preparing my Master's
bath!

sounds of jars clinking I'll set these bottles of oil down so I can
soothe my Master. *under her breath* My Master had better
soothe me, too. *whimpers* I don't think I've … EVER …
needed his touch so badly.

A little more water, and I'll go find him. *humming for a moment
and stirring the water*

gasps

Oh! Master! You're here! You've taken my hips in your
strong hands. I didn't hear you come in behind
me. *quivery* You shouldn't frighten your slavegirl, Mast-
mmmmphhhhhhh mmmphhhh *interrupted by a kiss*

a long, sensual kiss. She whimpers sweetly into the kiss

breathless Master. Each time you kiss me, I melt. I drip down my thighs for you. *a soft, needy little moan*

What am I doing? I'm preparing a bath for you, Master. *giggles* You can tell by the fragrant steam in the air and by the way your loving, collared pleasure-kitten is kneeling naked on the lip of the bath.

breathy, seductive Completely naked, Master.

Except for the collar on my throat. The brand you burned into my thigh.

You own me, Master. My tits lift and fall as I breathe, swollen with milk. My thighs are soft cream, ready for my Master's pleasure.

teasing It's almost ready, Master. Your bath.

I thought, since the baby is asleep and one of the dancing slaves is watching him … and since you've been so protective, caring for me, taking the baby the last few nights so your slavegirl could sleep … and then hiding yawns behind your hand all day when you thought I wasn't looking … I thought I would relax you and worship you tonight. By preparing the most sweet, scented, sensual bath for you. *teasing* Only don't fall asleep in the bath, Master. Because after I bathe you and rub the fatigue from your shoulders, my Master might desire to enjoy his sweet, scented, sensual kitten.

soft and seductive Would you like to enjoy your kitten, Master?

I'm not as sore now as I was. I ... I think I'm ready. *quivers* To be fucked.

You own me. You could have taken me any night you chose. But you let me recover and rest for weeks ... I love you, Master.

kissing

she "mmphhs" into his mouth, in startled arousal

breathless Master! If you keep squeezing my breasts like that, I'll be too aroused to focus on your bath!

a soft little cry as he pinches her nipples

Master! Please! My nipples are so sensitive. My breasts so full of milk. *whimpers* Please be gentle, Master.

moans Yes, Master ... ohhhhhh ... your mouth is hot on my breasts ... my nipples ... ohhh, when you suckle me, I feel like I could swoon. Master, Master ... leave some for the baby ... *moans*

panting softly

Oh Master. Oh Master. When you graze my nipples with your teeth! Mmmmnn! You're going to light a forest fire between my thighs, Master! I can't! I can't bear it!

soft whimpers

Yes, Master. You own my breasts.

My tits are for your pleasure. *giggles* Though you might have competition for them now. Your son is VERY demanding.

SMACK!

she squeals Ah! My tit!

improv smacks and squeals and quivers for a few moments

Yes, Master. Yes, I'm a good girl. I'm your good girl. Suck my tits, Master. As Master pleases.

moaning

Ohh your hands and your mouth are … hot. So hot.

Master! I'm supposed to be helping ease your stress! What kind of devoted bath-slave will I be if you reduce me to a wet, whimpering puddle?

moaning

Master, my blossom is SOAKED. I'm going to just cum apart at your touch, Master!

whimpering

What… what's that, Master? You … you want your slavegirl clean, too? What do you mean, Master? I'm already naked and sweaty in the steam, Master. I'm here to bathe YOU, Master.

a sudden cry, followed by a splash, and spluttering, as her Master throws her in the bath

spluttering Master! Master!

a feminine growl I have an EVIL Master. *growls* Come here, Master. Your love-slave wants to give you a kiss …

mmmphh

the sound of a kiss

whispers I think it's time for Master's bath. *giggles*

kissing

… I'll just grip your shoulders, Master, and …

heavy splash as she pulls her Master into the bath with her

her giggles

Now Master can enjoy his bath! And be as wet as I am! *giggling* Your garments, your sable cloak, your hair slick to your shoulders… *giggles* My Master looks like a god of the sea. *giggles* It's okay, Master, I needed to wash your garments anyway. Now, my Master AND his clothes will be clean. *giggles* Your devoted, clever slavegirl has completed two tasks at once, Master! *giggles*

a soft gasp

Oh.

Oh. That look.

Master? Is … is your kitten in trouble? I only wanted to bathe you, Mast- *she squeals* My hair! Oh! You're bending me over the lip of the bath! Master? Master?!

SMACK!!!

squeals Master!

SMACK!!

squeals Master! *whimpers* When you smack my ass, I get so wet …

SMACK!!

squeals Master, Master … *whispers* I've missed this … I've missed your hand on me. Spank me, Master. I'll be a good kitten.

SMACK!!

squeals Yes, Master! I'll be a good kitten!

SMACK!!

squeals Yes, Master!

SMACK!!

squeals YES, MASTER!

SMACK!!

squeals I'm your good kitten!

SMACK!!

squeals Your kitten!

SMACK!!

squeals Your pleasure-kitten!

SMACK!!

squeals Your kitten-slut!

SMACK!!

squeals

SMACK!!

squeals I love you, Master!

panting Master? Master, are you unfastening your ... ohhhhhhh, your ... your cock ... *whimpers in need* ... so hot and thick against my ass ... Master, I should be bathing you, Master! *quivers* Why are you reaching for the oils, Master? I'm wet enough for you, Master, I promise, I ... *a long, quivery, whimpery moan* ... ohhhh, your finger in my ass ... slick and firm in my ass ... oh gods ... oh dear ... Master ... my Master ... you're going to fuck your pleasure-slut in the ass, Master?

whimpers

Oh, Master, how you tower behind me, muscled and intense, gripping me by my hair, holding me exactly where you want me. Dripping water from your hair and shoulders, standing like a god in your bath, in the steam. Your eyes are FIRE, Master. *moans* Are you going to burn me, Master?

whimpers Your ... your cock.

Right there. Right there.

Master! Master, I'm so tight back there. Master, it's been so long since you've been in my ass, I don't know if I ... I don't know if your slavegirl can take it, Master! You might break me! You might ... *she cries out as he takes her*

Oh! It's big! *panting* It's big! *squeals* Master, you're so big!

a scream as he thrusts deeper

splashing bath water ... and wild, urgent thrusts against the side of the bath, and moaning, squealing cries from her as he takes her ass

she cries out at each thrust Master! My Master! My Master! Oh Master! Master! MASTER!

then, little whimpering squeals without words

SMACK!!!!

squeals Yes, Master!

SMACK!!!!

squeals Master!

SMACK!!!!

squeals Yes, Master, yes! I'll buck my hips like a good girl! I'll give you such pleasure, Master! Fuck my ass, Master! Fuck my ass! Let me be the tightest, hottest little collar-slut! I'm yours, Master! I'm yours! Yours, yours! Fuck your little slut, Master!

moaning You are so big in me, Master!

Take me! Take me! Take me! I want to give you pleasure, Master! I want to give you pleasure! I gave you a son! Are you proud of me, Master? Are you proud of your slavegirl?!

a squeal as he thrusts himself all the way into her ass

MASTER!

squeals

quivers So deep! So deep!

You're all the way in me … inside my ass. M-Master …

improv a fast, urgent anal fuck, her cries as he takes her

panting Yes, Master, yes, pull my hair. Make my tits sway and leap as you fuck your kitten. I belong to you, Master! I belong to you! I love you! I know you're close! I can feel you tensing! Cum in my ass, Master! Cum in my ass!

Master, please, please, PLEASE! I need your seed! I need to feel you throb in my ass! Please! Crush me under your muscled body and fuck me and bruise me and FILL ME, Master! Fill my ass! *moans* Claim your kitten!

more and more aroused Claim me! Claim me! Cum in me! Cum in me! Cum INSIDE me!

Master! Master! Master! Yes, yes! Throb in me! Give it to me! Master, please please please Masterrrrr *she cums* I yield! I yield! I YIELD!

she cums so hard, spasming around him

the water splashing goes calmer after a moment

soft and quivery after the water settles, almost tearful after the intensity of her orgasm I am your conquest, Master. You've fucked my ass. You've collared me and branded me and bred me.

whispers You've fucked my heart.

I'm yours.

I love you so much…

You own me.

panting What … what's that in your hand, Master? That object? That … *she moans* … ohh, you're pulling out of me … and pushing that thing inside me … into my ass … *a grunt and a whimper* Oh Master, it's big, it's big, it's big like your cock! It's … *squeals*

whimpers Ohhhhhh it fills me so full.

So full.

Keeping your cum inside me.

whimpers

Will I be wearing this all night, Master? While I bathe you? When you fuck me in our bed while the baby sleeps? Will I have your plug in my ass, keeping your seed hot and sticky inside me? Will I be full of your semen all night, Master? The morning sun will kiss my body and the new day will find your slavegirl exhausted and sweaty in your bed with your plug still in her. Completely filled by my Master.

whimpers

My Master. My Master.

soft, aroused sounds

Am I to bathe you now, Master?

Yes, Master. Sit back in the bath, my Master. My love. Watch my tits heave for you, leaking milk. My ass would be leaking your cum, but you've plugged me, Master. *heat in her voice* I can feel your cum in me, Master, warm in my ass.

Sit back, my wonderful Master. Relax. Breathe deep, like a god who has just fucked his nymph.

quivers You fucked me, Master. I'm yours.

I'll unbutton your garments … take the cloak from your shoulders … *sounds of disrobing*

moans From your muscled, powerful shoulders.

My powerful Master who ravishes me.

And I'll do anything to relax you and give you pleasure tonight, Master.

breathes Anything.

I am your slave-kitten.

Here … I'll get the oils …

bottles clinking

And sit in your lap like a good girl.

water splashing for a moment

Master.

slow, gentle kissing

Your mouth just takes possession of me when we kiss.

kissing

I love you, Master. Let me kiss the line of your jaw …

sweet, slow kissing

And your neck…

kissing

And maybe your wet little kitten will bite…

bites him

giggles

SMACK!

squeals I'm sorry, Master!

giggles Are my teeth too sharp, Master?

SMACK!

cries out I'm sorry!

giggles

kissing

she moans into the kiss

breathless with need I don't know how long we have until the baby wakes, but right now, Master, I am so ... completely ... yours.

Feel my tits press your chest, Master. Take them in your hands again, Master. Take my tits. *breathes* My tits are yours. *gasps* Squeeze them! *moans* Master. Grope me, Master. *whimpers sweetly*

kissing, moaning into the kiss

devoted My Master. My Master. Mmmpph.

kissing

How may I please you tonight, Master?

How may I give you pleasure?

sultry I want to worship you and fuck you and be your wet, obedient slavegirl.

kissing, moaning

My Master.

kissing

Enjoy me, Master.

kissing

the episode ends

13

Enjoy Me, Master

This episode opens with the soft, breathing and aroused whimpers of the slavegirl, and possibly with soft, exotic music.

How you stare at me, stranger. Yes, I am naked, leashed by my collar to this slave post outside the perfumer's pavilion, with my wrists bound tightly behind me. My Master has gone inside the pavilion to buy scents, leaving me here to await his return. My breasts lift and fall as I breathe.

breathing softly

I feel the cool metal of my collar and my slave belt, locked on my cunt. I am naked and my body glistens with oil. My Master told his dancing slaves to watch our son, and he brought me to the market today to display his slavegirl's beauty to the world.

Do you like my beauty?

Mmmm. I'm squirming against the post. See how the post is carved in the shape of a goddess's body, a goddess of love and delight and pleasure. A goddess who watches over slave markets and lights fire between the thighs of virgins, to make them long for a Master. Her breasts are full, her thighs parted and inviting, but I am more lovely than she. She is only sculpted wood, and I am warm, oiled, feminine flesh. Mmmnn.

I am my Master's sensual slavegirl. I delight my Master. He takes pleasure in my full young breasts, … my sleek thighs … in my small, soft mouth. *teases* My mouth opens for my Master's cock.

moans

Master told me to display his pleasure-kitten's beauty proudly to any who pass by, because he is so proud of his love-slave.

How your eyes burn as you gaze on my curves and my soft, heaving breasts. My nipples swelling with desire and delight in this afternoon heat. Aching for my Master's touch. They are pierced for his pleasure, and a delicate gold chain runs from one nipple to the other.

You mustn't step too close, stranger. I belong only to him. Look. I will turn my hip, let you see the brand of ownership my Master burned into my thigh. The night he bought me, he held me down by his hearth, covered my mouth, and burned his mark into my soft flesh while I screamed into his palm. Then he took me … and ravished me. He conquered me, with his hard cock deep inside me, while my flesh still burned for him. I am his, and he is my Master. Under my slave belt, I drip warm honey, craving his touch. He owns me.

soft little moans and quivers of arousal

Why do you step so near, stranger? I told you. I am for enjoying with your eyes, not your hands. *a soft, feminine sound, aroused but also nervous* You wouldn't dare. I don't belong to you. My Master would be furious with you if you touched me. He is not a forgiving man. You don't want to anger him.

aroused Just stand there and admire his pleasure-slut. *moans* Watch me squirm sweetly against this post, the way I'd wriggle against my Master's hard body.

defiantly Stare at me as you wish, stranger, you cannot touch my warm cunt. My Master has me locked, and only he holds my key. No one will ever touch me but the man I love, the man who owns me.

moaning

Ohhh, my nipples ache so for his touch. For his strong, loving hands.

whispers Oh Master, hurry back. How this stranger looks at me. I am so wet, so wet.

gasps No! Get your hands off me, stranger! No! *squeals* Don't tug the chain at my nipples! *SQUEALS* Don't! Don't! They're so sensitive! Please! *squeals* Yes, I'm kicking at you! How dare you, how dare you! Take your hands from my tits, or I will scream! I'll screa-

choking sounds

then heaving for air You animal! *starts to scream for help* Mast-

choking sounds

squirming and kicking

gasping for breath Mast-

choking

gasping Don't … don't hurt me, don't hurt me, please.

quivering Don't press your mouth to my throat … mmmmnnn! *whimpering with arousal* Stop, stop, stop! Ohhhhh your hands … *moans* … Don't you know who owns me? Don't you know who my Master is? He owns the villa by the lake, and seventeen dancing slaves, and me. He is the man who burned the houses of the wolf hunters and sold their wives and daughters to be pleasure-sluts. He burned the deep, dark forest, left the pale moon lonely at night with no werewolves to howl to her. My Master will cut out your heart!

quivering as he touches her

Why … why are you smiling like that? That…that is not a nice smile.

gasps Your … your eyes!

terrified I don't understand. Your eyes reflect the moon. I can see the full moon in your eyes! But the moon last night was a crescent! And she isn't in the sky right now. It's midday. You … who are you? Oh goddess! You… you're a wolf! You're a wolf, you're a wolf, you're a wolf!

Don't… don't hurt me …

Master, help! Mast-mmmphhh mmmphhh *interrupted by a hand pressed so firmly over her mouth, silencing her scream for help*

we hear a low wolf growl

she squeals into his hand in fright at the sound

then she whimpers tearfully into the werewolf's hand as he touches her … for several long moments, she whimpers, getting more and more scared

she gasps as his hand leaves her lips, and we hear running footsteps as the werewolf flees

tearful You better run, you animal.

sob

gasps, seeing her Master Master! Master, you're here! That's why he ran! Master, protect me!

Your hands cupping my face. Master, Master.

sobbing sweetly in her relief

sniffles Master, there was a werewolf here. He touched my breasts! He growled, and I thought he meant to rip out my throat! Master, Master! Keep me safe!

Master, that rage in your eyes. I'm all right. Master, I'm all right, he didn't hurt me. Master!

breathing quickly still

Master, come back!

… how you move, like a panther, stalking from tent to tent, demanding to know if any of the merchants saw a man molest your slavegirl.

breathing fast

Master, come back.

No one saw, Master. No one else cares what happens to a naked, vulnerable slavegirl. *whimpers* I have only my Master to protect me. Master. Come back to me. I'm scared. Squirming against this post, alone, naked, my heart pounding, my nipples still swollen from that beast's touch.

quivery

Thank you, Master. Thank you for coming back. I need you, Master. Keep me safe. Keep me-mmmmm

a deep, deep sensual kiss

quivery I love you, Master.

Yes, Master. Hold my breasts. *moans* Feel my tits soft and full in your hands. You own my breasts, Master. I don't want any other man or wolf to ever touch them. Only you, Master. Only ever you.

moans

My Master. *aroused little sounds as he cups her breasts* I was so frightened.

whispers When you cup my breasts in your hands, erasing his touch with yours, I feel so safe. So owned. Touch me, Master.

whimpers softly, sweetly

Caress me. *whispers* Caress me.

I love you, Master.

Please keep me safe.

soft little moans as her breasts are played with

whimpers Your hands are so warm, and so good. *a sweet little squeal* Yes, Master. Tug the chain you've strung from my nipples. *whimpers* Master, oh Master.

her voice overwhelmed with love I am your pleasure-kitten, Master.

another sensual kiss

whispers reverently Your mouth.

kissing

Oh! You're unleashing me from the post. But keeping my wrists tied behind me. Oh, Master. That growl you make. It makes me drip warm honey. Master, my Master.

Mmn! Pull me by my leash, yes Master. I understand. You're taking me into the perfumer's tent, because no werewolf is going to keep you from buying the gifts you have in mind for your pleasure-kitten.

Yes, Master.

But I know that heat in your eyes, Master! I know you mean to hunt that wolf later, that wolf who touched me, after you have me safely home. *quivery* Please be careful, Master. Please. He touched me, he must have meant to enrage you, to make you hunt him in the streets of the city. Please, Master, I'm scared for you. Please be so careful. If he ... if he hurt you, I ... I... mmmphhh!! *he interrupts her with a kiss*

she protests, muffled, into his kiss, then melts, whimpering sweetly into his mouth in the long, long kiss

she draws a few quivering breaths after the kiss

she breathes the word so softly Master.

the sound of him delivering a quick spank

a little squeal from her

quivers Yes Master. Yes. I'll be quiet ... and follow where you lead.

whispers Only promise you'll be careful.

sniffles Thank you, Master.

I love you so much.

Mmmm. It's cool in this pavilion, Master, and dim, with only that one red lamp. Do you like the glow of the soft, sensual light on my body?

overwhelmed with adoration and devotion Master ... in the red light, you look like such a god. Powerful and muscled. Your sable cloak thrown over one shoulder. Your eyes smolder. And I am your slavegirl, naked and voluptuous at my Master's side.

What do you wish of your slavegirl, Master?

giggles

You wish to try out scents on me, Master?

aroused While the perfume merchant watches and gives advice?

Master! The key! You're holding the key to my slave belt! I see it in your hand!

the sound of him unlocking her chastity belt

Master! Master, you can't … you can't mean to TAKE me! In here, in this tent, while the merchant watches you fuck me!

the rattle of metal as he pulls the slave belt from her

whispers I am so naked. So … so naked and wet. My cunt is wet as an OCEAN for you, Master.

whimpers

Yes, Master, I understand. Yes, Master. Yes, Master. *breathing fast* I will stand here, beautiful and naked and awaiting your pleasure, with my blossom swollen with need. You've already selected the scents, Master? Those little jars by the perfumer? Mmmm, citrus and cranberries. Lavender and chamomile. *a soft sigh of pleasure* Cinnamon, apple, nutmeg.

giggles Am I a dinner, Master?

low and sultry Am I a banquet of pleasure for my Master?

whispers Will you feast on me, Master?

moans How you caress my breast... Master, the merchant is watching us.

whimpers in arousal

Yes, Master, yes. I'll hold still. Though my thighs quiver.

My Master.

You're opening the jars, ohhhh ... those scents ... they smell wonderful. Mmmnn. The way you dab the perfumes and scented oils on my neck with your fingertips. *whisper* Oh, Master, your fingers are so gentle on my body...

moans

Oh, Master. And now you're dabbing citrus scent on my nipples.

soft, aroused sounds

Master. *her voice filled with erotic promise* Your slavegirl will press her soft breasts to your face tonight, Master, so you can breathe deeply of her. Mmmnn!

Oh Master, yes. Lean close, breathe in my scent.

quivers I don't care who sees. I am yours, Master. Smell the perfumes on my body, on my breasts that heave for you. Smell my heat.

Master, you make me so hot.

moans

Yes… your fingers on my thighs, dabbing lavender on the soft insides of my thighs … mmmnnn! And dripping chamomile … ahhhh … over my blossom and my sensitive, swollen little clit! *quivers*

Master … Master!

whispers Oh I need your touch.

Your hands on me smooth away every care, every fear. I barely remember what scared me outside; when you touch me like this, you are the only thing that exists in my world. Master, touch me. Love me, Master.

Master? Master?! You're crouching before me … why … ahhhhhhhhh … your warm breath across my folds … *whispers*Master! *whispers* You're breathing in the scent of my blossom, my body's own perfume, my wet cunt, more delectable and pleasing to my Master than any other scent. *moans* Master, your mouth on me! Your mouth! You're making it difficult to stand where you've told me! Yes, grasp my hips, don't let me f-fall, Master, Master! *moans* Your lips and tongue … tasting me … Master, my Master, enjoy me! Enjoy me! Taste my nectar, Master! My warm honey is for you! All for you!

improv her moans and whimpers as he tastes her for a few moments

panting Enjoy me … enjoy me …

The perfume merchant is watching my breasts heave as you taste me! Master! Master!

quivery, overwhelmed Master, I'm your conquest. I'm your love-slave. You own me, you own me, you own me!

improv her moans of love and devotion to her Master … as she approaches orgasm

Master, Master, Master, may I yield, Master? May I surrender? Master?!! May I fill your mouth with my warm honey, Master, please? Master, please! Thank you, Master! Master! Enjoy me, enjoy me, enjoy me! *she cums*

quivering My Master …

My thighs are shaking.

whimpers

Your hands holding my thighs… you make me feel so safe.

Yes, Master. Yes, I'll kneel.

Mmmmn. Here, at my Master's feet. *almost tearful with joy* This is where I belong, Master. With my wrists bound behind me, my breasts rising and falling and my thighs spread wide, my blossom soaked at your touch, my mouth soft and warm … and open.

Yes, Master. Yes. I'll spread my thighs even wider. You want my soft cunt displayed? You … you want the merchant to see what a wet, desperate fuck-kitten you own? *whimpers* You want him to see the warm petals you'll be dripping his perfumes over? *whimpers* Master! I'm so open. I'm so open!

breathing so fast

Master, my face burns! My cheeks burn at the way the perfumer watches me. But my heart burns with love and my cunt burns with need. Oh gods, you burn me. You brand me again with every touch. You make me yours, you make me so yours.

May I give you pleasure, Master? What do you desire of your slavegirl, Master? *whispers* I want to give you pleasure.

Mmmn. *kissing* Permit your slave-kitten to kiss your thighs, Master.

kissing

Mmmn. Your strong, masculine thighs. *lovingly* Master, Master.

kissing

Oh yes, Master, yes, I'll please you. I'll lick your cock, Master.

gentle licking sounds

quivers My Master.

licking

I will suck gently at my Master's balls.

sucking gently

The scents you've put on my body excite me, Master, but they're nothing compared to your musk. *sucking* Your musk makes me want to swallow your seed, Master. It makes me want your hot, sticky seed in my mouth. *whimpers of need*

licking

I'll kiss my way along your cock.

kissing

I worship you, Master. You are my god.

kissing

I love you.

kissing

That perfumer, maybe he owns a slavegirl too. But not one like me. I am so in love with you, Master. I will give everything to please you. My love. I will show that merchant how a true pleasure-kitten pleases her Master, and he will moan in his bed tonight, remembering.

kissing

pleading Master, fill my mouth. I love you.

soft, sensual blowjob sounds

I love you.

blowjob sounds, and sweet whimpers muffled around his cock

I love you.

Master. Master.

blowjob sounds

You own my small, wet mouth.

blowjob sounds

Master, I'm so wet. I'll moan around your cock.

she does

a sensual, slow blowjob, with her muffled, loving, devoted, needful moans

You make me drip down my legs. *whimpers*

blowjob

quivers Do I please you, Master? I love you. That merchant is so flushed, watching us. *teases* He wishes he could buy me. *low and sultry* I think he might release inside his garments, Master.

Will you release, too, Master? Will you fill my soft little mouth? Will you cum in my mouth, Master?

I want to delight you … *sucking* … and make you happier than any man in the world. *sucking more vigorously*

Your slavegirl is kneeling, bound and scented for her Master. Please fuck my mouth, Master. Please cum in my mouth. I am yours. I am y-mmmphh mmmphhh

a vigorous blowjob

we hear her muffled whimpers of "Master! Master! Master!" around his cock

then her pleading with him to cum: "Mm hmm! Mmm hmm!"

then her whimper as he fills her mouth

several loud swallows

breathing hard

Oh Master. Oh Master. I want your taste in my mouth every night. Oh gods, Master, I love you, I love you!

kissing Let me kiss your thighs, Master.

kissing

And your strong, powerful legs.

kissing

tearful with love and surrender And your feet.

slow, gentle kisses

whispers My Master.

kissing

Yes Master! Mmmn! Pull me to my feet! Oh!

Ohh. I'm leaning into you Master because I'm so … wet … I can barely stand.

Mmmm.

Yes. Your hands on my breasts.

moans

Master … did you hear the merchant groan? He did cum, watching us.

quivery Did I please you?

a deep, ravenous kiss, and she whimpers sweetly into his mouth. It is a long kiss.

quivers I love you, Master.

Will you take me home? And perfume me, and enjoy me? I want to open my legs for you and give you pleasure. At sunset, at dusk, at midnight. I don't want you to go hunting the werewolf, Master. I want you to protect me in our bed. I want you to fuck me. I want your weight on my body. I want your hard thrusts inside me, owning me. Filling me. I want your hand on my throat, telling me when I can breathe and when I must wait for my Master to give me air. Oh Master. I love you.

I am your pleasure-slut. Will you take me home, Master?

Mmmn! Tug my leash. Yes, I understand; you still have to pay for the perfumes. I will stand beautifully beside my Master, let the merchant gaze at my dripping cunt and my full tits and my lips swollen from your thrusting cock. *a whimper of arousal* How you make me blush. How my face burns for you, Master.

I am yours.

Enjoy me, Master. Enjoy me.

we hear her soft little sounds of arousal for a few brief moments

then the episode ends

14

Protect Me, Master

This episode opens with the soft, breathing of a sleeping slavegirl and the sounds of a rainstorm outside.

Then, we hear a wolf howl.

the slavegirl gasps and is startled awake

Master! Master! A wolf! There's a wolf! Nearby, maybe even in your pleasure gardens! Master, I'm scared! *gasps* The baby! Is the baby safe?!

In … a locked room. With the slave you've told to be his nurse tonight. Of course. Of course he's safe. And I don't want to wake him. I'm just … scared.

rustling of bedsheets

Master, no, no! Don't get up! Don't leave me, Master!

footsteps

whimpers Please don't leave me alone in the bed, Master.

the sound of a blade unsheathing

frightened for her Master You're going to hunt it. The wolf in your gardens. Master, be careful! Master, I love you!

a door creaking open, then shut

rattle of a key in the lock

her frightened breaths. She is almost tearful with fear for him

softly Master, Master. Oh, please be careful.

You've left me alone in your bedchamber. Locked in. And the window is high and … *quivers* … it frames the full moon. Oh Master. What if it's the wolf who touched me at the market today? When it was shaped like a man? *whimpers* What if it's the wolf that wants me? That wants to hurt you by fucking me … or … devouring me?

thunder

she whimpers

I'm naked in your bed. My breasts are soft and full, moving sweetly in the moonlight. And my thighs are bare, Master. The metal belt that protects your slavegirl's wet cunt is tossed aside on the floor by your hearth, because you fucked me so long tonight. All I'm wearing is your collar, locked on my throat.

quivery If a wolf were to … to take me … I couldn't stop the beast from forcing my legs open and …

whispers … and there's nothing protecting my pussy …

quivery Master. I'm frightened.

Come back.

Please come back.

I'm covering my soft, soft little cunt with my hand.

I'm so scared.

a wolf howl

she whimpers

That wolf. It wants to ravish me. It wants to rape me.

Master will keep me safe. Master will keep me safe. He cherishes me.

whispers Please keep me safe.

breathing, panting, as she listens

whispers Oh Master, come back.

sniffles I'm hugging myself, my arms under my full tits, my eyes on that full, terrifying moon. Oh Master. I can almost feel the forest moss again, the wolf's c-claws digging into my thighs, its … its cock … *whimpers* Oh gods.

the key in the lock

her gasp

the door creaks open

hasty footsteps toward her

Master! *tearful* Master, you're ba-mmmmmphhhhhhhhhh

his kiss is long and demanding as he crushes her to his chest. For a while, she just whimpers sweetly into his kiss, overwhelmed and so grateful to be held in his arms again

breathless Master. Master, hold me.

soft little feminine whimpers

whispers The baby's safe? Oh thank you, Master, thank you for checking on him. Oh Master.

Master, your garments are soaked. Where have you been?

Chasing the wolf through your pleasure gardens? In the moonlight, among the cherry trees and the marble nymphs?

It got away? *whimpers*

But you'll … hunt it, tomorrow?

Master, please! Hire others to! Please don't hunt it yourself! Please! Please!

Please, stay here tomorrow, with me. *scared, trying to be seductive* Send others after the wolf and stay in our bed fucking me all day until nightfall, Master. I will open my thighs for you and surrender my warm honey to your lips … and cock … and moan for you like I am being fucked by a god. *softly* You are my god, Master. Don't go. I'm scared for you, Master.

a deep kiss, but shorter this time

whispers Stay with me.

thunder

Mmmn. Master, your hair is dripping. And you've made me wet.

Let me ... get this sable cloak and this vest off you, Master. *sounds of her undressing him* You need a warm bed, Master. And a warm slavegirl.

still quivery but trying to take charge and care for her Master You shouldn't have been out in the rain in the middle of the night, Master. You're soaked. You'll get a chill. Master, lie down, my Master, I'll make a fire for us.

sounds of her gathering up kindling

gasps Master!

terrified Master, look! LOOK! There ... in the moonlight on the hearth ... Right there!

Master! It's a paw print! A wolf's paw, wet with the dew! Master! It was here! It was IN HERE. By our BED! It was WATCHING us while we slept! Master! Oh gods!

he pulls her to his chest

Yes, hold me. Hold me, hold me, hold me.

sobbing softly for a few moments

Oh Master, how you growl.

sniffles

I'm trembling. I'm s-so scared. Master, it was WATCHING us sleep. It could have … it could have … *sniffles*

he kisses her

she mmmphhs sweetly into the kiss

a soft little sigh My Master.

Mmmn. The way you kiss my eyelids, Master … kissing my tears. Master, what are we going to do?

softly Yes, Master, I know. I know you burned a forest to keep me safe. I know you would do anything to protect me. But it was right HERE. What if that wolf comes another night and hurts my Master, and … and takes his girl? *whimpers*

Oh!

rustling as she is thrust down on her belly on the bed

Oh, Master! You've thrust me down on the bed, on my belly and tits. Master! You're pinning me by my throat!

light choking

gasps Yes, Master. I know you'll protect what's yours.

Master, are … are you hard?

Oh GODS! Pressed to me right … there … Master?!!! Are you going to -

her cry as she is penetrated

Master! *a shocked, moaning cry as he thrusts DEEP*

squeals Master! You're so rough! So rough! Master!!

wild cries of "Master…! Master…! Master…!" at each thrust, startled and aroused and taken

Master…! Master…! Master…!

MASTER!!!

Oh, your cock in me! Your hand on my throat!

choking

gasps Yes, choke me, Master! Own me! Own me!

choking and whimpering at the thrusts

I'm yours! I'm yours! I'm your slave!

Oh you're so rough with me tonight, Master!

crying out as he takes her, for a few moments, without words

My Master! My Master!

Yes! Tell me that, Master, tell me no one will EVER touch me but you, no man and no wolf, until the hair on my head and the hair soft by my cunt is silver and I've cum ten thousand nights for my Master! Oh Master, my tight wet cunt is for you! Only for you! Master! Master! Fuck me! Fuck me! Fuck your pleasure-slut, Master!

wild cries of heat and need

Fuck me on your bed while rain drenches the world! With your body on me so *quivers* so strong and muscled and sweaty ... I feel so ... protected. Cover me with your body and fuck me!

Master!

How you grip my ass...

SMACK!

squeals

SMACK!

squeals

SMACK!

squeals

Yes, Master! Yes! My ass is yours! My ass is YOURS! *SQUEALS* Your thumb in my ass! MASTER!!!!

Master, may I ... may I squeeze and flood your cock? May I yield for you like a good little slut? Please, Master, please! I love you! Please let me cum!

light choking

Yes! Master, you own my breath!

choking

I don't need to breathe! I don't need to, I don't need to! I just need to be fucked by my Master!

choking

Master, Master! I'll break for you! I'll break for you, Master! I love you! Master, may I? May I? May I yield, Master, please, please! May I? Yes! Yes! YES! MASTER!

she orgasms passionately

quivering afterward

Master.

Master.

My Master.

a moan as he pulls out of her Yes, Master. Take my hair. I'll please you, Master, I'll please y-mmmmphhhhhhhhhhh

improv a quick, rough blowjob

in the middle, she gets a gasp of air and pants Yes, push your cock in my throat, Master. Use me. Use m-mmmphhhh mmmmphh mmmmphhhhhhhhhhhh

improv a rough blowjob, with her whimpers around his cock

gasp of air I love your cock! I love your mmmmmphhhhhhhh

blowjob noises

he fills her mouth and she squeals as it hits her tongue, then swallows in loud gulps

panting, just destroyed by his roughness

quivers Master. How you TOOK me.

whispers Yes, Master. I belong to you. I'm your conquest.

Yes, pull me into your arms. Oh Master, hold me.

a soft whimper My Master.

I love you.

I love you.

I can still taste your seed in my mouth. *a soft, soft moan* oh gods. Master, I want your taste in my mouth every night.

softly Ohhh, my thighs quiver. I'll be sore tomorrow from how you fucked me.

Seeing that paw print, you really wanted to claim me tonight, didn't you, Master?

kissing

I'm yours, Master. I'm here. I'm safe.

kissing

Oh, Master. Feel my small hands soft against your chest. Hold me. I am your slavegirl, your owned wet collared little slut, but sometimes you hold me and gaze at me with such warmth in your eyes, like I am your princess and not only your slavegirl.

kissing, and her soft soft moans into his kiss

Oh Master, yes. Mmmn. Touch me. My breasts are swollen

with milk. My nipples ache at your touch. Mmmnn.

moans as he touches her

You are my Master. You own me. I don't want anyone else's hands on me.

moans Only yours. Ohhhh, your warm hands.

Squeeze my tits, Master.

moaning

squeals When you pinch my nipples like that, I burn for you, Master!

soft little whimpers of need You make me … so … wet …

Everything that werewolf wants from me, everything it could never have, it is yours. I am all yours. My tight cunt, my womb, my mouth, my ass, it's all yours. You've claimed me.

kissing

whispers Please don't let any wolf get me.

Please. I want to lie here safe in your bed, in the arms of the man who owns me, pinned under your powerful hips, with you fucking me. With your cock so savage and powerful inside me. Master, please.

Protect me. Own me.

kissing

I'm in your collar. I'm naked and helpless in your arms. Let your slavegirl kiss your neck...

kiss ... with my small ... *kiss* ... wet ... *kiss* ... little mouth ...

kissing, with soft little noises

Master. I want to be so full of your cum tonight.

kissing his neck

moans I want to feel your hot, sticky semen leaking down my thighs.

kissing My Master. Let me curl my fingers around your cock. *breathy with need* This hard cock felt so good in me, Master. *moans* I love your hard cock, Master. I love how you fill me so full I could cry. Master!

softly Do you like my fingers soft around your cock?

My Master. I would give you anything. I am completely surrendered to you, Master. You own every beat of my heart.

kissing

How you harden in my hand... *moans* I need you, Master. Oh, Master.

Keep me safe, Master.

kissing

Keep me and the baby safe.

kissing

Protect us, Master.

Oh I need you, I need you. I want you in me all night. Open me again with your cock. I know no wolf can touch me or hurt me when my Master is inside me. Oh, Master. *worshipful* I love you. You own me. You bred me.

moaning into a kiss

whispers Please, Master, take me. Love me, Ravish me.

My Master.

soft kissing, and rain

the episode ends

15

Own Me, Master

Exotic music. The trickling of water.

Where have you brought me tonight, Master? This pool in the middle of the city … I've never been here before. It's lovely. But it's so late, Master; all the stars are out. The cypress trees are tall, and the wall around us is overgrown with moss and… *gasps softly* … oh, Master, that statue in the water. She's so tall. Her hands lift her stone breasts, and clear water runs from her cunt down her thighs, trickling into the pool. And I see how there are slave posts carved in the shape of naked, voluptuous women, set in a circle around the pool, posts with lamps balanced on their heads, small lamps filled with captive fireflies. By each post stands a man with a whip … *whimpers* … and a naked slavegirl kneeling by his feet. But they're gazing at ME as though I am the most desirable woman on this continent.

softly They can see my whole body, Master. They can see the flash of my warm cunt each time I take a step. They can see my nipples hard and swollen and needing your touch. *moans* I would almost cum if you touched them,

Master, if you so much as teased them with your knuckles. They're so sensitive. *whimpers*

whispers I need to be touched.

But Master, who are those men? Why do they look at me so? And that … that bag you've brought with you, Master, what's in it?

blushing I'm … I'm sorry, Master. It's just that your slave-kitten is terribly curious. And … and aroused … *whimpers* … and nervous.

What is this place, Master? What do you desire from your pleasure-slave tonight? You've had me prepared for you, oiled and perfumed, my body scented and aroused for your pleasure. *an aroused sigh* A gold chain strung between my nipples, delicate as spider silk. Your collar on my neck glistens in the starlight, but you've left my soft, wet little blossom unlocked, Master. My slave belt is at home by my Master's bed.

Yes, Master, I'll follow you to that slave post by the water. *breathing quickly* I'll walk beautifully for my Master, letting my hips sway and my breasts lift and fall sweetly as I walk. I must be elegant and beautiful and make my Master proud of me. Especially with all the other Masters watching me. *softly* MY Master owns the most beautiful, pleasing, loving slavegirl in this city.

I will prove it to them for you tonight, if you wish me to, Master.

Is that why you've brought me here? Do … do you wish me

to give you pleasure, Master? Here, by the pool, while those other Masters and their slavegirls watch me? *whimpers*

nervous Master?

What is going to happen to me tonight, Master?

Kneel by your feet, Master? Yes, Master. *taking a calming breath* It will be my pleasure, Master.

gasps Master, your hand in my hair! Yes, Master. Guide me. Whatever pleasure you desire will be my delight, Master. I love you. I surrender, Master. Let me please you.

Yes, Master. I'll free you of your garments.

rustling

Oh, Master. *reverently, very softly* Your cock is so beautiful, Master.

Yes, Master, I'll kiss your thighs. I'll kiss your body like such a … good … girl.

Gentle …

kissing

soft …

kissing

sensual …

kissing

submissive kisses …

kissing

… for my Master.

more soft, sweet, sensual kisses for his thighs … for a few moments

a quivery breath Master … what you're saying to the other men. Master, are … are you trying to make your slavegirl cry, Master?

softly tearful Telling them that your slavegirl wears YOUR collar and YOUR brand, that I've carried YOUR child in my womb. That tonight you … you will bind me to you, here in this holy place beneath the blazing stars, before the goddess of love and desire … that you'll bind your slavegirl to your heart and your hearth, forever and forever. *sniffles* Master.

barely able to speak the words, she is so overwhelmed I love you.

kissing his thighs again for a bit

And … you're telling them that many have challenged you for me, and those who did, *a momentary flash of anger* … those who tried to take your slavegirl, they are all dead. You're telling them I am YOURS, and you will burn and slay and destroy any who threaten me or the child I've given you.

breathless My Master. I am so in love with you, Master. Master, you make me feel so safe. How you cherish me.

sniffles Master.

kissing his thighs

Master, you're lifting the bag! … and pulling out …

she screams

quivery

That … that thing you've thrown to the feet of the other men, Master, it's … it's hideous. It's a wolf's … a wolf's h-head.

The last of the werewolves.

The one that … that touched me. *whimpers*

Master, you … *whispers* you killed it. The last one. *in wonder* They're … they're all gone. All of them. *whispers* All the beasts of the wild forest that wanted to hurt your pleasure-kitten. *whimpers* All the beasts that would have torn me apart.

a soft, soft moan at his touch Oh Master, your hand is so warm and gentle, caressing my cheek. My Master. My Master who protects his kitten.

sniffles Yes, Master. Yes, I understand. I have to be quiet. It's not for me to talk while you speak vows of ownership before the men of the city. I'll be quiet. *softly, slightly tearful, slightly overwhelmed* I'll be quiet and kiss your thighs, Master.

soft kisses and soft, soft little noises from her

whispers Oh, Master. Your thighs are strong, and your cock is swollen by my cheek. Mmmn. You're so hard, Master.

And your musk ... *breathes in his scent* ... Master, I'm wet. They're all watching me, but I am so, so wet for you. I'm dripping warm honey, my Master. For you. I love you.

kissing him

whispers Let me please you, Master. Let me show them all what a good pleasure-slut wears your collar.

Yes, Master? There's something I need to do first?

You need me to tell the other men and their slavegirls what I will do to please and delight my Master? I need to turn all these feelings in my heart into words, and say ... how ... how I will surrender to you, Master?

Master?

quivery Oh, Master. I kneel naked and collared ... and so wet ... and you stand over me like a god in your sable cloak with the stars above your head. With your hand holding my face so tenderly I could cry. My Master. When you look at me like this, with your eyes deep as the sea and intense as a forest fire, your eyes smoldering in the dark, I ... I melt, Master. I melt.

I am dripping warm honey down my thighs, and my ... my heart is dripping love and ... and Master, I melt. I melt for you.

I submit to you. I am yours. I surrender everything, Master. Everything.

Whatever you desire, Master.

If you tell me to lie down on my back like a good, obedient kitten-slut and open my thighs and show the whole world this wet, dripping cunt that my Master owns, I will submit to you. It will be my pleasure, Master. If you tell me to wade into the pool and close my eyes and not open them until dawn, no matter how you touch me, no matter if you even touch me at all, I will submit to you, Master. I will stand in the pool beneath the goddess's wet, dripping pussy while my own cunt drips down my thighs and I will not move or open my eyes until you tell me. I will obey you, Master.

If you tell me to walk around the slave posts in this circle and beg each man to whip my tits and my thighs and my soft, sensitive clit ... *whimpers* ... until I return and kneel, lashed and aching, at your feet to take your cock in my mouth, I will submit to you, Master. I love you, Master. If you desire my soft, small mouth around your cock, I will please you again and again while the stars burn and the fireflies dance above your head. Oh Master, I will tease ... and lick ... and caress your cock with my warm mouth. Gazing up at you with my heart shining in my eyes, Master. I will swallow your cum, again and again until my belly is full of your semen.

Or if you tell me to bend with my face to the earth and spread my ass open for you, Master, so that you may take me as hard as you desire, *trembling* oh Master. I will submit to you. My ass belongs to you. Take my ass, Master. Hurt me, and hold me if I cry. *quiver* I want to make you happy. So happy. I want to give you such pleasure, Master.

I am your love-kitten, Master. You own me. My breath, my

body, my everything. I am completely yours. Tonight, and every night until I die, Master. You ... own ... me.

I am your slavegirl.

whispers I would do anything for you, Master.

breathes the word Anything.

I am yours.

Yes, Master. Oh, Master. I see the ropes hanging from the post. *softly, submissively* Yes, Master. Bind me. Please bind me.

Bind me and make me give you pleasure, more pleasure than I have ever given before, more than I ever dreamed I could. Make me please you, Master, as you deserve. Take my body, Master. Take my everything. Take me.

Oh! *soft little noises as she is bound*

Oh, Master, the ropes are so soft yet so strong. Silk rope ... oh Master, it feels so good on my skin, holding me, oh my gods. Your ropes on my body, on my wrists ... mmnnn ... my arms ... holding me so ... so secure.

whispers So safe.

So yours.

Bind me, Master. I want to be tied up. *moans* You make me ... so helpless ... so submissive ... so conquered ... bind me ... yes ... tighter ... *whimpers* ... oh, if I squirm, the ropes don't give at all ...

more soft, feminine noises as she squirms, as she's tied

worshipful I'm tied in my Master's ropes …

her voice hot with love I don't ever want to be released.

You've conquered my heart, Master. I'm your captive and your love-slave, forever.

Oh! Yes, lift me to my feet, oh Master, let me press my full breasts and thighs to your body and mmmmnnn!!! *a rough, rough kiss, and her whimpers and moans into the kiss*

breathless My Master.

Oh! You're pressing me back against the slave pole … ohh, the wood is smooth against my shoulders and ass… *whimpers*You're binding me to the post. Master? Mmmn. Whatever you desire … is yours, Master.

nervous Oh … one of the men is handing you … a whip. *she swallows* Like the first evening in your pleasure gardens, Master, when you whipped me. You said you wanted every cell in my body to know who I belong to.

softly I know, Master.

I know with every beat of my heart who owns me.

You're going to whip me so THEY know. So they can see your marks on my body. Not only the brand you burned in my thigh, but the marks of your lash across my tits and thighs.

a whimper of fright, that she suppresses

And I'm so … naked and vulnerable. My wrists tied behind

me, my body bound to this post, your ropes holding me captive. No way for me to hide my body. And all their eyes on me.

Each breath I take lifts my breasts for the kiss of your whip, Master.

she takes two little breaths

Master.

I am yours.

Whip me, Master. Mark me.

whispers Please whip me.

the sound of the whip striking her

her sharp cry

a whimper

then, submissively determined to bear the whip I love you, Master.

CRACK!

she cries out

I love you, Master. *breathing fast* I can take it for you, Master. I can take anything for you. You are my owner and my love. I will bear each kiss of the leather across my soft breasts.

Mark me, Master.

CRACK!

squeals

I love you, Master!

CRACK!

squeals I love you, Master!

CRACK! I   love   you,   Master!   I   love   you
- *CRACK squeals* Master! I love you!

CRACK! I love you!

CRACK I love you!

CRACK I LOVE YOU!

panting Please, Master. Whip me. Whip me. Show them all how you own me. Whip me until I cry for you, Master. I love you!! '

CRACK!!!

she screams

gasping for air Your collar is on my throat, Master! Locked on me! My body is yours, Master!

CRACK! squeals

CRACK! squeals

CRACK! squeals

panting, whimpering Master, Master, I love you.

breathing hard, raising her voice All of you men watching, look.

Look. See these welts rising on my tits. I belong to him! *defiant* I am his slavegirl, and he is MY Master! And none of you EVER get to have me! I belong to YOU, Master!

CRACK

screams I LOVE YOU, MASTER!

CRACK

screams

I LOVE YOU!!

CRACK

a long wail

whispers I could die of how much I love you.

panting

You're … you're going to … whip my … my cunt?

a low whine

Yes, Master. You own my cunt. My thighs are drenched with my warm honey. Master, whip my cunt, Master, whip me, whip me, whip me …

CRACK!

a sweetly anguished cry … repeated after each crack of the whip

Masterrrr!

CRACK!

Master!

CRACK!

My Master!

CRACK!!!

Oh GODDESS my clit, my clit, Master!!!!

CRACK!

wordless squeal

CRACK!

wordless squeal

CRACK!

wordless squeal

CRACK!

shrieks I love you!!!

soft sobbing

after a moment, very softly Master … Master … mmnnn

he interrupts her with a slow, sensual kiss

she moans into the kiss

softly My breasts and my cunt are on fire, Master.

How you caress my cheek … and stroke my hair … *happycry sob* Master, I love you. I love you, I love you.

pleading Was I a good girl, Master? I wanted to take it for you like such a good girl.

another long kiss

breathless Master. Please kiss me again. Kiss me until the stars burn out, Master. Don't ever stop. Take my mouth. I love y-mmmmphhhhh

kissing

moans Your hands on my tits. Oh Master, yes, yes. Grip my tits. My tits belong to you. My tits will always belong to YOU. Master! Feel my breasts slick with scented oil for your pleasure … ahhh … and stinging from your whip … oh! Oh! Master, yes, kiss my neck, kiss my neck! Mmmn! Oh, I'm dripping for you, Master! Ahhhh … Play with my breasts, Master, they are yours, they are YOURS … *squeals* Yes, twist my … my nipples … I … I … I'm yours! *squeals*

kissing

she squeals into the kiss, muffled, in response to his hands on her. He keeps pinching and playing with her nipples, and she keeps squealing, muffled, into the long kiss.

she bites his lip

a tearful giggle I didn't mean to bite you, Master, I couldn't help it, your little kitten is wild with heat! … and pleasure

… and joy! … Master, oh Master! I wish I could devour you as you do me! *quivers* My nipples burn at your touch, Master! My cunt is on fire! Master! Please fuck me, Master! I don't want ANYone to doubt how you own me. I want the WORLD to know I'm yours. All the girls I grew up with, in my village, they were scattered like dust after the slavers took us, all of them lost out there in the wide world, but not me. Not me. Oh Master, I came home. I came home to my Master, who bought me and took my heart. I have a Master who will protect me always.

Please fuck me, Master. I will clench and ripple around your cock like I never have before. Fuck me against this pole, Master. I'm your tied-up little sex-kitten! Show them I'm yours.

moans Please let me prove I'm yours.

I am YOURS!

she cries out Yes, Master! Force my legs open! Oh, Master, oh Master! Your cock! *panting* Right there against my … soaked … little … petals! … Master! … I could … I could … could almost yield now Master, I could cum now, Master. Oh Master, take me! Take your slavegirl! Take your slut!

she screams in joy as he plunges his cock into her

Yes!

screams again

I'm so tight! So tight! So wet! Master, fuck me!

Fuck me!

Fuck me, Master!

Please! Pound me against this slave pole, Master! Make my tits bounce, Master!

quick little squeals as he thrusts, for a few moments

Gods, Master, feel me grip your cock! *desperate moans, wildly in heat* Feel me squeeze ... and milk your cock! Master, Master, pound me! Don't hold back! Break me, Master!

Yes! Yes! Take my throat! Master, Master!!!

choking

after a few moments of breathless whimpering, he lets her breathe, and she squeals Oh fuckkkkkk!

Master!!

You're so HARD in me!

My Master! My Master! *almost sobbing in her need to cum for him*

light choking

speaking quickly Master, ravish me! Don't let me breathe! Don't let me do ANYthing but please you! Master, I want to please you! I want to please you! Oh GODS I want to please you, Master! USE ME!

choking

choked whimpers as he fucks her

breathless Master! Master!

Yes, yes, yes, hold my face in your hands and roll your hips and TAKE me … the surge and thrust of your cock … oh Master, my tits bounce for you at each thrust! Oh, you're so hot in me, so hot … so hard … open me, stretch me … *squeals* … hurt me with your cock, Master!! Harder, oh harder … Master, I'm going to scream like a goddess for you, I'm going to flood your cock, oh Master, oh Master, nothing exists in the world but you! Just your cock in me! Your cock in me! Your eyes gazing into mine! Master, Master, I love you! I love you! Oh gods Master, yes! Yes! I love your cock! I love your cock! Oh gods, Master, harder, use me, Master, I'm your kitten-slut, I'm your kitten-slut, I'm your kitten-sluuuuut … oh fuckkkkkk , Master, I need to … I need to … I can't … I can't … please, please, please!!!!!!! *a rapid, desperate stream of words without much pause for breath* Yes! Thank you, Master! Than you, Master! THANK YOU, Master! I yield! I yield! I love you, I love you I love you I love you

she cums

MASTERRRRRR

quivering after her orgasm, completely surrendered

her voice trembling Master.

whimpers Oh Master.

wild female-animal grunts as he keeps fucking her

then, choking sounds

Yes, Master, take my breath, take me, take me…

choking

Oh, Master, I can see it in your eyes. You're so close. So close. Please, let go inside me. Fill me. *moans* Oh Master, fill me with your cum, Master, fill me with your hot … sticky … seed.

Oh Master, I'm bound to you. Forever and forever. Cum in me.

Cum in me, Master.

Cum in your kitten. Cum in your kitten!

moans Yes! Oh Master, yes, pulse … in … me! Please! Please! I need your cum so much, Master! Please! Please!

Yes! *she cums again, with him, squealing in her joy and surrender*

she is in a nearly ahegao state afterward, just demolished with joy and happiness and pleasure

she starts to cry softly

Mmmnn. *he kisses her, long and long*

her voice so, so warm with love and so soft with tears Master, you are my god. I'm floating … I feel so … happy … Hold me, hold me. … You keep me so … safe …

soft happy feminine sounds

whispers the word like it is so precious to her Master.

Stay inside me, Master, please.

Oh please.

Stay in me all night.

Stay in me forever.

My Master, my Master, I love you. I love you.

I love you.

kissing

Master, I wish you could feel what I feel right now … *tearful* … I love you so much …

kissing

so softly You keep me safe … and yours.

Mmmn …your ropes dig into my arms … mmmmnnnn.

You own me. You own me! Oh fuck, how you own me… You whipped me and marked me and fucked me. If I'd known when you bought me what it would mean to be yours I would have crawled to you that night on my knees, Master, and kissed your thighs and your feet and BEGGED you to brand me and breed me. My Master!

whimpers You make me so wet …

… and so happy …

soft quivers for a moment

gasps Oh! Master, look up! The other Masters, they've set the fireflies free from the lamps. *in soft, breathless wonder* The fireflies are dancing over our heads, Master, over the water … it's … it's so beautiful.

The other Masters are still watching us. *moans* They're watching you own me. Their slave-kittens are watching us. And they look jealous, Master. *a very pleased moan*

And that goddess in her pool is watching you bind me to your heart, Master.

Oh, my Master. I would rather die than ever leave your arms.

a little noise of pleasure Yes, feel me clench … mmmnnn … around your cock … Master … did I give you pleasure, Master? *moans* Did I please you?

Ohhhhh …

I'm tied up and so full of my Master's cock. I'm slick with sweat, Master. And my wet little cunt is squeezing you so tight.

Do you want to fuck me again, Master?

I can take it.

I can take ANYthing you give me. I am your sensual, surrendered slavegirl.

You can fuck me every night of our lives, Master, and every night I will try to give you more pleasure. *moans* I am my Master's SLUT. I am your wet little slut, Master.

kissing … moaning into his kiss

Take me, Master. Again. And again. Let me show that goddess in the pool how a woman in love fucks her Master!

quivers You own me.

kissing

Take me.

kissing

Take me, Master. Love me, Master. Love your slavegirl. Love me all night.

kissing

I love you.

the series ends

PART II –
THE MASTER'S TALE

1

On Display at the Slave Auction: You're the One I'm Buying Tonight

TAGS: [M4F] [Fsub] [Mdom] [Bondage] [Good Girl] [Examining her before purchase] [Teasing] [Hold the moan]

Ah, what's this? I'll stop here before returning to my seat for the bidding, and take a good look at you. You're much prettier than the others. I don't know quite what it is. Maybe it's your lips, slightly parted and so full, like a dream of pleasure; they would look so good around my cock tonight. Maybe it's the way your tits move so nicely with those quick, frightened little gasps of yours. Maybe it's how full and soft they look, or the gorgeous curve of your hips, or the sweet folds you're trying to hide between your thighs.

You're naked and I can see all of you.

But I think, after all, it is your eyes.

It is your eyes that have captured me.

They are so alive, your eyes. So full of fire. Nervousness and hope. You aren't broken like some of the others. You're on fire with life.

I want to taste that fire.

I want to feel it burn.

Yes, I'll take a good look at you.

We have a few minutes before it's your turn on the auction block, and most of the other buyers tonight seem focused on that wispy little thing from some northern village, the virgin they're bidding on right now. Poor little girl. She IS pretty. But I'd be afraid of breaking her at a touch.

I'd rather have you.

But let's take a good, long look. I want to explore this woman I'm buying.

There you are. Arch your back, lift your breasts. They've trained you well.

I'm leaning close, breathing in the scent of your hair, your soft skin, your… mmmm, is that arousal? I can smell you. You're in heat, pretty slavegirl. Mmmm.

Is my warm breath on your throat doing that to you?

What if I brush your neck with my lips? Bite the line of your jaw gently with my teeth?

Ahhh. That was a delicious little shiver.

You're so sensitive, aren't you?

Sensitive everywhere. I'll run this hand down your back … feeling the soft warmth of your skin … grip your ass and pull you closer. No, don't look away.

sound of a slap across her ass

I want your eyes up here, on mine, while I touch you, slavegirl. I want to see what my touch does to you.

slap

You keep your eyes on mine, girl.

slap

a low grrrowl Eyes … on mine.

SLAP

That's better.

You don't get to be shy tonight.

SLAP

You don't get to hide from my desire.

SLAP

You don't get to hide from my touch.

Mmmm, I love how you tremble when I tease the inside of your thigh with my fingertips.

That's a girl.

Yes, open those legs a little.

Let me have what I want.

Mmmm. *whispers in her ear* You be a good girl, and I'll be the one who buys you tonight.

Where did they find you? Your body is so… perfect. You're clearly not from here. Was your village burned? Did warriors drag you screaming from a hut in flames? Were you thrown into the slaver's wagon or did they enjoy you first?

Ah. There's that fire in your eyes.

Angry, are you?

Angry but … aroused.

No, you can't hide it. I can smell your sweet cunt.

growl this line, low and slow I know how badly you need to be … fucked.

Mmmm, your breasts feel so GOOD when I cup them like this. When I squeeze them in my hands and run my fingers across those hardening nipples. So soft, so feminine. Someone has chained a goddess here by mistake. A goddess for me to explore … and enjoy … *whispers* and fuck.

You feel delicious when you squirm against me like that.

They have your wrists shackled tightly behind you, don't they?

Such crude chains.

In my home, you would be as naked as you are now, but you would wear finer chains than those by far. Slender links of pure gold, that ring like music when you wriggle. Or silk ropes, teasing your wrists with their softness even as they hold you tight.

Pretty girl.

And these nipples. So hard. I love circling them slowly with my thumbs, like this. I may pierce them, if it pleases me. Attach the most dainty of golden chains, running from one nipple to the other. Mmmm. You deserve to wear jewelry like that. Some of these other slaves are for taverns or to display on the doorsteps of shops, to entice customers inside. But not you. You are lush and alive and radiant. Mmmm, voluptuous. You will be chained by your ankle to a bed covered in silk, your body decorated in rare jewelry, the best I own, and your juices running down your thighs.

You … deserve to be prepared for nights of pleasure.

Bathed in milk.

Oiled and perfumed.

And brought to my chamber glowing like an immortal.

Ah, it looks like they've sold off that little virgin. They're bidding on the brunette with the ample hips now. You'll be up soon. On display, as men compete for the right to HAVE you. Does that excite you?

Look at you quiver.

Mmmm, your body could make a man go mad.

We don't have long. It won't do for me to offend the slaver by delaying the bidding on you, though they do love when buyers … explore … the merchandise.

We only have a moment. But I need to know if I'm going to buy you tonight. I need to know if you'll be a joy and an excitement, if you'll make me roar with pleasure.

Now.

Let's see if I can kindle you.

Let's see if you burn with heat.

Mmm, yes, good girl, feel my hand slide up your sweet thigh, feel me cup your soft, warm cunt. That's a girl. I saw that little quiver. And you ARE wet against my hand. Mmm, you are such a good … tasty … slut.

Let's find out HOW wet.

grrrowls You hold very still, girl, and bite your lip so you don't cry out. I don't want any of the other buyers hearing how hot and wet and ready to fuck … my slavegirl is. I don't want anyone to try outbidding me tonight. Of course, they can try all they want. I'm still taking you tonight.

grrrowls You will be … MINE.

whispers I'm going to buy you, take you home, and FUCK you until you can't stand.

say this line slow, deep, and possessive I'm going to fuck you until you're a sobbing, begging mess on my bed.

You're going to scream for me tonight, girl.

I'm going to OWN you.

Now. Let's slide a finger thickly inside you. Mmmm. Like that.

Mmmm, I am pleased. You have a hot, tight cunt. I bet you would grip my cock so nicely. And by the gods, you are WET.

And so tight.

Do you think you can take another finger, girl? For me?

Let's find out.

Right now.

Mmmm. There we go. Two fingers thrusting into your soft, wet cunt. And you are doing so well, girl, not crying out. I hear you muffling those little whimpers in your mouth. Mmmm. Don't worry, girl. Tonight, once you're safely purchased and chained by your ankle to my bed, you can scream as loudly as you want when I make you cum.

growls And I WILL make you cum. Again and again.

But you're not going to cum right now.

You're going to have to wait.

You're going to have to be a good, patient girl for me.

I haven't bought you yet.

Only good girls get bought.

I want to try something. I'm going to lean close and bring my lips warm and soft to your clit. Let you feel my warm breath … and the brush of my lips … right there. Mmm, how you shiver. You are so delicious. I wonder what you'll do if I flick my tongue, warm and wet, across your soft little clit. Mmm, remember, don't cry out. Don't moan. Don't make any noise, girl.

he licks her clit

I'm going to lick you slowly, savoring you.

licking sounds

A good slave is worth taking the time to enjoy. I might enjoy you ALL night, luscious slavegirl.

more sounds of tasting her

Mmmm. There. That's all you get. No, no, don't whimper.

sound of a smack across her thigh

I told you to stay quiet. Disobedient girls get smacked. On their thigh *smack*

On their ass *smack*

On their sensitive clit *smack!*

You're going to be a good girl who does what she's told, aren't you?

That's right. Now I'm going to take my fingers out of your

sweet cunt and lift them to your mouth … and you're going to taste how fucking wet you are for me, aren't you, girl?

Mmmm. Good girl.

Your soft tongue feels so good.

I'll feed you something else later. Mmm, look at you standing there with your thighs SOAKED. And that look in your eyes, like you want to drop to your knees and BEG to be fucked, but you know better.

You have to wait.

You're going up to the auction block in a minute, and the bidding will start. Ah, look at that little spark of fear in your eyes. Your tits lifting and falling so sweetly as you breathe faster. You're going to be bought. Will it be by me? Or by another? Will your new Master be kind or cruel? Will you be sleeping tonight on a silk bed or in a cold kennel on a threadbare cushion? Will your new Master want to touch you, fondle you, caress you for hours, heating you slowly like a fine meal before tasting all your delicacies … or will he be abrupt, brutal, pinning you to the bed on your belly, his hand on your neck, his cock driven hard into your ass?

Well, we'll see.

I'll go back to my seat now. You keep breathing like that, girl, in soft, frightened, nervous gasps. It makes your breasts move so prettily.

sounds of his footsteps

seating himself

Mmmm. There, from this seat I have a good view of the auction block. It looks like they are just leading the previous lot away. My, she is a pretty thing. But I do like how that tight, delicious slut BURNED when I touched her.

laughs Well, my mind is made up.

Ah, there you are, slavegirl.

They're tugging you along by your bound wrists. They've leashed you. How delicious. There you are, straining a little against your bonds, showing off the sweet curves of your body. So naked. So helpless. So alive. You GLOW with life. I might have to outbid every man in this pavilion, you look so fucking hot. Mmmm. They have you standing on the block now. Is that a sheen of tears in your eyes? You look so good. We can see you clearly in the light of the lanterns over the block, lit up with their soft glow as though you're an angel captured and held here for the pleasures of men. But you can't see us. We're all in shadow. You won't know who is bidding on you. You won't know who you're sold to until he approaches the block to claim you. To make you his.

No wonder you're frightened.

They've started the bidding. Twenty gold coins. Thirty. Thirty-five. Forty. Look at you standing there so beautiful. You're listening to the voices, aren't you? Trying to imagine what kind of men those voices came from, what kind of men might buy you tonight. Or are you listening, perhaps, for just one voice? Are you listening for my voice?

raises his voice Fifty!

pause Fifty-five!

There, that's done it. There are only a few of us bidding now. You're looking toward me, though I know it's too dark where I'm seated for you to see me. Is that hope in your face? Ah, the slaver has just taken a fistful of your hair and tugged your head back, arching your body for us, showing off your breasts. His foot has kicked your ankles open so that your sweet cunt is visible to all of us. Mmmm, is that moisture I still see on your thighs? Gods, you are a beautiful slut. I AM going to have you tonight.

raises his voice Seventy!

Well, there are just three of us now. My competition seem to be a wrinkled old merchant and a woman with very intense eyes. Cruel eyes. Should I let one of them have you? You are trembling. And look at that … your nipples are so hard. You're enjoying this, aren't you, you sweet slut. You're enjoying hearing us bid on your warm, womanly body.

raises his voice Eighty! … Ninety!

growls You are costing me a LOT, girl. You had better writhe so prettily on my bed tonight. I'm going to make sure I get every coin's worth out of your sweet, wet body.

raises his voice Ninety-eight!

Just that woman and me now. She looks doubtful. How many coins is a wet, trembling slut worth, after all?

raises his voice One hundred! … … One hundred ten!

There we are.

Sold.

footsteps

Now to walk down to the block and claim you. Here, slaver, take this bag of coin. And I will take this girl.

Mmm, look at those soft, hopeful, nervous eyes. I'll cup your chin, lift your face, holding your face right where I want you.

say these next lines SLOW and DEEP ... the listener should feel these lines in her ear, in her bones, should feel his growl of ownership deep in her body

You are ... MINE, slavegirl. All .... mine.

I told you.

I'm the one who is buying you tonight.

I'm the one who is going to OWN you.

I'm the one who is going to FUCK you until you're soaked and sobbing from orgasms.

Now. I'm going to take my first kiss, first of many, and it is going to be a LONG kiss. I intend to enjoy you fully. And then, I will take you home to my bed.

I'll grip the back of your neck ... like this. Press your soft, naked body up hard against me, like this. Let you feel the thickness beneath my belt against your soft thigh. And I get to feel your breasts sweet against my chest. And I am going to hold you firmly, just … like … this.

long, hungry kiss, his moan of need muffled by her mouth as he takes her

growls I OWN you, girl. You … are … MINE.

2

Taking My New Slave, After the Auction

Ah, there you are. Standing in the doorway to my bedchamber. Naked. Your skin glistening with oil, glowing in the red light of the lamp by my bed. The warm summer breeze through the wide window must feel so good on your soft, sensitive skin. It's quiet up here. You can hear the music faintly from the dancing girls in the garden below. But there's no pavilion of men bidding on you here, no servants around you as there were when they bathed you for me in warm milk. There's no one else here. Just you … and me.

Your hair is unbound and tumbling down your back, scented. A little jewelry to emphasize how naked, how feminine, how vulnerable you are for me: that slender chain around your belly, the jewel at either ear, the silver anklet with the slave bells tinkling gently as you walk, letting me know my slut is here and ready for me. And, of course, the links of cool metal wound about your wrists, so delicately made yet holding you so tightly, your arms captured behind you, forcing your breasts up, lifting them for my enjoyment.

And the way your thighs and your soft folds glisten in the

red light ... is that from the oil that has been rubbed into your skin, slavegirl, or are you wet? Are you moist and dripping for me?

Mmmmmm, you have been prepared so well for me.

Let's take a good, long look at you.

You were the prettiest woman in that market. But by the gods, you are even more beautiful now.

I WANT you.

The inviting curve of your hips ... The swell of your breasts, rising and falling as you breathe in those soft little gasps. Everything about you is a delight. You are lush and womanly, and you are going to feel so good beneath my body tonight, once I have sunk my cock deep into that sweet, moist cunt I see between your thighs.

Mmmmmmmmm.

But again it is your eyes that draw me. That fire I see in them. The flicker of anger even as the scent of your arousal fills my bedchamber. You are so alive, slavegirrrl. I know part of you is furious, part of you wants to fight me, even as part of you wants to moan at a touch.

whispers I bet you ... are ... soaked.

voice low and grrowly I am glad I bought you.

Approach the bed, girrrl. No, don't hesitate, don't resist. You won't like having your sweet, soft skin kissed by my whip, slavegirl.

There you are. That's a good girl.

I see your eyes flicking about as you take in the room. The satin bed, the silk curtains, the bowl of warm wine on its stand by the bed, the moonlight through the window and the red, shaded lamp.

growls You're a long way from your village, woman. That little town the slavers took you from.

This is your home now.

This is your Master's bed.

This is where you'll be FUCKED.

And I'm right here, rising from the bed. Muscled, naked…because I'm ready for a night of taking my new slave. *growls* My eyes kindling with heat as I take your hips in my hands and pull your bound body firmly up against mine and press my mouth to your neck. I can feel your tits sweet against my chest. Your nipples are so hard. Maybe I'll take them in my fingers and give them a good tug … like this.

That's a pretty sound you made.

Make it again. While I tug on these nipples.

Mmmm. Good girl.

whisper I like having my hands on your tits.

You can whimper and squirm all you like, slavegirl. You aren't going anywhere. I bought you, and you're going to give me so much pleasure.

I'll take a firm hold on the back of your neck, press you into my hard body. Do you feel my cock hard ... and hot ... and thick against your thigh? *growls*

I was so hard when I bid for you.

When I bought you.

the sound of him breathing in her scent

grrrowls slowly Mmmmm, you smell like you need to be FUCKED, slavegirl.

Your skin feels so warm at my touch. I might brand you tomorrow, right here where my hand is on your thigh, mark you as my own. You are such a hot ... tasty ... slut, and I don't want anyone to doubt for a moment who you BELONG to. You are MINE.

An entire pavilion of men bid on you, every one of them HUNGRY to own you. And I outbid them all.

I'm going to HAVE you tonight.

You cost me so much, slavegirl, and I mean to take EVERY coin's worth from your sweet body.

I'm glad I saw YOU and didn't have to settle for of those little sticks some of the other men wanted. You're the one I want. Your body feels so full and womanly pressed to mine. You aren't going to break when I touch you.

low growl Unless I WANT to break you, girl.

Now.

Let's HEAT you a little more. I want a wet, hot fuck tonight.

he says these lines slow and deep and hot with lust I'm going to thrust you down on my bed … like this … on your back. Because I want to see your eyes when I make you MOAN. My body hard above you as I hold you down by your throat.

That's a girl. Whimper for me. You aren't going anywhere. You're MINE.

Mmmm, I can hear the music of your chains as you squirm.

growls I'm going to make you burrrrn, slavegirl.

Hold still now.

the sound of a smack across her ass

You hold STILL for me, girl.

SMACK!

I'm going to reach my other hand down and lock this bedchain to your anklet. Binding you to my bed by that length of strong, slender chain.

Mmmm, listen to you. I like it when you sound like that.

You looked so vulnerable and erotic on that auction block, naked to all of our eyes, your thighs soaked. I saw you quiver each time you heard me bid. Each time you heard my voice calling out how much I was going to spend to HAVE you. To OWN you. To FUCK you hard and fast on this bed.

You're here now. You're chained to MY bed. MINE to enjoy. MY slave.

Now let's see just how wet this luscious woman I own is.

I want to FEEL your soft folds… like this… touching you firmly… feeling how wet and soft you are against my fingers. Mmmmm, so soft.

breathlessly What a warm … wet … slut.

I bet it is so hot inside your cunt right now. Your eyes may flash with anger, but you are in heat. I can smell your sweet cunt.

NO. I told you. You hold still.

SMACK

HOLD still…

SMACK! SMACK!

…while I slide my finger deep and thick inside you. Mmmmm, you clench so prettily around my finger, girl. You're as wet as the sea. *laughs softly*

lower, breathless That's a good woman. You just take it.

You're … all … MINE.

Mmmm, feel my finger thrusting inside you. My eyes on yours, enjoying how you react. Mmmm, you wriggle like that, girl, and I WILL smack you again.

SMACK!

You be a good girl and take this for me.

I think you need another finger inside you.

Mmmm. There we go.

You feel so fucking hot around my fingers.

I'm going to FUCK you with my fingers. Right here on my bed. I want my bed to SMELL like you, to smell like you being fucked.

Like this.

Hard and fast.

Soak my hand, slavegirl. I want your juices running down my hand, down my wrist.

I'm going to thrust a THIRD finger in you.

I know you're tight.

You're going to TAKE this for me, slavegirl.

Mmmmmm. I'm just going to bring my face to your thighs while I finger you. So I can get at your sweet clit. Do you feel my breath warm, right there?

My lips brushing your soft thighs?

Mmmmm.

kissing her there

the sound of him breathing in her scent

You smell SO good.

I remember from the slave block. I remember how you taste.

tasting her

Mmmm. I like having my mouth on your sweet clit.

… sounds of him licking, kissing…the sound of him licking her, taking his time, savoring her slowly … this part should last a couple of minutes … get that slavegirl EXCITED

Mmmmm, that's a pretty woman.

You TAKE my fingers while I lick … and suck … your warm, wet clit. While I heat my slave for a night of enjoyment.

licking her, speaking to her in between moments of licking her

Mmm, listen to you moan. That's a girl. You hold STILL for me, but you can cry out now. You can scream. You don't have to stay quiet like you did in the slaver's pavilion. There aren't any other men here to bid against me. I already WON you. Now you gush over my fingers and you SCREAM, girl. SCREAM for me, slavegirl.

Mmmmmm.

licking

You want to cum on my fingers, don't you, girl?

You want to cum screaming for me… And all the dancing girls, all the guests in the garden below… they're ALL going to hear you SCREAM for me. They're going to hear you SCREAM for the man who OWNS you.

more sounds of tasting her

But not yet, slave.

laughs quietly You don't get to cum yet.

I'm going to take my fingers from you slowwwwly … mmm, yes, that's it, tremble for me, girl … feel me draw my fingers up along your folds … drawing that wetness over your soft petals … over your warm, wet, sensitive … clit …

Mmmmm.

That was a lovely little cry.

I want to hear that again. I'll just draw my fingertips back across your clit…

There you are. Mmmm, you're just a wet, quivering mess, aren't you, slavegirl?

You want more.

I can tell you want more.

Don't deny it. I can smell how much you NEED it.

You're going to have to earn it, girl. GOOD girls get to cum.

I'm rising and getting a fistful of your sweet hair and pulling you from my bed to your feet. Look how shaky you are, strands of your hair sweaty across your cheek, that wild desperate look in your eyes. That's a good slavegirl.

Let's taste your mouth.

the sound of kissing her hard

Mmmmmmm. You kiss well, slavegirl.

I must have bit your lower lip, because I can taste your blood. I can taste YOU.

You look so pretty with your hands tied behind you.

growls I'm going to hold that grip in your hair and hold your gaze with mine a moment. I OWN you. I want you to hear that. All through your body. Right down to the deep hot core of you. I OWN you, slavegirl.

growling in her ear I'm going to make sure you feel me so DEEP in you tonight that your cunt remembers who it belongs to for the rest of your life.

deeper grrrrrowl Let's get you back on my bed where you belong.

I'll get the back of your neck in my hand and throw you back on the bed, pinning you there on your sweet belly and tits. Gods, look at that ass.

He smacks her ass

I love the way you cry out. I bet they heard that all the way down in the garden. Now SPREAD those legs, slavegirl.

SMACK!

WIDER.

SMACK!

WIDER. I want you to FEEL the strain in your thighs. Get those legs open and ready to be FUCKED, girl.

That's right. You're getting FUCKED tonight. I own you.

SMACK!

SMACK!

SMACK!

Good girrrrrl.

grunts

You feel my body on top of you… pinning you down… my hand on your throat holding you RIGHT where I want you … my other hand squeezing your lush, warm tit … you are MINE slavegirl … grrrr … feel that cock rubbing against your sweet, soft pussy … You're going to take what I give you, girl. You're going to take it DEEP. I'm not courting you, I'm OWNING you. I'm going to fuck you until you cum apart. Now let's get the head of this cock up against your sweet, wet cunt and …

a loud grunt as he shoves himself inside her

FUCK. Yes. Good GIRRRL!

Fuck, you feel so tight around my cock. You feel me shoving myself so deep in you, girl? Going to force your head to the side so I can see those eyes. That's a woman. I fucking LOVE the fire in your eyes. The anger and the NEED. I BOUGHT you for those eyes. For the sweet quivering fiery woman I see in those eyes.

growls You fucking KEEP those eyes on mine, girl.

SMACK!

GODS, the way you cry out when I smack your tit.

SMACK!

You look at me, slavegirl, and you keep those sweet fiery eyes on MINE, girl.

SMACK!

Good girl.

grunting as he fucks her Mmff. Mmmff. Mmmfff. That's it. Take it girl. FUCK yes, I LOVE how your cunt squeezes my cock. Fuck, you're TIGHT. Mmmfff. Mmmfff. You take it for me, girl. You take that cock. Gods, that feels good. Mmmmm, your cunt is so worth it. I'm glad I bought you. Mmmff. Mmmff. Mmmmfff.

I got one hand on your throat and the other gripping your warm, sweet ass. Wonder if you'll scream prettily for me if I SMACK you while I fuck you. Mmfff. Let's find out.

SMACK!!!

SMACK!!!

SMACK!!!

his grunts and the sounds of him fucking her continue throughout this section … his words breathless and growly in between

Mmmm, listen to you scream. They're not going to be able

to even dance in the garden out there, listening to your sweet cries. I'll just cover your mouth with my hand. Mmmm, fuck, girrrrl, your mouth is so warm and moist and open and vulnerable against my palm. Mmm, there you go. *grunting* You scream all you want into my hand while I fuck you. You feel like soft wet silk around my cock, like a heaven made entirely out of pleasure. Like the sweetest thing I've ever owned. Mmmmff. Mmmfff. That's a girl, grip my cock. Roll those hips for me. Roll those hips like a hot ... *a grunt as he thrusts* ... tight ... *grunt* ... slut ... *grunt*

I'm so DEEP in you, girl.

I'm going to pinch your nose shut with my thumb. Even your breath, even your air, belongs to me, slavegirl. I OWN you. You ROCK those hips for me if you want to breathe, girl.

Mmmmm. You get to breathe on the count of ten, girl.

grunting each number as he thrusts into her, ten thrusts

One.

Two.

Three.

Four.

MMMMMF. FIVE.

SIX.

SEVEN.

EIGHT. You … tight … sexy … slut. NINE.

TEN!!

There. Now I'll let up with my thumb. You get a few little gasps, girl. Fuck, you feel so good and tight around my cock.

growls Your cunt is worth every coin…

You got a breath or two, girl? Good? I'm taking away your air again. My hand over your soft mouth, my thumb pinching your nose SHUT. You don't get to scream. You don't get to breathe. You don't even get to wriggle much, pinned HARD under me. You just whimper prettily into my hand and TAKE IT LIKE A GOOD GIRL.

MMmfff. One.

Mmmff. Two.

Mmfff. Three! Four! FIVE.

SIX. *grunting passionately, like a beast, taking her*

SEVEN.

EIGHT.

NINE. FUCK, you are so WET.

TEN.

BREATHE, GIRL!

GOOD GIRRRRRL.

You are such a good girl.

FUCK. The air smells like your cunt and it smells like fuck and it smells GOOD. I'm going to leave you a sobbing, soaked MESS on this bed, slavegirl.

We're going to do this one more time, slavegirl. You get a last little gasp of air and then you fucking hold your breath for me.

Mmmff. Mmmfff. That's right, SOAK my cock with your juices.

Scream into my hand.

Good girl.

a low, intense growl Now I'm taking away your air again.

I own EVERY PART of you, girl. Your cunt. Your ass. *SMACK!!!* Your breath.

You get to breathe if I SAY you get to breathe.

Now TAKE it, slavegirl.

TAKE it.

One. Mmmfff

breathless, so close to cumming Two. Three.

Four. FIVE.

SIX.

SEVEN.

EIGHT. MMMFF. MMFF. *groaning* I'm going to CUM in you, girl.

a whispering moan as he just barely holds back I'm going to cum in your tight, slick cunt.

NINE!!!

grunting as he rides her

I'm cumming in you, girl!

TEN!

Breathe!

his low, masculine moan as he empties into her, filling her

panting afterward

Mmmmm, fuck.

Grrrrrrr. I love the way you spasm around my cock.

Mmmm. Such a GOOD girl.

Now you just breathe for a moment. That's it, you whimper into my hand. Good girl. You don't get to talk yet. You just breathe while I catch my own breath, and then I'll fuck that sweet ass of yours.

SMACK!

Mmmm, the way you jump when I do that.

SMACK!!!

I bet your ass is going to feel SO tight around my cock.

Mmmm, you are such a sweaty mess. And you smell so fucking hot right now.

Now you just breathe. You're going to need every breath you have when I fuck your ass in a moment, girrrl.

That's it, breathe.

Breathe.

Good girl.

whispering in her ear We're not done yet, slavegirl. I'm going to make sure you KNOW who owns you.

One hand on your mouth … I'm going to slide my other hand underneath your body and fondle that sweet clit I own. That's a girrrrl. Moan into my hand for me.

a slow growl in her ear That's right. You're chained tightly and your sweet cunt is full of my cock and you aren't going anywhere. You just whimper for me, girl. My fingers circling your clit … rubbing your clit … that's right. The way you move is keeping my cock HARD. Such a good girl.

whispers I AM going to brand you tomorrow. Burn my mark right into your thigh. I own you, and I'm going to KEEP you.

You … are … MINE.

breathing hard Now I'm going to keep rubbing your soft clit while I ... *groans* ... slide out of your warm cunt. Mmmm, you soaked my cock with your juices. That'll help. You feel me shifting my hips ... mmm, pressing my hard tip against that sweet little pucker of your ass. Grrr, I bet you're going to feel ... so ... tight ... there. Fuck.

I'm going to fill you so FULL, girl.

I OWN you.

You're going to hurt for me. You just stay focused on my fingers on your clit ... I want you on FIRE, slavegirl.

Mmmm, I'm just going to ... *grunts* ... slide in ... slowly ... fuckkkk, yes, GODS you are tight. Mmmm, fuck yes, cry out into my hand. *panting* Feel that hard, HARD cock sliding into you. Gods. You grip me so tightly there it's almost painful. But it feels SO fucking good.

groaning FUCK, you tight, sexy woman.

starting to grunt as he fucks her, more slowly this time, but deeply and HARD

Gods. Yes. Take it. Mmmff. Mmmff. Mmmff.

whispering hotly in her ear You REMEMBER who you BELONG to, girl.

Mmm, your clit is so SLICK against my fingers.

grunting

Fuck. You hear those revelers down in the garden? The guests and their servants and the naked dancing girls? You hear their music and their laughter outside? They KNOW you're in here on my bed getting FUCKED. They know I BOUGHT you. They know you're taking it hard like a hot … wet … slut.

Now I'm going to take my hand from your mouth and squeeze your tits and you SCREAM as loud as you want, girl. You let them KNOW your Master is fucking his new slavegirl in her ass. SCREAM for me, girl. I'm going to tug on your nipples and I'm going to … PINCH … your clit. Like that. And AGAIN.

You cum for me, slavegirl.

You CUM, pinned under me on my bed and FUCKED.

TAKE it. TAKE that hard cock in your ass. Mmmff. Mmmff.

panting, grunting … taking his time … this should last a minute … possibly improv grunted words in her ear, like "take it," "that's a girl," etc.

breathlessly I'm going to cum in your ass, slavegirl.

I'm going to cum in my slut's ass.

Take it.

groaning as he cums

Take all of my cum.

Take it in your ass.

groaning as he finishes

Good GIRL.

he smacks her ass with his hand

GOOD girl.

Mmmmmmmmmm.

low and deep in her ear You are a goooood fuck.

talking slowly, post-coital and pleased and growly Mmmm. I am glad I bought you.

You just rest, now. You'll get to please me again soon. You just catch your breath.

You just lie under me all shaky and sweaty. My body covering you, holding you under me … SAFE … and OWNED.

I LOVE that shocked look in your eyes. That look like you're CONQUERED. Like you KNOW who you belong to.

Mmmm. That's a girl. You just breathe. Cry if you need to. Or moan softly.

I've got you.

You aren't going anywhere.

You're safe in my bed. Safe in my chains. In my arms.

With my COCK in your ass.

You're MINE.

I OWN you.

My good girl. Mmm, I am so pleased with you. You are SUCH a hot, good woman. SO worth owning.

Just breathe.

I've got you, slavegirl. All … MINE.

Good girrrrrrl.

3

Taking My New Slave Girl After She's Had a Fright

Mmmm, now there is the sight I like best. Stepping back into my bedchamber in the heat of the afternoon and finding my woman right where I left her, waiting for me. Bound to the bedpost, standing, your wrists tied behind you, your full, supple breasts and sweet thighs turned toward the door. Your nipples swollen. That blush in your cheeks. Mmmm. Your skin glistening with oil. Your beautiful hair loose about your shoulders, a few strands sweaty across your face, showing me that you've been squirming against your bonds before I entered.

soft laugh You're not getting loose, slavegirl.

rustling of clothes Let me get these trousers off. So I can stand naked and hard as a god. And you can see how the sight of you, the smell of you, the sound of your little gasps excites my thick cock. How I swell and throb with the need to FUCK my tight, naked woman. Right now, in the sweat-heat of the day.

grrrowls

My business at the gate kept me. It's been too long since I've gripped your sweet body in my hands. Mmm, I'll just walk naked toward you. Press my hard body into yours, capturing you between me … and the bedpost. Mmm. Your tits feel so full and so *good* against my bare chest. And your hips cradle mine so sweetly. Do you feel me hard, engorged with hunger, throbbing with heat, against your soft mound as I press into you? As I take your warm tits in my hands?

That's a girl. *growls* Give me your lips, slavegirl.

kissing her roughly, possessively, a growl of need into her mouth as he kisses her

That is such a good girl.

Mmm, do you hear the music of water in the fountains, through that wide window? Those are my pleasure gardens down there, where the dancing slaves will perform by moonlight later and … entertain … my guests. The water you hear trickles from between the thighs of marble nymphs who stand naked in the pools, cupping their stone breasts or reaching out to beckon the guests near.

a quiet laugh You haven't really seen the gardens yet. I've hardly let you out of my bed. I'll amend that. Soon.

But for right now… Gods, your breasts feel GOOD in my hands. Your nipples like warm berries pressed against my palms. I want to bite those sweet, succulent berries.

He does, growling as he bites her

Mmm, that's a pretty woman.

That fire smoldering in your eyes. Fire and heat ... and a little fear. And you're trembling. More than usual. Mmm. Why is my slavegirl shaking? Is it because of the man I just told off, at the gate? Did you hear some of that through the window? Yes ... he DID want to buy you. He made a handsome offer on you. He's from further up the hill. He's richer than me, I admit, but ... *a low, possessive growl* ... if he wanted to buy you, he should have been at the auction.

Not that it would have mattered.

I would have sold the entire city to own you.

My voluptuous slavegirl.

passionate kissing

You're still trembling, girl. No. *SMACK* Don't avert your eyes. I'll cup your chin in my hand and lift your face so I can see those bewitching eyes. Those slavegirl eyes. Those fire-at-midnight eyes. Mmm, fuck, I love your eyes, slavegirl.

You're not trembling just because of the man at the gate, then. Or not only because of that. Hmm.

Are you trembling because I made you dance on my table last night before all my dinner guests, tossing your veils aside, one after another, until you stood naked and glistening? Is it because of the ravenous hunger in their faces as they gazed up at you while we ate? As their eyes looked right up at your naked, wet cunt while you danced? Is it because I told you, in front of all of them, that I might fuck you right there on the dinner table in my banquet hall, for dessert? That I might let them watch, since they were such good, well-mannered guests? That I might let them hear your screams when I pounded you against the oak of my table? Is that why you're trembling, girl?

No? Not just that, either?

Well … is it because I branded you … after dinner? My hand is on your thigh right now, feeling that sweet mark in your flesh. My fingertips caress you there. Mmmmmm. Gods, you SCREAMED so sweetly when my brand burned your flesh. When I seared my mark of ownership into your body. Your tits HEAVED with your sobs. Grrr. I remember kissing the tears from your face, while my hands took firm possession of your breasts. I remember how you moaned into my mouth when I took your lips with mine.

a long, growling kiss

And how you sobbed sweetly in my arms afterward, how you came and CAME, spasming around my cock while I fucked my wet slut on the branding bench.

Grrrrrr. I hear from your sweet gasps how well you remember that.

But that's not why you're trembling. I can see that.

Mmm. I'll just … tease … your mound with light brushes of my fingertips, while I watch your eyes.

Ah, I see. You're trembling because of what happened at the market this morning, when I took you out with me for the first time to show off my sexy slut. Dressed in nothing but a transparent silk veil around your shapely hips, walking a step behind me, swaying prettily. Your full, delicious tits bounced, naked and desirable, as we walked. You looked so fuckable. My brand on your hip declaring to the world whose slave you are, who you belong to. A necklace of gold, delicate as spider silk, clasped around your lovely throat, declaring that you belong to a man of wealth and authority and power. As you should, pretty slave. Only a man who could buy and sell cities could afford such a woman as you. Let the world see how treasured you are, as you walk half naked behind me in the crowded market streets. No wonder you swayed so sensually, so proudly.

Yes. You're trembling because of what happened THEN, in the market, when that torn-cloak, back-alley slaver tried to steal you while I was haggling with the silk merchant. He probably thought if he could sell you for half what I bought you for, he could buy his own auction pavilion and make some real coin. You were waiting so sweetly behind me, and he grabbed you, forced a gag in your mouth and a dark hood over your head, pulled you off the street. You screamed for me but it just came out as whimpers under the hood. You must have been terrified. His hands so strong on your body, his whisper in your ear to "shut up, girl." Your feet kicking as he dragged you. Alone, in the dark, his breath loud near your ear ... You couldn't see me running after him down the alley. Couldn't see the moment when my blade took him through the gut, though maybe you heard his choked cry.

When my hands touched you, you whimpered, so that I ached to hear it. And when I lifted the hood from your face, there were tears in your eyes.

And I kissed you. Like this.

a deep, long, possessive kiss

Slavegirl, you're home now.

You're safe.

I'm not going to let ANYone run off with my hot, wet slave. No one is going to steal or buy you from me. The winning bid at that slave auction was MINE. And YOU are MINE. I OWN you.

Mmmm, feel my fingers teasing your soaked, naked pussy. Caressing your folds … your clit … circling … teasing your entrance with one fingertip.

My sweet slut.

You are so … soft. And SO. Fucking. Wet.

That's a girl. You show me you NEED it. You rock your hips into my hand. Like a good girl.

whispers in her ear Wet, good slavegirls get … FUCKED.

growls

My other hand is in your hair, tugging your head back, my mouth hot on your neck. *kissing*

You keep your eyes on mine, girl. See in my eyes how I value you, how I WANT you. And I want to see YOUR eyes. I bought you for those eyes. Those eyes bright as a sunrise before battle.

Mmm. You're a long way from your village, but you are NOT going to be just used and cast aside or sold. I've marked you as mine. I own you.

growls And I will make you a promise, my sweet, tight slut.

You will never be neglected, my hot slavegirl. Not a night will pass without my thick ... hard ... fingers deep inside your cunt.

Like this.

with a grrowl, he thrusts two fingers into her

Yes. You clench and grip those two fingers. Good girrrl. I'm going to fuck you so hard with them. My hand grinding against your clit as I curl these fingers inside you. Take it, girrrl. Soak my hand. Show me your body KNOWS who OWNS you.

Mmm. That's it.

These fingers are fucking you so deep. And so FAST.

I want my teeth on your breasts. Your nipples.

growling as he bites her

a quiet, growly laugh The way you buck and squirm and whimper when I bite your tits. Fuck, slavegirl, you delight me. You delight me so. RIDE my fingers, slut. You are so fucking TIGHT around my fingers. Grind into my hand.

And give me those tits... *growling, biting sounds*

And your throat… *growling, biting*

And the line of your jaw… *growling, biting*

And your lips… *growling, biting*

Mmmmm, I can taste blood where I've bitten you. YOU are wine and fire and woman, and I will DEVOUR you, slavegirl.

his voice a slow, powerful growl You TAKE those fingers, girl. Those fingers DEEP in your CUNT.

I am going to BREAK you.

I'm going to make it so you get DRENCHED, your juices dripping down your smooth legs, when you so much as hear my voice … Or my low grrrowl …or my footstep at the door. I'm going to own you so thoroughly, you get soaked just from hearing me breathe. You. Are. Mine.

whispers I am going to break you, slavegirl.

You CUM on my fingers, girl. You flood my hand. I am going to fuck you with these fingers until I hear you SCREAM. You are MINE. MINE, slavegirl. MINE, pleasure-girl. MINE, slut. Cum for me.

improv a growling, ferocious, possessive fingerfuck, with possessive things growled in her ear

That's a girl. Wet as the sea, and MOANING.

You are so beautiful when you cum, slavegirl.

And yes. You. Are. Mine.

You are my own, and I will COVER your body in my marks today so that you KNOW it.

Let me … grrrrr… pull these fingers out of you for a moment.

That's a good girl. You whimper, dripping, wet, MINE, tied to that bedpost. I am going to get something from that wall.

Mmm. There we are.

Yes, girl. It IS a whip.

No, you haven't done anything wrong. *his voice low and intense* This is so you can feel my ownership WRITTEN on your body.

Mmmm.

You're going to feel each snap of this whip, each mark burning in your skin, and each time this whip lands, I want to hear you cry 'I'm yours, Master.' If you're a good girl and you scream those words for me, I will stop soon.

Once your body is well-marked.

Mmmm. Look at you tremble. That is a GOOD tremble. Not fear of being sold or stolen now, but that simpler fear of your Master's hand, of his whip on your flesh. And it is making you wetter, isn't it? I can see your juices running down your legs, girl. I can SMELL how desperately you need to be FUCKED.

Snap of the whip across her thighs

Good girl. That was a lovely cry. Again.

Crack!

Good girl. That landed SO prettily across your breasts. Tell me who you belong to.

Crack! Crack!

Mmmm. Such pretty red marks, right across your thighs. Louder.

Crack!

I said LOUDER, slavegirl. Who do you belong to?

CRACK! CRACK! CRACK!

GOOD girl. MMMMM, good girl. Three more. I'm going to step to the side so I can get a good angle on your ass with my whip. That sweet ass needs to be whipped SO HARD. SCREAM for me, slavegirl.

CRACK!

CRACK!

CRACK!!!!

You. Are. Mine.

And one last crack of the whip, right … across … your mound.

CRACK!!!!!!!

Mmmmm.

There we are.

Mmm. Such a sweet slave.

I'll cast this whip aside… Mmmm, take your face in my firm hands. Kiss the tears from your eyelids and cheeks.

kissing

My hands on your body, caressing, soothing, everywhere my whip burned you. Soothing away the pain with my fingers…

Or giving pain … as I choose … Taking your nipples, twisting them in my hands … YES … on your toes, like that. Whimper for me.

Good girl. My good girl. Such moist, beautiful eyes. You are safe. You are home. And you are mine. And I will keep you, slavegirl.

Mmm, these tears. Shhh. Shhh.

kissing

growls The way you MELT into me when I kiss you … Gods, that pleases me.

YOU please me.

Feel me pressed into you, naked and hot and hungry.

whispers I own you.

kissing her hard

Now. I'll step away just to retrieve my knife from the bed where I left it. There we go. … Let's cut those ropes, cut you loose from this post. Grrrr. That's it. How deliciously shaky you are, like you've just been shattered. Mmmm. And look at your thighs glistening WET in the afternoon sunlight.

I'll pull you to the bed where you BELONG, slavegirl. Lie down, tuck you in tightly beside me on your back, your head on my arm, your belly and breasts and sweet womanly hips bare for me. Mine to touch and fondle and enjoy. Feel the HEAT of me pressed to your body. My cock hard against your hip.

breathes in her scent I fucking LOVE how you smell, girl. I love how you whimper and moan and flood my fingers when I touch you. I love how your tits are heaving. Do you hear the water trickling between the naked thighs of the nymphs outside? Do you hear my deep, full breathing? Do you hear the grrrowl in my chest as I hold you?

growls

My knife is naked and unsheathed like my cock… Let me lift the blade above your eyes so you can see it flash in the sunlight.

Mmm, I see your eyes widen, slave. As I touch the edge to your cheek … This is a warrior's blade, LONG and SHARP. That man who tried to take you today, I cut him open with this sharp, lethal edge.

Mmm. That is a very sexy gasp.

This is a knife that protects what I own. This is a knife I use to keep my woman safe.

Come here, slavegirl.

I'm pulling you closer to me by your hair, your breasts against my chest. Teasing your cheek with the cold flat of the blade. Cold steel against hot woman.

his voice is low ... and slow ... and deep, almost mesmerizing I own you, slavegirl. I can do anything I want with you.

I'm going to teach you how safe you are in my hands, slavegirl.

I'll run this blade along the smooth curve of your throat ... just letting you FEEL it.

Grrrrr.

Letting you FEEL how powerless you are.

Just a ... flick ... of my wrist and I would HAVE you in a different way, slavegirl. That's how completely I own you.

Now I'll run my knife down from your collarbone ... run the cold flat of the blade along the top of your breasts ... grrrrr ... Looking right into your eyes. Now, girl. Ask your Master to keep you safe. ASK me to keep you safe, slave.

listens Mmmm. That's a good girl.

slow grrrowl I OWN you. And I will ALWAYS keep you safe.

I take the knifetip and just circle your nipple playfully with it. Not cutting, but I'm letting you feel the press of that sharp tip against your so-sensitive skin.

Mmmm. *almost a whisper, hot with desire* How you quiver. I am so proud of you, girl. You're safe. My hands are firm and sure.

Now I'll tease your other breast with the knife. The sharp, cold steel tip. Pressing the edge under your nipple to let you FEEL … grrrrrr … I want your little gasps. Don't move. Don't. Move. Just take it like a good girl. You're going to take ANYthing I give you. That's my girl.

Grrrrr. Now I turn the knife so the flat of the blade is against your skin. Running it down over your sweet belly… Do you know where I'm going with this knife, slavegirrrrl?

Mmmmmmmm.

Hold very still, slavegirl. I will keep you safe.

slowly I'll tease the flat of this blade slowwwwly across your mound… Take the blade down along the smooth inside of your thigh, which is still slick from when you came like my hot slut. And I turn the knife and just TEASE the insides of your thighs with the edge, the sharp edge … as if I'm shaving you.

Good girl.

Grrrrrr.

Nothing is going to hurt you unless I WANT it to, slavegirrrrrl. You just hold still and take it for me.

grrrowls Whimper for me … as I slowwwwwly and gently and so carefully tease the flat of the knife back and forth across your clit …

Letting you feel the cold metal against your hot … wet … flesh.

Good girrrrrrl.

I OWN you, slavegirl.

I own this sweet little clit of yours. And I own your wet cunt. I bought you and I own you and I will do with you what I want. Feel the blade rubbing back and forth across your clit, the cold metal igniting every nerve ending you have, slavegirl.

Burrrrn for me, girl.

Good girrrrrl.

Now this knife … has a really … long … hilt. It's a warrior's knife. It's a tool, not a toy. And I'm turning it in my hand now so that the hilt of the knife teases your sweet clit … and your soft folds … and your wet slit. Grrrrrr.

whispers I'm going to fuck you with this knife, slavegirl.

That's what I'm going to do. Right. Now.

Feel that hilt tease your entrance … mmmm, I'm taking a firm hold of the guard and I'm SLIDING several INCHES of hide-wrapped hilt inside your sweet body. So thick inside you. Mmmm, it's thick like my cock, slavegirl, and it's warm from my hand.

Good girl.

My other hand rests on your mound so my fingers can tease … and pinch … and circle your swollen little clit … while I FUCK you HARD and FAST with that hilt. The knife blade is so close to your thigh and the hilt is inside you and I am thrusting it back and forth, TAKING my girl.

Good girrrrrl.

Taking my girl with my knife … Fucking her sweet wet cunt with the hilt of my knife … mmmmm …

My fingers tease your clit …

My breath warm in your ear: I want you to FUCK that knife, slavegirrrrrrl, and I want you to CUM screaming on that hilt. You. Will. Scream. For me, girl.

That's my good girl. Good girl.

I'm thrusting that knife HARD inside you. Nipping your jawline with my teeth … because I told you, I will hurt you the way I WANT to hurt you.

Biting your ear.

Grrrrrr. I want you to CUM on this knife.

My breath hot on your skin. My mouth hot on your throat. My fingers hot on your clit. The inside of your cunt must be so fucking HOT right now. And that knife is fucking you as fast as my cock will. Just taking you RIGHT HERE on my bed, on the silk sheets that you're going to SOAK with your juices.

You'll get my cock soon, slavegirrrl. But right now, you're going to please my knife with your cunt, because I TOLD you to. SQUEEZE it. MOVE your hips. FUCK that knife.

Feel that hilt fucking you hard. So hard inside you.

Good girl.

whispers You are MY ... sweet ... slut ...

My slut. My pleasure-slut. My fuck-slave. My slavegirl.

I'm turning the hilt now, rotating the hilt inside you as I thrust, wanting to caress every part of your insides with it, just ROTATING that hilt and thrusting it and screwing it deeper, FUCKING you with that knife, FUCKING you HARD with my knife, biting your neck. BEG me, slavegirl. BEG me.

YES. Good girl. You MAY. Cum on my knife. CUM on my knife. I want you to SHATTER as I keep fucking you hard with that knife.

GOOD girl.

Teasing your clit.

FUCKING you with that knife ... I'm making sure that hilt RIDES you through that orgasm.

Mmmmm.

There you go.

Good girl.

I'm easing back … it's all right ….

You're safe. You're safe. You're safe … and owned … in my arms, slavegirl. Nothing is ever going to hurt you unless I decide it.

I'm taking the knife from your hot, wet little cunt … Lifting it and teasing the hilt across your clit for a moment, letting you feel how SOAKED it is with your juices.

And I lift that hilt to your lips … Kiss the hilt that FUCKED you, slavegirl.

Mmmmm.

That's a GOOD girl.

Now THANK your Master. *growls* Thank me for letting you cum on my knife.

Good girl. SUCH a hot, sweet slut.

Now I'll set this knife aside … Gather my wet, quivering girl into my arms, pulling you close, close and captive, kissing your throat and jaw where I've bitten you… Grrrr, you're going to have so MANY bruises, slavegirl. You're going to wear the marks of my enjoyment all over your body. … good girl … such a GOOD girrrrl …

That's it. You just breathe and whimper.

I'm going to cup your sweet cunt in my hand … mmmmm, that's my slave, wet and hot and soaked from your orgasm … *whispers* Your cunt feels so … fucking … hot in my hand.

I am glad I BOUGHT you, slavegirl. My arms are where you are going to STAY. You'll stay where I put you, and SCREAM when I fuck you, and cum all night when it pleases me. You're safe, and you're mine.

NOW.

I want a TASTE of the girl who just came on my knife.

SMACK!!! Keep those thighs open for me girl.

I'll lay you back, move down your body, my breath warm on your belly … your thighs … your soft mound … That's it, you wriggle and squirm and arch for me. You KNOW what I'm going to do to you, slavegirl.

whispers You KNOW what I'm going to make your body do for ME.

I'm holding you pinned by my powerful hands on your hips. You haven't BEGUN to cum enough to satisfy me, slavegirl. I want you reduced to a wet, whimpering animal. Grrrrr.

breathes softly across her clit Mmmm, feel my warm breath on your swollen clit.

This clit is MINE.

licking

growls

Fuck, you are so WET against my mouth. Mmmmm. You ARE going to cum for me again soon, girl. You're going to cum as often as I want. You don't get any say in it. You just squirm and squeal and flood my mouth with your juices, slavegirl.

You. Will. Cum. For me.

I will MAKE you cum, as often as I please.

Now. Let's light your cunt on FIRE.

licking … kissing … sucking

improv at least 5 minutes of intense, grrrowly oral sex. Really TASTE that woman. She is YOURS. Make her SQUIRM. Say sweet things to her like "Buck those hips for me, slut" and "You are MINE" and "You taste so fucking good, slavegirl." Growl. Kiss. Lick. Smack her thighs hard and tell her to take it for you.

Make her CUM

That's a girl. You CUM in my mouth, slavegirl. You flood my lips and chin with your juices. I want you to soak me AND the bed, slut. Cum for me, girl. Now.

SMACK

NOW, slavegirl. *sucking, licking* Give me what I want. Give me your juices and your cum. Give it to me, slave. You are MINE.

another minute of sucking and growling and licking … make damn sure she DOES soak that bed for you

Grrrrrr.

warm, quiet laugh That's a girl.

So. Fucking. Wet.

You scream so prettily when you cum.

Good. Girrrl.

panting

And NOW.

It's time for me to FUCK my slavegirl.

You're going to please me SO WELL.

My hands on your hips flipping you onto your belly ... pinning you down HARD where I want you. Those sweet thighs and that sweet ass are still RED from my WHIP.

SMACK!!!!!

That's a girl. SCREAM for me.

SMACK!!!!

Mmmmm. You feel so warm under my hand. I'm just going to GRIP your ass a moment, feel the fire I've lit in your skin. The heat from my whip.

Open those legs for me, slut. *SMACK!!!!* Open them WIDE. The way I LIKE it. The way I like you open and hot and READY.

SMACK!!!! WIDER.

SMACK!!! SMACK!!!

That's a girl.

Now I'll drop my weight on you hard … *grunts* … Fuck, you feel so soft and warm and wet under me… Feel my cock against your soft folds … I'm crushing you to the bed. You don't need to worry about breathing right now, girl you just need to fucking PLEASE your Master's cock. I spent a fortune on you, pleasure-slave, and every night that I want it, I WILL have EVERY coin's worth from your tight body.

grrrowl My cock is so hard against your wet slit … grrrrrr … One thrust and …. MMMFFFFFFFFF … FUCK … You feel SO. Fucking. Good. So tight and so wet. Mmmfff. Fuck. Gods. Like sinking my cock DEEP into wet, soft silk.

Now you're going to GRIP my cock with your cunt, slavegirl. You're going to give me EVERYthing I want. My hand on your neck and my hips riding you HARD.

improv a hard, wild fuck, grunting as he ravages her against the bed

You are SO worth owning, slavegirl.

You please me SO much.

Mmmmmfff. Mmmmfffff.

Feel my hand gripping your throat as I RIDE you.

Feel me squeeze.

Feel me OWN you.

My slave girl. Mmmff. Mmmfffff.

Note to the voice/performer: improv the wild abandon of this hard fuck … take her EXACTLY how you please, as roughly as you please, she is YOURS

Yes, I'm fucking you HARD. Taking you as I PLEASE. Because I OWN you. Because you are MINE.

You TAKE it, girl.

Mmfff. Mmffff.

improv for several minutes, riding her hard, telling her he owns her

You feel my naked, warm cock so DEEP in you… grrrrr… I'm going to CUM in you, girl … I'm going to BREED you, slavegirrrl… You're going to feel me pulse so hot and thick inside your cunt …

Grrr … I'm covering your mouth with my hand … my firm, warm hand … SCREAM into my hand for me, slavegirrrrl.

Spasm around my cock, girrrl. You're going to take ALL of it. Mmmfff. MMmfff. Fuck. I'm going to fill you. I'm going to breed you. I BOUGHT you. I've FUCKED you. I OWN you. You. ARE. MINE.

Take it, GIRL. SCREAM into my hand!

his orgasm, loud and intense and savage

panting

Fuck.

Mmmm, slavegirl.

Mmmm, listen to you whimpering and gasping so prettily under me. Soaked in sweat, mine and yours. And sooo well-fucked.

My slavegirl.

My own.

My tight, wet, helpless slut. Mmmm, you SMELL well-fucked.

Grrrr.

I'm going to take my hand from your mouth … get a fistful of your hair and force your head to the side, see the sweet, conquered look in your eyes … and TAKE your mouth with mine …

kissing her HARD, a low masculine groan into the kiss

Mmmmm. That's a good girl.

a second kiss, even rougher

Mmmm. You. Are. Mine. No one is going to steal you or buy you from me. I will own you until you have borne me children and you are silver-haired and sweet and still so FUCKING beautiful when you clench around my cock. You are MINE, slavegirl.

grrrrowls

Now you just rest under my body until I'm ready to have you again. *panting* Feel my COCK softening slowly inside you. Feel my weight on you. My hand in your hair. You are owned and safe.

And after I've spilled my seed into you again later, I'll have you bathed in milk and oiled and I'll have blossoms woven into your hair and golden chains hung from your nipples, and I'll have you dance naked for my guests at dinner again.*grrrowls* Because I fucking LOVE how you dance, woman.

And I'll buy some sweet girl for you at the market this weekend to bring home and keep chained at your side, so she can lick and tease and suck those sweet nipples in her soft, warm mouth. So she can lick your cunt with sweet little flicks of her warm tongue, and whimper with her mouth around your swollen clit, and keep you wet for me while I'm away from this bed, keep you sobbing with orgasms until I return. I own you, and not a day is going to pass without you spending half of it soaked and cumming on this bed. You are here for pleasure, slave.

This is your home. And I OWN you. And you are safe. Grrrrrr. So you keep panting under me so prettily while I take your tits firmly in my hands and squeeze ... mmmm, how you whimper ... and you breathe while you can. Because you're going to please me again real soon, slavegirrrrl.

grrrowls

PART III –
FURTHER TALES
OF CAPTURE AND
CONQUEST

Ravished Among the Burning Tents: Squirm All You Want, You're Mine

Once he starts telling her his dream, we hear, faintly, the sound of distant flames.

The male speaker and his lover are in bed. His voice is low and growly and hot with desire, and husky after sleep.

Good morning, sweet girl. Mmm. I dreamed of you in the night. Such a vivid, luscious dream. Mmm, yes, I'll tell you about it. But first … *he grunts* … I need to get your hot body underneath mine. There. Mmm. You need to be pinned under my body while you hear about this dream. You hot, fuckable woman. *growls* I'm going to tell you this story, and you're going to take it like a good girl.

Yes, my cock is hard. *whispers* And hot.

That's what happens when I'm cooped up with a wild, beautiful woman. My body burns with energy, with strength and passion and heat. *growly and husky* I'm going to fuck you, sweet girl. But I'm also going to tell you this story of what I dreamed in the night. *a low grrrowl*

Open your legs, sweet girl.

That's it.

Fuckkkk.

Good girl.

Now, just feel my body hard and strong on top of you. My hands on you. My cock against your thigh. *growls* I will tell you what I dreamed. We were in the past. Mmm. Maybe I knew you then. Tents were burning. I can still smell the flames. *breathing in deeply* And I can smell you, your wet heat. *aroused* In my dream, you were fleeing in a brief dress of soft hide, weeping with fear, shaking with adrenaline, your hair in disarray. I chased you. Hunted you, my blood hot, taking joy in the lush curves and running body of the woman I would capture. I herded you like a soft, sweet doe among the tents of your people until you were caught between me and the flames.

Then you faced me, trembling, your eyes wild and hot, your dress torn away from one breast where I had seized you earlier. Before you pulled away and ran. Now there was nowhere to left to run. No one to help you. Just me. Laughing with pleasure, I strode to you, getting my hands on your soft body. Gods, you're soft, you sweet, fuckable girl. That's it, you moan for me while I grip these warm tits, while I tell you this story. I had hold of you, and you cried out. I threw you to the ground on your belly, a knee firm in the small of your back as I forced your wrists behind you, crossed them, and bound them in a leather cord.

rustling, sounds of binding

Mmm, like this. I tied you … just like this. *growls* Yes, you squirm for me, girl. Squirm all you want, you're mine. These bonds are tight, you're not going anywhere, girl.

Then I grabbed your tit and your hip, like this, and flipped you onto your back, my hot rape-captive. I tore your dress the rest of the way from your breasts, kissed and bit them …

grunting and kissing as he does just that with her, taking her tits as he pleases and igniting her body

… and gripped them in my hands while you writhed and squealed and begged. *growls* Fuck, I love how your nipples harden. How you thrash and wriggle for me. *breathing hard* Do that, my captive. Fight me. You're tied. You're mine. I've got your tits in my hands and my cock against your thigh. I own you, you hot captive slut.

Your soft cries in my dream delighted me, and I laughed and took your mouth, hard, as you squirmed in the dirt between the tents. My body covered yours, brutal and strong, my hands stripping you ruthlessly while you writhed and whimpered into my mouth. My hands peeling you naked, hot, gripping your soft skin. Like this.

a hot, savage, violent kiss, his muffled growls into her mouth

it is a long, plundering kiss

breathless and hungry Then your squirmings excited me beyond bearing. I lifted my mouth from yours and thrust your legs apart.

grunting and rustling

low and hot That's it. I want that naked little cunt. Feel my fingers opening you… Mmm, fuck. Tight girl. *whispers* Take it.

breathing hard I freed my cock. Your breasts bounced beneath me as you quivered and kicked. Oh fuckkk. Just like your tits are bouncing now. Fuck, I like your tits. My tied up little rape-slut. I covered your mouth with my hand, like this, mmm, my palm hot and firm against your soft lips. *his arousal is burning hot now* Yeah, you whimper into my hand like a GOOD girl. I love how soft and vulnerable your mouth feels. That hot little mouth is MINE. Mine to kiss and bite. Mine to fuck. Mine to shut up when I please.

in these next lines, he grunts the word "thrust" as he thrusts into her, and the lines that follow are delivered in his breathless growls, telling his lover the story of her rape among the burning tents while he rides her in their bed

I covered your mouth and I THRUST myself into you violently. Unnnh! Taking what I wanted. Unnh, unnh, unnh. Forcing such sweet squeals under my palm. Unnh, unnh. Yeah, cry out for me. Squeal into my hand, my hot slut. Fuck. Fuck, YES. Unnh. Unnh. I took you and TOOK you, savage in my heat … unnh … and urgent, needing to enjoy my rape-captive quickly before the fires spread. Fuck, you're tight. You're so fucking tight. With your eyes wild above my hand and your thighs squirming and your tits rubbing against my chest. Fuckkk. You're MINE. Mmm, fuck, fuck, FUCK. You're so hot. Squirm all you want, you good girl, I'm raping you. My cock so FUCKING hard in your tight cunt. Unnh, unnh. *grunting like a beast as he fucks her, as he tells the story* There among the burning tents, my thrusts bruised your thighs, my hips rolled as I plundered your warm, wet cunt. I felt you grip me so tightly. You begged and wriggled, exciting me as I mastered your body. Your mouth soft beneath my hand, your breast warm in my grip, your tight cunt a wild delight as I pounded you against the soft earth. Unnh, unnh, unnh! I gazed down into your hot eyes as I raped you, until you could only grunt and whimper, a sweet female animal being fucked and mated by her captor.

low grrrowl Mine.

Yeah, you writhe while I fuck you. Buck those hips. Make this exciting. Fuck, how you smell, how you feel. My captive slut. You're going to take it like a good girl.

a few moments of savage grunting and thrusting, taking her urgently

Yes, yes, fuck yes. Whether you squirm or submit, you're going to just cum apart under the surge and roll of my hips. Mm, fuck. Fuck. That's it, scream into my hand, little girl. You're mine, mine, MINE.

There in the grass, I held your gaze as my balls tightened. I plunged so deep, unnnh, your softness a wild caress along my cock. Then deep again, unnnh, and then again, unnnh. Fuckkkk. Then I spilled all my pleasure and battle joy and heat into your body, spurts of my seed, the pulsing of my cock hot inside you, filling you with my hot cum while you wailed sweetly into my palm. Unnh. FUCK. Like this. My cock naked and primal. You CUM for me, you hot slut. You CUM like a good girl. Cum, cum, cum. I'm cumming in you.

I'm cumming in you, girl, mmm, fuckkkkk …

he cums, groaning and filling her

his orgasm is powerful, and afterward he is sweaty and hot and breathing hard

Mmmm. Yes.

Oh, yes.

a quiet, pleased laugh

How you clenched around as I came, as I filled my captive slut. Mmmm. We could hear … the tents … burning. The fires getting closer. I had poured such fire from my cock into your body.

Mmm, you like that? *growls* Yeah, mewl into my palm like a good girl while I finish this story.

slow and breathless I rested on top of you a moment, panting, my head resting on your hot, sweaty breast. I turned my face and bit your nipple,

he does, grunting as he bites her,

… mmm, because I loved your squeal into my hand. Good girl.

I pressed my lips to ear and breathed … two words … just like this …

My.

Slave.

Mmmm. My slave. I breathed those words by your ear with my cock inside you. Claiming you.

Mmmm. Then I pulled myself out of you, enjoying your whimper.

he moans as he pulls out

I got to my feet, pulled you up roughly by one of your bound arms. My other hand took your hair, like this, mmm, and pulled your head back savagely, arching your beauty, displaying your breasts to any fellow warriors we might pass. I marched you through the burning tents as you sobbed and said incoherent things, conquered and distressed and overcome. My seed trickled down your thigh. The smell of your wet heat excited me, making me hard again, almost too hard to walk.

growls You excite me, woman.

Soon the burning tents were behind us and I was forcing my bound captive through the long grasses. In a dip of the land, other captive women lay together, bound, their clothes torn or stripped from their writhing bodies. Some were gagged tightly with cloth. Some were struggling, their breasts bouncing, and begging. Some were weeping softly. Some were staring back at the burning tents with wide eyes, or gazing up helplessly at the warriors guarding them. One woman with raven hair was kneeling before one of the warriors, looking up at him … sweet and fearful … surrendered … opening her soft, wet little mouth while he freed his cock. Maybe she hoped he would protect her and be gentle with her. Or maybe … maybe a desire to be owned burned in her heart.

I threw you down among the other women, naked and hot and well-fucked. My cum on your thigh. Your face sweaty and flushed, strands of your hair stuck to your cheek. I thrust your legs apart again ... like this ... mmmm. You moaned. With my fingers ... like this ... ahhh ... I drew some of your wet heat from your pussy and smeared it across your cheek, so my rape-captive would smell her arousal while awaiting my return. Mmmm. Then I took a fingertip of dark paint from a pouch at my belt and drew my sign on your left tit, ... right ... here ... tracing my finger along your tit ... mmm ... marking you as my captive, my property. I gripped your other tit hard ... mmm ... and kissed your hot fuckable little mouth, plundering you, biting your lip, tasting blood and tears and woman.

Like this.

his kiss is primal and intense, biting her, owning her, taking her mouth as thoroughly as he wants

How you moaned into my mouth! My captive pleasure-slut, who would soon be bound and helpless in my bedding, warming me in my own tent, all winter. I kissed you like I wanted every cell in your body to know I OWNED you.

kissing her hard, again

Then I thrust you to your back among the other captives, and I stood and strode back toward the tents on fire, to help with the looting. Behind me ... mmm ... the sounds of soft sobs and gasps, the sounds of the raven-haired slave sucking at a warrior's hard cock. The sounds of my own woman whimpering and squirming in her bonds, wet and hot and leaking my cum … your pussy clenching and hot as you wondered what would happen to you. The sky was red from your burning village, and you could feel each blade of grass, each breath of wind across your thighs … and tits. The leather cord tight around your wrists. A Master's mark on your breast. Yes, you're going to stay tied. Just. Like. This. Knowing at any moment I may return, hungry and hot, and thrust your legs apart. To rape you. To own you. Good girl, squirm for me. You are my luscious, sweaty little prey. Torn from your tents and put to my use. My bite marks on your tits and my cum leaking down your leg.

growls Oh fuck, that's hot. Let me get my fingers in you … *grunts as he does* … fuckkk, so wet. So wet. You liked my dream. Good girl. Let me just fuck with my fingers while I get my cock hard again. SUCH a hot, tight little fuck. *growls*

Do you smell the fires in the tents?

Do you see my eyes smoldering in the blaze?

Get used to your new life, little dream-slut. Helpless pleasure-slave. Every night, your body is going to surrender under my wild rape.

kissing her hard

Because you are captured.

a savage kiss, growling into her mouth

Owned.

kissing her again, growling

growls MINE.

another rough kiss

the scene ends

Ravished in the Conqueror's Tent: Scream into my Hand All You Want, Pretty Girl, You're Mine

Once he starts telling her his dream, we hear, faintly, the sound of a campfire.

The male speaker and his lover are in bed. His voice is low and growly and hot with desire, and husky after sleep.

Good morning, sweet girl. Mmm. I dreamed of you again in the night. Such an intense, sensual, savage dream. Mmm, yes, I'll tell you about it. But first … *he grunts* … I need to get your hot body underneath mine. There. Mmm. You need to be pinned under my body while you hear about this dream. You hot, fuckable woman. *growls* I like how soft you are, captive beneath me. Give me that soft little mouth.

he kisses her, growling into her mouth, his intensity rising, hot and primal

a hot whisper How you kiss.

growly I could devour you, woman.

I'm going to tell you this story, and you're going to wriggle under me while I do. *breathy* I'm going to make you writhe.

Yes, my cock is hard. *whispers* And hot. I fucked you in my sleep, all night. That's what happens when I'm cooped up with a wild, passionate woman. My body burns with energy, with strength and lust and heat. *growly and husky* I'm going to fuck you, sweet girl. But I'm also going to tell you this story of what I dreamed in the night. *a low grrrowl*

Open your legs, sweet girl.

That's it.

Fuckkkk.

Good girl.

Now, just feel my body hard and strong on top of you. My hands on you. My cock against your thigh. *growls* I will tell you what I dreamed. We were in the past. Mmn. I can still smell the cookfires and hear the wind against the sides of my tent. My warriors and I had conquered your people. Your village burned in the night. And you … *an aroused growl* … you had been peeled out of your clothes, left standing in my tent as naked as the night. My warriors had prepared you for me. These luscious tits had been oiled for my pleasure. They dripped perfume here, behind your ears … *breathing in her scent* … here, on your soft neck … *kissing her, slow and sensual but hungry* … mmm … here, on your nipples … *we hear him kissing, suckling* … at your navel … *kissing* … and lower … they dripped warm, scented oil over your clit and your hot virgin cunt. Right … here.

Mmmn.

You were so ... *whispers* ... wet ... and slick against my fingertips.

a hot whisper Just like you are now.

Beautiful girl.

You came into my tent the night of your capture, naked, sweetly scented, holding a bowl of hot wine. You were trembling. Some of the wine spilled over your soft hands. I lay naked on the furs and beckoned you near. The softest whimper in your throat. Your eyes were soft and wide like a captive doe's. I told you, girl, if you didn't kneel and offer me that wine, I would tie you to the earth outside my tent, pour that wine over your tits and cunt, and let my men lick it off your body.

You moaned and knelt swiftly. Lifted the bowl to my lips. I drank deep, then knocked the emptied bowl from your hands and grabbed a fistful of your hair, like this, and drank from your lips.

he kisses her hard, and growls into her helpless little mouth as he plunders her

his voice low and hot and intense You were caught. My arms savage. My mouth hot on your throat and breasts as I pulled you down to the furs. As I held you down and kissed your breasts, I told you to sing for me, sing one of the love songs of your people. You cried softly then, and I was rough with you. You shook your head and I slapped your tit ...

smack!

Like this.

smack!!

growls And I held you by your hair and told you to SING for me, virgin girl. I want to hear that hot voice before I ravish you.

an intense, animal growl I don't care if you don't want to. You … WILL … please me.

Smack! SMACK!!!

Sing, my hot little rape-captive.

growls That's a girl. That's a … good … girl.

a growl of pleasure

husky Your voice does things to me.

…good girl.

You could feel my cock harden against your hip. These soft tits were heaving with fright. *whispers* And excitement. I slid a hand between your thighs … like this … mmm … and teased open your virgin slit … like this … and told you: You sing like an angel in heat.

I'm going to make you SING at each violent thrust, babygirl. I own you tonight. I'm going to rape you.

Yes, squirm for me, girl. Just like I dreamed. Your little fists hit at my shoulders when I forced my mouth on yours.

he kisses her, growling

And I reached for a sash by my bedding ... like this ... wound it about your wrists ...

we hear him tying her

That's it. Just like this, I bound your hands in front of you, right here between your tits, like you're praying or begging for pity. That's my pretty girl. *growls* I like you tied. Helpless and hot, squirming and sweaty. Ready to be fucked.

he growls

I made the knots ... tight.

Like this.

Mmn. Pretty girl. Yes, your eyes shone with tears in the firelight ... just like that. Wriggle for me, babygirl. Feel how tightly I've bound you. Feel my hard body pinning you. *growls* I killed so many warriors today, to get at you, to get my rough hands on your tits and thighs. *growls* You're mine. Now open that hot little pussy for me. Open those soft thighs.

rustling

I'm too strong for you, girl. You're going to be as open as I want. *growls* I'm going to have everything I want. I plundered your village tonight, and now I'll plunder YOU.

I like how you beg. Delight me, and I'll keep you, I won't throw you to my men like a strip of hot meat.

kissing her savagely

That's it. Tremble for me, virgin girl.

almost whispering, on fire with lust for her This cock rubbing against your cunt ... hot ... and thick ... you're going to take it now, deep and violent. This hard cock. I'm going to rut in you like a beast.

Feel my hand cover your mouth, you hot captive girl. *whispers* You're going to be bred tonight. Squirm all you want, babygirl. Scream into my hand. This hot cunt is mine.

In my dream, I held you down while you writhed and bucked and I ...

he grunts with pleasure as he thrusts into her

... THRUST into your virgin slit. Fuckkk, like this. Oh fuckkk. Such a tight, hot rape-captive. Mmn, I could feel your cunt soft as a kiss around my cock, and tight as a fist. Fuckk. I like this cunt. *growls in her ear* I own your cunt now, girl. Unnh, unnh, this cunt ... unnh ... belongs to ME.

he grunts savagely as he thrusts into her, wild and violent; we hear him grunting, thrusting, enjoying her while he delivers the lines that follow

Oh, how you squirmed. As I took this hot cunt. *groans* The scent of you made me a wild animal. My eyes smoldered above yours. My hand pressed over your mouth so hard, your teeth cut your lip. And I rolled my hips and violated you, bruising your thighs as I thrust savagely into your body, unnh, again and .. unnh .. again! Fuckk, you feel so fucking hot. I would burn a city to own you. I would leave an entire tribe bleeding in the dirt to pin your squirming body under mine and own this hot cunt.

growling, feral Squirm, captive girl. I'm RIDING you. You take each pounding thrust. I'll kiss your neck …

kissing her hungrily, savagely

husky You're not a virgin anymore. Unnh. You're a woman. Unnh. MY woman.

I pressed my mouth to your ear, unnh, and whispered three words, unnh …

whispers, hot and fierce, a conqueror You're. My. Slave.

That's it. That's it. You moan into my hand, slut. You're *thrusting* My *thrusting* Slave. *thrusting*

he pounds her

Squeeze my cock, good girl. Kick those knees against my hips. Buck those hips. Writhe, you hot rape-slut. Make me work for it. Make me work to breed this fertile cunt. I'm going to breed you, you know. No condom, no pulling out. In my dream, there were no condoms, just my savage cock in you, the roll and surge of my hips, just my hand hot on your mouth and my semen spilling hot into your womb. I hear how you whimper into my hand. You're going to have your conqueror's baby. You're getting bred, babygirl. You're getting BRED. I can't wake from that dream and not breed you. It's today. I'm breeding you TODAY, in this tent, on these furs, in this bed, while you squeal into my palm like a wild captive bitch. *groans* I'm close, babygirl. SQUIRM. This is your last chance … *grunting* … to wriggle loose, to get my cock out of you. *growls in her ear, his voice gone feral, primal in his heat* Scream, babygirl, into my hand. Scream. No one can hear you. No one is left to help. There's just my cock. Just my cock. All that's left in your world is my wild pounding cock and my chest crushing your tits and my hand on your mouth. You take this cock! You take this cock DEEP, girl! UNNH! This is it. This is fucking IT. Kick and fight me and SCREAM, I'm going to plant my seed in you, slave! I'm going to cum in you! I'm going to CUM in you!

Grunts

… right …

grunts

… fucking …

grunts

NOW.

he starts to cum in her, filling her, taking hot joy in it

Ohh fuck. You're mine.

he thrusts

Mine.

thrusts

MINE.

thrust

panting as he finishes

whispers in her ear Slave.

I've claimed you. *growls*

Feel my seed in you.

just breathes the words My captive bitch.

These soft tits will grow full and tight with milk. This belly will be round for my delight.

whispers in her ear You're going to bear my child.

Mmmn. Yes. You just whimper into my hand, you sweet voluptuous rape-slut, while I finish my story.

still panting a little

Bound and raped and soaked with sweat under me.

a contented grrowl

I gazed down at my captive slut, at your eyes wild above my hand, at the glow of the firelight on your trembling body. I bit these sensitive little nipples, wanting to brand you with my teeth.

he bites her, growling

How you quiver.

more biting, growling

Too sensitive, are we? Mmn. In my dream, you cried softly. You'd been … conquered.

I slipped my hand between your legs … mmmn … scooping up your virgin's blood on my fingertips. Then I lifted my hand and smeared that blood warm across your lips and cheek. Showing you what I'd done to you. I slid my fingers into your mouth and made you taste it. Like this.

Yes, suckle my fingers, babygirl.

That's a good girl. Mmn, look at you, so sweetly shattered, your wrists tied, strands of your hair stuck sweaty to your cheek, your tits rising with each panting breath, your soft helpless little mouth suckling my fingers. Good girl. Good girl. I'll keep that hot mouth full from now on. When you aren't singing me the love songs of your people, you can use that hot mouth to please me.

Suck these fingers, babygirl. Taste your hot molten honey. Mmmn. Good girl. You taste hot after you're ravished, don't you? Mmmn.

whispers, hot in her ear I've raped you.

I've burned your village. There's nowhere for you to go. At dusk, I'm going to ride from here with you bound in my saddle, and you … are going to warm my furs every night, out on the wild steppes. You're going to delight me with your soft heat. You're going to lick … and suck … and squirm. And bear warrior-children for me.

whispers I've bred you.

You're mine.

Now give me that soft mouth.

he kisses her, growling like a beast, muffled and feral

It's a long, demanding kiss

This hot little mouth is mine. This hot cunt still squeezing my cock … is MINE. This ass, if I choose to rape it, is mine. You … are … MINE.

Smack!

These hot, smackable tits are mine.

Smack! Smack!

growls All. MINE.

smack!

Mmn, such pretty sounds you make.

Now. Breathe in the scent of the cookfire. The scent of my male musk. The scent of your own soaked cunt, what I did to you, what I made your body do for me. If you listen, you can just hear other captive girls in the other tents, squealing as my warriors conquer them. Now … mmmn … while I squeeze these tits, mmmn, while my cock rests inside you, warm and so good inside you, mmn, you be a good girl and kiss my throat and chest. Lick my skin with your soft little tongue. You're tied, but you can bring me so much pleasure with your mouth, luscious slavegirl. Show me you're the kind of breeding slave who gets caressed and fed and treated well, not the kind of slave who gets her tits and thighs and her hot little clit smacked until noon.

SMACK!!!

growls Open your mouth.

SMACK!!

he kisses her, hard and hot

he growls into her mouth

Mmn. Good girl. When I kiss you, you open your mouth like a good slave and give me EVERYthing.

he kisses her, voraciously, like a warrior starving for his slave, starving for HER

There you go. Mmn, you're so … soft.

These tits. Mmmn.

Now, lick and kiss my neck and chest. Delight me, my rape-captive. *growls savagely* Give … me … pleasure.

moans

Good girl. That's a good girl.

growls That's it. Get me excited and I'll fuck you again. I'll fuck you until you can't stand, slavegirl. *he grunts as he thrusts*

That's it.

grunts

Take it.

grunts

Take it.

he kisses her again, growling

You're MINE.

hot, almost violent kissing

the scene ends

Welcome to My Master's Tent, Sir; Master Says I Must Give You Pleasure Tonight

In this erotic tale, a captive librarian who has been made into a pleasure-slave is thrown to her Master's guest to give him pleasure and keep him entertained the night before important talks. The guest is hot, and her Master is cruel; as the guest (the listener) forces orgasm after orgasm on her, the slavegirl starts to beg the guest to make her Master an offer and buy her and take her away to a better life. A life far from this desert tent, with books to read and a gentler Master.

Will Sir give in and buy her, or will she be left to her Master again in the morning? She will have to do everything she can think of to please and entice the listener, desperate for him to say "Yes, you are mine."

The script opens with the sound of her being thrown to the carpets on the floor. She whimpers. Shaky, she starts to speak. She is both frightened and aroused, quivery.

Hello, sir. Welcome to my Master's tent. There, he has left for another pavilion now, it … it's just us here. *softly* Just me … and you. Alone. I … *hesitates, frightened* … My Master has thrown me naked to your feet because he wishes you to feel welcome, a most honored guest and highly esteemed, and ...

a brief hesitation, her tone showing that the words are false ... because my Master is a generous man with a warm heart.

seductive, though frightened He wishes me to please you ... with my body ... with my soft young breasts ... with my warm mouth ... with my tight little cunt ... and *whimpers* with my...my ass, if...if you wish it, Sir.

I have to be completely obedient and completely pleasing, or ... or I will be beaten and ... and thrown to my Master's men to be enjoyed at their pleasure all night. *whimpers at the thought*

Please, Sir. Please look on me with favor. Let me kneel prettily for you ...

Here, like this.

With my... with my knees spread wide and my soft, warm cunt on display for you. Like Master taught me. I'll tilt back my head and roll my shoulders back and lift my breasts like they're aching for your touch. Do ... do you see my breasts lift and fall as I breathe?

the sound of her frightened, aroused breathing

Do ... do my naked thighs and my full breasts please you, Sir?

listens a second, then responds to a question My name is whatever you want my name to be, Sir. … Yes, you may call me that tonight, Sir. Is that name special to you, Sir? I will be her tonight. *a seductive little moan* I am whatever you need, Sir.

How may I give you pleasure, Sir? How may I make your night wonderful?

Yes, Sir. Yes, I'll sit in your lap. I will sit naked … and warm … and soft in your lap. *trembly* It will be my pleasure, Sir. Here, just relax, Sir, settle back on these silk cushions, and watch me rise gracefully to my feet, slow and sensuous, taking care to let you have a long, teasing glimpse of my soft folds. Taking care to lift my breasts attractively. Turning slightly and glancing at you over my shoulder. Letting my hips sway as I turn and step closer.

her voice lowers So close.

Master taught me to be graceful and delicate … to make sure every movement of my body is feminine and sensual and gives men pleasure.

Feel my fingertips trail … so gently … ahhh, so teasingly … down your muscled arms …

And I'll lift my soft little hands to your shoulders and lean in toward you … letting your warm breath caress me, … mmm, your breath across the full swell of my breasts…

a soft aroused sigh

I'll settle so gently into your lap, mmm, one leg to each side, so if Sir wishes he can touch … and caress … *gasps* … and fondle my soft, naked cunt. Yes … *almost tearful, aroused and frightened all at once* Yes, like that, Sir. Ohhhh … your fingers are so … warm. And firm. Does … does my naked little cunt please you, Sir?

moans

You may slide a finger inside me if you want, Sir. Master says all my holes are for your pleasure tonight, Sir. If I deny you anything, Master will be furious with me. *whimpers* Take from me as you wish, Sir. I am yours until the sun rises. You can… ahhhh!!!!!!

moans

I can feel your finger pressing … right there. Do … do you enjoy teasing me, Sir?

How else may I give Sir pleasure?

Mmm, cross my wrists behind my back? Like this, Sir? Is that how you want me? *softly, seductively* My arms behind me as though I'm a freshly captured slave, or fresh from the auction block, bound in your rope? Naked and helpless and open to your every touch, to fondle as you please?

gaspy little whimpers Oh, how you touch me… how you play with me and fondle me … *moans* … yes, I'm your pleasure-toy tonight, your plaything … to be touched as you wish … as firmly or roughly as you wish. I am yours.

these lines are slow and seductive You can do whatever you want. You can touch me. You can taste me. You can … fuck me.

moans Ohhh, yes, you can kiss my breasts, just like that. *gasps softly* Yes, Sir. My… my tits. I will call them that if it pleases you, Sir. My soft young tits. Touch my tits. Squeeze my tits. Ah! Squeeze my tits. *shuddering moan* My tits are for your pleasure … my tits are here for your mouth … ahhh … your lips and teeth … *moans* while you finger me, Sir.

Aren't my tits sweet … and perfumed … and slick with oils, Sir? Mmmmm … Look how hard my little nipples are. Do you see how my tits glisten in the lantern light? You can fuck my tits later if you want, Sir. You can command me to push them together around your cock and I will beg you to cum between my tits, Sir, to give me a necklace of your seed. If that's what you want, Sir.

wet sounds

moans I am here to give you pleasure. Do you hear how wet I am?

wet sounds Do you hear how I wet you make me? *moans*

a sudden cry Oh!! You … you found my clit.

Oh yes, Sir. Yes, Sir, I love how you touch me. I do. I will do whatever it takes to please you tonight, Sir.

Yes, Sir. Yes, you may kiss my mouth. My mouth belongs to you. Kiss my mou-MMMMPHHHHHH *a long, long, deep kiss ...* *she moans into his kiss*

after, she is breathless Ohhh. You ... you do NOT kiss like Master does. You kiss like ... like you want to devour me, all night.

soft and low Do you want to devour me, Sir? Do you want to ravish me? You're a guest in my Master's tent, and ... EVERYthing he owns ... is for your enjoyment and your pleasure tonight. *whimpers* Especially me.

teasing You can tie me up if you want to, Sir. There are ropes there by the cushions.

Oh? You ... don't want to tie me? You ... want me to keep my wrists where you tell me to keep them? *quivery* Is that how you like your slavegirl, Sir? Obedient and ... *whimpers* ... and wet while you fuck her with your finger?

moaning Oh...your finger in me ... mmmm, and your mouth on my tits... *gasps* Oh! You bit me. My nipple. *quivery whimpers* Ohhh ... I'm so wet.

I heard you talking with Master earlier, I know how important the talks tomorrow are to you ... to both of you... I wasn't supposed to eavesdrop but I couldn't help it. *low voice, sharing a secret with him* I watched you through a tiny tear in the wall of the tent and I watched. And listened. I wanted to get a peek at you because I knew Master might give me to you tonight and I was frightened, not knowing what you would be like, kind or cruel, weak or ... strong...

a sudden gasp, then a low sultry moan Ohhhh … your finger is moving so fast in me … ah … oh … yes, I'm … I'm very sensitive in that spot right there…

And when I saw you in the light of the lantern, you did NOT look weak. You looked so handsome … and muscular … like … like a lord from the stories I read as a girl …

giggles Yes, Sir, yes, I can read. I wasn't always a slavegirl with my thighs spread open and wet for the pleasure of men. I used to … *frightened* Does … does Sir want to hear this? I … I don't have to talk if Sir doesn't like … *breathing easier* Yes, Sir. If it adds to your pleasure, Sir, I'll tell you about how I became a slavegirl.

I was a librarian. Yes, I'm blushing. *surprises herself with a giggle* I wore a little dress and I helped the people in my village get things to read, I was the mayor's youngest daughter, and … I was a virgin. And I loved my books. *softly, reverently* I loved my books so much. I miss the stories. I miss the smell of the pages. Oh Sir. *longingly* I used to read in the library at night for hours and hours… by the light of a small lantern like this one here in Master's tent. Except I wasn't naked.

softly If I were reading a book right now, in this tent, on these silk carpets, I guess I would be reading naked. On my elbows and belly, with my book open in front of me, and my ass ready for the firm grip of a Master's hand, my feet in the air while I get lost in such a good story.

But ... *distressed, speaking the next words in a rush* Master doesn't have any books. Not even one! If... if I please you so well tonight *pleading, seductive, gentle kisses on his neck and lips* ... mmmmmm, if I kiss you so well ... if I ... if I fuck you so well ... if I'm so good for you, Sir ... will you bring me books? From your country? Next time you visit my Master? Please, Sir? Please will you bring me a book? Even just one book...

No, Sir. *gasps, frightened* I'm ... I'm sorry, I didn't mean to demand anything of you, Sir. Forgive me, Sir. I didn't mean to be an impertinent pleasure-slave, I'm so, so sorry.

a moan of delight Yes! YES Sir, yes, thank you for thinking about it. Thank you, thank you, thank you.

kissing him sweetly, lingeringly

Yes, Sir. I... I'll finish my story, Sir ... *moans* while ... while you finger me. *gasping* It's hard ... to ... to talk, Sir ...

I ... I was a librarian. And then my ... my village was raided ... ahhhh ... and desert riders took me ... and all the young women ... but they didn't rape me. They ... they raped one of the other young girls who wasn't a virgin. Over and over in the night.

frightened, quivery, a little angry at the memory, aroused by Sir's touch on her

I listened to her cries and I shivered naked under the blanket where they'd left me tied up, near their campfire, under the cold stars, while men fucked another girl, near me, all night in the dark. They wanted me to be a virgin for the auction, so they could sell me for more. But the next morning, one of them made me take him in his … in his mouth. I'd never done that before, and I choked, but he didn't care. He made me take it.

He fucked my mouth.

And then he did it again, but this time he was more patient, and he started teaching me how to suck, how to please him, how to be a good little slavegirl.

softening her voice, gentle I… I could do that for you, Sir, if you wish.

I could take you in my mouth.

I could take your cock in my throat. And swallow everything you give me.

moans Yes Sir yes, I'm very wet. I'm so very wet. My pussy is so wet. They didn't touch my pussy, Sir. They trained me … and sold me at auction … and Master bought me and brought me here to his tent, a few weeks ago. And he took my virginity so violently, right on those cushions over there, Sir. There's still a stain of blood on one of them from when Master tore open my virginity. I can show you later if you want, Sir. You can see where I was deflowered.

whimpering moans for a little while

Oh your finger … your finger .. your mouth on my tits … you're teasing me so. Exciting me more than I can bear.

whimpers

Yes, Sir. I … I watched you tonight, talking with Master. And you looked just like a lord in the books I read. But also I was so scared, because you looked so stern.

I'm still frightened. Very. But Master had me aroused and oiled and perfumed for you. Do you see how my skin glistens, how hard my nipples are from the teasing I've endured, and from the way you're fingering me now? I am very wet. Master said he needed to make sure I would quiver and moan at your touch, no matter how frightened I might be. He said that I had better be a dream of pleasure to you, as far into the night as you wish to enjoy me. That if you don't walk into negotiations tomorrow with a grin on your face, I will be severely punished. And he held my legs open and caressed my soft folds until I writhed and whimpered for him, and he smacked my little clit … *whimpers* … and told me to be such a good girl for you.

SMACK a sharp cry

Yes! *squeaks* Yes, he smacked my clit just like that.

SMACK she cries out

Yes, like that, Sir.

several sharp smacks followed by whimpery little screams from her trembly Yes, yes I'll be a good girl, Sir. I'll be a good girl. May I? May I be a good girl for you, Sir? Please, Sir? Here I am, naked and trembling and wet, in your lap, and you can have your way with me, Sir.

cries out Oh, two fingers in me. *squeals* Th…th..three… oh, I feel so full. I can't…I'm still too tight… I'm young and tight and…

SMACK

screams Yes! Yes, I'll be good, Sir. I'll be good. I'll clench down on your fingers … *moans* … with my tight little cunt and I'll be SUCH a good girl for you, Sir. With my hands behind my back. With my tits heaving as you rape me with your fingers.

moaning … improv getting close to orgasm as he fingerfucks this sweet slavegirl

Oh, Sir … Sir … you're going to make me cum … If you keep … If you keep doing that … you're going to make me cum, you're going to make me cum …

Yes, yes, I'll flood your hand, I'll soak your hand, I'll cum on your finger,s if that will give you pleasure, Sir … oh my GOD how you're fucking me … with your hand … oh Sir oh Sir oh Sir …

muffled suddenly as he kisses her

whimpering into his mouth, sounds of a ravenous kiss … then, she squeals into his mouth as she cums around his fingers, still submitting to his kiss … the waves of her orgasm take her and her wild cries of pleasure are smothered by his mouth … only when she is done and quivery does he lift his mouth from hers

Oh God. Oh God. Oh God.

Yes, Sir. Yes, I'll unfasten your trousers and … and take out your hard cock … ohhh my God, your cock is … so thick. You are … so thick. You made me cum so hard with just your fingers, that cock is going to break me. *whimpers* What do you want to do with me, Sir? How may I give you pleasure, Sir?

Yes, Sir. Yes. I'll lift my hips and … ahhhhh!!!!!! … mmmm … *whimpers* your cock is against my folds and you are SO hard … yes, Sir, yes Sir, I'll lower myself on you.

Will Sir be gentle?

I've only been raped by my Master a few times and I am still so tight … and so tender … will you be gentle with me, Sir?

Yes, Sir. *frightened but aroused* I know I have to please you in whatever way you choose. If you want to fuck me like an animal … if you want to fuck me until I scream … if you want to fuck my ass … *whimpers* … I am to give you such pleasure, Sir. Whatever Sir wishes. Do you feel how soaked I am, Sir? Wet … and hot … and soft as silk against the head of your cock? I'll just… curl my fingers around your hard shaft … and I'll rub myself back and forth across the head of your cock … oh, I'm so wet … and ease you inside *gasps* me … *a soft, sweet cry as she penetrated*

Ohhh … I don't know how to take your cock, it's so thick … *whimpers* I … I'm lowering myself … ohhhh … just a little at a time … oh, you're going to hurt me … Yes, Sir. Yes, I'm crossing my wrists behind me again. Oh! You're … your taking my hips in your powerful hands … your strong, warm hands … please be gent-AHHHH!!!

a wild cry as he sheathes himself fully inside her

ahhhh … you're … you're inside me. You're completely in me. You've forced me open around your cock. *whimpers* Yes, Sir. Feel me ripple around you … mmm, squeezing you. I've been practicing around my own finger. Grip and release … and ripple … I know how to please a man. Master says I have to be SO good at pleasing a man.

Do I please you, Sir?

Do I please you, the way I squeeze your cock, holding and gripping you inside me like I don't ever want to let you go, like I want you to fuck me until dawn and then fuck me until noon and then fuck me until night and leave me a wet, sweaty, sobbing mess in my Master's tent?

moaning Yes, Sir, yes, I'll ride your cock. I'll ride your cock. Will you help guide me with your hands, Sir? Since my own are behind me, bound by your will, as surely as though you've taken me and tied me to be your rape-captive tonight? Will you guide me, Sir, control me, show me how to ride your cock, how to do it so well for you?

moaning … wet sounds … sweet cries Ohhh, each time you lift me, until just the head of your cock is touching my cunt and then … AHHHH! … *panting …* you penetrate me again … you fill me, you fuck me … like I was made to be your slut … like I was made to please your cock … fuck me, Sir … fuck me as hard as you wish, Sir … make me take it … I want to give you pleasure!

breathing faster Oh fuck … oh fuck … oh fuck …

Do you like how my tits bounce for you, Sir?

Oh Sir! Oh Sir! Do you like my cunt? Do you like my cunt gripping your cock? Do you like how my insides squeeze and caress you? Fuck my cunt, Sir, fuck my cunt. Oh God. Oh God, you're so big me. Break me, Sir. Enjoy me. Ravish me.

May I cum for you, Sir? May I cum screaming around your cock?

panting, desperate Yes, Sir, yes, I'll obey, I'll wait, I'll wait, I'll wait…

Here, Sir, kiss my breasts. Kiss my tits. *whimpers* Kiss my mouth.

hungry kissing…her whimpers of need muffled by his mouth

moaning, frantic Sir, I need to cum, I need to cum, I need to cum, I don't think I can obey, I'm still a new slavegirl, I'm just an innocent librarian girl who was stripped and sold and fucked and told to be so pleasing. Please don't be mad. Please. Please let me cum. Please let me cum on your cock. Please!!! PLEASE!

YES!

YES! Thank you, Sir, thank you! *screaming* I'm cumming! I'm cumming for you, Sir! I'm cumming!

her passionate, wild orgasm

soft whimpers ah, ah, ah, so wet, so wet … oh Sir, I've soaked your cock … please cum in me, Sir … please cum in me.

I'm going to keep rippling around your cock.

I want your cum, Sir. I need your cum. I need you to cum in me. I need you to make me yours.

You can imagine I'm your captive, Sir, if you want. Maybe this is your tent. Or maybe you're one of the desert riders who TOOK me. Maybe you've dragged me from the library and thrown me naked over your saddle. Maybe you've carried me away into the desert … until we're far from anyone who can help me, anyone who can save me or hear me scream. Maybe you've made a fire and you've lain me bound beside it, my tits heaving in terror…

moaning as her arousal becomes intense

Are you going to rape me, Sir? Am I here to be raped? Are you going to empty your seed into me? Into my soft, *panting* … fertile, … virgin cunt? *whispers* Is that what you want? Do you want me impregnate me? Do you want to breed me? Do you want to cum in me?

Cum in me, Sir. Please cum in me.

Please cum in me! Cum inside me! Cum in me, cum in me, cum in…

Yes! *gasps* Yes! I feel … I feel you pulse in me … feel me squeeze you … cum in me … oh god fill me, cum in me … ah, ah, ah…

she cums again

panting

say these lines sweet and slow … Mmmmmm, feel me just … mmm, just pressing my body to you…lying here with you, clasping your cock inside me … where I'm warm … and soft … and so wet. My tits pressed soft to your hard chest. Ahhh, do you feel my nipples rub against you as I breathe? Mmmm, you came inside me like a god. You are so big in me, Sir. Let me kiss your neck …

soft kisses

softly, so soft Did this slavegirl please you, Sir?

Did I give you pleasure?

Did you like cumming in me?

softer, almost but not quite a whisper You could take me away from here, take me with you … *moans* own me … You could buy me from my Master.

talking fast, a little desperate He wants tomorrow's talks to go well, he wants it so badly, I KNOW he wouldn't refuse you if you made an offer for me.

breathing soft, warm across his skin

You could buy me, Sir.

kissing him

You could buy me and have me and fuck me, … every … night.

Here … ahhh … feel me … mmm … squeeze your cock again.

Please buy me. My Master is so cruel. You could take me away somewhere … to your own country … where there are books.

hopeful I could read naked for you…while you watch.

If you … if you bring me books, I will read naked to you every night until you're excited and you have to ravish me.

whispers Please bring me books.

You could rescue me. You could make me yours.

Here, let me just … *shifting* … I'll lick and kiss at your neck … *kissing and licking* … with my soft, wet little mouth … *kissing*

Mmmm. And your ear … *kissing*

a hot whisper in his ear Buy me, Sir.

I will be SUCH a good girl for you.

I will do anything to please you. To please your cock. To give you pleasure. Whenever you need it. I will be your good … wet … obedient … slavegirl.

whispers Make me your slavegirl.

gasps No, no, no! Don't tell my Master, don't, please, please, please don't tell him. Don't tell him I asked you to buy me. Don't. *frightened* He'll beat me so. Please … please, I just want to please you. I just want to be so good for you. Let me be good for you. Aren't I good for you?

Yes. *almost ready to faint with relief* Thank you. Thank you so much. Yes, Sir. Yes, I'll … I'll please your cock … with my soft, warm mouth … while you think about it.

Mmmmm.

I'll … ahhhh … pull myself out of you … *whimpers* … oh God you're so big…

a soft moan near his ear Your cum is leaking out of my cunt … your seed is dripping from me, Sir …

soft, seductive whimper I want to earn more of your seed …

Mmmm. Kiss my way slowly down your chest …

kissing her way down his belly

Run my fingernails across your nipples … mmmmmmm…. over your muscled arms…

You are so strong … mmm, so masculine, so powerful. I am so helplessly yours, Sir.

Mmm … let me kiss your thighs…

kissing

My mouth is so wet … and so small … you might bruise my lips, Sir … so small …

kissing

Mmm, do you like how I kiss you?

kissing

Does my soft mouth feel good?

kissing

May I please your cock, Sir? May this helpless young slavegirl please … and lick …

licking sound

and kiss …

kissing sound

and suck …

sucking sound

… your cock?

Mmmm, thank you, Sir.

Thank you for letting me suck your cock. I want to make you feel like a god. Let me just … breathe … across the tip …

she does

Mmmmm. And lick…

she does

You taste so good, Sir. So good.

I'll just close my mouth around … mmmmm …

sucking

softly Do you like my mouth on your cock?

slow, gentle sucking for a minute

Do I please you, Sir? I'll tease your balls so gently with my fingernails … ahhh, I felt you twitch against my lips … I felt you THROB. Your cock is so hard. Still so hard. I'm going to make you harder, I promise, Sir.

sucking

Yes, Sir, yes, I'll gaze up at you while I take your cock deeper …

moaning around his cock as she sucks … moaning as if to make him cum with her voice

Mmmmm … I love your cock … mmmm, I love your cock in my mouth …

I could do this every evening for you, Sir, every night, every morning, if you buy me … if you take me with you…

frightened Yes, Sir, I'll focus on your cock. I'm sorry, Sir.

sucking vigorously… sounds of gagging on his cock

Oh god, you're so big.

sucking

So big.

Sucking … choking

Oh! Your hand in my hair! Are you going to fuck my-mmmmphhhhh mmmphhh mmmphhhhhh

a vigorous, rough, wet blowjob for a couple of minutes

Mmmphhh mmmphhh feel me caress your balls, and feel me taking everything you give me, please please cum in my m--mmmphh mmmphhhh mmmphhhh

talking with her mouth full cum in my mouth, cum in my mouth, please cum in my mouth, cum in my mouth, cum in my mouth…

squeals as he fills her mouth

gulping, swallowing sounds

gasping for breath

Mmmmff. *pulling her mouth gently from his cock* Ohhh. You tasted sweeter than Master, sir.

softly I … LOVED … tasting your cum.

whispers I loved swallowing your cum. Swallowing ALL of it.

I loved your cock in my throat.

Did you like how I moaned around your cock? Am I a good, sweet little pleasure-slave?

Here, let me just… mmmm, just lie here with my cheek against your cock and my soft, wet pussy against your shin. Oh Sir, oh Sir, look at me gazing up at you. My face soft in the lantern light, my lips reddened from how you fucked my mouth. Sirrr… See in my eyes how I yearn to be your good, obedient slavegirl. I will be such a good girl for you.

softly, scared, hoping Please buy me. Please buy me. I want to be yours. Your pleasure-slave. Your slut. Your everything. Anything you need. Buy me. Buy me.

Yes, Sir. *a disappointed whimper* I know it's time to rest. Yes, Sir, you'll think about it tonight and tell me in the morning. Thank you, Sir. Thank you. Please, please, please say yes. Please say you'll buy me. Please say you want to fuck me every night. Please. *whimpers* Yes, Sir. I'll… I'll just kiss your thighs while you rest. I'll show you what a GOOD slavegirl I am for you.

slow, gentle kissing of his thighs

Your good, sweet, captive librarian girl…

breathing softly across his thigh

with her soft tits…

breathing softly across his skin again

and her wet, fuckable cunt…

kissing

You are my Master, Sir. My only Master, if you want to be.
I am yours.

kissing, licking slowly

softly, pleading with all of her talent for seduction, every ounce of it Will
you buy me? *kissing* Will you buy me?

Waking You in Your Bed With My Hand on Your Mouth and My Cock Inside You

this episode opens with him grunting softly as he penetrates the sweet listener... throughout, he is breathless and almost in awe at how much he's enjoying her, at how hot she is, this helpless woman he's waking with his cock. He gets the script's lines out in short phrases as he thrusts, his rhythm deep and slow at first, enjoying her. This is a man who has her exactly as he wants and is enjoying every moment, every soft whimper, every movement of her sweaty, hot body. There's nothing trivial about this night ravishing. He has wanted her and wanted her, and now he has her, and everything about her is so delicious to him. You can hear it in his voice. You can hear it in his breathing. You can hear it in his growls and his grunts as he thrusts in her. He is taking her, completely, in the middle of a hot night.

his voice low and husky at her ear as he thrusts Mmn. Mmn! Wake up, that's it. Shh. That's a girl. Shh. Whimper into my hand. Mm hmm, you don't get to scream right now. You don't get to beg. You just get to take this cock. That's a girl. That's a good girl. *grunting as she squirms under him* Shh, shh, feel my hand tight over your mouth. You squirm all you want, you're still getting this hard cock. Mm, that's it. You're not going anywhere, babygirl, you're not going anywhere. You're getting FUCKED.

Mmmm. Your body is so hot, wriggling under me. This hot ass and these sexy tits. Oh fuck. You made it so easy, babygirl, naked in your bed with your window open like that. It's hot out. Was your air conditioning broken? Oh shh, shh, shhh. Mmm, it was so EASY to just climb on top of you in your bed and slide this thick cock into you while you slept. Mm. But I love that you're awake. I love that you're squirming. Oh, you good girl. Unnh. Unnh.

Your mouth feels so sweet under my palm. I love those little screams you're making. Oh, keep doing that. Mmm fuck yes.

Mmmm, this tight cunt, mm fuck how you squeeze my cock, mmm. I understand about your window, it's a REALLY hot night. But now I'm going to have a hot night. Aren't I, babygirl? Oh yeah, take that cock, mmm, take that cock, mmm, you're all mine now, mine to fuck. My cock is in you, sweetheart. My cock is so deep in you, you are so full of my cock. Mm yeah, fight me, fight me, you hot slut. I bet you've dreamed of this, dreamed of waking to a hot cock inside you and a hand pressed over your mouth and a man so hungry for you he just has to take you right here in your bed in the middle of the night. Ever since I saw you, I couldn't get you out of my mind. I had to HAVE you, babygirl.

breathing in her scent Oh my god. You smell so good when you're being fucked, you smell so good. Unnh, unnh, unnh. Oh, you're taking it like a champ, sweetheart. Yeah, you cry and beg and whimper, but you're taking it like a champ.

Mmmm, fuck this sweet pussy is so tight. You weren't a virgin, were you, kitten? Oh fuck, it doesn't even matter, unnnnnh, just take this cock, babygirl, take this cock. I'm enjoying you so fucking much. Oh you're so soft and hot, unnh! Yes.

You just whimper into my palm like a good little slut and squeeze this cock for me. That's it. Mmm, fuck. You are so soft ... unnh ... and warm and ... unnh ... tight. Mmmn. It's so good to be inside you like this, just thrusting, fuck yes, unnh, no condom, just my hard naked cock. That's a girl. You struggle if you want. You kick. You scratch at my hand over your mouth and buck those sweet hips. Fuckk, you are such a good ride, kitten. But here's the thing. You're not getting me out of you until I've fucking bred you. That's right. I want to watch you for the rest of the year, watch your tits swell and tighten, full of hot milk. Watch your belly grow round with child. Then I'll come back, just like this, in the middle of the night, and cover your mouth and wake you with my cock and fuck your lush, pregnant body. I bet you'll cum screaming into my hand when I do that. Your nipples and hot cunt will be so sensitive in that second trimester, every cell in your body wild and alive. I bet you'll be the hottest rape I could ever imagine.

getting more excited, fucking her faster Oh yeah. Unnh, unnh. My pregnant, juicy fuckbitch. Oh fuck. So yeah, you squirm for me like a good girl. You put up a fight. Kick and scratch and bite my palm if you can. I'm still fucking this hot little pussy. I'm still getting you pregnant. Mmmn, fuck, how you squirm. I'm going to fill you with hot, sticky seed, little girl. Oh yeah. Fuck. Let me get a handful of hot tit. Fuck yes.

Oh this nipple is so fucking hard. You like this. You've probably squirmed in your bed imagining being taken, hungrily like this, night after night with your soft fingers between your thighs lighting fires you can't quench, burning up with need to be held down and fucked and mated in the dark, pounded and shattered in your own bed.

Let me get my fingers on that swollen little clit. That's it. Oh yeah, I'll just keep my other hand firm over your mouth and fuck this cock deeper into you, fuck, fuck. Mmmn that's it. Buck those hips. Your sweet pussy is soaked, just fucking SOAKED, oh babyGIRL you're so fucking wet. When I caress this helpless little clit ... mmm yeah ... you can't hide the animal grunts and moans you make. Yeah, that's what you are. A hot sweaty female animal about to be bred, about to be fucked full of my cum. Go ahead. Moan into my hand. Soak my cock with your hot juices and clench down on me and moan. It's okay, babygirl, it's okay. I've got my hand on your mouth. No one can hear you. No one knows what an animal you are. What a hot needy little bitch in heat, squeezing my cock. No one knows but me. Moan, babygirl. Moan for me. I'm close. I'm going to cum in your hot cunt. I'm going to impregnate you, pour my seed into you, a hot sticky gift. Yeah that's it, squeal into my hand like a bitch. I'm riding you so hard. No one can hear you. No one can help you. Let go. There's nothing you can do but take this pounding cock and cum and cum and milk me dry. That's a girl. It's time to breed you. It's time to breed you, you hot sweaty squealing bitch. You cum for me, babygirl. I want to feel you fucking CUM on my cock. Here, I'll help. I'll pinch this sweet clit, mmm yeah, and pinch your nose shut, take your air. Yeah, you can't breathe, you can't breathe. Just whimper under my hand and squirm on my cock. Fuck! Mmm! That's a girl. You don't need to breathe right now, you just need to cum on this cock.

You get to breathe when you cum, babygirl. You get to breathe when you cum!

That's it. That's it. Squeeze my cock. That's it. Cum for me. Cum on my cock..cum on my cock. You want to breathe, then cum! Cum on my cock, you tight fuckbitch. Cum for me, cum on me, cum, cum, cum on my cock, breathe babygirl breathe! Yes! Fuck! Yes! Give me that hot cunt, give me that cunt, give me that cunt, yes fuck fuck fuckkkkkkk

he cums in her, intensely, swept away in the heat of her

Fuck yes. Unnh, unnh, unnh.

pleased, breathless laughter

Ahhh. I love unloading my hot seed in your cunt. God, you're a hot bitch. Such a beautiful hot bitch. Oh yeah, oh yeah, take that cum. Take that cum. Fuck yes. Good girl. Good girl!

That's a girl... it's okay, you can cry. You can cry. You put up a good fight. I can feel your thighs shaking. You were such a good girl. Mewl into my hand and just, mmm, just feel my cock soften slowly inside you. Fuck. I've never had a fuck as hot as you. You really made me work for it, squirming and squealing into my hand. Such a good girl.

whispers But even good girls get bred.

And now you're MY good girl. You just breathe through your nose, babygirl...you came so hard, I can feel you still spasming a little around my cock. Such a good girl. Such a good girl. Shhh. Let me kiss your hair.

kissing

Mmmn. Your hair is such a sweaty mess. You're a hot mess, babygirl. Your bed is soaked under you. My hot little animal. Mmmm. This ass feels so good against my groin. Mmmn fuck. You have a really really hot cunt. *whispers* I like it.

kissing her hair and cheek

I like how you whimper into my hand.

kissing

Oh, is this little clit too sensitive? Too bad. I'm going to keep rubbing it. I like it. I like the sounds you make into my hand.

Cry into my hand, sweetie, it's all right.

That's it. Mm, good girl. It's okay to cry. You're so well-fucked and bred and so full of my cock. And I know you've never cum like that. I could tell from your animal yowls muffled under my hand. You came like an angel on fire. Mmm fuck. My good babygirl. I know it was intense, having that orgasm forced from you, wave after wave of it crashing through you. Oh, you good girl. You cry all you need to. Shhh. I've got you. I've got you.

kissing

Mmmn, this little clit is so slick and hot under my fingertips. Are you cumming again? Are you cumming while you cry, babygirl? Go ahead, do it, cum on my cock and sob into my hand and show me what a good hot little breeding bitch you are. That's my girl. Cum for me. Mmm. Feel these fingers on your hot little clit and cum, cum, cum...

Mmmn, good girl.

Good GIRL. My good girl.

MMMM.

Fuck yes. Oh fuck. You got my cock SO wet.

kissing

What a hot slut you are.

kissing

a low, delighted laugh Mmmn, don't worry, I'll go in a moment and let you cry yourself to sleep like a good girl, let you feel my cum trickle down your thigh all night. Mmm. And don't worry, I'll come back soon, sweetie. Sometimes it takes more than once to get a hot bitch like you pregnant. I need to pump you full of my semen until we're sure.

Yeah, let me kiss those hot tears from your cheek.

Mmm. Good girl. My good girl.

kissing

Shh, whimper into my hand. Mmm, you're so wet. Shh. You

stay wet for me, babygirl. You keep this tight little cunt slick and wet for my cock. Mmmn.

kissing

Good girl. I'll be back.

kissing

the scene ends

Stealing a Woman

The original cast for this erotic audio drama included voice actresses RuthieRen, FieldsOfLupine, Funfettikitten, and two zealous male raiders.

An audio performance can be found at:
https://www.reddit.com/r/gonewildaudio/comments/fazpr7/fffmm4m_stealing_a_woman_kidnapping_capture/

SCENE 1 – CAPTURING HER

We hear the gentle sounds of the ocean shore in the distance, and the sweet humming of the woman who will soon be CAPTIVE. She is cooking inside the cottage. We might hear stew bubbling, a knife chopping carrots. She sounds wistful.

The two raiders, men, are talking to the listener in hushed voices outside her window, not wanting her to hear them. They are very close to the listener. Perhaps he hears one in each ear.

RAIDER 1. *hushed* What, are you nervous?

RAIDER 2. *hushed* It's natural to be nervous. I was nervous my first time, too.

RAIDER 1. *reassuring* There's nothing to be afraid of. Just look through the window at her. She's beautiful. Humming while she cooks in her cottage by the sea. Sweet, hot little thing.

RAIDER 2. She's got lovely tits. Mmm. Just think, you'll be squeezing them in your hands tonight.

RAIDER 1. Don't worry. Every one of us had our first time stealing a woman. Your heart races. Palms go sweaty.

RAIDER 2. But then you grab her and she's hot and soft in your arms.

RAIDER 1. Throw her over your horse.

RAIDER 2. Ride back to your tent.

RAIDER 1. And enjoy her. There's nothing to it.

RAIDER 2. We'll help, you know. *blushes* Oh, I … don't mean with the enjoying. You'll do all the enjoying.

RAIDER 1. He means with the capture. A man should have his friends with him when he steals his first girl. We're here. She's going to be yours.

RAIDER 2. *sighs* She is beautiful. Chopping carrots by that fire. Listen to her. She has no idea we're here. Look how her tits move beneath her blouse when she breathes. You chose well, my friend. My first slavegirl wasn't half so lovely.

RAIDER 1. *amused* Mine was pretty. But … you've done better. She's hot. Come on, let's get her.

CAPTIVE. *a soft sigh* My father spends such long nights out on the water fishing. And it gets so cold and quiet in this cottage after dinner. I should … *blushes* … I should invite the woodcutter's son over sometime to … *flustered* What am I saying?

RAIDER 2. Oh ho, what's this? Do you hear this? Oh, she wants a man.

CAPTIVE. He does have such strong hands. And it would be … warmer, if he was with me. Here in my father's cottage. *breathing faster, aroused, her voice soft* Maybe he'd even kiss me. That would feel … warm. *whispers* So warm. Being kissed.

RAIDER 1. *whispers* She wants to be kissed.

RAIDER 2. *whispers* And touched.

RAIDER 1. Oh, look, look.

CAPTIVE. *a soft moan*

RAIDER 2. She's touching her breast.

RAIDER 1. Mmmm.

RAIDER 2. Do you think she knows she's doing it?

CAPTIVE. *moans* Oh yes, touch me. Touch me …

RAIDER 1. She knows.

CAPTIVE. Ohhh … ohhhh … your hand on my bosom is so … so delicious … and decadent … mmmmm … we shouldn't …

RAIDER 1. I bet she tosses in her bed at night until the sheets are soaked. She needs a man, the way you need a woman.

The girl moans softly during the lines that follow.

RAIDER 2. Here, you take the rope. You'll need it when you grab her.

RAIDER 1. I know you've never tied a girl, but we saw you practicing on one of your father's slavegirls.

RAIDER 2. No, it's all right.

RAIDER 1. We know you didn't touch the girl. But you made her kneel and hold out her wrists so you could practice the knots.

RAIDER 2. *amused* Your father knows, too. He doesn't mind. He's proud of you. The chieftain's son, getting ready to take his first woman.

RAIDER 1. Gods, I bet she's slick and hot between her thighs right now. *groans*

CAPTIVE. *gasps!* ... Is ... is someone out there?

RAIDER 2. Uh oh.

RAIDER 1. She heard us.

RAIDER 2. Go on. Make us proud. Up through the window! We'll follow!

CAPTIVE. Oh no. Oh no!

RAIDER 1. Go steal that woman!

CAPTIVE. *clattering, grabbing up a knife* Stay back! I'll cut you! *gasps* No! Let go of my wrist! *struggling* Let me go!

RAIDER 1. That's it, hold her.

CAPTIVE. Who … who are you men? Please! Please!!

RAIDER 2. I'll take that knife, girl.

CAPTIVE. No, no, no.

RAIDER 1. You've got her, son. Go ahead, pull her arms behind her back.

CAPTIVE. *squirming* Get off me! Let GO of me!

RAIDER 2. Yes, force her arms behind her. You can cross her wrists and hold them in one firm hand. That's it. Mmm. This is a pretty little knife she had. Flashes in the light from her fire. Silver, isn't it? To keep werewolves away? *laughs* We're not wolves, girl.

RAIDER 1. Well, not that kind of wolves.

RAIDER 2. Mmm, let me trail this knifetip along her cheek.

CAPTIVE. *frightened sob* Don't hurt me.

RAIDER 1. Wouldn't dream of it.

CAPTIVE. *frightened* That blade is so cold against my cheek. *whimpers* And you're … you're in leather riding clothes. You're … you're raiders! Raiders from the high steppes!

RAIDER 2. That we are.

RAIDER 1. This young man's our chieftain's son.

RAIDER 2. And you're his woman tonight.

CAPTIVE. No. No! *squirming*

RAIDER 1. Hold her firmly. She's a feisty wildcat!

CAPTIVE. Get OFF me! Help! HELP! FATHER! HELP ME!

RAIDER 1. Don't let her scream like that, though.

RAIDER 2. The fishermen will hear her over the water.

RAIDER 1. Here, get your hand over her mouth.

CAPTIVE. *She screams, and the scream is interrupted as the listener claps his hand firmly over her lips, muffling her cry.* Mmmphh!!!!!!! Mmmph!

RAIDER 1. That's it, keep her quiet.

RAIDER 2. Mmm, feel her squirm against your body.

RAIDER 1. Those lush curves rubbing against you. She is ALL woman. She's so worth stealing, isn't she?

CAPTIVE. Mmmmphhh! *whimpering and fighting*

RAIDER 2. Ah, feel her mouth so soft and warm and wet, open and helpless under the palm of your hand. She's squirming, but she knows she's yours now. She knows you're going to take her.

CAPTIVE: Nuh uh! Nuh uh!

RAIDER 1. Here, get a handful of her warm breast. She'll squeal for you.

CAPTIVE: MMMMNN!!!!!

RAIDER 2. Gods. That's it. Look at her sweet fearful eyes. Here, hold her still, I'll cut the laces and we'll get that blouse off her tits.

CAPTIVE. *frantic, muffled protests*

The quiet sound of the laces being cut.

RAIDER 1. Oh gods.

RAIDER 2. Beautiful.

RAIDER 1. Such full tits.

RAIDER 2. You really have good taste. I'm glad you picked her. Here, I'll hold her arms for you.

RAIDER 1. Lift your hand from her lips a moment. I'll cover her mouth for you.

CAPTIVE. *protesting a moment as one hand is lifted from her lips* Father, help! Help m – mmmphhh! *another hand clapped over her mouth*

RAIDER 1. There.

RAIDER 2. Now tie her quick so you have your hands free to get a good feel.

RAIDER 1. WE won't feel her. She's all yours.

RAIDER 2. Your slavegirl.

CAPTIVE. *sobs and then screams several times, muffled, and squirms*

RAIDER 1. There you go. Right around her wrists.

RAIDER 2. It feels good binding a girl, doesn't it? Knowing she can't slap or scratch or do anything but squirm and wiggle and make her tits bounce.

CAPTIVE. *sobbing softly, with muffled, breathless protests*

RAIDER 1. There you go. All tied up and helpless.

RAIDER 2. Her tits naked and aching for your touch.

CAPTIVE. *begging, muffled*

RAIDER 1. There's nothing to be afraid of. You heard her craving a man's touch.

RAIDER 2. She needs you, just as you need her. She might not know it yet. But go ahead, you can touch her. You can touch her soft tits.

CAPTIVE. Nuhh uh! Nuh uhh!

RAIDER 1. You're stealing her.

RAIDER 2. She's YOUR pleasure-slave. That's it, son, take her tits in your hands.

CAPTIVE. Mmmmphh!!!!!!

RAIDER 1. Gods, just FEEL her tits.

RAIDER 2. How she bounces and squirms when you do that. Mmm. Feel her in your hands, her soft warm flesh.

RAIDER 1. She's so young.

RAIDER 2. So good.

RAIDER 1. *his voice warm and encouraging* She's going to be so tight around your cock tonight.

CAPTIVE. *squeals at those words*

RAIDER 1. Squeeze her.

CAPTIVE. *moaning helplessly*

RAIDER 1. Just milk those soft, full tits in your hands.

CAPTIVE. *moaning*

RAIDER 2. She's yours. You own her.

RAIDER 1. Once you put the collar on her anyway.

CAPTIVE. Mmmph?!!!!

RAIDER 1. You have the collar, don't you?

RAIDER 2. Don't make him nervous. It's right on his belt. Go ahead, put it on her. Claim her. No man in the camp will touch your girl when they see your collar on her neck.

RAIDER 1. She has such a sweet neck.

RAIDER 2. Here, I'll pull back her hair. Kiss her neck. Get

her ready for your collar. Go ahead, kiss her soft skin.

CAPTIVE. *whimpers a few moments at the kisses on her neck*

RAIDER 1. Oh, how she quivers. She likes your mouth on her. Lick her neck with your tongue.

CAPTIVE. *a startled, frightened, helpless moan into her captor's hand*

RAIDER 2. Just breathe in her scent. Mmm, doesn't she smell good?

CAPTIVE. *whimpers*

RAIDER 1. She's yours. You can enjoy her as you please.

CAPTIVE. *muffled pleading*

RAIDER 2. Each day after a long ride, miles and miles over the steppes, when you're tired and sore, she can kneel naked by your fire and suck your cock.

CAPTIVE. *a muffled squeal, terrified and excited at the thought*

RAIDER 1. You chose her.

RAIDER 2. Go on, put the collar on her.

RAIDER 1. Make her your collared slavegirl. That band of soft leather, with your mark on it. It'll fit so snug around her throat.

RAIDER 2. She'll feel it every morning when she wakes on the furs by your feet. And she'll know who she belongs to.

CAPTIVE. *tearful pleading*

RAIDER 1. That's it. Right around her throat.

CAPTIVE. Mmmphh mmmphhhh

RAIDER 2. She's yours.

RAIDER 1. All yours.

RAIDER 2. Go ahead, lock it shut. Lock it on her.

CAPTIVE. Nuh uhh! Nuh uh! NUH UH!!

The sound of the lock clicking shut

CAPTIVE. *a muffled wail as she hears that sound and feels the collar snug around her throat*

RAIDER 1. That's it. Ah, her tears are so pretty on her cheeks.

RAIDER 2. Don't worry. They all cry at first. It's probably scary when a man first takes them.

CAPTIVE. *muffled begging*

RAIDER 2. But once you've had her a few nights, and fed her morsels of venison on your fingertips, and she's slept naked and tied in your arms, she'll know she's yours.

RAIDER 1. She knows it now. She's just frightened.

RAIDER 2. Be gentle with her tonight. It can hurt a little for her at first.

CAPTIVE. *sobbing*

RAIDER 1. Come on, let's get her to your horse and ride back. Before any of the boats return.

RAIDER 2. We're going to bring the horses around to the door. You hold her a moment until we get back, all right?

RAIDER 1. I'll take my hand from her mouth. You keep her silent, though.

CAPTIVE. Mmmphh mm – Please, I won't scream, I won't scream. Don't cover my mouth. *sobs*

RAIDER 2. We'll be right back.

The sound of the door, and their receding footsteps.

RAIDER 2. *his voice faint, receding, outside* He found a really luscious one.

RAIDER 1. *his voice also faint, outside* Did you SEE her tits?

CAPTIVE. *pleading softly* Please, please, you don't want to take me away from here, away from my father. Please. No, don't grip my breasts, please. Oh, oh. Your hands are so strong. *whimpers* So strong on my breasts. Please, you have to let me go. Please be merciful! Please? Please? *she gasps, then moans* Ah! No! Please, my nipples are so sensitive, don't … *moans* … don't pinch them between your fingers like that, please!! *struggling* Oh, why have you tied me? And … and collared me? *sobs* Please let me go! No, no, don't pull at my nipples! *she squeals, then is panting with arousal and fright* Oh, this can't be happening. Ah! You've … you've taken hold of my chin. *breathless* And your eyes are so very deep. … You are unnervingly handsome for a barbarian who has my blouse cut open and has me tied … and panting in your arms. *whispers* The way you're looking at me. Are … are you going to … mmmmmm mmmmm mmnnnnn *she moans and whimpers, muffled, against his mouth, as he takes a long, sensual kiss … afterward, she's gasping* … You … you kissed me! You took a kiss from me! mmmphhh mmmm *he kisses her again, and she whimpers into his mouth, then moans passionately as he fondles her* … oh, you're kissing me … and fondling me … *whimpers* Your mouth is so warm on mine … your hands … *speaks in a desperate whisper* … please, before the other men come back … please hear me … I don't want to go. I don't want to go to your tent out in the wilderness. I want to stay here, in my father's house. Please. *He kisses her again, and she protests weakly into the kiss* Mmmmn, mmmmn. *gasps as the kiss ends* Please? *her voice pleading, so innocent and gentle* … Please don't take me?

The door creaks open, and we hear the whicker of horses

Oh no, they're back! Please, no, no, don't pull me through the door, no, no, no! Father! Father! Help! Hel-mmmmmphhh! mmmphhh!!!!

her muffled squeals into his hand as she's dragged to his horse, a muffled sobbing cry of frustration and fright

RAIDER 1. Here. Use this cloth to bind her mouth.

RAIDER 2. She might work it out from between her teeth in a bit, but it'll keep her quiet til we're away.

CAPTIVE. Mmmphh Please, plea-mmmmphh mmmphhh *gagged again*

RAIDER 1. All right, here, up you go, son.

The horse whickers. We hear the listener mount up.

RAIDER 2. We'll lift her up to you. So you can hold her across your saddle as we ride, your freshly captured woman.

The sounds of the captive being thrown across his saddle.

CAPTIVE. *muffled "oooomph!" as she's put there.*

Suddenly, a wolf howls, cold and feral in the distance.

CAPTIVE. *a muffled cry of fright*

RAIDER 2. The werewolves are out.

RAIDER 1. Girl, you're lucky our friend has you, and they don't.

Another wolf howl

CAPTIVE. *sobbing softly, muffled*

RAIDER 2. Aw, she's so frightened. *gently, advising the young man* Here, look, you can take the reins in one hand and, with your other hand, stroke her hair softly, caress her cheek, while we ride. It'll comfort her.

CAPTIVE. *whimpers and sniffles*

RAIDER 2. That's it.

RAIDER 1. I bet her hair's very soft.

CAPTIVE. *soft little mewling*

RAIDER 2. It's all right, lovely woman. You're being stolen at night by a chieftain's son. He's a good young man. He'll treat you so well.

CAPTIVE. *whimpers*

RAIDER 1. He'll give you strong babies.

CAPTIVE. *a squeal of horror*

RAIDER 2. Mount up.

We hear the other raiders mount.

RAIDER 1. Let's ride!

Hoofbeats. And the captive's soft, helpless whimpers at the jostling of the horse and at her captor's gentle touch on her cheek. And wolf howls in the distance.

The scene ends.

SCENE 2 – PREPARING HER

We hear the faint sounds of the camp. The hoofbeats slow and stop, and we hear everyone dismount. The woman's soft little muffled whimpers.

SLAVEGIRL JULES. Oh! What have you men brought us?

RAIDER 1. The chieftain's son has stolen his first woman.

SLAVEGIRL LUPINE. *admiring* Ah! She's so lovely!

CAPTIVE. *begging faintly for help, muffled*

RAIDER 2. Girls, take her into the slaves' tent, get her ready. She has a mighty young warrior to please tonight.

CAPTIVE. *squeals*

RAIDER 2. And she better please him well!

CAPTIVE. *sobs*

SLAVEGIRL LUPINE. Hush, darling.

SLAVEGIRL JULES. It'll be all right. Here, come with us.

SLAVEGIRL LUPINE. Don't be afraid. We've got you.

SLAVEGIRL JULES. We'll get you ready for him.

SLAVEGIRL LUPINE. Come inside the tent, darling.

CAPTIVE. Mmmmmphh! Mmmph!

Their footsteps, and the sound of a tent flap drawn aside and then falling back, silencing her whimpers as they retreat within.

RAIDER 1. I'll take care of the horses and be right back.

RAIDER 2. Sounds good.

footsteps

RAIDER 2. *softly* Wait, my friend. Where are you going? To your tent to get ready? Wait a moment. Don't you want to … see her first? While they prepare her? *amused* You can. There's a little rent in the fabric, in the back of the slavegirls' tent. They don't know about it, but we do. Come on, I'll show you.

footsteps

RAIDER 2. *whispers* See, a rent in the fabric. Look through it. Go on. But you better be so quiet. As you discovered at the fisherman's cottage, slavegirls have good hearing. There, do you see them, by the light of that red oil lamp? Our two women, naked and hot, and your tearful captive, in just her skirt, with them on the furs?

CAPTIVE. *soft whimpers*

SLAVEGIRL LUPINE. Here, darling, let's get that gag out of your mouth.

CAPTIVE. Mmmphh mmphhh *draws in a breath and releases it with a sob* I want to go home. I want my father. *whimpers*

SLAVEGIRL JULES. I know.

CAPTIVE. I'm scared.

SLAVEGIRL JULES. I was scared my first night too. I'm Jules.

SLAVERGIRL LUPINE. I'm Lupine.

CAPTIVE (RUTHIE). *sniffles* I … I'm Ruth.

JULES. Beautiful, sweet Ruthie. Do you understand what's happening?

LUPINE. Oh, look at you shake your head. You sweet, shy girl. Don't worry. You won't be alone.

JULES. We'll be your sisters.

RUTHIE. *trying to think clearly* You're both naked, and … you have collars. You're … you're captives. Like me.

LUPINE. Oh, darling. We haven't been captives in a very long time.

JULES. We're slavegirls.

LUPINE. *softly* Yes, we are.

JULES. We sleep in the furs with our men and give them pleasure.

LUPINE. And the comfort of our bodies after a hard day's ride.

JULES. They've been very kind to us. My Master kisses me awake each morning. And he sings to me and tells me I'm beautiful.

LUPINE. Mine holds me and caresses my hair if I have nightmares. And … and look … my belly has begun to swell.

RUTHIE. *gasps*

JULES. Yours will, too. And mine. *wistful* I hope. *sighs softly* Come on, dear Ruthie. Let's get you naked.

RUTHIE. *gasps* No! No!

LUPINE. Shh, it's all right. It's all right. Poor girl. Here, press your cheek to my breast. Mmm, like that. I'll hold you and stroke your hair. You have such silky hair. Shhh, it's going to be all right.

RUTHIE. *crying* I just want to go home.

JULES. *gently* That's not going to happen, sister.

LUPINE. A man of the steppes has stolen you away and collared you.

JULES. He would kill a hundred men before he'd ever give you up.

LUPINE. He chose you. He wanted YOU.

RUTHIE. *whimpers* What am I going to do?

JULES. He'll want you soon.

LUPINE. We have to get you ready.

RUTHIE. *squeaks* Ready?

JULES. You'll need to be perfumed.

LUPINE. And oiled.

RUTHIE. Can … can you untie my hands?

JULES. I … I'm sorry.

LUPINE. I don't think we should. The men might not like it.

JULES. We're not supposed to untie each other.

LUPINE. He'll want you brought to his tent bound.

RUTHIE. *tearful* To his … his bed?

LUPINE. Oh, they don't have beds here, darling.

JULES. You couldn't carry a bed on a horse.

LUPINE. You'll be laid down naked and soft …

JULES. … and tied …

LUPINE. … on his sleeping furs.

JULES. And now we're going to help get you ready, so you'll please him, and … so it won't hurt much.

RUTHIE. *whimpers*

JULES. Shh, just feel my fingers so gentle at your waist. Will you lift your hips, beautiful Ruthie? I'll shimmy this skirt off you.

LUPINE. Good girl.

rustling of her skirt being tugged down

JULES. There you go. You're so brave, sister. So brave and so good.

LUPINE. Just keep resting your cheek against my breast and breathe, beautiful girl. We've got you.

JULES. I'll just unfasten these undergarments … *rustling* There.

RUTHIE. *trembling* I'm naked.

LUPINE. *gently* So are we, darling. Except for these collars on our throats.

RUTHIE. It's so snug on mine.

LUPINE. *gently* You belong to a man, now.

JULES. Open your thighs, sweetie. Just a little. Ahh. Oh, wow. Lupine, look.

LUPINE. Oh. You're … beautiful.

JULES. That little tuft of red hair. Like soft flame between your thighs.

LUPINE. *so softly* He's going to really like that. Get the oils, sister.

JULES. Mmm. Here. Do you see this flask? It's full of warm, scented oil. I need to rub it into your skin so that you are soft and yielding …

LUPINE. And relaxed.

JULES. And glistening.

LUPINE. And ready for your Master.

RUTHIE. Will it hurt?

LUPINE. Not at all, darling.

JULES. Here, spread your legs more. Shhh, we're going to help. I promise.

LUPINE. Here, I've got you. Tilt your head back a little. Feel my lips soft against your cheek. *kissing* Your temple. Mmmmm. Good girl. I'm going to kiss under your jaw while Jules oils your legs and feet.

sound effect: the shlick of oily hands on Ruthie's body, and Lupine's gentle kisses on her neck, so gentle and warm and good

RUTHIE. *soft, soft little moans*

Distant in the night, the howling of a werewolf.

RUTHIE. *gasps* Oh no, oh no.

LUPINE. Shhh, it's all right. You're safe.

JULES. The werewolves do love to hunt and breed young women, but …

LUPINE. … this camp is full of strong men. No werewolf would dare.

JULES. You're safe, Ruthie. You're … so … safe.

RUTHIE. *tearful* Oh, oh.

JULES. *her voice sweet and reassuring* Sister.

LUPINE. We've got you. Just rest your tied hands against my thigh. Mmm, right there. And lie back against my body. I've got you. I'll hold you. I won't let you go.

JULES. We'll get you so ready.

RUTHIE. *breathy* Why are you being so good to me?

JULES. Because you're our sister.

LUPINE. You don't ever have to be alone, darling. Now, close your eyes. You have such beautiful eyes. But you need to just relax … feel Jules's hands rubbing the oil, warm and slick, into your legs … your thighs.

RUTHIE. *moans*

JULES. I'll help soothe away the fear, beautiful Ruthie.

LUPINE. Yes. You are beautiful … and good … and brave … just breathe. Jules, give me some of the oil. Here, pour it into my cupped hands.

JULES. Here you go, sister.

LUPINE. Mmm, I'm going to rub it into your shoulders, your arms. Mmmm.

RUTHIE. *soft little noises*

LUPINE. That's a good girl.

JULES. Such a good girl. Your legs glisten so. Your oiled body just glows in the red light of our lamp. If only your Master could see you like this, right now.

RAIDER 2. *whispers in the listener's ear* Little do they know. *a quiet, aroused sigh* See how beautiful our women are?

We hear quiet footsteps, and then Raider 1 crouches beside the other man and the listener.

RAIDER 1. *whispers* What did I miss?

RAIDER 2. Shhh.

RUTHIE. *softly* What's going to happen to me?

LUPINE. You're going to be kissed and loved.

JULES. *trying to speak gently, but a little excited* And we're going to help you get really, really wet. It will hurt less if we get you soaked.

RUTHIE. Your touch on my body. I've ... I've never felt ... *gasps, then moans* ... OH my gods, your hands on my breasts!

LUPINE. Shhh. Just breathe, darling. Keep your eyes closed.

JULES. Just ... feel.

LUPINE. *her voice soft and reassuring* Mmm, lovely girl, so lovely. Men can be rough on our breasts, but my hands are soft ... and firm ... and warm with oil. Just the way you need. Feel me caress ... and squeeze ... your soft, soft tits. My darling.

RUTHIE. *moaning* Oh, what are you doing to me?

JULES. Mmm, you're starting to moisten, sister. I can smell your pleasure oils. You have ... the most beautiful, delicate flower. Its petals are opening a little.

RUTHIE. *whispers, blushing* Oh, don't look at me.

JULES. Shh, sister. Shh. I'll just kiss the insides of your thighs. *Kissing*

RUTHIE. Mmmmn! *she starts breathing quite a bit faster*

LUPINE. Mmmn, look at these lovely nipples, swelling at my touch.

RUTHIE. *a long moan*

JULES. Ohhhh … when I press my fingertip here … *whispers* … right here …

RUTHIE. *a wild, moaning, startled cry*

JULES. … she IS wet. So wet. I … I want to taste her. May I, sister?

LUPINE. You may. But lick her very gently. I don't think she's ever done this before.

RUTHIE. What … what are you … I don't under-OHHH!!! *squeals in shocked, alarmed pleasure*

JULES. *sweet licking sounds*

LUPINE. Spread your legs more for her, darling.

RUTHIE. *helpless, soft moans*

JULES. *licking, then she moans, too* Oh, sister, the hair by your blossom is so soft against my cheek. Your petals are so sofffft against my lips. *licking* I love the way you taste.

RUTHIE. *panting* Oh my gods.

LUPINE. Here, I'll lay you back on these furs.

RUTHIE. *sudden fright* Don't leave me!

LUPINE. *warm as sunlight* Oh, I won't EVER! My darling, I'm not going to leave you. I'm going to lay down with you, my breasts … mmmmnnn … soft against yours …

RUTHIE. Ahh-ahh!!!

LUPINE. Your breasts so soft beneath my fingers. Mmmn. *gently* My hair falls about our faces like a veil. And I'm going to kiss you. *so, so softly* Like this.

The two women kiss, and it is long and sensual and takes their breath away, and they moan, muffled, into each other's mouths, while Jules licks at Ruthie's flower and makes the sweetest sounds of enjoyment as she does.

From here through the end of the scene, Slavegirls Lupine and Jules sound more and more aroused and breathless. (They have begun touching themselves while they touch Ruthie, as they reveal soon.)

JULES. I'm going to take hold of your hip, beautiful sister. While my lips tease your sweet little clit out of its hood. *kissing her sweet blossom*

RUTHIE. *helpless moaning, overwhelmed by these sensations of wild pleasure*

LUPINE. You're tied, darling. Tied … and licked. All you get to do right now is breathe … and enjoy … and be enjoyed. You're safe. It's all right. You can let go.

JULES. *exhales softly* I'll breathe gently across your clit. Isn't my breath soft and warm? *she exhales again, slowly, teasingly*

RUTHIE. *panting* Sister! Sister!

JULES. Mmmmm. Sister. *giggles* I'm going to lick your clit now. *licking*

RUTHIE. *coming undone, gasp after gasp, a series of short, rising moans until she cries out breathlessly:* I never knew! I never knew!

LUPINE. Mmm, and I'm going to kiss this warm, swollen nipple. *kissing* … And lick. *licking* … And suckle. *suckling* Mmmmmmmmn. *suckling* … And nibble. *she bites*

RUTHIE. *squeals*

LUPINE. … While I tease your other nipple with my nails. Mmmn.

JULES. Your thighs quiver! *sucking softly* Are you going to cum for us, beautiful Ruthie? *sucking … her voice is full of pleasure and yearning* I want you to cum. I want you to gush wet and warm against my lips. I want your warm honey dripping down my chin. I'll tease your thigh with my fingertips. While I lick at your sweet … *licking* … mmmm … nectar …

RUTHIE. *beside herself with pleasure, panting this word softly:* Sister, sister, sister …

LUPINE. *moans* We're going to cum with you, darling. *quivers* Look where my other hand is. *moans* I have my fingers between my soft thighs. *whispers* I'm touching myself for you, darling.

Ruthie is moaning as they enjoy her

JULES. *moans* I am, too. *moans* You're exciting, sister! *sucking warmly at her, and moaning as she does*

LUPINE. You excite us! Please cum for us, Ruthie. Feel my mouth hot on your breasts. *suckling and moaning as she does*

JULES. Please cum, please cum, sister! Please cum on my face, sister!

LUPINE. Please!

JULES. Please!

RUTHIE. So … so hot! So hot! What is happening to me? What is HAPPENING to me?

LUPINE. *quivery* Just breathe and let it happen.

JULES. *suckling* Mmmmm. You look so beautiful, arching your back. Yes, lift your hips! *suckling* Mmmn. mmmn. Rub your soft blossom into my mouth. Oh yes, Ruthie, oh yes. *moans* Please cum for me, sister, please. *suckling*

LUPINE. Surrender for us, darling.

JULES. You are so good and so brave and we love you! *suckling*

LUPINE. We love you, sister.

RUTHIE. *whimpers* Kiss me.

LUPINE. *moans* With all my heart.

Lupine kisses her, and we hear her moans and Ruthie's muffled cries, and Jules's sweet suckling and muffled moans.

JULES. Cum! Cum! *vigorous cunnilingus*

RUTHIE. Oh, I … I … I!!!!!!!!!!!!!!

Ruthie squeals in orgasm!

Lupine and Jules cum a moment after Ruthie starts to. Their sweet cries fill the tent.

Soft little afterglow sounds from all of them.

JULES. *breathless* Oh wow. *quivers* Oh wow. *so tender* I love how you taste, Ruthie sister.

RUTHIE. *sobbing softly, overwhelmed*

LUPINE. *so gently* It's all right. It's all right. We've got you. Beautiful girl. *giggles* Beautiful, sweaty, oiled girl.

JULES. You are so good, sister.

LUPINE. So good.

RUTHIE. *whispers* Oh my gods. Oh my gods.

RAIDER 2. *quietly, reverently* Wow.

RAIDER 1. *Whispers* Come on. We better go.

We hear the footsteps of the men, and the soft sounds of the three women recede and then are silent as the men leave.

RAIDER 1. *hushed* She came screaming. With your bonds on her wrists. Your collar on her throat.

RAIDER 2. She's going to be very hot for you tonight.

RAIDER 1. A hot, soaked slavegirl. Dripping for you.

RAIDER 2. They'll bring her to you soon.

A werewolf howls in the distance.

RAIDER 1. Cursed wolves. It's that full moon in the sky tonight.

RAIDER 2. *cheerful* You'll keep her safe from wolves.

their footsteps stop

RAIDER 2. Here we are. Your tent, my friend. We'll leave you here.

RAIDER 1. This part, you do yourself.

RAIDER 2. You get to enjoy your woman.

RAIDER 1. Gods, you chose a luscious woman! *pleased* Aren't you glad you stole her from her father's cottage tonight?

RAIDER 2. *claps the listener on his shoulder with his hand* We are so proud of you.

RAIDER 1. She's going to open for your cock, and you are going to have SUCH a hot night.

RAIDER 2. *gentle, reassuring* Don't be nervous. She'll be brought here sleek and naked with her hands tied. Perfumed and ready to be fucked. And she'll feel YOUR collar on her neck and her love oils dripping down her thighs. Her whole body flushed and hot. And she'll BELONG to you.

RAIDER 1. Just … enjoy her.

RAIDER 2. And if you're nervous at all, just remember how she whimpered sweetly into your hand when you covered her mouth.

RAIDER 1. Remember the soft swell of her tits in your hands.

RAIDER 2. And remember how she squealed when she came, a few moments ago.

RAIDER 1. Go on. Wait for her in your tent. You can tell us about her in the morning.

RAIDER 2. You make us so proud. You are a warrior of our people, and you will conquer her tonight. Your first woman.

RAIDER 1. She's going to be so good for you.

RAIDER 2. And she'll be yours.

RAIDER 1. Go in and wait for her.

The sound of a tent flap drawn aside, and falling back after the listener enters. The footsteps of the other two men receding.

The scene ends.

SCENE 3 – ENJOYING HER

The sounds of a flickering oil lamp. The tent flap is drawn aside and the three women enter. We hear their soft breathing. Ruthie sounds frightened. They all sound aroused. Slavegirls Lupine and Jules bring the new capture into the tent, tied, between them.

SLAVEGIRL LUPINE. Hello, Master. We've brought your woman.

SLAVEGIRL JULES. We've aroused her.

LUPINE. She's flushed and hot.

JULES. Her body is perfumed and ready for you.

LUPINE. She's dripping down her thighs, Master.

RUTHIE. *a tearful, whisper* I'm so scared. *whispers* But so wet.

LUPINE. *shyly, submissively* Master, may … may we stay? We told her we wouldn't leave her.

JULES. *hopeful* May we stay with her, Master?

LUPINE. While you enjoy her?

JULES. She's our sister.

LUPINE. Our own Masters won't mind if we stay with her tonight. They are so proud of you and they want you to have the most wonderful night with your woman.

JULES. We'll help! Please, may we stay?

LUPINE. *responding to his reply* Thank you, Master! You are kind.

RUTHIE. *tearful, grateful* Thank you. Oh thank you! My sisters.

LUPINE. Your slavegirl is very lovely. See, her skin glows with warmth in the red light of your lamp, Master. Her wrists are tied behind her body, her breasts and thighs are slick with oil, and her nipples are swollen.

JULES. Her tits lift and fall with her little gasps of excitement. And there, between her thighs, such sweet red hair, so gentle to touch, and her virgin blossom is so … soffft. Do you want to touch her? Do you want to conquer her tonight, Master?

RUTHIE. *trembling and frightened, but also still very aroused* Is …
is that what's going to happen to me?

In the distance, several werewolves howl.

RUTHIE. *trembling* Am I going to be ravished on your furs,
here in your barbaric tent, far from my father's cottage, far
from any help, while hunting wolves howl to the full moon
outside? *whispers* Are you going to deflower me tonight? Is
that what's going to happen? I've never felt so … helpless.
So feminine. So frightened. *gasps* You've grabbed my arms!
Pulling me up against your hard chest. *breathless* The way you
look at me. *whispers* So hungry. *softly* Please, will you … will
you spare me? *sniffles*

LUPINE. *a tone of caring but mild rebuke* Sister!

JULES. *gently* He needs you tonight, sister. You're the first
girl he's stolen.

RUTHIE. I don't understand.

LUPINE. Look at his face. He hungers for your body, yes
…

JULES. … but look. Oh, look. He's so … nervous.

LUPINE. He's our chieftain's son.

JULES. He's never conquered a woman before. You're …
gently … his first.

RUTHIE. *gasps* I'm … his … ?

LUPINE. *gently but firmly* Kiss him, slavegirl. He's
frightened. Comfort him.

RUTHIE. *quivering* I hardly know what to think … I …

JULES. Kiss him.

Ruthie presses her mouth to his, a shy kiss that becomes warm and sensual. She begins to moan softly into his mouth.

RUTHIE. *whispers* I'm sorry. I … I didn't even think. *in wonder* Are … are YOU scared, too? *so shy* I … I'm a virgin too. I've never been stolen by a man before. And … tonight, in my cottage, when you pressed your mouth to mine, that … that was my first kiss. *quivers* Yours are the first hands I've ever felt on these breasts. *whispers* Why did you take me? Why did you choose me? *she listens for a moment, then whispers* You just WANTED me? *breathing soft and quivery* You … you're going to kiss me again, aren't you?

JULES. Call him Master.

RUTHIE. *trembling* Are you going to kiss me, Master?

he does, and we hear her whimpering sweetly into the kiss

LUPINE. You don't have to be shy. She is yours.

JULES. Take her mouth, Master. Kiss her until she's trembling in your arms.

The kiss gets fiercer. We hear Ruthie's muffled, frightened, excited whimper into his mouth.

RUTHIE. *moans, then the kiss ends* I can hardly breathe. The way you kiss me. Oh, … your hands. Your hands on me. Mmmmn. In the slave tent, my sisters said my breasts are full and lush and pleasing. Are … are my breasts pleasing?

kissing

JULES. Do her breasts feel good in your hands, Master?

LUPINE. *happy* You get to enjoy her all night.

The kiss ends, and we hear Ruthie's quivery, excited, nervous breathing

RUTHIE. *softly* Yes. I know you want me. You fastened this collar so snug around my neck. I feel it each time I swallow. *she swallows* I feel its firm leather holding me. … *quivers* … Locked on me.

LUPINE. *so softly* We'll undress you, Master, while you touch her.

JULES. Feel our small, soft hands on your body, Master.

the rustling of his clothes, and Ruthie's soft sounds of rising desire

RUTHIE. *whispers* You're naked. *gasps* No, no, it's all right. *reverently* You're … you're beautiful. I … I never knew a man's body would be so beautiful.

LUPINE. Press yourself to him, sister.

JULES. To his cock.

RUTHIE. *moans, and her voice gets tender* I … I'll be gentle with you, too. *gently* Master. *soft, sweet kisses* Do my lips feel good on your neck? *kissing his neck a few moments … then she whispers* Your lips felt SO good on mine. In the cottage. I was scared, but … *whispers* … you made me wet.

LUPINE. Feel her body, Master. She's oiled and slick …

JULES. … and so warm.

RUTHIE. *a soft moan* Oh, your hands on my ass. Pull me more firmly against you. Mmmn. I can feel you and … *whimpers* you are SO hard. You've tied me. I'm helpless in the arms of a naked warrior. *moans* I'm squirming a little. Rubbing my breasts across your chest, my soft, warm mound against your cock. I can't help it. Your touch burns me, warrior. *breathes* … Master.

Soft moans from Ruthie throughout the lines that follow

JULES. Look at her eyes shining for you. We prepared her for you.

LUPINE. She's yours, Master.

JULES. She wants to be taken.

LUPINE. She wants you to conquer her.

JULES. *ever so softly* We'll help. We'll lick … *licking* … and kiss your neck … *kissing* …

LUPINE … and your powerful shoulders, Master … *licking and kissing*

JULES. *licking and kissing* I'll caress your balls, Master.

LUPINE. I'll tease your thighs with my nails. *moans* Be so hard for her, Master. She's never been under a man's body before. You'll be like a god to her. *kissing*

JULES. *kissing* You were so brave, stealing her.

RUTHIE. *whispers* You were. You were so bold. Coming through my window, seizing what you wanted. Covering my mouth. Taking me away while I squirmed. *whimpers* Your cock is so thick against my soft mound. Master … *so softly* will … will you hurt me tonight? Will I bleed?

For an answer, he kisses her again

RUTHIE. *moans* Yes, my thighs part for you. Letting your hand explore me. *moans*

LUPINE. *quivers, at his ear* She's so wet on your fingers, Master. She'll soak your hand if you're gentle with her.

RUTHIE. *moaning* Please be gentle, Master. *moans* Oh, your fingers, your fingertips at my … my clit … my .. .ahhh … ahhh …

We hear Lupine and Jules kissing his neck and shoulders and moaning very softly while Ruthie gasps and squirms, feeling so very hot.

LUPINE. Lay her down on the furs, Master.

Rustling, and soft gasps from Ruthie as her Master lays her down, naked and helpless, on the furs and lowers his body onto her.

RUTHIE. *gaspy little breaths* You're on top of me! I'm pinned under you on your soft furs. So helpless. I can't believe this is happening. *panting* I'm captive in a barbarian's tent, and you're going to ravish me!

Ruthie moans helplessly, squirming sweetly during the lines that follow

JULES. We'll lie down to either side and snuggle close, naked and warm, while you're on top of her.

LUPINE. *her voice soft, in one ear* We'll kiss your neck. *kissing*

JULES. *her voice soft, in his other ear* Grip and squeeze your ass while you have her. *moans*

LUPINE. *pleads* Oh, have her, Master. Have her.

JULES. Have our sister!

LUPINE. Open her, Master.

JULES. Open her thighs, Master.

RUTHIE. *moans*

LUPINE. She's so wet.

JULES. Our virgin sister is so wet for you.

LUPINE. *whispers in his ear* Touch her.

JULES. *whispers in his other ear* Take her.

LUPINE. *whispers* Own her.

JULES. *whispers* She's yours.

RUTHIE. *gasping* Oh no. Oh no. Please. Wait. You … you're so big. I'm … I'm scared.

LUPINE. Shhh. So is he, darling.

JULES. Come here, sister. I'll cup your cheek, and … *whispers* … everything's going to be all right. I promise.

Jules kisses her, and Ruthie and Jules moan softly into each other's mouths, two slavegirls on fire. While Lupine breathes softly, aroused.

RUTHIE. *breathless after the kiss, and moaning softly with arousal* Oh, Master, your cock is right there. The tip of your cock at my soft blossom. I feel so small and wet. *whimpers* I know one thrust would open me. *whispers* And you're so powerful. You don't know it yet, you're as nervous as I am … but you are SO powerful. You've brought me here. You have me tied up, my legs forced open around your hips, and I'm sweaty and oiled and dripping. *aroused* And you're going to have your way with me. *breathing faster … she says so softly* Conquer me. Ravish me. Make me your slavegirl.

She cries out as he penetrates her

Lupine and Jules moan in arousal

Wet sounds as he takes her

RUTHIE. *gasping for air* You … you moaned my name! My name! When you thrust in me! How did you … *she cries out again, breathlessly, as he thrusts a second time* Master! *panting* You're so … thick! You're inside me! *gaspy* You're inside me! I have a man's cock in me. *whimpers* Oh … I'm so full of your cock. *whispers* I'm so tight! *reassuring, aroused, pleading* You don't have to be nervous, you don't have to be. You're so good in me. It hurt for just a moment, only a little, and you feel so good in me. I'm tied, and soft, and hot. *pleading* Do what you want with me. *whispers* You can do what you want with me. … Master. *a thrust makes her scream* Master! *another* Master! *another* Master!

LUPINE. Oh, you're so good to her. *kissing his neck*

JULES. Make her scream, Master, make our sister scream. *kissing his neck*

LUPINE. *moans* You can just grab her hips and pump yourself into her sweet young body. We'll hold her breasts and lift them for you.

JULES. We'll each cup one of our sister's breasts, Master, in our soft hands.

RUTHIE. *moaning*

JULES. Kiss her tits, Master.

LUPINE. Her breasts are for your pleasure, and to feed the babies you'll put in her. Suckle her, Master.

RUTHIE. *squeals*

JULES. She's arching her back for you, Master!

RUTHIE. Oh, Master! Oh, Master! How you thrust in me!

LUPINE. *moans* Oh Master, feel her lift her hips into you. She needs more.

JULES. Thrust in her, Master. She wants you. Even as you want her.

RUTHIE. *sobbing moans* I do. Gods help me, I do! You powerful, ... *breathless* BIG ... beautiful virgin warrior! Oh take me! You've conquered me! You're inside me! I'm yours! Let my tight young body please you! Please! Please! They were right! You are like a god to me! You're my god! Ravage me! Please ravage me!!! *squeals*

LUPINE. *gasps* You bit her!

JULES. You bit our sister!

LUPINE. You bit her tit!

RUTHIE. *panting wildly; Ruthie moans through the lines that follow*

LUPINE. How you roll and surge inside her.

JULES. I can feel the muscles in your ass clenching, Master.

LUPINE. You must be so full of cum.

JULES. You must need to spill it in her so badly.

LUPINE. *quivering* We'll rub ourselves on you, Master, while you thrust in her.

JULES. Our men said we could. They want you to be so happy tonight. They're so proud of you, Master.

LUPINE. We're so proud of you. Look at our sister's face, so flushed. Strands of her fiery hair stuck sweaty to her cheek. Look at the pleasure you're giving her!

JULES. She's going wild beneath you, Master.

LUPINE. She's yours. Your woman, wild and wet! Own her.

Jules and Lupine rub themselves against him and moan softly throughout the lines that follow

RUTHIE. Take me, Master! Take me! Oh, you beautiful man! Your beautiful, beautiful cock! Oh, it fills me! *moaning* I never knew it would be like this. I never. I never. Master, Master, bite me again, please, please, please, I'm on fire.

squeals Your teeth in my shoulder! Yes yes yes YES! Master, Master, cover my mouth, please please please, I need something to bite, and I'm tied and I can't reach YOUR shoulder! Please put your hand over my mouth, let me bite your palm! I'm clenching down so tight on your cock and I'm so wild with heat, if I can't bite or scratch, I'll die, Master! Please! Mmmphh! MMMPHHH! *she bites, then squeals into his palm … gasping wildly through her nose and grunting like an animal as he ravages her, and on throughout the lines that follow*

LUPINE. *whimpers* Master, we're so wet.

JULES. We're so wet!

LUPINE. *moans* May we touch ourselves while you ravish her, Master?

JULES. Please, Master, please? May we slide our delicate fingers between our thighs?

LUPINE. And into our soft heat? Please, Master?

JULES. Please, Master!

LUPINE. Please!

LUPINE and JULES. Yes! Oh yes, yes, yes … *moaning helplessly, so, so aroused*

LUPINE. Make her cum, Master! Make her cum!

JULES. Make us cum!

Their moans rising

LUPINE. Your groans are so hot, Master! You're going to cum in her. You're going to cum in her!

JULES. Fill our sister!

RUTHIE. Mmmphh MMPH! *Ruthie bites his hand again, and his hand lifts. She's panting and desperate.* I'm spasming around your cock! I'm cumming! I'm cumming! Kiss me! Kiss me! Fill me! *squeals* I belong to you! Kiss me, Master! Mmmphh! Mmmphhhhh!

LUPINE and JULES. Cum in her! Cum! Cum inside her!

Ruthie squeals in orgasm, muffled by the kiss.

Lupine and Jules cum, in delicious abandon.

Afterward, Ruthie whimpers sweetly into his mouth, and he keeps kissing her.

LUPINE. *softly* I'm so sweaty.

JULES. *a soft sound of pleasure* My juices are dripping down my leg.

The kiss ends.

RUTHIE. *gently, sweetly* Neither of us are virgins anymore. *she swallows nervously* And you are my Master. *shaken* Your cock. It pulsed in me. Your seed is in me. *kissing him*

LUPINE. *moans* Oh, you are so hot. You are both so hot.

JULES. *admiringly* You conqueror.

RUTHIE. *softly* You conquered me. *breathless, awed* What you

DID in me. … I'm your slavegirl. *sniffles, aroused and vulnerable* What's going to happen to me? I don't know … if I'll ever see my father again … or the cottage … *moans* … I feel so … alive … and shaken. With your cock in me. *whispers* What's going to happen to me, Master?

JULES. You're going to lie sweaty and bound underneath his body, Ruthie, here on the furs.

LUPINE. Mmmm. Until he's ready to ravage you again.

JULES. Tomorrow, you'll ride in his arms, on horseback, far across the steppes. Our people move like the wind. You're part of that now.

LUPINE. You'll be very far from your father's cottage.

JULES. But always, always home. With us.

RUTHIE. *trembling* My Master.

Outside, wolves howl.

RUTHIE. *gasps* Those wolves! I feel so helpless, my wrists tied. Will you keep me safe tonight, Master? *softly* You won't let the wolves get me? *submissively, melted* Thank you, Master. *moans* Oh, where are you reaching with your fingers? *Moans*

LUPINE. He's scooping up some of your virgin's blood on his fingertips.

RUTHIE. *gasps* And bringing it to my lips. You … *quivery* … you want me to taste? *whispers* You want me to taste what you did to me? *louder* How primally you claimed me? *softly* Yes, Master. *She licks his fingertips, then moans* Yes, I understand. My virgin blood smeared across my lips is proof that my Master owns me. *moans* You are such a … MAN. I don't know what's happened to me. *tearful* You make me feel like an animal. Like an animal rutting in a tent. Kiss me, you beast. Yes, grip me by my collar with your cock still in me, and kiss me. Mmmphh.

A passionate, ravenous kiss, and we can hear her need. After the kiss, Ruthie makes gaspy little sounds, conquered.

LUPINE. *breathes* You warrior.

JULES. The oil in the red lamp is burning low, Master. Soon it will be dark inside the tent.

LUPINE. And we'll lie with you on the furs, soft …

JULES. And naked …

RUTHIE. And wet. *whimpers* And sore. *vulnerable* You stole me, Master. Please stay inside me. *moans* Rest your head on my breasts. Mmmn. *softly* Let my breasts soothe you tonight, soft against your face as you sleep. They're bruised from your biting, Master. I'm so exhausted. I … I'm going to sleep beneath your hard body, here on these furs. Yours to wake and ravish when you please.

LUPINE. *warmly* Welcome to the tents of our people, sister. *kisses her warmly*

Ruthie moans softly into the kiss

JULES. Good night, sister. *kisses her warmly*

Ruthie moans softly into the kiss

JULES. We love you, sister.

RUTHIE. *helplessly tearful* I love you, too.

Outside, wolves howl again.

RUTHIE. *sleepy and shaken* My Master. Hold me. Kiss me.

kissing

RUTHIE. *tenderly, trembling* I'm your slavegirl.

kissing

the scene ends

BUY ME, MASTER

EPILOGUES –
DEVOTED, COLLARED,
YOURS

BUY ME, MASTER

You Own Me: May I Please Wear Your Collar, Master?

This is a romantic script for a loving, devoted slavegirl who is yearning to tell her Master how much he means to her and how much she is his, and to ask him a big question…

Optional sound effect: the ocean, soft and gentle and quiet. Other sound effects that occur later in the script: a zipper, and the click of a small lock like a padlock.

Here I am, Master. Kneeling. Naked. At your feet, here on your deck by the seaside. The ocean's breath caressing my body for you, making goosebumps on my arms and my tits. My nipples are hard … and my thighs are wet. My lips are open and soft. And I'm gazing up at you with all the warmth of my heart, because I adore you so much. Kneeling here at your feet, ready to serve and delight you, is all I could ever want, all I could ever need. You melt me. You fill me. You fill me SO full, there isn't room left for anything but loving you. Just loving you. I am your slavegirl, Master, and I love you, Master. I love you. I love you so much.

Master, just hearing your voice … your low growl … your footstep at the door … your soft breathing at night …

makes me wet. Makes me drip down my thighs for you. My Master. My lord.

The first time you cupped my chin in your hand, and tilted my head up in your firm grip, and held my gaze with yours, I felt like you were looking right into my heart, into the deepest core of me, and I was open and naked and yours. I melted for you, Master.

The first time you kissed me, I moaned into your mouth. I couldn't help it. I knew you owned me. I hadn't known it until that moment, but you did. You owned me. You own me now. You own all of me.

The first time you TOOK me, I came almost the moment you entered me, almost the moment I felt the warmth of your cock FILLING me. Do you remember, Master? You had wooed me … and pursued me … and you were so patient … and so certain you would HAVE me. And when you finally had me naked, when I finally undressed and was trembling and warm in your arms, you teased me … and edged me … for hours. Until I was sobbing with my need to be fucked. With my need to be fucked by YOU. And when you took me, I squeezed your cock and I came, I came, I came screaming a word I had never said to ANY man before. Never dreamed I COULD ever say to a man.

I came screaming, "Master!"

whispers I came so much, that night. … And every night since that you've taken me. I … am drenched for you. I am SOAKED.

whispers, very softly Master.

You own that word from me.

No one else will ever hear it.

Only you.

Master.

You … OWN … that word.

You own my lips. You know you never have to ask; you simply take a fistful of my hair and pull me close and kiss me and KISS me until I am whimpering and wet in your arms.

You own my soft, full breasts. And my nipples that are swollen and needing your touch. If you want to kiss them, or … *gasps* … twist them, or … *whimpers* … clamp them … or smack them with your hand, you never have to ask. My tits are yours, Master. My warm, sexy tits belong to YOU.

You own my sweet cunt that is dripping for you right now. My cunt is ready to welcome your cock whenEVer you need my cunt, Master. I will moan as you take me, and I will squeeze and clench and caress your cock with every hot inch of my wet, naked cunt. You own my cunt, Master. My cunt is yours.

You own the tight heat of my ass. It is yours. To take whenever it pleases you, Master. Even if it hurts, I'll be hurting for you. I'll be pleasing you. If I'm too loud, cover my mouth with your hand and fuck my ass as hard as you need to, Master. Let me scream into your hand. And I will take it. I will take every hard, spearing thrust. I will take whatever you give me. Because I am yours. You own my ass.

You own my body.

You own my breath. The first time you covered my mouth with your firm hand and pinched my nose shut with your thumb, while you were fucking me on your bed … and you told me I couldn't breathe until you allowed it, that I just had to take it for you, that you owned even the breath in my body, … I whimpered for you, Master. I couldn't help it. I whimpered and I came SO HARD on your magnificent, hard, cock.

I trust you with my breath. You own my breath.

You own my pleasure. When you tell me not to cum all week until you see me on the weekend, I don't want to obey, I don't, but I do. I do. Because I want to please you more than anything. Because I'm melted for you. Because my pleasure is a gift from you, and I would never steal it from you, Master. You own me. And so I squirm in my bed at night and I edge and I edge and I whimper your name, and I beg you, I beg you with my all my desperation and passion and love to please PLEASE let me cum. But you aren't there with me yet, and I don't have your permission, so I don't, I bite my pillow and whimper and sob in my need but I don't cum, even though my fingers are drenched with my NEED for you.

Because I'm yours.

You own me.

You own my heart.

My heart is as deep as the sea out there, and I am ALL yours. I've seen you hold me so firmly, so lovingly, whether I'm calm or whether I'm shaking with tempests of emotion. I've come home snapping at you and bitchy from the WORST day at work, and you've just bent me over your knee and spanked me until my ass was red and then held me for an hour, stroking my hair and kissing me. And somehow it made everything better. Like no matter how awful I feel, you're ready to take me in hand and take care of me and hold me. You aren't afraid of my feelings. Because you trust my heart. It doesn't matter what mood I'm in, nothing daunts you, you just take control and you love me and want me and own me. You dance with me the way your boat dances with the waves. No matter how upset I am, you hold me and take me where you need me to go. And you make me feel … SO … safe.

My heart is as full as the sea. The way you look at me. The way you talk to me. Like I am SO treasured and SO wanted. The way you admire my work and encourage me and the way you let me thrive as my own person, accepting all of me, desiring all of me, yet when you want me in your arms you can make me wet and submissive with just a look.

Oh Master. I am so full of love for you, Master. So full.

I would do anything for you, Master. You can tell me to do ANYthing, and I will do it. You could whip me, and I would cry out, "Thank you, Master!" each time the whip cracked across my body, across my full tits or my soft, soaked thighs, or my warm mound. Even though I had tears in my eyes, I would say, "Thank you, Master!"

You could brand me. And I would scream from the pain of it but then I would sob, "Thank you, Master," because I want your mark on my body. I want the world to know you own me. If you want to brand me, I will surrender to you, Master.

You could breed me. And I would rock my hips for you while you filled me with your seed, and I would beg you to give me a baby. To impregnate me. To make me even more YOURS. To make my belly and breasts grow round and full for you, Master.

You could tell me to make you breakfast each morning and bring it to you naked in bed. You could tell me to wake you with my mouth around your cock, to blow you and pleasure you until you burst in my mouth, until you give ME a hot, sticky breakfast.

You could tell me to be waiting for you naked, on my knees, at the front door when you come home each day from work. I get home first, and I could. And I will, I WILL, if you command it, Master. I will wait so that when you open the door, the first thing you see is me … naked … kneeling … my legs spread with my cunt already dripping onto the floor, my head tilted back and my soft, warm eyes gazing up at you lovingly as I open my soft mouth for your cock. I will do ANYthing for you, Master.

You could tell me after you fuck me to step outside your home and walk naked down your street with my breasts bruised from your kisses and your cum dripping down my leg. With my chin lifted high because I am YOUR beautiful slavegirl and you want the whole world to know what a beautiful, submissive, trusting woman you own. And I would do it for you, Master. I would say, "Thank you, Master," and walk, naked and dripping your cum, out the door for you, Master.

You could tell me to dance naked on your dining room table while your friends are over. You could tell me to sway and pivot and display my nude body, to cup my breasts and offer them to you, to be soaked for you while your friends gaze openly, heatedly at my naked, warm cunt. You could tell me to beg … for your COCK … while I dance for you, while they watch.

whispers Take me for dessert, Master. Fill me with your cock, Master, please, please fill me with your cock. Please fuck me. Fuck me, Master. I need it. I NEED it. I need to be fucked. I need your hard cock in me. I need you to fuck my cunt. Fuck me, Master, fuck me, please.

moans I would beg for you, Master. Just like that.

You could tell me to brag to your friends about how GOOD you feel in me, how thick and how hard and how hot, and how much I am IN HEAT for you, Master, how much I NEED your cock inside me.

You could tell me to lie down on my back on the dining room table after dancing, and spread my thighs so wide, and touch myself for you, while they watch. You could tell me to cum. You could tell me to squirm … and moan … and flood your table … and I would lift my tits and throw back my head and scream with pleasure for you, Master. With my fingers so deep in my cunt for you, Master. While they watch.

You could tell me to BEG you to let your friends fuck me. And I would beg. I would plead for you to let them thrust their hard cocks inside me. In my mouth. In my pussy. In my ass. Between my breasts. As much cock as I can possibly take. I would beg you to let them cover me in their cum, until I'm drenched in it, until my whole body is sticky and I lie panting and shaking and dripping with their seed. But my eyes would be gazing at you, the whole time. Only you, Master. Only you own me.

And though I would beg so prettily for you to let them fuck me, because I would want to please you, I would hope with my whole body and my whole cunt and my whole heart that you would say No. That you would keep me for you. For you only. Because yours is the only cock I want in me. Because I want you to keep me possessively to yourself. Because I want you to fuck me on your dining room table in front of your friends, in front of all your friends who watched me dance and watched me finger myself and cum screaming for my Master, in front of all your friends who want me and can't have me.

I am so yours, Master. I belong to you. I am so in love with you, Master. I would be so overwhelmed at your desire for me, being FUCKED on your dining room table while your friends watch, that I would give you the hottest, wildest, most loving fuck you have ever had. I would clasp your cock so tightly inside me and grip your shoulders and your ass, and slide a finger inside your warm ass ... and I would kiss you breathless ... and I would bite ... and I would fuck ... and I would SOAK your cock ... and I would arch my body and lift my whole self into you because I want you, I want you, I want you to OWN all of me, I want to be your joy and your pleasure, I want to be YOURS. And I'd scream for you, Master. I'd scream for you. I'd be SUCH a good fuck for you, Master. I'd be such a ... GOOD ... slavegirl. I would roll my hips and squeeze you and let my cunt ripple around your cock and I would cum for you and CUM for you, fucking you like my whole body and my whole heart belongs to you, like I'm melted, like I'm yours, like every beat of my heart is for pleasing you, Master. I would fuck you like your friends have never even DREAMED of being fucked. I would fuck you like they never knew a woman COULD fuck. I would fuck you like you OWN me.

Because you do. You OWN me.

Master. My Master.

moans I WANT to obey you.

Mmm, feel me rubbing my cheek into your hand, your strong, firm hand, like a kitten. Because I'm YOUR kitten, Master. I want to please you. I want you to be proud of your slavegirl. I want you to be SO delighted in me.

And that's why I need to ask you something, Master. I need to ask you. A question that burns in my heart. I can't, I can't, I can't go through tonight without asking you.

And I'm so scared to ask it, but I need to, I yearn to.

Will you please let your slavegirl, your kitten, ask you a question, Master? Please, Master?

... Thank you. *whispers* I love you, Master.

breathlessly Master ... Master ... I am YOURS. Will you tell the world I am yours? Will you let me wear your collar, Master? May I wear YOUR collar on my throat?

Will you collar me, Master?

Will you collar your sweet, loving, obedient slave?

Please, Master.

Please collar me, Master.

Please ... make me your kitten. Your owned slavegirl. Own me completely. I want to wear your collar ... when I'm at home, when I'm in bed, mmmmmmmm when I'm in YOUR bed, ... when I'm walking down the sidewalk, when I'm shopping, when I'm out with my friends, when I'm at work. I want to be ... YOURS. Completely.

When I wear your collar, when I feel it around my throat each time I draw in a breath, each time I gasp, each time I swallow your cum, I will be YOURS. You will own my heart. Any question you ask, I will answer. Any secret I have, I will whisper in your ear, because you own all my secrets. You own all of ME.

You will own my cunt. It is yours. Any time you want pleasure from me, any time you want the heat of my body around your cock, you may use me. I won't say No. I have given myself to you completely. Because I trust you. Because I feel so safe with you. Because I love you. Because I would rather kneel here, naked, at your feet, with my thighs spread wide to display the sweet naked cunt you own ... I would rather be completely vulnerable and completely open and risk all the ways you could ever hurt me ... than go one more night without being COMPLETELY owned by you, without being yours completely. I trust you. I TRUST you, Master.

I love you.

I submit to you.

Please, Master, please put your collar on me.

softly Please claim me. Please own me. Own me, Master.

Oh! Yes! I see ... I see the collar you've just drawn from your pocket ... oh my ... Master ... You had one ready? You ... you knew I would ask? You knew what I wanted? Oh Master, Master, Master, I love you ... Oh Master, it's beautiful. That black leather, and that tiny heart-shaped lock. It looks like it will be soft on my skin ... but so strong. The way you are often gentle with me ... but so strong when you hold me, when you bend me to your will.

breathless Oh Master. Please ... please ...

Yes, Master. Yes. You own me. I will obey ... every ... word. Snap your fingers, Master, and I will kneel. Gesture at your bed, and I will lie down naked with my legs spread and beg you to fuck me. Pat your thigh once, and I will strip and bend over your knees and thank you as you spank me hard. Gesture for the whip, and I will bring it to you, on my hands and knees, clutched in my teeth. Anything you choose to do with me, Master. Any pleasure you decide to give me. Any discipline you decide I need. I will give you everything, Master, holding nothing back. I belong to you, Master.

Please, Master. Put it around my throat.

moans softly Oh, the leather is so soft. And so warm from your hands, Master. I feel ... so held. Like it is your hands holding my throat, like it's your hands holding my heart.

Please, Master, please lock it on me. Lock your collar on your trembling, wet, obedient slave. Lock it on this woman who is yours, yours, always yours. I love you, Master. I want this. I want to give myself to you.

a loud, cold click, like a padlock

gasps

Ah!! That … that sound. That click of the lock. Oh my god. It's LOCKED on me.

I … I could cry. I'm so happy. I feel so safe, I feel so safe. So wanted. You DO want all of me, you DO. Master!

It's… it's locked on me. I am LOCKED … in YOUR collar.

Yes, Master, keep the key. The key to my collar is yours and yours only. I can't remove this collar, only you ever could. And I trust, I trust you never will. I trust you. I love you. I WANT you.

I am yours, Master. I love you! How may your slavegirl please you, Master?

… YES, Master. It will be my pleasure, Master.

the sound of a zipper

Oh Master, your cock is so wonderful. Your cock is so BEAUTIFUL. The round head of it, mmmmm, and the warm GIRTH of you and the way it is so strong and thick and the way you throb so warmly when I brush my cheek along your shaft… So strong and warm, like you …

Oh Master. Your cock is so beautiful. Your cock gives me SO MUCH pleasure. I am SO wet for your cock, Master.

You OWN me with this cock. With your every touch, with your every word whispered in my ear, with your every THRUST in my tight cunt, you OWN me.

I LOVE your cock.

repeat, slower, warmly, lovingly I … LOVE … your cock.

I want to worship your cock.

As I worship and serve you, my Master.

I'll just reach for you … with my warm, gentle hands … mmmm, and breathe softly over the head of your cock. *she does*

And lick… *she does*

And kiss… *she does*

And tease the head of your cock with my soft, wet mouth … mmmmmmmmmmmmmmm

a few moments of gentle sucking sounds

Mmm, I LOVE the taste of your cock, Master. I love the SCENT of you. I love you in my MOUTH. OH Master, Master! I am SOAKED right now, kneeling here, licking your cock, wearing your collar. Use me, Master. You own me; please use me.

gasps Oh! The way you're gripping me by my collar. YES, Master. Yes, make me please you the way YOU want. Teach me to please you, Master. Teach me, M--MMMPHHHH!!!!!!

for several minutes, improv a very rough facefuck, her choking and gagging and moaning around his cock … a tearful, rough blowjob … interspersed with lines like the following:

MMMPHHH MMPHHHH Do I please you, Mas-MMMMPHH MMMMPHHHHH

MMMMPHHH Yes use my mouth, use my MMMMPHHH MMMMPHHHHHHHHH

MMMMPHHH I love your cock, oh god, I LOVE your COCK!!! MMMMPHHHH

after choking hard It's … it's okay. I … I don't need to breathe right now. I just need to please you, Master. I love you. Use me however you want, Master. I love you. MMMMPHHH MMMMPHHHH

repeat "I love you," muffled around his cock, saying "I love you" desperately, with your mouth full, several times

MMMPHHH MMMPHHH Please cum in my mouth, please cum in my MMMPHH MMMPHHHH

she moans "please cum in my mouth" over and over, muffled by his cock, until, he does, and then we hear her whimper, overwhelmed as he fills her mouth. We hear her swallow, and again, and again.

gasping for breath

Oh, Master.

Oh Master. Yes. Yes, I swallowed all of it. Did ... did I please you, Master?

Mmmm. I LOVE when you call me that. Yes, Master yes, I am YOUR good girl. YOUR kitten. Your ... your collar-slut.

I am whatever you need, Master.

I promise.

I am yours. I love you. I LOVE you.

Mmmm, let me lean in and kiss your thighs. Please. I want to kiss your thighs.

kissing ... lots of gentle, loving kisses for his thighs

sighs softly My Master.

a brief pause as she listens

giggles What's that?

You're ... you're taking a few days off work? And you're ... taking me out in the boat, Master? So you can be alone with your collared slave and fuck her, out there on the beautiful ocean, as often as you want? Oh Master! Yes! Yes, make love to me, own me, let me rock beneath you while the waves rock beneath us both. Make me spend the week naked aboard your boat. Make me edge and beg you to let me cum. Make me suck your cock while you chart our course. Fuck me … SO hard … out there, on the ocean, where the only thing that exists in my entire world is you. Just you. My Master. My love. My lord.

Take me out there tonight, Master.

Fuck me on the moonlit sea.

Own me.

I love you. Take me tonight, Master. *breathless* I submit. Take my body. Take my wet, soaked cunt. Take my breasts and my ass and my mouth. Take my breath, take my everything. Take my heart. Take *me.* Take me.

Take me.

Do You Need My Mouth, Master?

We hear the soft breathing of a sleeping slavegirl, soft little noises, and the quiet clinking of her chain as she shifts in her sleep

we hear her wake

so sleepy Mmmn, Master. Master. It's late. Mmmn. You woke me. Your naked slavegirl, with my ankle chained to your bed. Mmmn. Your hands on my tits … ah-ah-ahhh!

gaspy little breaths as he arouses her, for a few moments, as he fondles her

breathy You own me.

rustling and clinking chain as she shifts in the bed

barely above a whisper, so aroused My thighs open for you, Master. As you touch me … in your bed … in the dark.

he takes her mouth with his

kissing, long and sensual, while she moans sweetly into his mouth

Mmmn. Kissed awake by my Master.

breathing softly, aroused

Yes, Master. My mouth is for your pleasure. *whispers* You can have my mouth.

he gives her another powerful, mastering kiss, and she whimpers softly, yielding and surrendering, giving him everything with that kiss

breathless How may your sleepy slavegirl please you, Master? How may I delight you?

gasps

Your hand in my hair!

quivering Master?

the sound of his cock smacking her cheek

gasps Your hard cock!

the smacking sound again, and again, followed by cute little gasps

Do you need my mouth, Master?

Do you need my soft, wet little mouth? For your cock? My mouth is for your cock. You own me. Use my mou-MMM! MMPHH! MMMPHHH!

he fills her mouth with his cock and pumps his hips vigorously, we hear her little grunts and whimpers and muffled sounds as she takes it for him

a rough blowjob

an I-just-woke-you-up-because-I-need-to-FUCK-your-mouth blowjob

Mmmphh mmmphh mmmphh!

he doesn't let her speak

she is aroused, moaning and whimpering sweetly, muffled, around his cock

maybe she talks a little with her mouth full, just the word "Master" or an "I love you" muffled by his cock

the blowjob gets rougher

we hear the sounds her throat makes as he fucks her throat

no words

just … throatfucking

just a naked, hot, quivering slavegirl letting her Master use her throat

as long as he wants

then he pushes her down all the way, his groin against her nose, his balls against her chin, and we hear her whimper, then no air. No breath for ten seconds. Just little rustles as she squirms in the bed, maybe the chain clinking, maybe near the tenth second a desperate whine around his cock.

he lets her up

we hear her sucking in air through her nose, desperately, with his cock still in her mouth

she whimpers

more rapid throatfucking sounds

so fast

then he stops abruptly, and she makes a muffled little noise of surprise

a whimper at another thrust

she swallows, loudly

we hear another thrust

she gulps … several swallows

we hear her breathing through her nose and making soft, submissive, overwhelmed little sounds, muffled around his cock

after a few moments, he takes his cock from her mouth

she is panting softly

whispers Master.

The taste of your cock. The taste of your cum. *moans*

softly You own me.

the sound of his cock smacking her cheek

a soft little sound

Yes, Master. I'll go back to sleep. With the taste of you in my mouth. It's going to be so hard to sleep, you have me so … on fire. My nipples are swollen like hard little berries. My hips are rocking. *whimpers* I … I am so wet, I am so wet. Please, please touch me.

his cock smacks her cheek

whimpers I have to wait. I have to wait. I know, I know you need rest. *whimpers*

Yes, Master. Yes, Master, I'll be a good girl. I'll be a good girl for you. I'll try to sleep. I'll be your good girl. I love you, Master.

soft little whimpers

so softly I'll obey my Master.

whimpers

My Master.

for a few moments, we listen to her quick, aroused little breaths and whimpers and squirms as she tries to get into a restful position in the bed and obey. Maybe the clinking of the chain. Rustling in the bed. She is so wet and can hardly keep still.

trying to keep quiet I'm so wet. Oh god, I'm so wet. I'm so wet for you.

soft little whimpers Master. Master.

aroused breathing

the scene ends

(Aftercare)
You Conquered Me

soft, gentle kisses on his neck

Mmm. I love just lying in your arms, naked and sweaty, kissing your neck after we play. *kissing*

soft and sweet What we just did, what you just heard, the way I bucked and moaned and screamed in your arms ... *a soft little sigh of happiness* ... I just want you to know, I'm all right. *giggles* I am so very all right. It was wonderful. *giggles* I'm so breathless.

kissing

Thank you for taking me.

quivery Thank you. You just ... conquered me.

a sweet little sound in his ear I'm your conquest. Helpless in your arms.

Your hands are still on my body, gripping me, holding me, and I love it.

I love your hands.

Oh GOD, how you FUCKED me.

Here. *kissing* Just feel my soft, full tits pressed naked to your chest. *whispers* Feel my nipples. Feel my cunt wet and so, so soft against your thigh. And just relax … let me kiss you. *kissing, with a soft little moan into his mouth* Let me kiss the man who FUCKED me. *kissing* Let me kiss your lips … *kissing and moaning into the kiss* … and your neck. *kissing* You took me so hard. You ravished me.

And now you get to relax.

I love when you're flushed and sweaty like this. Your cock still hard from spilling your seed into me. *whimpers* The way you pulsed inside me. I want to feel that all night. That sensation of you cumming in me.

Let me hold you. Take care of you. *breathy, quivery* I am so thankful. You … you just TOOK me. I feel … mmm, so open. So good. You make me feel so safe. So safe. And so wet. Thank you. Thank you. I almost cried when I came, it was so intense. *softly* Thank you for doing that to me. For making me surrender like that.

I know it was intense for you, too. Please … just close your eyes. Listen to my voice.

Feel my whole body pressed to you right now. Feminine and soft and naked.

whispers And yours.

I'm pressed to you because I feel so safe with you. Oh Master. You're so strong and so good. The way you took me … the way you growled … the way you held me down and fucked me, exactly as you pleased. *whimpers* You were so … dangerous.

whispers And I loved it.

I loved it so much.

I loved each pounding thrust of your cock in me. You're so BIG in me.

Oh god, how I came. And came. You MADE me cum. You made me cum so hard.

I opened like a flower to the sun. I OPENED for you. Oh my god, feel how wet I still am, pressed to your thigh. Oh Master. How you took me.

whispers Take me again.

And again.

As often as you want.

I know you would never hurt me. It was just a fantasy. It made me so wet.

I don't always get to just let go and … feel. You MADE me feel. You made me feel SO MUCH. *moans* You made me squeal for you.

You're so strong and so confident, the way you just TAKE me, I can just let go, I can just yield and surrender and FEEL. I can take everything you give me.

quivery Let me kiss the line of your jaw.

gentle kissing for a little while

And your neck.

kissing

You make me so wet.

I would do anything for you right now. Anything to please you. You've conquered me. You've taken me. Ravished me. I'm yours. So entirely yours. I'm so happy. You make me feel desired.

I would do anything you wanted.

You could do anything to me, and I would moan "Yes."

Oh, yes.

whispers Unless you want me to say No.

giggles Unless you want me to squirm … and wriggle … and squeal into your firm hand over my mouth. Mmmmmm.

she makes a soft little whimper or two, to demonstrate

so aroused You make me so wet.

Mmm.

You make me so safe.

You're such a good lover. Such a good man. A good, strong man who keeps me safe. You know just how to take me.

Your cock feels so fucking good in me. And you are so aware of what I need. Oh my god, you give me JUST what I need. You took such good care of me.

quivery Thank you.

Thank you so much.

I'm so happy.

Hold me. *a soft little feminine noise* I surrender.

You just breathe … and relax … and let me worship you with my soft, small mouth …

kissing

Kissing your neck.

kissing

whispers I'll kiss your thighs if you want me to, Master. I'll kiss your cock. *breathy* I will love your cock with my warm, wet mouth.

kissing him

When you're ready, take me again.

Please. Do what you want with me.

I feel so safe in your arms.

Just take me and fuck me and make me please you. You don't have to ask. Just put your cock in me. Do what you want with me. I trust you. I trust you so much. I've never trusted anyone so much. Where you lead, I'll follow. I promise. I'm yours. I just want to lie with my legs open and my cunt wet and inviting and yours, and submit. *soft little whimpers of need* I just want to submit to you. Own me. Use me. I submit, I submit. Open me and open me until I'm so open I cry when I cum. I want you in me. That's all I want, all I want. All I could ever need. Just you filling me so full, your body thrusting on top of me and your eyes so deep above mine and your hands holding me exactly where you want me. Just you in me, making me take it, making me take what you know I need.

moans I'm open. I'm hot and open for you. I'm so ready for you. Please fuck me.

I need you so much. I need your cock. I need your kisses. I need you to TAKE me.

kissing him, moaning sweetly into the kiss

breathless Ravish me.

Ravish me.

kissing him, moaning into his mouth again, more aroused

the audio ends